D1015709

ADVANCE PRAISE FOR *UNBLEMISHED*

"A breathtaking fantasy set in an extraordinary fairy-tale world, with deceptive twists and an addictively adorable cast who are illusory to the end. Just when I thought I'd figured each out, Sara Ella sent me for another ride. A wholly original story, *Unblemished* begins as a sweet melody and quickly becomes an anthem of the heart. And I'm singing my soul out. Fans of *Once Upon a Time* and Julie Kagawa, brace yourselves."

—MARY WEBER, AWARD-WINNING AUTHOR OF
THE STORM SIREN TRILOGY

"Lyrically written and achingly romantic—*Unblemished* will tug your heartstrings!"

—MELISSA LANDERS, AUTHOR OF *ALIENATED,*
INVADED, AND *STARFLIGHT*

"Self-worth and destiny collide in this twisty-turny fantasy full of surprise and heart. Propelled into a world she knows nothing about, Eliyana learns that the birthmark she despises is not quite the superficial curse she thought it was—it's worse, and the mark comes with a heavy responsibility. Can she face her reflection long enough to be the hero her new friends need? With charm and wit, author Sara Ella delivers *Unblemished*, a magical story with a compelling message and a unique take on the perils of Central Park."

—SHANNON DITTEMORE, AUTHOR OF
THE ANGEL EYES TRILOGY

"*Unblemished* is an enchanting, beautifully written adventure with a pitch-perfect blend of fantasy, realism, and romance. Move this one to the top of your TBR pile and clear your schedule, you won't want to put it down!"

—LORIE LANGDON, AUTHOR OF THE AMAZON
BESTSELLING DOON SERIES.

"Unblemished had me from the first chapter—mystery, romance, and mind-blowing twists and turns that I SO did not see coming! The worlds Sara Ella builds are complex and seamless; the characters she creates are beautifully flawed. Readers are sure to love this book and finish it, as I did, begging for more!"

—KRISTA MCGEE, AUTHOR OF THE ANOMALY TRILOGY

unblemished

sara ella

THOMAS NELSON
Since 1798

Published in Nashville, Tennessee, by Thomas Nelson. Thomas Nelson is a registered trademark of HarperCollins Christian Publishing, Inc.

Special thanks to Jim Hart of Hartline Literary.

Map by Matthew Covington.

Thomas Nelson titles may be purchased in bulk for educational, business, fundraising, or sales promotional use. For information, please e-mail SpecialMarkets@ ThomasNelson.com.

Publisher's Note: This novel is a work of fiction. Names, characters, places, and incidents are either products of the author's imagination or used fictitiously. All characters are fictional, and any similarity to people living or dead is purely coincidental.

Library of Congress Cataloging-in-Publication Data

Names: Ella, Sara, author.
Title: Unblemished / Sara Ella.
Description: Nashville, Tennessee : Thomas Nelson, [2016] | Summary: "With a birthmark covering half her face, Eliyana has always recoiled from her own reflection in the mirror. But what if that were only one Reflection—one world? What if another world existed where her blemish could become her strength?" Provided by publisher.
Identifiers: LCCN 2016017932 | ISBN 9780718081010 (hardback)
Subjects: | CYAC: Fantasy. | Birthmarks--Fiction. | Abnormalities, Human--Fiction.
Classification: LCC PZ7.1.E435 Un 2016 | DDC [Fic]--dc23 LC record available at https:// lccn.loc.gov/2016017932

Printed in the United States of America

16 17 18 19 20 RRD 5 4 3 2 1

For my mom,
Mary Elizabeth (1956—2012).
You always said I'd write a book.
And, as always, you were right.

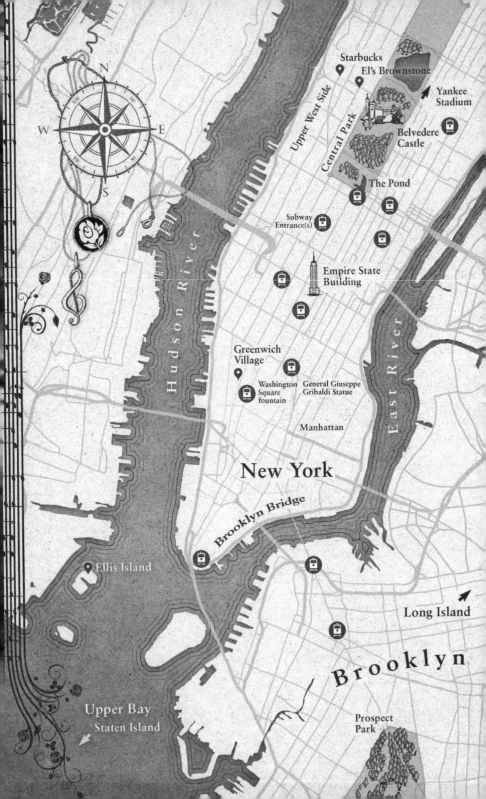

To the Crown until death

Canyons &
Desert lands

Dewsti Province

Shadow
Territory

The Forest
of Night

Midnight
Lake

Onhuds River

Pireem
Mountain

Stae River

Wichgreen Village

Fountain
Threshold
Lancaster Ryan Statue

Wichgreen Province

Second Reflection

Broken Bridge

Gnol Island

Lisel Island
Nathaniel's Brownstone

Old Maple Mines

Lynbrook Province

Sea

Haven Island

Forest of Tromes

Once upon a time is ne'er what it seems.
And happily ever after oft a mere device of dreams.
What wicked snares are vines, and thorns cause many throes.
But peer beyond the surface; you may there find a rose.

—THE REFLECTION CHRONICLES, FIRST ACCOUNT

prelude

This is all my fault.

She'll lose her soul because of me.

I stare at the Verity's vessel and search his stony eyes for some sign he'll do what he must, some sense he's finally decided to let go.

Do it, my soul pleads. *Save her*, my eyes implore.

One, two, three breaths before he nods.

Sigh. This is it. The steady adagio of my beating heart plays the coda in my final act.

His face is drawn, pale. The sight pulls at my heartstrings, overtuning them to the point of snapping.

My eyes want to close. I will them to remain open. I won't abandon him in this. The burden is ours to bear. Together. No turning back.

The enemy raises his sword as the Verity's vessel creeps toward him. The extended note of hesitation ushers in the last cadence of my life. There will be no encore for me. No reprise or standing ovation. This is my final performance. The curtain is closing, and the audience is taking its leave.

His sword comes flying down.

ACT I

Home

monster

I t can't be true. I've known the news for a week, and still it hits me as if I'm finding out for the very first time.

Elizabeth Ember, Up-and-Coming Artist of the Upper West Side, Dies at 34.

The bold headline on the front of the *New York Times* obituaries blares up at me, a black-and-white photo of Mom posted beneath. Was it only last month this exact photo adorned another section of the paper? Even with gray skin, her dark hair swept into a messy bun, Mom's organic beauty radiates from the page. Why she hated being photographed, I'll never understand. I flip the paper upside down. When I die, will my portrait grace the news?

Of course not. My face looks as if a toddler scribbled on it with a red Sharpie while I was asleep. No reporter in his right mind would put my picture in the paper. Not unless it was a Halloween edition.

Mom used to sit in the rooftop garden of our brownstone, a cup of hot Earl Grey in her hands, and gaze out over Manhattan. She adored this city for its energy and symphony of cultures. "It's always alive, always moving," she'd said.

Now, every consolation from a complete stranger invites a fresh wave of sobs. My chest heaves with each one, rising and

falling like the steady tumult of the Hudson on a stormy day. I
drive back the waves with smiles and nods and deep, controlled
breaths, all for the sake of appearances. To be the hostess Mom
would've been. The one I'll never be.

"I'm so sorry for your loss . . ."

Smile.

"She'll be missed . . ."

Nod.

"It will get better with time . . ."

Inhale.

"You know we're all here for you, dear . . ."

Exhale.

Nothing more than empty words from phony people who
can't even look me in the eye as they give their condolences. Can I
blame them? I don't enjoy looking at me. Why should they?

My phone vibrates, dancing along the granite countertop in
our—my kitchen. The screen lights up, flashing the name and
selfie that hurts and comforts in one ping of mixed emotions.

Joshua.

My fingers curl around the orchid-colored case, squeeze. I
asked him to stay away, to give me space. Time. He agreed with a
solemn nod, giving me what I wanted.

If it's what I wanted, why do I long to go next door and fall into
his arms?

I close my eyes, mentally pushing away the cacophony of
voices echoing around our—my home. It doesn't work. This is all
just too much.

A sea of catered dishes covers the kitchen island. Nothing
offers comfort like platters of prosciutto and tartlets, right? What
is this, a cocktail party? And could it be more obvious these people
know nothing about me or Mom? Prosciutto? Really? Gag me. I
haven't touched meat in ten years, and I'm certainly not going to
start now.

Beyond the bar, the sunroom with its large bay window, upright piano, and ornate fireplace is set up as an art gallery. Mom's recently commissioned dealer, Lincoln Cooper, took care of all the details, despite the setback his recent gallery fire caused him. How very noble of him considering he's known us less than a month. Where did he find all these people? Do they even know who they're mourning, or are their sympathies part of the show?

Easels display oil-pastel renderings and watercolor paintings, along with a few of Mom's charcoal sketches. Most of the pieces featured are from her *Autumn* collection, Lincoln's idea of staying on theme with the current season. He negotiates prices while admirers speak overtly about the tragedy of such a talented artist dying so young.

"What better way to remember Elizabeth than to display and sell her masterpieces at the wake," he'd said with enthusiasm. "Eclectic art is all the rage now."

I nodded my consent, but I knew better. Lincoln Cooper couldn't care less about paying tribute to Mom. He hardly knew her. All he cares about is his big fat commission. And considering he's priced each painting well beyond what Mom would approve of, I don't think he'll have trouble getting what he wants. Sheesh. Maybe this *is* a cocktail party. Let him have his fun. I only want one painting for myself, along with Mom's sketchbooks.

The essence of her surrounds me. In every brushstroke and ebony pencil rub. In the scent of canvas. In the crinkle of brown paper as Lincoln unwraps a new piece to replace one he's just sold. My lower lip quivers, and I suck it in between my teeth. Mom would want me to be brave now, but how can I be? She'll never again sit on our roof and paint the sun rising over Central Park. Never send me down the block to pick up a new box of pencils from Staples or sketch me while I do my homework.

At once I can't breathe. I'm suffocating, but no one notices. I can't be here anymore. I won't do this. She's not dead. She can't be.

Nausea takes over. I cover my mouth with one hand, bolt from the kitchen. My empty stomach lurches, but I welcome the chance to escape. I shove past the mingling art enthusiasts in the sunroom who turn their attention to me for a moment before I enter the bathroom across the hall. *Slam, flip, click.* Finally having a moment of privacy and solace, I collapse to the floor, clutch my throbbing head in my hands, and cry.

"Mom . . ." Sob. Swipe. Sniff. "Mom, I need you."

"Beneath winter's icy sadness lies spring's blooming joy."

Mom's poetic words breeze across my heart. She was always repeating things like this, urging me to remember them, to write them down.

"Not this time, Mom." Not this time.

Tap, tap.

I jerk my head up. Hold my breath. If I don't answer, whoever it is will go away eventually.

Tap. Tap, tap, tap, tap—

"Occupied," I call out. "There's another bathroom—"

"El? Are you in there? It's me."

I roll my head back against the door. He's here? He's here.

"Come on." A hint of humor mellows Joshua's tone. "I brought pizza. I know how much you hate fancy hors d'oeuvres."

My stomach rumbles. I've hardly eaten in days. Still, I can't bring myself to budge.

"If you don't come out, I'll start singing."

He wouldn't dare, not with all those people around.

"One . . ."

I stand and push the tears away with my palms.

"Two . . ."

I force myself to look in the mirror, and my heart tumbles to the floor. What did I expect? Crying and mascara streaks would actually help my appearance? I can't let him see me this way.

Shattered. Broken.

I've fallen apart in his presence once, and all it brought was more heartache. Never again.

"Three."

I glance at the door and wait. One, two heartbeats. Footsteps depart. I sigh. Guess he gave up. It's for the best. I'm a wreck.

My gaze returns to my reflection. The strange crimson birthmark winds up the right side of my face in creeping, curling tendrils. Like vines choking my skin. Thorns drawing blood in trickles, permanently staining my complexion.

I'm a monster.

I lift a hand and let it hover there. Now I look almost normal. Too bad I can't walk around this way all the time. Or better yet, wear a paper bag over my head. My only trinket of beauty is the silver treble clef–heart pendant Joshua gave me last spring. The one he made me swear never to take off—a token from a time that will never be again.

I swipe my fingertips beneath my eyelids to extract some of the runny mascara goop. My ombre hair, mocha melting into blonde, hangs in drab sheets to my shoulders. Mom's idea of something wild for senior year, though it just makes me feel as if I'm trying to be someone I'm not. I comb my fingers through my full bangs, the ones I cut to cover my forehead, to help me blend in. Some birthmark covered is better than none covered at all.

The soft picking of guitar strings breaks the silence. A familiar melody floats under the crack beneath the door, cradles my heart, and lifts it off the ground.

Joshua sings out pure and strong. The chords to "Daydream Believer" are the first he taught me to play—G transitioning into A minor, then B minor to C. I could play the song in my sleep. He's not being fair.

More notes. Closer. Louder. His dynamic tenor beckons me as it crescendos at the chorus.

I place a palm on the door. A smile surfaces for the first time in a week. In the three years I've known Joshua, he's never once sung in public.

I turn the lock and open the door to a crowd gathered around a boy and his guitar. The boy I love.

No. The realization is a slap in the face. The confession may be internal, for my heart alone, but it's there. Complicating. Everything.

When he finishes the song, everyone applauds. Once they disperse, trickling from the foyer back into the sunroom, Joshua smiles and shrugs in his boyish way.

"I thought you weren't coming," I say to the floor.

"You asked me not to."

My head lifts. "And yet here you are."

He takes a step closer. "Here I am."

The silence between us is easy. Comfortable. The first bout of normalcy I've had since Mom died.

"You didn't think I'd let you deal with these suits alone, did you?" He hitches his thumb over one shoulder, then lays the guitar against the stairs and crosses the hall, closing the remaining distance between us.

"Thank you." The words release on a much-needed exhale. Maybe I misunderstood what happened between us the other night.

"Of course." He smiles and his fingers brush mine. An accident? Aside from the times he had to position my hand on the guitar, Joshua has never initiated physical contact. I search his eyes for some confirmation the touch was intentional.

A throat clears. Joshua shoves the hand that grazed mine into his pocket. The moment, whatever it was, is gone.

An elderly gentleman with a pocket square and a circa-1970s briefcase steps forward, a manila folder tucked beneath his right arm. "Ah, Mr. David. Glad you could make it. I just need your signature on a few more papers."

Joshua glances between me and the man. Scratches the back of his head. His dark hair is a mess, and his black-and-green plaid shirt is rumpled. The disheveled look is out of character for him. "Right." He takes the folder from the man. "Thanks."

My eyebrows pinch. "What's that? Who are you?"

"Forgive me." The man sets down his briefcase and offers a hand. "My name is Wallace Matthews. You must be Eliyana. Elizabeth told me so much about you." I can't help but notice he doesn't meet my eyes. My face.

I cross my arms, not bothering to shake his hand. "Joshua? Do you know this guy?" My eyes don't leave Joshua's stubbled face, but his gaze remains downcast.

"So very sorry," Wallace mumbles, retracting his hand and letting it fall limp at his side. "I am Elizabeth's attorney. And Mr. David here is your legal guardian now." He picks up his briefcase and flips his wrist to check his out-of-date watch. "Strange she never mentioned any of this to you—"

"Is this why you're here?" I snap at Joshua, cutting Wallace off. "Because you have to be?" My expression tightens.

Joshua's cerulean eyes widen and finally lock on mine. "What? Of course not. El—"

"How long have you known?" My words slip through clenched teeth.

He hesitates. "Awhile."

"So all this time we've been friends, it's been a lie?"

"No. We were friends first. It was only a month ago Elizabeth came to me and asked if I'd be willing to take responsibility should something happen to her."

"Responsibility?" My voice quivers. "Are you serious? I'll be eighteen in less than a month. I can take care of myself."

"That isn't quite accurate," Wallace interjects. "Your mother left everything to Mr. David. The home. Her bank accounts. She wanted to ensure you'd be looked after by a responsible adult.

Someone who could work and provide while you finish high school and begin college." A lady in a ridiculous black feathered hat taps Wallace on the shoulder with her dragon fingernail and he excuses himself.

Once we're alone again I say under my breath, "You're only three years older than me. How much more responsible can you be?"

"I'm going to take care of you. It's what your mom wanted." He bends the folder and shoves it into his back pocket.

I step back. Shake my head. Why would Mom keep this from me? And why isn't she here so I can ask her?

"El." Joshua reaches for me. "I'm sorry. We should've told you. If it bothers you that much, I'll find someone else to be your guardian. I'll do whatever it takes to make this transition as easy as possible. To make you feel safe. That's all I want."

Someone else. Transition. Easy. Safe. The words blur together as I retreat into the bathroom. Lock the door. Invisibility is the only way I know how to survive. Because if I let him see how much this hurts, if I let him witness the broken heart on my sleeve, he might find someone else to care for me.

Then he'll leave me too.

And there it is. The truth. As much as I hate for him to stay out of guilt or pity or duty, it would be worse to see him go. Mom's death is the hardest thing I've ever endured. If I lost Joshua, too, I don't think I could bear it. I'm not that brave. So I'll do what I'm best at. I'll pretend. If he sees I'm okay, he'll stay.

And I won't have to feel this way ever again.

T W O

think again

Someone's in my room.

I lie unmoving atop rumpled sheets. Sweat sticks to every crease and pore on my skin, reminding me I fell asleep with the space heater on again. Floorboards whine beneath my intruder's weight. I keep my eyes closed and feign sleep. My breaths release as if rehearsed.

The light flicks on. An orange glow penetrates my eyelids.

"Happy birthday!"

I open my eyes. *Mom?*

So this isn't real. Just a memory. A dream. Still, I'll take what I can get.

She floats over to my bed. A Crumbs Bake Shop cupcake with a single lit candle rests in her palm. Blackout—my favorite flavor. Mom sits, her ageless smile beaming. "Make a wish."

How could I forget? Every year it's the same. At midnight on my birthday Mom wakes me and insists we begin celebrating. Except my birthday is still three months away. I laugh. "It's not even September."

Her brown eyes twinkle. What's she hiding? "I know, but I thought we'd start the festivities early this year."

Wax drips down a purple candle onto chocolate frosting. "Three months early?"

"You only turn eighteen once." She says this every year, about every age. "As far as I'm concerned, all of autumn belongs to you this year. Now make a wish."

"Hold on. I have a surprise for you too." I open my nightstand drawer and withdraw the latest copy of the *New York Times*. Beaming, I pull out the "Arts & Leisure" section, pass it to her.

The paper crinkles as she unfolds it. "What's this?"

"Your surprise." I sit up and cross my legs, unable to contain the bouncing five-year-old inside. "I know you've postponed your dream because of me. Now you don't have to." I tap the paper. "Look."

Mom gasps, covers her mouth with a trembling hand. All color drains from her face. "Eliyana, what did you do?"

My excitement falters. "I entered one of your paintings in an art competition. You know, the one that fancy gallery downtown holds every year? The one you've always wanted to enter but never have." I nudge her with my elbow. More than just my mom, she's my best friend. She deserves this.

Mom remains silent.

I shift uncomfortably. Weird. I thought she'd be excited. "Um, anyway," I continue, the rush gone from my words, "you were selected as one of twenty artists to exhibit your work. They wanted to include your picture with the other winners, so I sent it in. I didn't think you'd mind."

She sets the paper down, her emotionless expression gives nothing away. Is she angry? Embarrassed? Finally she says to the wall, "You know how private I am."

I do know. I had to sneak a candid shot for the contest because she's always hated having her photo taken. Won't even let me get my picture done at school, insisting she do my portrait herself, which means no yearbook photos for me. I've never argued against her protectiveness. Who'd want to remember my ugmug anyway? I have no Facebook account, no Twitter or Instagram. Not that I'd have any friends or followers if I did.

"Mom, your photo is in the paper because you're an amazing artist." My hand finds her shoulder. "I thought you'd be happy."

She stands, tightens the tie on her robe. "Go back to sleep, Eliyana. I'll see you in the morning. We have back-to-school shopping tomorrow. You need your rest."

"Mom—"

"Good night." She blows on the candle. The flame extinguishes. And so does my dream.

The doorbell chime pulls me out of unconsciousness. I open sleep-infested eyes to a room veiled in darkness. Shards of moonlight pierce the cracks in my window blinds, scattering like broken glass on the floor. My mouth is dry and has that distinct cardboard flavor of dehydration. I smack and lick my lips. *Bleh.* I need water.

What time is it? I reach over and fumble for my phone, but it isn't there. Why—? Right. I left it in the kitchen. My best guess is it's sometime after eight at night. Then again, it could be two in the morning for all I know.

I lie still for a minute, allowing my body to wake. One eye itches and I rub it hard. Comb sleepy fingers through my hair and try to inhale some of the wind I just had knocked out of me. The dream—the memory—was so real.

The doorbell rings again. There's movement downstairs. I'm familiar with the growing pains of my lifelong home—the arthritic pops of loose floorboards, the senile complaints of unoiled hinges. Joshua must be moving some things over from next door. If he's going to be my guardian, he has to play the part.

I swing my jean-clad legs over the edge of my bed. A half-eaten granola bar with its trail of crumbs leading off the cliff of my nightstand begs to be rescued. My middle cramps, answering the cry audibly, but I can't bring myself to pick up the square of oats and honey. I'm hungry, but I'm also not. No other way to put it.

I stand, and my ankles creak. What is it about grief that makes everything age? My muscles ache, pleading with me to get back in bed. It's as if I'm being sucked deeper and deeper, swirling down a never-ending drain. Every time I slosh my way back to the ledge, life pulls the plug.

I walk over inside-out tees and unpaired socks on my way to the door, switching off the space heater as I pass by. Wrinkled papers and forgotten textbooks spill from my backpack. The pile of clothes and homework will only continue to grow. I have no intention of cleaning, or returning to school, in the near future. I've completed all my required classes anyway. What's the point in going back?

An off-kilter smirk surfaces. Quinn's going to have a fit.

All the more reason to stay home. She may be my best girl-friend, but that isn't saying much. Frenemy is more accurate.

Muffled voices drift from the first floor. I turn the glass knob on my bedroom door and open it a pinch. What's going on down there? Is Joshua already having guests over?

An invisible knife rips through my chest. He has friends. Friends who aren't me. Friends who probably include girls. Why am I only realizing this now?

My sockless toes curl when I step out onto the cool hallway floor. The brownstone is longer than it is wide, so the top of the stairs is just a stride away. I creep to the railing and peer into the foyer. Empty. The voices are too distant to be in the sunroom. They must be coming from the kitchen.

I skirt the banister's curve and tiptoe down the stairs, careful to avoid the testy spots.

"You need to find someone else. I can't do this anymore." The voice is undeniably Joshua's.

I pause on the bottom step.

"There's no time," a deeper voice says. "I already have my hands full with the other situation. You said you could handle this. Bring her back. Tonight."

The metronome in my chest triples. That voice. I've heard it before. But where? I peer around the corner. Only Joshua is visible, standing on the other side of the bar, his back toward me. Even from here, the stiffness in his shoulders stands out.

"Tonight?" Joshua's voice jumps up an octave. "Give her a chance to recover from the last life-altering event. Besides, she's safer here."

I step back. Why's he talking about me? He can't really be trying to find me an alternate guardian. Can he?

"Tonight."

My breath catches at the finality in his tone.

Déjà vu registers somewhere in my brain's encrypted files. I fight the impulse to peek around the corner again. I can't just storm in there and throw a fit. No. Then Joshua will know I've been eavesdropping. I'll have to talk to him about this tomorrow. When I can reason with him like the adult I almost am.

Step, creak. Step, creak.

I take a silent leap over a touchy floorboard and enter the dark bathroom across the hall. I've spent a lot of time in here lately.

Leaving the door ajar, I watch for movement in the foyer. Joshua enters first, his face paler than Mom's pastel paintings.

The other man follows. He's a head taller than Joshua with charcoal hair and intense eyes—eyes so recognizable, they stir something inside me. A memory? The man places a hand on the doorknob but doesn't turn it. "What aren't you telling me?"

Joshua scratches the back of his head. The way he does when he feels uncomfortable. The way he did earlier today. And the night everything changed between us. "I don't know what you mean."

At last, the man turns. One corner of his mouth slants north. "I think you do. I think you need to consider what it means that you've fallen for her. The consequences those feelings will bring."

My pulse ceases to exist. Think again, dude. Joshua can't possibly—

"You know she's just a job, Makai," he snaps. "It's all she can ever be. Frankly, I'm ready for this whole thing to be over."

My heartbeat returns. Fears confirmed. I've never heard him speak that way to anyone.

Makai gives a scarce nod. "Are you certain?"

Joshua crosses his arms. "I am."

I back into the shadowy confines of the bathroom and grope for the toilet seat. When I find it, I sit. How many times will I cry today? I hate his ability to storm every fortress I work so hard to construct.

The front door thuds closed, followed by the dead bolt's distinct *click*. Joshua and Makai are gone. I rise and enter the deserted hallway.

Why do I know that man? I close my eyes. His face is clear, but not in color. Black and white. Lines and shadows. Mom.

I lurch up the stairs and head straight for her room. The door has remained closed for a week. I haven't been able to bear going in, but now I can't wait. I enter and wince. This room smells more like her than any other.

Mary-Poppins tidy, just as she left it. A hope chest at the foot of her bed contains piles upon piles of sketchbooks spanning nearly two decades. I grab the key from Mom's nightstand and unlock the chest. The older books are at the bottom. White sticky labels date each one, the corners curled and peeling. I've looked through them countless times. I know exactly what I'm hunting for. I need the book from the year before I was born.

I kneel by the chest and lift its lid. Well-greased hinges move in silence. The scent of old paper and charcoal wafts upward, growing staler as I shift the top layers aside. There it is. I turn my back against the trunk and slide down, then cross my legs and open the cracked spine. Some of the pages float to the floor. So much of her early work is in here. Mostly landscapes. Some journal entries too.

And then I find it—a portrait occupying the final page. The likeness is younger, but the intensity in the man's gaze is unmistakable. Mom's careful cursive transcribed two words at the top left-hand corner.

Makai Archer.

The book falls. My lungs inflate and deflate rapidly. Could Makai be my dad?

Nathaniel Archer was my grandfather's name. I never met the man, only know he left us this house in his will because of my father—someone else I've never met. Mom didn't talk about him either, but she kept her own last name so I can only guess their relationship didn't end well. But then why would she keep this drawing of Makai?

I have to find him. I have to know. Joshua may think of me as a job, whatever that means, but this Makai person might have the answers I need. I snatch up the book and race down the stairs. A peek out the foyer window confirms what I'd hoped. Joshua and Makai are on the front steps, still talking. Perfect.

My cell phone is in the kitchen. I retrieve it as well as my keys from a hook by the back door. A glance at the time—8:37—reveals my theory was correct. I shove my feet into my gray-and-lavender Chuck Taylors, hopping on one foot and then the other to get my heels in. I return to the front of the house to wait. When Joshua goes next door for more boxes, I have my chance.

Makai heads west down Eighty-First. With as much stealth as possible I unlock the door, step into the frigid air, and secure the dead bolt. I shove my keys and phone into my hoodie pocket, still clutching the sketchbook in my right hand, and follow my target.

I speed-walk to keep up with his long stride. Once we're out of sight of Joshua's place, I'll make my move. Mom would've killed me for going out at night alone. It's early November, and the twinkle lights for the trees aren't up yet. Pockets of light spill from streetlamps, and illuminated windows blush at random, breaking up the shadows.

Makai turns left onto Amsterdam, and I jog to catch up. I reach the intersection and follow his course. He went left, right? I squint. Nothing. I turn around and go the other way. He's not there. He couldn't have made it to the end of another block already. Not possible.

My shoulders slump. I guess I won't be getting any answers tonight. My phone vibrates against my middle. I pull it free and open a text from Quinn.

hi! sorry i couldn't b there 2day. just got back. hang 2nite?

I tap out a quick reply.

too tired. rain check?

Quinn's response flashes back almost instantly.

k.

I end the conversation with a smiling emoji and pocket my phone. When I look up, a chill wraps my body and I shudder. A sense of panic sends a jolt of electricity through my veins. I take a step and then I stop. Then I walk in the opposite direction of my house.

I'm only wearing my "Beauty School Dropout" pajama tank beneath an aqua New York City hoodie. My thin jeans aren't exactly helping ward off the cold either. Cars pass by, their headlights blinding me as darkness burrows in for the night. But the temporary sight paralysis isn't my worst problem.

The bigger issue is the hooded guy four sidewalk squares behind me—the one who stands in the middle of the sidewalk, impeding my path home. The one who's been following me for nearly a block.

BE HAPPY

Don't panic. Panicking will only make things worse.

Think. I need people. Starbucks, just another block away.

I focus on my destination and walk at an even pace. I scan the sidewalk—nothing but a plastic grocery sack, a discarded Kit Kat wrapper, and a little doggy surprise someone left by a tree. Stupid tourists. No native would ever be so inconsiderate.

Not a single warm body in sight. Nobody is dumb enough to go for a late-night stroll alone in this city—except me. They say the Upper West Side is family friendly, but creepers are everywhere.

And I've attracted one.

Should I run? No. Don't alert the guy and speed up the mugging. Just drop the wallet and let him have it. I reach into my pocket. *Snap!* I was so fixated on following Makai, grabbing it didn't cross my mind.

What if my stalker's not after money? What if his intention is something else? I've never even kissed a guy. The thought of some stranger taking what he wants raises bile into my throat.

"Do not let fear control you. You're my brave girl."

Thanks for the vote of confidence, Mom, but it doesn't do a thing for me right now.

I chance it and glimpse over my shoulder.

Hoodie keeps his head bowed, his features invisible, his hands buried in his sweatshirt pockets. He doesn't look at me. Doesn't he notice our too-close proximity?

"Don't be afraid. I'm here."

You're not here though, Mom. Not even close.

I tuck the sketchbook under my arm, slide my phone from my pocket, and tap out 911 on the dial screen. My thumb hovers over the green Call button. My chest thuds. I might as well have a troupe of stomp dancers living inside it. I practically hear booming drums as the steps grow more complicated.

Hoodie walks right past me.

A much-needed sigh hushes my heart. I wait a full minute, then click off my phone and tuck it away.

Hoodie enters an apartment building.

Why was I so paranoid? One look at my face and the guy probably would've bolted. I should've just turned and said "boo."

A car alarm shrieks blocks away. Cabs pass at regular intervals, and the occasional *beep* of a locking vehicle diminishes my feelings of isolation. My breaths form clouds in the night air.

I pull my sweatshirt hood over my ears, wishing I'd brought earbuds for my phone. Music would be nice right now. Something to take my mind off Mom. And Joshua. Does he really think I'm just a "job"? Do our three years of friendship mean nothing?

Stop feeling. Stop caring. Stop loving. At least then it wouldn't hurt so much when someone leaves—or wants to leave.

When Broadway's lights come into view, approaching footsteps interrupt my thoughts. My peripheral vision reveals nothing, so I look back.

Return of Hoodie—Episode Two.

What am I doing? Why didn't I go home after he passed me? I was too focused on my own heartache to use common sense. Stupid.

I'm not athletic, so running won't save me. I nearly collapsed during the tap-dance number in *Anything Goes* at school last year.

My talents are much better served singing from behind a curtain while some pretty face lip-synchs the words. Our drama teacher stole the brilliant idea from *Singin' in the Rain.*

A hand grabs my arm.

I whirl. The sketchbook goes flying. My hands grasp Hoodie's shoulders and my knee meets groin in a move I didn't know I was capable of.

Hoodie lets out a guttural noise and a string of curses.

Adrenaline takes over. I turn and book it. My sneakers slap pavement, and a rush of cold floods my ears. Scaffolding drapes historical buildings in the midst of facelifts. I weave in and out of lanky metal poles, orange cones, and painter's plastic. By the last few feet my throat burns and my breaths come in gasps. When I'm finally basking in Starbucks' glow on the corner of Broadway, I allow myself to pause and glance down the street. I've lost Hoodie—for now.

I open the glass door, and Michael Bublé's charming romanticism welcomes me. Go on. Rub it in, why don't you? "Everything" plays low over the coffee shop's speakers, perfect ambience for lovebirds and local authors pulling swing shifts. Torture for me. The barista glances up, then looks away. Nothing I'm not used to. I prefer it, actually. Better to be ignored than taunted or teased.

The whir of bean grinders and the whoosh of steam wands create a much more soothing melody. Caffeine is the last thing I need. My blood brews through my veins like it's bursting from an espresso machine gone haywire. I can't resist the intoxicating scent of fresh Colombian though. Now I really do wish I had my wallet.

A hand touches my shoulder. I jump three feet.

"What the bleep, El?"

I pivot on my heel.

Quinn Kelley stares back at me. Her ice-blue eyes bulge out of their black-lined frames. "What's the matter with you?"

I shake my head. "I thought you were someone else. This guy . . . he tried to attack me on my walk here."

Quinn's raised eyebrows turn down. "What do you mean 'on your walk here'? I thought *you* were too tired to go out."

Of course *that's* the part she focuses on. How do I explain? I've only known her a few months. We may have been fast friends, but I can't tell her I was following some strange man who might be my father. I'd sound crazy. "I . . . changed my mind. I decided to take a stroll to clear my head."

"You should've texted." Her tone patronizing, she passes me. "I would've come to get you. Creepers are everywhere, you know."

I know. "I didn't think of it, I guess." I make a face behind her back. I'd like to see her execute such an escape.

Quinn isn't listening. She's already at the counter, prattling off her convoluted modifiers to the barista. Sometimes I think she drinks her coffee that way so she sounds cool when she orders it.

Man, she pulls off the Goth look. Real Goth. Turn-of-the-century, vintage Goth, not *The Rocky Horror Picture Show* kind. She's really not who I'd expect to see dressed this way. Lacy black stockings cover her never-ending legs and disappear into matching lace peep-toe heels. Black lace overlays her maroon party dress. Of course she adds her own touch to the look. Cherry-red lipstick instead of black, a silk rose pinned at her hip to match.

When she saunters back, she flips her platinum ponytail over one shoulder. "I ordered your drink for you."

I stare at my drab shoes. She'll hold this over me somehow. "You didn't need to."

Quinn rolls her eyes. "How else are you going to party with me all night if you don't get your fix?"

"I'm not going to a party, Q. I just need to catch my breath, and then I'm going home."

"You can't sit home and mope for the rest of your life."

The barista calls her name, and she's gone again.

Now I'm tired, the adrenaline rush evaporated. Mope? Is she serious? I didn't fail a chemistry exam. My. Mom. Died.

She returns with drinks in hand and passes me one.

I should stand up to her, tell her exactly where she can take her snide comment. Instead I say, "Thanks, but I'm really not in the mood for a crowd tonight." I sip and sigh. How can someone who makes me feel worse about myself most of the time know me so well after only a few months? The three-sugar soy latte is perfect.

"Oh, enough sulking. What you need is a little fun." She drinks her customized iced chai through a green straw, leaving an imprint of red lipstick when she pulls away.

"I'm not sulking. It's been a long week." I let the words hang. I shouldn't have to explain myself.

"You're coming with me, and that's final. You owe me for the drink anyway."

Why am I even friends with her? She latched onto me the moment we met and hasn't left me alone since. I'm a glutton for punishment. Or maybe I know I don't have any risk of heartbreak with Quinn. Either way, with or without her, I'm miserable.

I open my mouth to protest again, and the last person I expect to see traipses through the door. His hands hide within the front pouch of his navy Yankees hoodie, and his shoulders nearly touch his ears.

Joshua's gaze locks with mine. His shoulders fall. Is he relieved? Angry? I can't tell. He walks over. His slow gait gives the impression of uncertainty. "Hey. I thought you were asleep."

Quinn speaks first, as always. "You wanna come with us?" She's made it clear she disapproves of Joshua, so her invite is out of place.

"Where to?" His eyes never leave mine.

"A few parties. Maybe a club or two. You in?"

Joshua doesn't even peek at her. "Did you walk here?" Does he think we're the only two people in the conversation?

I level him with a deadpan gaze. *Keep it together, El.* "I'm sorry. I didn't realize I needed your permission to leave the house."

He inches closer. "You could've been hurt." He has no clue how true his statement rings. "I would've walked you if you'd asked."

"Is that your *job* now? To chaperone me everywhere?"

For once, he doesn't have anything to say.

"Am I missing something here?" Quinn steps between us. "Did you two break up?"

Ugh. She has no filter.

"We're just friends."

Don't feel. Don't care. Don't love. Don't let him see how much his words affect you.

Quinn narrows her eyes. "Whatever. Are you in or not?" She plants her hands on her hips, almost knocking the silk rose loose, and taps her peekaboo toe against the tiled floor. Lips pinching, she sweeps her glare over him. She doesn't really want him to join us, so why is she inviting him?

"Maybe another time." Joshua scarcely looks her way and then addresses me alone. "Come back with me. There are some things we need to discuss."

I should. I need answers. Does he know if Makai is my dad? Where did they want to take me tonight?

I almost say yes, but I can't be around Joshua right now. If I go back with him, we'll argue. I'll break down. Then he'll leave for sure. He already told Makai to "find someone else." Which is exactly why I need to figure out who Makai is and how he's linked to me. And I need to find out on my own.

"Like Quinn said, we're going out." Did I just agree to do the thing I don't want to do?

She grabs my hand, pulls me toward the door, and waves at Joshua. "See you, Josiah!"

I don't even bother correcting her.

⌒∞⌒

The air in the cab is drenched with the stale smell of body odor and exhaust fumes. The contents of Quinn's Coach bag pile between us on the bench seat: lip gloss, mascara, an antique compact, a half-eaten roll of Life Savers, a pocketknife, and a faded receipt. She opens her compact and begins retouching her already flawless makeup job.

I rest an elbow on the window ledge. Lean my face against my fist. I made Quinn tell the driver to take us back up my street first. But it was already too late. Mom's sketchbook was gone. Now we take West Side Highway all the way downtown. As we near the insomniac area of the city, the Hudson illuminates. Like yellow brick roads, columns of light create golden paths along the surface. If only they led someplace over the rainbow. A place where even an ugly girl could catch a break.

"What are you wearing under that potato sack?"

I glance to my left. Quinn gathers her things, returns them to her bag.

"You mean my sweatshirt?"

She nods.

"A tank top. Why?" I suck in my cheeks. I have a feeling I know her answer. *Whatever she says to persuade you, just say no.*

"Lose it."

I cross my arms. "Are you joking? It's freezing outside." How can she stand to go out in November wearing clothing no thicker than lingerie?

She tucks a loose strand of hair behind her ear. "We're not going to be outside, are we? Now take it off. I'm not walking into the party with a mannequin from Old Navy."

"My hoodie's from Aéropostale."

"Whatever. Blake Trevor's the most popular guy in school. We can't walk into his party looking like rejects. His college friends will be there."

I stifle a groan. Blake Trevor? The guy has made my life a living purgatory since freshman year.

"Your rack is your best feature, El. Flaunt it."

I loosen my clenched jaw. Is she serious? She hasn't asked about Mom's wake or how I'm feeling. What am I doing here anyway? Once we drop her off, I'll take the subway back. Except . . . ugh. My MetroCard is in my wallet at home. No way am I wasting money on a return ride to the Upper West Side. A girl's got to have principles. And double no way am I asking Quinn for cab fare—just one more thing for her to hold over my head. I'll have to deal. It's only a few hours, right?

Her face relaxes a smidge. "Look. I know you've had a hard day, and I'm sorry I couldn't be there. I'm just trying to help you get your mind off it. Okay?"

No. It's not okay. But I nod anyway.

She smiles. "Good. Be happy. You know I heart you."

I offer a semigrin in return. For all her faults and selfishness, Quinn has stuck by me even though I'm not exactly the most popular choice for company. Besides, she helped Mom make her first big art sale. For that I am indebted indefinitely.

"I heart you too." And despite everything that's happened today, I almost mean it. But how can I face a roomful of Blake's jerky friends? The cab slows and my stomach acid roils. Maybe I should've eaten the granola bar after all. At least then I'd have something to throw up.

park and cold

The windows are going to explode. Blake has the bass setting on his stereo way too high. When we pull up to the curb before his loft, the cab seats vibrate from the volume as Michael Jackson sings "Smooth Criminal." Quinn gets out first and pays the driver, adding a nonchalant "Keep the change" like any Fifth Avenue regular.

I open my door. Take a deep breath. I can do this. I can become more familiar with *The Perks of Being a Wallflower* for a few hours while Quinn mingles with guys way too old for us. Of course, who am I to talk? I'm in love—*was* in love—with Joshua, and he just turned twenty-one in September. Maybe she's right. Maybe I do need to have some fun for a change. Or, at the very least, I need the distraction. It will give me time to figure out how to find Makai anyway.

I rise from the cab and tie my sweatshirt around my waist, then tug my tank top over my jeans so my midriff doesn't show. This is the exact opposite of being invisible. Thankfully, the purple cotton neckline brushes my collarbone. The trivial modesty does nothing to pacify my rock 'n' roll nerves. Someone could plug me into an amp for all the reverberations under my skin.

The renovated firehouse is plain and out-of-date on the outside, but once we pass through the garage, climb the stairs, and enter the loft, it's like stepping into an Upper East Side apartment.

Everything from track lighting to custom crown molding screams money. This kind of place is Joshua's utopia. As an architecture major at Columbia, he loves taking something most people would see as junk and rendering it beautiful again.

Too bad I'm not a building.

"Hey, you made it." Blake Trevor in the flesh greets us with outstretched arms and a sloshed grin. Wasted already. Where are his parents? Would they even care to learn their teenage son is a lush?

Quinn pushes him against his chest. Her black fingernails dig lightly into his fitted polo shirt. "Of course. We wouldn't miss it."

Blake smiles wider, then turns his attention to me. His smile scrunches into a sneer.

I hug my chest and shift.

"Well, if it isn't Bloody Mary." Blake slurs one of the many nicknames he's used for me over the years.

"Blake, be nice." Quinn tosses out the comment. She's standing up for me, but she's not. Maybe she only brought me because she knew I'd be sober enough to call a cab at the end of the night.

Blake belches. This dude has no shame. "C'mon, Quinny. I was jus' havin' some fun." His letterman jacket has a beer stain on the front, but he doesn't seem to notice—or care. Plastered much?

I can't stand here any longer. "I'm going to get a drink." I have to yell over the music. "Do you want anything?"

"I'm good." She links one arm through Blake's, and they disappear into a swarm of alcohol-infused partyers. What does she hope to gain from hanging with a guy like him?

Music is my thing, but the heavy metal garbage now blasting from the speakers isn't music. Mom always said if you can't understand the lyrics, it's just noise. So true.

I meander through the crowd. Dancers holding red plastic cups of skunky amber liquid bump me as I pass. When I finally exit the maze of bodies and reach the kitchen, I feel as if I've been hula hooping for all the twisting and turning I've had to do.

I open the fridge and scan the drink choices. All two of them—beer and light beer. Gross. I grab an empty cup and fill it at the tap on the refrigerator. The cold water soothes my throat after the hot coffee. A stack of pizza boxes sits on the counter. My mouth waters. I can't put it off any longer. I open the top one. Yuck. Nothing but grease-caked cardboard and stringy bits of cheese.

The next two boxes, same thing. In the fourth I find a few slices of cold pepperoni. It'll have to do. One by one I pick off the processed-meat circles and toss them onto a napkin. When I take my first bite, I sigh. It might be cold, but my stomach doesn't care. When was the last time I ate?

Once I've finished my slice, a guy with an Amazin' Mets tee layered over a long-sleeved thermal, horrid acne, and a mess of blond waves joins me. "Anything good left?"

Out of habit I angle my face so my hair falls over the right side. "I only got down to the fourth box."

He searches the stack. An entire pie topped in veggies lurks at the bottom. "You want one?"

I glance at him past a curtain of dark locks. "Sure."

He leans against the counter and hands me a slice. "I'm Ky."

"El." I take a bite. Much better.

He smiles and chews. "You go to Upper West Prep with Blake?"

I nod. "Yeah." Unfortunately. "You?" I've never seen him before. Maybe he's new.

The volume lowers a smidge. U2's "With or Without You" combines couples across the loft.

"Blake and I share a mutual friend. I just started at NYU."

A college guy? I guess it's the acne that makes him seem younger.

Ky shifts. "You wanna dance?"

I consider him, waiting for the punch line. No one has ever asked me to dance. Even those considered freaks and geeks tend to avoid me. I am literally the last person on anyone's dance card.

Except, this time, the punch line doesn't come. Ky just smiles crookedly, waiting. Confidence emanates from his relaxed posture. In the way he doesn't hide. It's as if he doesn't care what he looks like. So I find myself saying, "Okay."

Before he takes my hand, he reaches forward and tucks my hair behind my ear. His bold move stops my breath in my throat. "Cool tattoo." He smiles. Doesn't flinch.

Cool tattoo? What planet is this guy from?

On the edge of the floor, Ky wraps his arms around my waist, and I put my hands on his shoulders. We sway in silence, which is fine by me. I'm not up to talking. When Bono's voice trails off, we part and stand there. Ky clears his throat, rocks back on his heels. We open our mouths in synchrony.

"Go ahead," he shouts over the vocal stylings of Jimmy Eat World.

"I'm going to use the restroom. Do you know where it is?"

He points toward the loft's north wall. A line has formed in front of what I assume is the bathroom door. Great.

"I'm gonna grab a drink. Meet me outside? This music is going to make me go deaf."

I nod. What else do I have to do while I wait for Quinn to have her fill of this scene?

I make my way back across the ocean of gyrating bodies and stand in line behind a girl doing the potty dance. Hilarious. I'm probably the only one here who needs to pee out from under the influence of alcohol.

The line moves at a larghissimo cadence—or as Mom would say, "Slower than midtown traffic during rush hour."

I pull out my phone and dial Information.

The operator's nasal voice grates through the speaker. "City and state, please."

"Manhattan, New York."

"What listing?"

I enunciate each syllable. "Muh-ki Ar-cher." I wait with suspended breath for her response.

"I'm sorry. I'm not showing anyone by that name."

"Can you try Brooklyn?" The line inches forward, and I move with it.

Another beat. "Nothing in Brooklyn either."

"Try Staten Island." I visually rummage the crowd for Quinn. It's impossible to tell who's who in this jungle.

The operator sighs. "Nothing for Staten Island either."

I bite my lip. I'm annoying her, but I have to know. "Union City, New Jersey?"

Two more beats. "No."

Hope dwindles. "Okay. Thank y—"

Click.

The line continues to shorten every few minutes. While I wait, I comb the popular social media sites for Makai Archer. It's a pretty unusual name, and the search quickly turns up nothing. Next, I Google and then Bing him. Zilch. Only junk spams the palm-sized screen.

I give up. The arched window overlooking the street is as tall as it is wide. Down below a guy opens a cab door for a girl with blonde hair more blinding than the sun. I'd recognize that mane anywhere. Quinn. She throws her head back, and I can almost hear the peal of her laughter over the music.

I put all thoughts of Makai Archer and peeing aside, leave the line, and dart for the exit. Again I have to worm through the overcrowded party. I call Quinn. *Pick up, pick up, pick up.* It rings once, goes straight to voice mail. Why am I not surprised? It's not like this is the first time she's done this to me.

"Everything okay?" Ky is lazing against the wall outside the door.

"Not really." I take the steps two at a time to the garage. When I'm at the curb, Quinn is long gone. Now what?

Ky appears beside me. "Was that your friend? The blonde?"
She's not my friend. "Yes."

He clasps his hands on top of his head, looks up and down the street. "Oh, man, I would've stopped her if I'd known. Sorry."

"*Call Joshua.*" Mom's voice inside my head chirps loud and clear.

No. I don't need him to rescue me.

"It's not your fault," I say to Ky. "It's just . . . she was my ride." I remove my sweatshirt from my waist. Shrug into it. Zip it to my chest. At least now I can wear what I want.

"Listen, I'm parked down the street. I could give you a lift."

I gape at him. "You have a car?"

Ky lowers his arms and shrugs. "Give me a break. I just moved here."

A foreigner. That explains it. "It's fine. I'll wait. Maybe she'll come back." Not likely.

"Nonsense. I'll drive you. It's really not a big deal. I was looking for an excuse to escape anyway."

"*Call Joshua now.*"

I've got this. I have to learn to do things on my own.

"My car is this way." He gestures to the end of the block, starts walking.

He seems nice enough. What's the harm?

"*Stop, Eliyana.*"

Mom—

"*This is a bad idea.*"

I'm fine. "Lead the way," I say.

After about half a block I can't stand the quiet any longer. "So where'd you move from?"

Ky laughs. It catches oddly. "I'm sure you wouldn't know it."

"What do you mean?"

"You haven't been there in a long time." He runs a hand through his blond waves. "I think you were just a baby when you left."

"Run. Now."

I stop. Something isn't right. My senses enhance. Everything, from the smell of asphalt to the water swishing in the sewer below, intensifies. Except my vision. That starts to blur.

Ky stops too.

I slide my right foot backward.

He turns. "This is me." The blinking red stoplight ahead flashes in warning.

I slide my other foot back an inch. My cold hands already nestle in my sweatshirt pocket. I clutch my phone, a lifeline. "I think I might wait for Quinn after all. I'd hate for you to go out of your way."

Ky looks down and shakes his head. A devilish grin spreads across his zit-flecked face. "It's not out of my way, Eliyana. In fact, you are the *only* reason I'm here tonight."

The sound of my name on his lips—the name I didn't give him—finally kicks my butt into gear. What was I thinking? I free my phone, press hard on the Home button, and blurt the first two words I can form. "Call Joshua."

"I wouldn't if I were you." He moves toward me. His hands clench and unclench.

One ring. Two. My whole body falls asleep, from shoulder to toe. What's happening?

"El?" Joshua's voice jets over the line on the third ring.

I try to speak through my quavering. "I need you to come get me." I attempt to move back again, but my feet remain glued in place.

"I'm on my way. Keep your phone on. I'll track you."

Since when did Joshua become so tech savvy? "Okay."

Ky doesn't attack. He just creeps toward me like Sweeney Todd waiting for the right moment to cut a throat. I try to look away, but for some reason, I can't. I can speak and blink, but otherwise I'm completely paralyzed.

Then I notice it. Same walk. Same height and build. His sweat-shirt is gone, but it has to be him. Hoodie.

Joshua is asking me something, but his words don't register. *Focus.* I may have only seconds left to speak to him.

"El, can you hear me? The guy. What does he look like?"

How does he know about Ky? "Blond. Pimples. Kinda skinny."

Joshua growls. "Kyaphus Rhyen. Makai warned me about him. El, whatever you do, don't look into his eyes."

Too late. Ky knocks the phone out of my hand. It bounces off the curb and into the gutter. He breathes hot air onto my face. Traces it with one finger. For the briefest moment I almost think I catch a hint of regret in his eyes, a flicker of a wordless apology. But then it vanishes, leaving a determined glare in its place. Dark and cold.

My insides squirm.

He bares his teeth and licks his lips. "Come on, I won't bite." He reaches his other hand up to my neck. Then my world fades to black.

childhood

You'd think by this point I'd be used to getting ditched. The never-ending pattern of disappointment should have taught me to expect it. But despite Quinn's selfish behavior, I thought she'd at least get me a cab before she left. Why do I bother hoping for the best in people? Aside from Mom, most everyone else has proven the only thing they're capable of is letting me down.

I met Quinn the first day of senior year. Though it was only a few months ago, it feels like a lifetime.

"Is this seat taken?" A way-too-pretty-to-be-speaking-to-me blonde dressed as if ready to attend a funeral stands by my lab table. With one hand planted on her popped hip, she waves the other over the empty stool. A small black purse dangles from her overturned wrist.

I shake my head.

"Great." She slides onto the stool next to mine and lays the purse on her lap.

I return my attention to the open textbook, pretending to study the periodic table of elements. I'm the only one in AP Chem without a partner, which means double the work. Like last year in Physics, no one chooses me unless assigned.

"I'm Quinn, by the way." Marilyn Monroe meets Helena Bonham Carter sticks a fingerless-gloved hand between my nose and the book.

"Um, El." I don't look up.

"I just transferred from East Prep."

I snort inwardly and flip the page. "You probably don't want to advertise that information to the general public."

"Why not?"

Poor thing, so innocent. So clueless.

I sigh, shut *Advanced Explorations in Chemistry*, and swivel to face her. "Because if word gets out you used to go to East Prep, you'll be stuffed inside a locker before day's end. Century-long rivalry, ya know?" Prep students may be of a higher breed, but they're not above the occasional mutt-like behavioral slipup.

"Thanks." She unsnaps her purse and applies fresh gloss to her poison-apple lips. *Smack*. "I'll keep it in mind. So what class do you have next?"

I hate to ruin the possibility I might gain a friend my last year of high school, but . . . "You probably don't want to be seen talking to me either." I'm a glutton for punishment, but it wouldn't be fair to sentence the girl to my personal purgatory on her first day.

She removes a bottle of black polish and begins coating her already-ebony nails. The ammonia odor wafts toward me. "Why not?"

I smother a choke. This is why I go with the natural look. "Seriously?" I glance at Mr. Newman. Will he reprimand her for using class time for personal pampering?

No. He's sitting atop his desk reading *The Prisoner of Azkaban*. Again. Technically we're supposed to be studying for the exam tomorrow. Really it's just our twenty-three-year-old chemistry prof's excuse to pretend he's teaching at Hogwarts, rather than our "completely mundane Muggle institution." Yes, those words have literally flown from his mouth on more than one occasion.

Quinn blows on her nails, leaving my question without its obvious answer.

I roll my eyes. She has to notice my birthmark—a homing

beacon for ridicule and rejection. "Let's just say if you hang with me, there's no way you'll get in with the popular crowd." Do I really need to spell it out for her?

She hops down from the stool.

Sayonara. Been nice knowing you. Oh wait, I didn't.

The stool legs scrape linoleum as she scoots her seat closer to mine. It's only a few inches away when she resumes her perch.

Well, that's new.

"So, are you a native or a transplant?" Chatty, this one.

I shrug, hunkering into the Yankees sweatshirt I borrowed—a.k.a. stole—from Joshua last Friday during our all-night *American Idol* audition marathon. Making fun of fifteen seasons' worth of people dressed as cows who sing rap-remixes of "Old MacDonald Had a Farm" is what we do best. "I've lived in the city since I was a baby," I tell her, taking a whiff of Joshua-scented fabric. Only four more hours, then I can have the real thing. "You?"

She slides the bottle of polish toward me and stretches her right hand beside it. "Same. Live with my mom. Dad left when I was little."

"Me too." I lift the brush, wipe it against the bottle's lip. *Drip, drip.* Paint splatters the tabletop. It's black as well. Mr. Newman won't notice.

"My mom works in fashion. What's yours do?"

I move from her pinky to her thumb, giving each nail an even coat. "She's an artist, a painter. Mostly watercolors and stuff like that."

"Hey, there's this really high-end art dealer who lives in my building. Lincoln something or other. I could totally introduce your mom to him if you want."

"I don't know. She kind of likes her privacy." The art contest incident from last week is still fresh. Since then things have been awkward between us. I hate it.

"Oh, come on," Quinn says. "Every serious artist needs a dealer.

At least meet him." She gives a nonchalant smile, as if changing people's lives is something she does all the time.

"I'll think about it." What would it hurt?

"Great." She plucks a phone from her purse, careful not to smudge her freshly inked nails. "What's your number?"

I prattle off the digits as she taps them into her phone. My own phone vibrates. I glance at Mr. Newman, then withdraw it from my backpack. One new text.

hit the bux after school?

I smile and reply. Quinn's screen flashes almost instantly. This must be the equivalent of passing notes in class, something I've never done.

Just like that, for the first time since childhood, I have a friend.

I arise from the groggy haze of my memory-slash-dream. I'm lying on the back seat of a car. Oily leather sticks to my face and carries the faint smell of coconut. I try to cry out, but my mouth's gagged, my feet and hands bound. Is this what being drunk feels like? Street-lamps blur by. I'm going to be sick. I really have to pee now. Lovely.

"Ugh." I groan against a throbbing migraine. I'll never forgive Quinn for this.

"It's not much farther, princess."

I blink several times and try to zero in on the driver. Ky. Or what did Joshua call him? Kyaphus? How could Joshua know that? Does this have something to do with the conversation I overheard before I left the house?

The car's steady vibration attempts to lull me back into oblivion. I open my eyes wider. Gotta stay awake. I have to scream the minute Ky lets me out.

He doesn't have the radio on. The eerie silence is louder than Blake Trevor's stereo. I need music. Now. Music mollifies me, helps me focus. Beethoven's "Moonlight Sonata" comes to mind. I tap off the notes on my numb fingers. At least I have muscle control again.

One, two, three. Breathe in through my nose. *One, two, three.* Breathe out through my mouth. Oxygen enters my lungs, surfing smoothly on each wave of notes. My head bobs to the steady rhythm I've heard so many times. Mom's favorite for me to play on the piano.

The melody repeats three times over before Ky brings the car to a slow stop.

Where are we?

When he comes around the side and opens my door, panic returns. He's put his hoodie on. Stalker identity confirmed. A blade glints at his side—is it made of glass? He reaches for me.

I shut my eyes. Tight. Blood. Please don't let him draw blood.

The glass blade is cold against my sore wrists. Every muscle seizes. Teeth grind. Lungs fail.

But Ky doesn't hurt me. He frees me.

With my hands and feet loose, air greets raw skin. *Ahhh.*

"We walk from here." He helps me sit. "Don't try anything. This is no ordinary blade. I'd hate for you to get hurt." His voice softens. If I didn't know any better, I'd think he means it.

Ha! Not likely.

"Understand?"

I nod. Sweat trickles down my temple.

Grazing my cheek with the knife, Ky severs the gag. He presses the tip into my side. I don't dare scream. "Get out. Slowly."

I obey to perfection, stalling as much as possible. Will Joshua know where to find me? I don't have my phone, so he has no way of tracking me. He recognized Ky's name, so maybe—

"Move." Ky forces the point closer, if possible.

I wince.

We're standing on the edge of Central Park's south end, right outside the Artist's Gate. A statue of José Julián Martí on his noble steed guards the entrance. This is where he brings me? We're closer to home now than we were downtown. A surge of hope bursts from my chest. I know this area of the city as well as the chords to "Daydream Believer."

"Um, I don't think you can leave your car parked on the curb." I point to a red-and-white No Parking Any Time sign. "You'll get towed."

"Unimportant." He wraps one arm around me. "Smile, princess. For the next few minutes we're in love."

Groups of various sizes cluster around the Park's perimeter. I refuse to smile and he draws me closer. He nuzzles his nose into my hair, and I gag.

His blade cuts through the cloth of my sweatshirt. "Smile." The hiss, as sharp as the knife, punctures the air.

This time, I force a small grin. Doesn't anyone notice us? Don't they see I'm being forced against my will?

He leads me down a flight of steps into the park. A canopy of pin oaks envelops us as we descend. Their splayed, fingerlike branches clutch a beautiful fall wardrobe of leaves in oranges and reds that will soon become last season's garb. Beneath them, old-fashioned lampposts cast a white glow from every angle.

If I can get away, Central Park has plenty of hiding places. I know them well, and I'm betting if he just moved here he doesn't.

"Do you come here often?"

"No."

A few more steps. "How long have you lived here again?"

"Keep your mouth shut," Ky snaps. Annoyed. Good.

"I was just wondering why a college student would want to throw his life away by kidnapping a teenager."

He stops. Shakes his head. Laughs. "You stupid girl. Do you mean to tell me Elizabeth told you nothing?"

Whiplash. "What do you know about my mom?"

"Wow. She's dumber than you are." He drags me forward.

The insult raises several choice words to mind. How dare he say that about Mom. But I don't speak again. Somehow this all fits together. Joshua knowing Ky's name. Ky knowing Mom. These are the outer corners of one complicated puzzle. If only I had the middle pieces so I could see the entire picture.

We pass more late-night loiterers. A shifty-eyed man stomping out a cigarette at the base of a tree, attempting to hide his totally illegal act. A couple in matching joggers walking their Border collies. Three girls about my age passing a bag of Skittles back and forth as they chat. Laugh. Gossip. Oblivious in their own little bubble.

I will someone to look at me. To ask if I'm okay. To care.

As if reading my thoughts, Ky laughs, low and mocking. "People only see what they want to see, princess. They ignore what's right in front of them. No one is going to save you."

I swallow. Having been the target of bullies like Blake, I know too well most people would rather look the other way than try to help and risk their own skin.

The Pond is in clear view. He lugs me to it, then stops on the soggy shore. "Get in."

His demand is very stage left. Is he going to drown me? "What?" I avoid eye contact.

He digs the blade deeper, breaking skin. I try to lean away, but his grip is too firm. "Either get in or be dragged in."

"What am I supposed to do?"

"When you can't touch the bottom anymore, swim down. Haman will be waiting on the other side."

The other side? Haman? Maybe Ky is some psycho, escaped from a mental hospital. Of course, that doesn't explain his freeze-ray eyes. Still, if I play along I might be able to escape. "You're not coming?"

"No."

"Why not?"

"You and your questions." Ky spits to one side.

This is my chance. "So I just go out to where it's too deep to stand and then swim to the bottom?"

"Yes." Ky looks around, back toward the path. "Now hurry up."

What's he so nervous about?

I feign compliance and shrug, suppressing a grin. "Okay. But you'll have to let my arm go first."

He releases me with a shove, and I tread the freezing shallows. My sneakers become instant weights. I'll never gain distance in them now. I remove each one and chuck them ashore.

Ky is a statue, arms crossed, watching me.

I move forward, ignoring the shivers already taking over. My feet sink with each step. Once the water reaches waist high, I push off from the muddy bed and swim. Something squirms by my leg. I jerk away. *Gross.*

When I point my toes and can't reach the bottom anymore, I glimpse the shore one last time. Ky hasn't moved. I take a deep breath. Then I dive. The water is dank. Murky. I can't see a thing.

If I can get deep enough, I'll be able to swim forward and hide beneath the Pond's bridge. I'll wait in the shadows until Ky leaves. When it's safe, I'll swim to land. Go home.

A hand grabs my ankle and yanks me down.

I claw for the surface. Chest tightens. Lungs burn. The grip on my ankle is too much. Down, down, down. How deep is this thing anyway? I'm dizzy. I'm going to pass out.

And then, out of nowhere, another hand grabs me, but this time around my bicep. I'm a rope in a tug-of-war, and Team Ankle is winning. I kick with every modicum of feistiness and teenage angst I have left. I don't know if the other contestant is friend or foe, but he's yanking me in the direction I want to, no, *need* to go.

Thwack! My heel meets bone . . . a nose? I'm free.

With my rescuer's help I swim for the surface. When I break it, I gulp. Lie on my back and float. I can't swim anymore. Then I'm dragged along until I finally reach earth.

Whoever saved me is propping my head now. *Cough. Spit. Gasp.* "Thank you." Was that my voice or did I trade with a toad?

"Quiet now. We don't have much time."

Mom?

I look up. My vision blurs. Blink, blink, blink. Oh my—"Mom!" This can't be real.

"Hi, brave girl." She looks different, older somehow.

I scramble to sit. I cry out, and something reminiscent of a seal bark protrudes. "Mom, what's happening?" Sob after chest-jolting sob spills forth. I clutch the fabric of her clothes, afraid if I let go she'll vanish with my next breath.

She strokes my wet hair, finger-combing the tangles. "I need you to listen to me now. We may have only moments."

Choking fear wraps jagged talons around my heart. "What do you mean?"

"I thought keeping all of this from you was the best thing. But I was wrong. You need to know the truth so you can guard your heart against the lies." She cranes her neck.

I follow her lead and search for Ky on the opposite shore. He's gone. *Good riddance.*

She grips my shoulders, and we lock gazes again. Her stare bores into my soul. I brace myself.

"You are not of this Reflection, Eliyana. I brought you here to hide you from those who seek to use you. In hopes you'd have a normal life. I wanted you to have a choice."

Reflection? Normal? Nothing about any of this is normal. "Why would anyone want to use me?"

"Because of this." Mom touches four fingertips to my birthmark.

I shudder. "I don't—"

"This"—she traces my cheek—"is not what it seems. These markings on your face make you a target. The enemy knows about you now. It's not safe here for you anymore."

"Enemy? Target? You're not making sense." Has someone drugged her?

Mom sighs. Moonlight reflects off her pooling tears. With a shaky breath she says, "I'm sorry. I was wrong. I never should have kept—"

Splash! She doesn't have the chance to finish. Whatever just broke through the water is coming right at us.

SIX

far away

An arrow—an *arrow*—darts by, inches from my face. Pings the maple tree behind Mom.

"Run!" She yanks me to a stand. We trip over stones and midget bushes along the shore up a small incline to the winding path around the Pond. A copse of trees rises beyond the sidewalk. Mom sprints into it, literally dragging me. She's going to dislocate my arm. Who'd have thought she could run this fast? When we're somewhat sheltered, she stops, grabs me by the shoulders, and looks past me, wild-eyed. "Give me your sweatshirt."

I'm panting. I grip my aching side to keep from falling over. "What?"

Mom sheds her navy-blue, open-front cardigan. The same one she wore last time I saw her. "Trade me."

We're both soaked. What good will trading clothes do? "Why?"

She seizes my hoodie's zipper, pulls it down, and peels the whole thing off in one swift move the way she did when I was young. She thrusts her cardigan at me and dons my sweatshirt. "You are to stay here until Joshua comes to get you. Do you understand me?"

"What?" I choke on the word. "No."

Mom wraps me in a tight hug. "I'll see you again. I promise. But right now the most important thing is keeping you far away from Jasyn Crowe."

The hug doesn't last. Who's Jasyn Crowe? I don't care. Only Mom matters. How can I let her go again? I won't. "No." I snatch her hand. Draw her deeper into the trees. "We're going home. Together."

She slides her fingers out of my sweaty ones and backs away. "I love you."

I blink. She's gone.

I love you too.

Fwit. An arrow sticks out from the ground before me.

I fight the urge to run after her, or better yet, start screaming so the shooters will come for me. What just happened? A dream? Did I fall victim to unconsciousness and am now drowning at the bottom of the Pond?

Fwit. An arrow grazes my arm, tears right through Mom's sweater. I hiss through my teeth. Touch three fingers to my stinging skin. When I lift them, bright red blood paints their tips.

Not a dream.

I press my hand over the wound. I'm a duet of nausea and panic. What should I do? Mom said to wait here, but what if I could save her? I bend and scoop up the arrow. Where'd the other one go? I shuffle around the dirt and twigs with my bare feet. *Got it.* With both arrows in my free hand, I dart in the direction she went.

There's too much light on the path. Some spills from the lamp-posts. Some streams down from Fifth Avenue. I stay on it anyway. Where were the arrows coming from? How did Mom just . . . vanish?

An arm materializes in front of me, jerks me into the trees. Now I really am getting whiplash.

I whirl, arrows pointed like spears.

A tall man in a black trench coat frowns down at me. "Makai?"

"Yes." He squints, focusing on something behind me. A quiver of arrows is slung over his back, a bow held close at his side.

Now I've seen everything.

He shoves a hand in his pocket, removes a white handkerchief, and hands it over. "Wrap it around your arm to stop the bleeding. Stay here. I'll be right back."

I remain, helpless as a toddler in a playpen. I'm not stupid. I'm not the girl in the horror flick running up the stairs in her underwear when she should be running out the door. I have enough brains to know when to act. When to stay put. But I'm tired of everyone treating me like a baby.

I unfold the white square, one-handed. Shimmering blue thread embroiders three initials in one corner—E.K.C. I drop the arrows, roll the cloth into a loose line, and tie it around my arm. The pressure pinches, a good, stay-alive pain.

Target. Enemy. Reflection. The words switch around like the notes of an unfinished composition. How can I believe any of it? How can I not? After everything I've seen tonight, my disbelief morphs closer to conviction each second. A boy with the power to render his victim immovable. Arrows soaring through Central Park. Mom appearing and disappearing. This isn't just weird, it's otherworldly.

A not-so-distant scream pierces the night. *Mom.*

I won't stand behind the curtain while Mom's fight scene takes center stage. Dumb or not, I have to help her.

With an arrow in each hand, I stumble onto the path and move north. Wet bangs stick to my forehead and hang before my eyes. I part them, push them off my face. Where's Makai? How does he keep disappearing? Water laps the shore to my left. Arrows zip by between interludes. Shouldn't I hear shouts—something to alert me of the raging battle?

The bridge rises just ahead. I stop and wait. Silence. I cross. I'm jogging now, don't slow when I cross paths with another unobservant pedestrian or two. Should I really be surprised when no one offers help? Wonders why a sopping girl is walking around barefoot, arrows fisted in each hand?

I'll give you that one, Ky. Most people *are* totally self-absorbed.

The gritty sidewalk scrapes my bare feet. I ignore the blisters, the skin stripping off layer by layer. It would be worse to walk around in soggy shoes. I'm almost where I started with Ky. Where is everyone? Where are the arrows coming from? What—?

A single arrow shoots from the water, into the air. The battle is . . . underwater?

One deep, gulping gasp. Mom's head surfaces. She screams again. Flails and disappears—pulled under?

Drawing in a huge breath, I dive after her. When I open my eyes, they burn against inky water. I swim forward. Down. My oxygen supply dwindles. What am I looking for? Guess I'll know when I find it.

A pinprick of clear, green light beckons me deeper. I swim closer and the light grows, first into a beam, then a pool. When I'm directly above it, the glare is almost too much. Like a glowing emerald treasure lost at sea, the light sparkles and shines. Draws me in. Mesmerizes me.

And then it really is sucking me deep into its whirlpool. I let it take me. For Mom. A hand reaches out from the light's nucleus. A head appears. There she is. Her face contorts, her eyes closed, her teeth clenched. Someone, or something, is hurting her.

Not if I have anything to say about it.

I kick hard, aiding the whirlpool in consuming me. I ignore the pain in my lungs, forget I can't breathe. I have only one goal, one purpose—save Mom. I stretch for her, but she's sucked into the light. Faster. Deeper. Closer. Green surrounds me. I have to reach her. I *have* to.

Another whiplash. I'm hauled backward, up and out, away from the light. Away from Mom. *No!* I try to scream, but opening my mouth only floods my lungs. Wiggle, squirm, kick. I don't need rescuing. I need to keep going. But I'm not strong enough. Whoever's gripping me refuses to relent. I don't give up. I resist all the way to the oxygenated surface.

When my face hits the cold night air, I release the arrows and cry out. Relieved. Agonized. I couldn't help her. She was right in front of me. I should've fought harder.

"Eliyana, are you okay? What in the world were you trying to do, get yourself killed?" A blend of relief and anger salts Joshua's voice. He has hold of my hand, his fingers threaded through mine. I've always imagined our hands intertwining this way. So what.

I wrench away, but he won't let go. "I was trying to save my mom."

He shakes his head. "El—" He squeezes my hand.

"I'm not crazy. She saved me. I *saw* her."

"It's not that. I don't think you're crazy. I know she's alive."

"You do?" And you didn't tell me?

A slight nod. Is that an apology in his eyes?

"Then we have to go back down there. We have to—"

"We'll get her. I promise. But not that way."

My mouth opens in automatic protest. Before I can argue he says, "I'll explain everything, but first we need to get to safety." He pulls me against him, and I stop breathing mid-exhale. Our bodies touch from chest to hip. His face is so close to mine our noses nearly brush.

My entire body is percussion. All beating organs and thrumming nerves. Is he trying to distract me?

And then it's over. Joshua turns and pulls my arms around his neck. Even dripping wet, he smells of autumn—cedar sprinkled with cinnamon and cloves. "Trust me. Okay?"

Mom's words. I let my muscles relax. Rest my head against his back and take in his heartbeat's steady rhythm. My own pulse slows to match. A single, traitorous sob escapes. Joshua's shoulders tense. He felt it. Does he care?

More than you know, sweetheart.

Yet another assurance of Mom's I can't believe. Since that night I've done my best to pack all our memories together in a box marked Do Not Open—a box I stuffed away in the attic of my emotional storage unit. Being close to him makes me want to peek inside that box, sort through those times. Examine them. What went wrong?

"How'd you find me, anyway? I dropped my phone back at the party."

"This was the most likely Threshold they'd use." Before I can ask what a Threshold is, he adds, "There's also a tracking device implanted in the necklace I gave you. Insurance. In case something happened to your phone." He clears his throat. "You can let go now." His voice, deep and husky, rumbles through his chest.

I release my grip, and we walk the few feet to the shore. I cover the pendant resting against my collarbone with my palm. Not a gift, then. Part of his job. Another ruse. Another lie. Was any of it real?

When I'm standing ashore, drenched inside and out, I glance at the water. It's still. Ordinary. No arrows. No battle raging beneath the surface.

Nothing aside from the silent procession accompanying the second funeral I've attended this week.

cﾟ⟨∞⟩ﾟ

This is the longest silence in the history of long silences.

Joshua busies himself with what could be a kindergarten construction project. A leaning stack of peanut butter sandwiches tops my kitchen island. He adds slice after slice of bread, spreading the tan paste like mortar over spongy white bricks.

I run a brush through my damp hair, water droplets pelting the floor. The wound on my arm has been properly bandaged, Makai's handkerchief tucked in the back pocket of my jeans. "Care to explain?" I try to hide the anger shading my voice. If Joshua hadn't intervened, if I'd had one more second, maybe Mom would be standing here too.

He doesn't look up. "When we're safe."

Why won't he look at me? He goes from summer to winter as often as Mom runs out of pencils. "We're not safe now?" And what about Mom? What about *her* safety?

He stops midspread. The corner of his mouth twitches. "No."

The doorbell rings. Neither of us moves. All the lamps in the house are off, per Joshua's instructions. Only the range light under the microwave glows pale gold.

Bing-bong.

He circumvents the island and pauses when he reaches me. "Get down on the floor. Don't move until I come for you."

I nod, lower myself to the refinished wood. I've never seen him so serious, so focused. This may be just a job to him, but he's good at it.

Every step he takes echoes through the brownstone. The sounds give his positions away, each call unique. One floorboard pops this way, another protests that way. When he's by the door, I picture him peeking out the window to see if the person on the other side is friend or foe. The door creaks open. Must be safe to reappear.

"I cannot believe you'd be so careless as to let her out of your sight like that. You know better than anyone what her life is worth." Makai is back. And he's pacing. His boots squeak as he clunks across the foyer.

"I made a mistake. I didn't want to force her into the middle of all this. It's not her battle to fight."

Makai emits a cynical laugh. "Like the Void it isn't."

I may have just developed a heart murmur. Battle? Void? "Okay, what on earth is going on here?" I enter the foyer.

Joshua's jaw tightens. "I thought I told you to stay put."

"I'm not a child. I don't need you to protect me." Except I *so* do, but I'll never admit it.

Makai stops midstride and offers a discreet bow. "Eliyana. I don't believe we've been formerly introduced. I'm Makai Archer,

Commander of the Guardians. I've watched over you and your mother since just after you were born."

His greeting is so formal I almost curtsy. "It's just El. " I draw his handkerchief from my pocket. It's wrinkled and stained. Maybe he won't want it back.

Makai accepts the damaged cloth, rubs it between his thumb and forefinger, before stowing it inside his coat. His expression sinks from angry to solemn. "I apologize we couldn't meet under better circumstances. I did what I could for your mother." His eyes glow, the orangey-brown color of cello wood. "I followed Crowe's men through the Forest of Night, but I had to turn back. I vowed I would always protect *you*, first and foremost." Why doesn't he sound too happy about that arrangement?

I shake my head. Just listening hurts. "I have no idea what you just said."

Makai looks at Joshua. "You haven't told her?"

Joshua shrugs. "I was getting to it. There hasn't exactly been a good time—"

"Eliyana, Joshua is your personal Guardian. He came here to assist me in protecting you when we discovered Crowe might have gotten a tip as to your existence."

Three years? Joshua has been my Guardian for—I can't even.

"The situation has escalated recently. We believe someone on this side discovered your location and has been sending him information since."

I shake my head again. "English please. Who is Jasyn Crowe? Where's my mom, and why was I led to believe she was dead? What do you mean by 'this side,' and why does this thing"—I point to my birthmark—"make me a target?"

"These are all very good questions," Makai says. "But they have to wait. We must get you to the Haven before Crowe discovers you are not the one his men apprehended."

Oh my—"Mom. She took my sweatshirt. They think she's me."

"Soulless." Joshua nearly vomits the word. "Vile, emotionless creatures, but too focused on themselves to see past their own noses."

"My best guess," Makai continues, "is Crowe faked Elizabeth's death to throw us off. He wants you alone and vulnerable. Elizabeth escaped because she knew he would send his men for you next. She wouldn't have been able to do it on her own. Crowe's castle is swarming with guards, which means your mother has an ally on the inside—good news for us."

"How do you know my mom?" The question bursts free before I can stop it. "Are you my dad?"

Makai scratches his cheek. "No. I am not your father, but I knew him."

Finally, some answers. "Who is he? Can you take me to him?" Maybe he can help us.

He frowns. "I said I knew him. I do not anymore."

"We really need to get going."

No way. Ignoring Joshua's interruption, I plant my feet, place my hands on my hips. "I'm not going anywhere until one of you gives me a straight answer."

Makai sighs. "Your father's name was Tiernan Archer. He was my younger brother."

Was. I grieve inwardly for the man I never knew—never will know. "What happened to him?"

"Tiernan disappeared seventeen years ago, but I have no delusions about my brother. About what he . . . became." The muscle beneath Makai's right eye twitches.

I lean forward. "And?"

His face softens for the first time since he walked through the door. "Tiernan turned Soulless." A pause. A shift. "He's never coming back."

tragic place

It's 10:00 a.m. but this makes no difference. No matter the time of day, the subway tunnels always smell like urine.

Joshua shoulders two backpacks—he refused to let me carry my own. I'm wearing my gray parka, unzipped over a long-sleeved aqua V-neck tee. Mom's black Uggs are warm and cozy around my toes. We always shared clothes. Is there a chance we will again?

A hobo with fingerless gloves and Santa Claus whiskers lies incapacitated against the wall, a poster advertising an MTA smart-phone app above him. We pass him. Stop a few feet behind the yellow safety line. Wait.

The subway isn't empty on a Sunday by any means. It just attracts a different sort of crowd. A mom with twin boys in matching plaid shorts and polo shirts trots down the steps, followed by a dad with an umbrella stroller in one arm and a wiggling toddler in the other. CEOs dressed for a morning on the green and child-free nannies enjoy a day off. Columbia students with lattes in hand chat about the upcoming Thanksgiving and winter breaks. It's a day of recreation, a day to forget the busyness of the week ahead. For everyone but us.

I lean toward Makai. "How far are we going?" Translation: How long until I'm in the same vicinity as Mom?

He's still carrying his bow and quiver. Nobody looks at him twice though. It's New York. Weird is normal.

"We'll get off just before the tunnel passes beneath the East River. Then we walk." An omniscient smile spreads across Makai's face. For the first time he looks less than intimidating. Something tells me when he says "walk," he doesn't mean above ground.

When the train screeches toward us, Joshua enfolds a protective arm around me. I should shrug him off, still unable to completely forgive him for thwarting Mom's rescue, but his nearness fills a longing inside. "Stay close. We're not sure what awaits us at the Threshold."

Threshold? There's that word again. The doors slide open before I can ask. People pile in like remote-control droids. I start in after them, but Joshua's embrace tightens as Makai extends an arm in front of us. It's the same gesture Mom always made when a bus came to a sudden stop. The doors are about to close. We're not going to make it. Then I'm rushed forward. We leave the platform just in time before being captured by the car's metal jaws.

The car rattles into darkness. Joshua grasps the bar above his head. I can't help but lean against him when the momentum impairs my balance.

Makai inclines his head. "Six o'clock."

Joshua nods, then glances back and to the right.

I follow his gaze through the mass of bodies. A blond boy with nostrils flaring watches us from the car's other end. My small breakfast of coffee and toast churns in my gut.

Joshua draws me closer. "Kyaphus. What do you suggest?"

Makai's cool expression doesn't alter. He'd be a good Buckingham Palace guard. "Follow my lead."

Thump, thump, thump. Is that my heartbeat or Joshua's? It palpitates faster, louder. I know what Ky is capable of. I never want to feel trapped inside my own body again.

When the train stops at Rockefeller Center, we exit. I'm expecting to book it up the stairs, but we just stand there, straddling the line between train and platform. What are we doing? We have to *move*.

Natives shove past, casting us dirty looks for blocking the exit. I glance between my protectors. Their eyes communicate understanding, while I remain clueless. Hello? Won't someone fill me in?

Ky exits three doors down. Strides our way. Makai shoves Joshua and me onto the train. The doors close, reducing us to spectators while Makai enters the lion's den.

I push against the doors, dig my fingers into the crevice between them. Worthless. My strongest link to Mom is going to sacrifice himself to save me. Us. What is Joshua doing? Why won't he fight?

"Stop, Eliyana." An eerie sort of calm, a resolve, laces his voice. My face flames.

Beyond the glass, Ky pulls his glass blade from his sweatshirt pocket and lunges.

Makai vanishes. Where'd he go?

Ky grabs what appears to be thin air, struggling against an invisible duress. He jerks his head left, right, as if avoiding a punch to the face.

Now I've seen everything.

The train lurches and glides. Ky plunges his knife into nothing. Makai reappears, the dagger sunk deep into his shoulder.

As the tunnel ingests us, I turn into Joshua. Let the walls crumble in this tragic place. I have a good excuse. I bury my face into his chest, and he strokes my hair. We don't speak. We don't have to. We spend the rest of the ride this way, clinging to each other. Somehow I know, in this moment, he needs me as much as I need him.

"Kyaphus won't be far behind." Joshua grasps my hand as we exit the train.

I won't read too much into it. It's part of his job, keeping me close.

We stand aside and wait for the train to leave. Joshua shrugs my backpack off his shoulder, passes it to me. "You should eat."

I accept the purple JanSport and sling it over my back, sliding my arms through the loops. Our hands separate, but he joins them again the moment my backpack is in place. "Not hungry."

"I'll carry it, El. I just gave it to you so you could eat."

I shake my head. "We'll be faster if we're balanced. I'll pull my own weight."

He knows I'm right. It's why he doesn't argue.

Once the train slithers away, he hops off the platform onto the tracks and reaches for me. "We need to hurry. Our window is small."

I plant my hands on his shoulders, and he lifts me down. When I'm on firm ground, he takes my hand again, leads me into darkness. Nobody stops us or tries to wave us back. Welcome to the city of minding your own business.

Joshua removes a Maglite from his backpack and clicks it on, illuminating our trail. Then he picks up his pace.

I have to double my steps to keep my short legs in sync with his long ones. We veer close to the wall, maintaining a sizable distance from the third rail. Gulp. Becoming underground roadkill is one thing, but electrocution is probably the last way I'd choose to die.

"What are you thinking?"

What if Mom is already dead? What if we're too late? It's my fault Makai's gone. "Nothing."

"Don't lie to me, El. I know you."

"Do you?" I try to free my hand.

He holds on tighter. "More than you know." I can't see his face, but it doesn't matter. I know every expression, every furrow and frown.

Grating metal resounds through the tunnel like fingernails on chalkboard.

We share one glance. Our hands part. Then we're running,

backpacks bouncing against our spines. Why does everything involve this stupid sport these days?

Slap. Slap. Slap.

We avoid the rails. Stay to one side. Our footsteps echo, lost beneath the scream of the approaching train. One thing's for sure—*if* we survive this, I'll never ride the subway again.

"There it is!"

Huh? Oh. An alcove, ahead and to the left. We'll have to jump over the tracks to get there. Peachy.

Light floods the walls. The train rounds the bend. "We're not going to make it," I shout.

Joshua swerves and I follow. We hurdle left, my entire body seizing when I leap over the "death rail." We duck into the alcove at the exact moment the train whooshes by. The backdraft nearly blows me off my feet. Joshua steadies me. Then I lose my footing. I'm falling. He's falling. We greet the ground with the breath knocked out of us.

"Are you hurt?"

Not physically. "I'm fine. You?"

He doesn't answer. Instead he gets up, grabs my hand, and helps me do the same. When I'm upright, he releases me.

To the right there's a metal door with the word Maintenance posted on it in peeling white letters.

"Follow me." Joshua pushes down on the handle, opens the door, and enters a narrow hallway. We follow it, Joshua in front, me behind.

Drip. Drip. Drip.

Leaky pipes and wire webs encase us. A caged lightbulb flickers on the ceiling. *Rap, rap, rap.* We follow the path, Joshua's flashlight beam guiding our way. We don't speak. Minute shadows silent minute. The walls seem to close in. Is it hot in here? My chest constricts. Hard to breathe.

The hall turns a sharp left. A dead end. Now what?

Joshua crouches, removes a grate about the size of a doormat, and sets it to the side with a *clang*. "I'll go down first to make sure the rungs are stable. Don't follow until I say."

I nod.

He rotates, descends backward into darkness.

I lean over the opening, waiting with breath on hold.

Squeak!

"Joshua?"

No response.

I swallow. One. Two. Three. "Joshua David, you answer me right now, or so help me—"

"I'm okay."

Exhale.

"Just slipped. I'm fine. Almost there."

Tick-tock, tick-tock. Hurry up. I can't take it anymore.

"All right." His voice is an echo in a canyon. Far. Small. How deep does this go?

I repeat his steps, turning first then climbing down. Narrow, round, and somewhat slippery, I take each bar with painstaking care. Left foot, right foot. Left foot, right foot. It's just a ladder. No big deal.

At the bottom Joshua grasps my waist, helps me down. Fingers loiter for a millisecond too long.

Scratch that. It's not hot in here. It's sweltering.

"This way," he says.

More long halls. Pipes. Railing. Stairs. Lightbulbs here and there. Who knew such a labyrinth existed below the city?

Finally, *finally*, we reach a padlocked door marked Restricted. Now what? "Do you have a key?"

"Don't need one." He walks straight through as if it isn't there.

My jaw goes slack. Now he's showing off. After everything I've seen tonight, I don't question it. I follow.

A chorus of rushing water echoes riotously. I'm standing on

the shore of a crystal-clear pool nestled in an open cavern. Grass greener than any I've seen carpets the floor. The air is so clean and pure I want to capture it in a bottle and drink it in. A rainbow of wildflowers dots the scene. At the center of it all is a great and glorious waterfall, a curtain of foamy white cascading from an opening in the rocky ceiling.

"Beautiful, isn't it?" Joshua leans against a boulder taller than he is.

I'm speechless—almost. "What is this place?"

He clasps his hands behind his back, like a tour guide at the Museum of Natural History. "This is a Threshold. It's a gateway between Reflections, or alternate universes, as you might recognize them. You saw a door blocking our way because you didn't know what to look for. You saw what you expected to see, not what was really here."

"People only see what they want to see." Ky's words release on my own whisper.

"What?" Joshua cocks his head.

Three quick blinks. "Never mind. Please don't tell me I have an alter ego floating around somewhere in there?" I gesture toward the water.

"No, no. Unlike worlds, souls cannot be duplicated." He chuckles.

Phew.

"Each Reflection has a series of Thresholds leading into the next one. The world you know is the Third Reflection, from which you can pass to the Second or Fourth." He speaks about it with ease. Has he given this speech before?

"How many are there?"

"Seven in all, but no one has ventured beyond the Fifth in years. Not since King Aidan was alive."

I don't even want to know.

"You almost passed through a Threshold last night."

The glowing green light at the bottom of the Pond.

"If you had passed through it, you would've fallen right into Crowe's hands. That Threshold leads into the Forest of Night—Shadow Territory."

Ugh. I can't keep up with him. Threshold. Reflection. Shadow Territory. "Where does this one lead?" If I wasn't witnessing an underground Eden, I wouldn't believe it.

"Lynbrook Province. It's on the outskirts and overlooked enough, no one should notice our entrance."

I face him. "Listen. Before we go any farther, I need to know a few things."

"Okay." His jaw bulges.

I step closer. "No more lies?"

"No more lies."

"Ever?"

He looks me square in the eyes. "Eliyana Ember, on my honor as a Guardian, I swear to be as honest with you as possible from here on out."

His use of my full name is so formal. Cold. I ignore the pinch in my chest and say, "I need to understand something. Mom said I'm not from here—the Third Reflection. You're not either, are you?"

"No. I'm not."

"The day we met . . ." I swallow, my courage gaining momentum with each word. "It wasn't an accident, was it? Every encounter, every time you called or hung out with me, it was all part of your"—another swallow—"job. Is that right?"

His Adam's apple bobs. "Yes."

"You're my best friend." Or you were. "Was any of it real?" An enormous lump presses on my vocal cords.

He runs his fingers through his hair. Averts his gaze. "I care for you. I can't deny that. But my duty comes first. Your *safety* comes first. You must understand—"

I lift a palm to stop him. "I got it, thanks. No need to elaborate."

Lips pursed, he nods, turns toward the pool.

"One more thing."

His body shifts, but he doesn't meet my gaze.

"From now on, if it comes between saving my life or Mom's, you'll save her."

No eye contact. No answer.

"Joshua?"

Nothing.

"Look. At. Me." When he doesn't, I add, "I'm not taking another step until you agree." My feet plant, arms cross. He can be stubborn, but so can I.

"You have no idea what you're asking."

"Promise me."

His eyes narrow. "Don't be childish. You've no clue what's at stake here."

"Why don't you tell me?"

He doesn't move. "It's not so simple."

"You promised no more lies. Prove it. Fill me in on why my life is so much more valuable than Mom's."

Still he ignores me.

"Answer me!"

That does it. He zips over to me like a bullet train. I've pushed him over the edge. He raises an open hand. For the smallest, stupidest moment, I think he might hit me. But he doesn't even come close to touching me. "I can't tell you. I won't put you in more danger than you're already in."

I roll my eyes. "Stop making excuses. You swore to be honest. How can I trust you if all you do is lie?"

His hand closes into a fist that he lowers to his side. "Don't you see that everything, *everything*, I've done is because—"

The pool bubbles, gurgles. The water turns green, a rerun of last night's show, but in a new venue. I blink rapidly. My palms go clammy. This is bad.

A man with greasy, slicked-back hair emerges. He's clad in leather pirate garb, and water cascades from his frame, from a holstered gun on one hip and a sheathed sword on the other. A black patch covers his left eye, completing the Davy Jones effect. Some kind of weird tattoo creeps up his neck and stops at his jaw. Like long black claws going for the kill.

Joshua assumes a protective stance in front of me.

"Joshua, my old comrade." The man leers. "It's been too long."

ACT II

I'm not
that girl

EIGHT

Hands Touch

My back smashes wall. Joshua's frame is a stalwart tower separating me from Jack Sparrow's much older and less attractive cousin. Why do I get the feeling my shivers are caused, not by the chilled stone icing my skin through layers of clothing but by greasehead's frosty glare?

Joshua reaches back, wraps an arm around me, and draws me closer. "It hasn't been long enough, Haman. And do *not* call me comrade. You betrayed the League of Guardians to follow Crowe and the Void. As far as I'm concerned, you were *never* on our side."

Haman steps ashore, his gait slow and uninterested. "Details, details." He smiles. A silver tooth fits like a single black key among a row of sparkling ivories. "I'm here for the girl. But you already knew that." He sighs. "There's no use stalling. You can't win this, boy." Haman titters. "The Void grows stronger each moment. With each heart that turns black. With each soul that gives in, my master moves closer to victory." He laughs again, a mocking, disrespectful sound.

Joshua huffs. "You've chosen your side. As far as I'm concerned, you and Crowe deserve each other, you two-faced son of a swine."

This time Haman snickers. "You have some nerve pointing out my shortcomings. Tell me, Joshua, how does it feel to be a murderer?"

Now he's flat-out lying.

"You. Tell. Me."

Joshua's rage emanates straight into every fiber of my being. With each word, each lie, my own anger escalates. It's like he and I are one entity, a series of melodies and harmonies woven together to create one intricately beautiful, yet complicated, piece.

Haman snaps his fingers.

Joshua collapses to the floor, writhing in pain.

I scream. This time the waterfall's roar drowns the echo. "What are you doing to him?" I throw off my backpack and kneel. Joshua kicks me hard in the thigh. I ignore the bruise already forming and place my hands on him. Calm down. He'll be okay.

He twists and turns in silent agony.

I glower at Haman. Sweltering tears spurt from my eyes. "Stop it!"

His good eye twitches. Hesitation? Could my pleas convince him?

"Please! I'll do whatever you want. I'll come with you, but please don't hurt him."

He lifts a hand and examines his fingernails.

I cover Joshua's entire body with my own. What do I do? What do I say?

"Be brave," Mom whispers.

I can't. I don't know how.

I lie next to Joshua, hold him. I'm useless. I couldn't save Mom. I can't save him.

"Please," I breathe into his neck. "Please."

Joshua goes still.

I sit and lift his head into my lap. His eyes are closed. His face is no longer contorted but peaceful. "Joshua." I trace his brow. "Wake up."

"He can't hear you." The voice is not Haman's.

I jerk my head toward the door we came through. Ky stands there, plus one swelling eye, minus a hoodie. He's got a tan pack slung over his back. Blood stains the front of his Mets shirt. Makai's blood.

"Are you alone?" Haman asks.

Ky nods. "Archer won't be a problem."

They both turn to me. "What about her?" Ky asks with a jut of his chin.

"Also not a problem."

Ky comes at me then.

I close my eyes and hold on to Joshua with all the strength I have. Arms stronger than mine wrench me away. I'm kicking and screaming, never looking directly at Ky.

Snap.

My intestines feel as if they've been ripped from my gut, twisted into knots, and then thrown back in. My forehead sears. My ears ignite. Every bone, nerve, and muscle shrieks against the torture. Make it stop. Please.

"What should I do with the rebel?" Ky transfers my dying body to Haman's arms.

I'm released from the pain the moment his hands touch my skin. Just before I pass out for the second time today, Haman answers, "Toss him in the water."

"A fire destroyed Lincoln Cooper's gallery. As far as we know, your mother was the only one inside. We've yet to uncover her remains, but we have two witnesses who saw her enter half an hour before the blaze began. We suspect arson. Did she have any enemies? Any suspects we can follow up on?"

I stare with blank eyes past the NYPD officer relaying the information of Mom's disappearance . . . death? I can't look directly at him. Too real.

Now I'm wandering aimlessly through Central Park. How did I get here? I don't remember leaving the house.

"El?"

My numbed heart flutters. I rotate in slow motion.

Joshua takes a hesitant step toward me. "I saw the cops outside your house. El, I'm so—"

I close the distance between us, fall against his chest, and cry.

We stay that way awhile. He doesn't push me away, but he doesn't fully embrace me either. He lets me be, and for a moment, it's okay.

Until it isn't. I want more.

My snot and salty tears soak his flannel shirt. I can't even think about how my face looks right now. I won't think about it. I sniff and dry my cheeks with my jacket sleeves. My forehead only reaches his chin. When I look into his eyes, I'm home.

This is right. This is real. I still have Joshua.

I rise on my toes, close my eyes, and—

"No." Joshua pulls away, taking all warmth and life with him. He scratches the back of his head, avoiding eye contact.

Tears burn. I trip over myself. I'm gone.

I open my eyes, attempt to recover from the all-too-real flashback. I try to breathe in, but I can't. No air underwater.

This must be the Threshold. What do Haman and Ky plan to do with me once we get to the other side—Reflection?

Drowning doesn't get easier with experience. It's like shooting up with a dose of panic. Walls close in while the surrounding space remains vastly empty. It doesn't help that my body is wracked with sobs, involuntarily welcoming my death sentence with every gulp of water.

An arm secures my waist, pulling me down, down, down into

the whirlpool of green. I don't bother seeing who has hold of me. Bubbles rise as I fall. Then a body disrupts the still water above. Joshua's limp and unconscious form sinks in slow motion. I reach for him, wince at the pain the small movement causes. I don't care. I keep reaching, keep fighting.

He'd do the same for me.

An ache resides deep within my chest. He can't die. There has to be help on the way. More Guardians. Someone. Anyone.

Past the green light at the bottom of the whirlpool waits an exact reflection of another. When I think I'm swimming down, I'm suddenly swimming—being dragged—up. Disoriented much?

I'm dumped on a shore of mud and reeds, turn on my side. My lungs burn, expelling water as I cough and choke and . . . is that blood? "Josh . . . ooo . . . waaaaah!" I scream-cry-wail, though it sounds nothing like it feels. My voice is too hoarse to do the agony inside justice. I feel as if I've been run over by a Mack Truck. Then dropped down a manhole. Then swept away with a horde of sewer rats.

Dead. I'd rather be dead.

An awning of branches, leaves, bark, and needles shades me. Trees. So many trees. Tall and wide and towering, and they all have . . . doors?

The chirping chorus of a middle-of-nowhere morning sings all around me. It's a foreign noise. Irksome. One I've heard on the sound machine by my bed, but never in real life. Engines revving and tires screeching. Horns honking and sirens blaring. A butcher spraying down rubber mats. A native cursing at a cab that won't stop. Those are the tunes on home's soundtrack. Not incessant twittering.

My parka is long gone, lost somewhere between Reflections. I'm soaked and muddy and—yuck—Mom's Uggs are waterlogged. My toes squish in my socks. But the discomfort is nothing compared to the numbness closing in. The blackness that threatened to swallow me after I thought Mom had died returns. And I don't even care.

"His Sovereignty won't be happy when he learns you used your Calling on the girl." Ky speaks in a low, agitated whisper, his voice fading in and out. I can't see him, but he isn't far.

"I did what was necessary to apprehend her," Haman says. "His Sovereignty has access to . . . medicines. The castle hosts some of the most talented Physics in this Reflection. She'll be taken care of once we reach our destination."

No. She—I won't. I let my hand fall back into the water. Cool. Inviting. Deadly.

"No medicine or Physic can reverse what you've done." Ky again. As much as I detest him, I hate Haman more. "His Sovereignty was adamant—he wants her alive. I'm an accomplice in this. Your careless actions affect me too. Crowe will have our souls if we ruin his plan."

I blink away black and orange spots. Glance at the water. Come on. Plenty of unbelievable stuff has happened recently. Any minute Joshua will break the surface. He'll turn up alive, just like Mom.

I inhale and flinch. The small movement of my ribs expanding, pushing against my skin, confirms my condition is bad. Am I really dying? My fingers wiggle in wetness. All it would take is one willful roll and I'd be back in the water. With each second that ticks by, the truth sinks deeper, anchoring me in reality. He's not coming. He's—*gulp*—gone. How can I keep going when Joshua is—?

"Like I said, His Sovereignty can cure her. One way or another, he always gets his way. Surely you have discovered that by now."

I inch my foot over, off the ledge and into the water.

"And if he doesn't?" Yep. I detest Ky less. He won't back down, even from a bully as detestable as Haman.

"You dare doubt our master? Be careful, Kyaphus. You know what His Sovereignty does to those who defy him. If he's willing to lock up Elizabeth, I guarantee he will not hesitate to do far worse to you."

Mom. I lift my hand and foot from the pool. Darkness rolls away in thick clouds. Light filters in as my vision begins to clear. I can't go through with it. Mom needs me.

Quiet. The argument is over. *Clop, clop, clop.* I try to sit. Excruciating. Crunches were never my thing, but this is ridiculous.

Two hands grab me beneath my arms. "Wait," Ky says. "You'll never be able to do it on your own."

I want to lurch away, but I can't even do that. "Don't touch me."

He laughs, almost to himself. "No way around it. Either you let me help you, or you die right here. Your choice."

I stare at my feet, guarding myself from his paralyzing gaze. *Mom. Do it for Mom.* "Fine."

It takes a drawn-out process of grimaces, pauses, and slow breaths to get me vertical. Ky is soaked through too. His jeans suction against his legs, his wet blond hair curling in places.

The pool is nestled in a circular clearing with trees bordering all sides. The hues of autumn quake in a dainty breeze. Red, orange, yellow, and brown all wave hello. A greeting from my favorite season, but I can't bring myself to appreciate it. It's meaningless without the ones I love by my side.

Two horses wait on a path ahead, one ebony and the other spotted gray. I have one arm around Ky, and he nudges me inch by inch. Wait. My feet dig like roots into the rich, moist soil.

Joshua. I didn't get to say good-bye.

Ky presses his lips against my ear. "Don't even think about it." He guides me forward, and I have no choice but to fall into step beside him.

Do it for Mom. She was always the goal.

I know, I know. But as we move farther and farther away from the Threshold, the pain around my heart deepens. Joshua is gone. If this is the price of love, it's one I can't afford.

My hand lifts to my collarbone. But the space is bare. No. "Stop. We have to go back. My necklace . . . it must have come off in the water." The gift may have been Joshua's way of keeping tabs on me, but it was so much more to me. And it's all I have left of him.

For a portion of an instant, Ky pauses. Will he at least give me this?

No. We're moving again.

Heartless jerk.

When we reach the horses, Haman strides into view. He mounts the black steed with ease, then turns up the collar of his jacket before he takes the reins.

"I'll lift you up first." Ky helps me get a foot into one stirrup, then boosts me onto the freckled horse.

And then I'm falling.

He catches me. Didn't see that one coming. He's stauncher than he first appears.

I won't thank him.

Once I'm finally sitting seven feet above the earth, Ky mounts the steed in one smooth move, pulls me into his chest.

I hate that I need him. "Don't get any ideas. Just because I'm not strong enough to fight you right now does not mean we're friends. You killed Makai. And . . . and Joshua . . ." My voice trembles. I swallow and steady it. "You're a murderer, just like Haman."

"Be careful, princess," he says in my ear. "I don't tolerate being accused of crimes I didn't commit." One breath. Two. "But for what it's worth, I'm sorry."

The empty condolences from Mom's wake fill my mind. He's sorry? I want to punch him. Slap him. Anything to cause him pain. But I can hardly move, so I say, "I hate you. I will never forgive you for this."

His head nods against the side of mine. "Duly noted."

The horse's jarring trot increases my discomfort, but it isn't as painful as trying to walk. We pass over a cobbled lane, weeds shooting up through dislodged stones. Every ten feet an unlit lamppost stands, all with glass shattered. The trees curve inward, creating a tunnel effect. These have doors, too, and are stacked together like row houses, tall and slender, with hardly any room separating one trunk from another.

I need to learn as much about this world as possible, so I ask, "What's with the trees?"

"What do you mean?" Ky's chest vibrates against my back.

"I mean the doors. Why do the trees have doors?" Each one is different, but all are weathered. Red doors, black doors, natural doors, some tall with squared corners, some short and rounded.

"How else would you get inside?" He might as well say "duh." Then he adds, "But this is Lynbrook Province. All these tromes were abandoned during the Revolution."

Tromes? Tree homes?

I examine each one as we trot onward. Do people, *did* people, really live in these? I look up. Windows glimmer high above in each trome. When a shock of blue flashes in one of the panes, I do a double take. On second glance, nothing's there. But I saw . . .

The horse stops.

The tree line ends just before a drop-off. The beginning of a dilapidated bridge stretches straight ahead. Thin branches arc and intertwine, consumed by overgrown and deadening ivy.

Haman dismounts. "We've reached the Broken Bridge. I will have words with the Troll."

Troll? As in mythical creature that doesn't exist?

He walks to the bridge's mouth and halts before earth changes to wood. Thirty feet ahead I can see the bridge is broken in two, a wide, impassable gap dividing our side from the other. Beyond the gap, a gray, rolling fog obscures the bridge's other half. I wait, my breath in limbo. Any minute some beast straight out of Middle Earth will emerge.

Not even close.

A striking woman with cascading blonde hair and wintry-blue eyes materializes from the mist. I'm immediately reminded of Quinn. Did she make it home okay? Did she ever try to call, drunk and slaphappy, to check on me?

No. She didn't.

The woman walks over the gap as if it's not there and approaches Haman.

A gasp escapes me. "How in the—?"

"It's a façade." Ky's lips graze my ear and I flinch. "An illusion created to ward off trespassers."

"Haman Skinner." The woman's lyrical voice turns even *his* name pleasant. Black dresses her hourglass frame from shoulder to toe, a flowing, almost ethereal fabric billowing around her. "What brings you so far from home?"

Haman bows. He respects her. Why? "Sovereignty business, Mistress Isabeau. My lord—"

A porcelain hand silences him midsentence. "You know better than anyone I do not make exceptions for Jasyn Crowe. Why are you really here?"

"We need to cross."

"And this concerns me how?"

With all the presentation of a hotel concierge, Haman sweeps an open palm back toward us. "The girl, m'lady. She is Elizabeth's child."

Isabeau's expression changes. Recognition? Hatred? Awe? "You are sure? Do not toy with me." Pink sneaks into her ashen cheeks.

His bow deepens. "I would not lie to you."

Isabeau looks past Haman, her glare penetrating.

I lean deeper into Ky's chest. What is it about this woman that makes me so afraid?

"So this is my late husband's unfaithfulness incarnate. She will make a fine slave."

In your dreams, lady.

With a trepid laugh Haman speaks again. "I'm afraid that isn't possible. His Sovereignty has plans for the girl. The mark—"

"I'm well aware of what her mark indicates, Haman, though it holds no value for me. Get on with it. What is my recompense?" Isabeau crosses her arms and tilts her chin. Pretty high-and-mighty for someone living on—or underneath, as the tales go—a bridge.

"What is it you desire most?"

Haman already knows her answer. Why this long-drawn-out conversation?

A pearly smile lights Isabeau's face. "How can I be sure you will keep our bargain?"

"I do not welcome your wrath. You have my word. I will deliver payment." He reaches out a hand.

Isabeau nods, her incisors a little too sharp within her satisfied grin. She places her dainty hand, palm up, in Haman's. "I bind you to your vow."

He bends, places a kiss to her palm, looks up. "By a kiss I am bound."

What just happened?

"We have an agreement." She leers at me. "Safe passage across the bridge in exchange for Elizabeth's unborn child."

NINE

Eyes Meet

The mist consumes us as we pass over the false gap in the Not-So-Broken Bridge. Clopping hooves and our breathing are the only sounds. It's daytime, but the shadows give the illusion of twilight. There's no hour or season. Just clouds. The arcing branches of the bridge act like a cage. Trapped.

Elizabeth's unborn child.

The second I'm able to move on my own, I'm figuring out a way to save her. From Jasyn. From Isabeau. The woman had to be lying. Mom would never have an affair with a married man. And she's sure not pregnant. When I find her—and I will find her—she'll set me straight.

She's lied to me before.

But she wouldn't lie again. Not about this.

Ky shifts behind me. I have to use him to learn what I can. If this were New York, I'd have no trouble with direction. I hate to admit it, but I need his knowledge of this place, this Reflection, if I'm going to escape . . . and survive.

"I always thought trolls were crude, hairy ogre-monsters." Keep it light.

"Not everything is visible on the surface, princess."

Do I hear spite? "How so?"

He tightens his hold on the reins. On me. Annoyed? Frustrated?

"I mean, appearances can deceive. A jagged surface doesn't always allude to what truly lies beneath."

You and the boy have something in common.

It's what Mom would say if she were here, but I won't believe it. Ky and I are nothing alike.

Better keep a tab on things I can use to my advantage. Weaknesses. Isabeau is Haman's weakness—someone he fears.

Check.

Now what's Ky afraid of?

"Can't we go any faster?"

"You ask a lot of questions."

"Is that a crime?"

He breathes in. Out. "The wounds Haman inflicted start deep, then work their way to the surface. You're bleeding internally now. Eventually your skin will rupture and you'll bleed out." He explains it like a doctor diagnosing a terminal patient. How does he know so much about this? "We're trying to get you to the castle without speeding up the process. Any sudden movements will only worsen your condition. It's why we continued through the Threshold into Lynbrook Province rather than taking you back to the Pond. The alternate Threshold would've left us practically at Crowe's doorstep. But this way is safer. Your Reflection has too many obstacles when it comes to getting from here to there."

Be still. If what Ky says is true, I'll be dead before I have a chance to save Mom.

"What does Jasyn want with me? Why all this trouble to bring me here?"

"Shhh!"

I raise my voice. "Tell me. Or I swear I'll throw myself off this horse—"

"I said be quiet!" he whisper-yells.

The black horse stops. Rears. Whinnies wildly. Ours follows like a tipped domino.

I clench its mane so I don't fall. Crud, that hurts. "What's happening?"

"Whoa! Easy, girl." He pulls on the reins, digging his heels into the horse's rear.

Something emerges from the fog ahead. Is it an animal? A bird?

Haman's steed bucks him off, bolts forward past the—

A large winged creature with an eagle's head and lion's body stands on all fours, the front two feet talons, the back two paws. It snaps its razor beak and claws the ground, ready to pounce. Something brown and lumpy is strapped to its back. But none of these oddities sticks out as much as the brilliant blue feather growing from its mane.

The window. A sudden flash of blue. But the beast is huge. How could it fit inside the trome? "What is that thing?"

"Griffin," Ky snarls.

Haman stands, adjusts his collar, and snaps his fingers.

The griffin charges.

It thrashes its head, flinging Haman to the side like a rag doll.

Serves you right, scalawag.

An anxious thrill grips me. Friend or foe? Either way, this thing has overcome a man I revile. I could run up and kiss it.

We back up. Turn. Race across the bridge. Ky kicks the horse hard. Twists the reins around his knuckles. Leans forward.

I crane my neck as the griffin lifts off the ground, beating its enormous wings. It's gaining. Is it . . . smiling?

Two sets of talons grab me, yank me, lift me off the horse. Ky strangles my foot and rises too. I kick him. A searing pain shoots up my leg. I still.

He tightens his hold. So much for not speeding up my internal injuries.

The griffin breaks through the branches and we climb up, up, up into the fog. We're rising above it. For the love of New York pizza! To the left is the forest of tromes, a canvas of warmth and spice. Then there's the vision on the right, hidden until now. As we soar over the gray into the horizon, the lens adjusts to perfect focus.

A mixture of forest and brick, trees and towers, comprises the skyline. The colors fade from black in the distance to gray and then green beneath us. To the untrained eye it's just an oddly tinted woodland landscape, but to my widening stare, it is precisely the opposite.

It's my favorite painting come to life, the single piece I kept out of dozens of Mom's creations. The paints she used were more vibrant, but even with the change of hues I recognize the likeness. I slacken my jaw. I let out a small yelp, but the current of wind sailing past my ears muffles the sound. No wonder I loved that painting so much.

The landscape below, rising and falling like a web of never-ending staircases, is a reflection of New York.

∽∞∾

I'm from the Big Apple. I'm not afraid of heights.

My arms feel ready to pop from their sockets where the griffin clutches. My foot has fallen asleep thanks to Ky's death grip. But I'm flying. Pain and discomfort are obsolete.

As I look down on the Second Reflection, I pick out where things should be. Central Park, the Flatiron Building, Belvedere Castle. Everything is there, but it's also not. A towering mountain replaces the Empire State Building. A neighboring canyon instead of Yankee Stadium. This place is distorted, contorted, changed, and identical all at once. It's larger, broader, a state to New York's city. But it's New York. It's home.

Over land, forest, and sea we glide. A trip that would take twenty minutes in the city takes at least an hour here. When at last the griffin descends, it's around where Staten Island would be—if

Staten Island were a small state. Forest swathes this version on all sides. Where are we supposed to land?

The griffin dives.

Ky's eyes are slammed shut, his face fifty shades of green. Why didn't he let me go? He didn't have to tag along. Why would he risk his life to stay with me? What's so important?

I close my eyes, waiting for branches to catch on my clothes, for leaves to pummel my face. When I'm sitting on firm ground without so much as a bruise or scratch added to my injuries, I lift my lashes.

Ground was the wrong word. *Platform* is more accurate. A circular landing covered in autumn foliage matches the forest exactly. Clever. A camouflaged helipad.

Ky lies on his back, eyes sealed, one hand still wrapped around my ankle, the other clutching his pack like a lifeline.

I try to breathe past the stabbing in my veins. It's not getting worse. Really.

At least my clothes have dried, dangled from the griffin's talons like jeans hanging from a wire. My boots are still damp though.

"You okay there, Maverick?"

Ky doesn't laugh. He blinks. When he shoots a glare toward me, I look away. "Don't you mean Goose? He's the one who died midair."

Wait. He actually gets the *Top Gun* reference? I thought—never mind. "Why'd you hold on if you're afraid of heights?"

He sits. "I'm not afraid of anything." His words are shaded.

"Whatever."

"This little chat is cute and all, but we need to move before we blow our cover." Another voice, female, joins the conversation.

I glance up and just as quickly look away. The girl on the platform is 90 percent buck naked. The brown pack hanging from her shoulders and a tattoo of a crown over a crossed arrow and sword above her right breast make up the covered 10 percent.

"Hello, Wren." Ky stares up at her.

Two questions. One, where'd the griffin go? Two, why's there a nude girl standing in its place?

"Kyaphus." She avoids eye contact. With him and with me. "For a second there I thought we might lose you."

Doesn't sound like that would've bothered her in the slightest. When I look at her again, she's dressing, removing articles of clothing from her pack and covering her olive skin. She tips her head as she shakes loose the folded clothes, and a single streak of sapphire shines amidst tangles of midnight hair. She slips on a pair of fudge-brown, skintight pants, then an auburn ribbed tank top. An army-green jacket with an abundance of loops, buckles, and pockets completes the ensemble.

"In your dreams, Song." Ky may not be able to trick this girl into a staring contest, but why doesn't he draw his knife? I haven't seen him with it since he stabbed Makai. Did he lose it?

She opens her mouth, never looking directly at him, but I interject, "Hold on." I meet Wren's scowl. "You're the griffin? How did you—?"

"She's a freak."

"You should talk, Rhyen. At least I use my Calling for good—to serve the Verity. You're nothing more than Crowe's lapdog. A slave of the Void. A waste of oxygen. Go on, little puppy. Go home to Daddy."

Ky leaps to his feet. Growls, "I am no one's slave."

"Enough!"

We freeze. An insanely muscular man steps onto the platform's ledge. An army guy cliché with his buzz cut, green jacket, combat boots, and at-ease stance. At his hip rests a sheathed knife, the handle wrapped in what looks like snakeskin. Behind his ear hangs a short, thin, dark-blue braid secured with a leather tie.

"Wren, report to the Physic's cabin. He'll check you out and clear you for your next assignment."

Griffin Girl dips her head, limps past G.I. Joe, and disappears behind him. Stairs maybe?

"As for you, Kyaphus." The man lugs Ky to his feet, cinches his arms behind his back. Like Wren, he never makes eye contact with Paralysis Boy. "You are headed straight for the Crypts. I've wanted to throw you in there since you abandoned the Guardians. Looks as if I will get my chance at last."

Ky puffs out his cheeks. Twist, jerk, pull. Fail.

Ha. It's not fun when you can't control your own body, is it?

"You're in over your head, Gage. Just wait." Ky's jawbone bulges. He levels Gage with a bloodthirsty glare.

I watch the exchange, spying something I didn't notice before. Ky's eyes are two different shades, one green and one brown. Strange. Beautiful.

It's almost as if he senses me staring. He whips his head in my direction, and for the briefest moment our eyes meet.

I scowl at my boots. What am I thinking? He's a scumbag. There's nothing beautiful about him.

"Careful now, traitor." Gage lifts Ky in the air as if he weighs nothing. "You wouldn't want me to lose my patience." His regard remains just out of Ky's line of vision. "And if I find out you had a hand in whatever is delaying Archer and David . . ."

Joshua. Kill me. Kill me *now*. If just hearing his name unravels me, how am I supposed to . . . ?

Mom. Concentrate on Mom.

Gage whistles like he's hailing a cab, and a girl of maybe fifteen appears. She's wearing a sky-blue Bohemian-style skirt and a cream-colored peasant top with a drawstring neck. A waterfall braid pulls luxuriant brown hair off her face, only a stripe of lavender resting against her cheek.

For the first time Gage smiles. Says to me, "Welcome. I am Lieutenant Commander Jonathan Gage, but you may refer to me as the latter."

"El," I say.

He gives a slight bow. "Commander Archer sent word we should anticipate your arrival." He withdraws a small scroll from his pants pocket and hands it to me.

It's literally torture to unfurl the yellowed paper, which is actually two pages rolled together. My lips move silently as I bite back the pain and read the first page. I skim Makai's short explanation—he and Joshua are returning, and they're bringing a girl. Me. He even warned Gage we might be compromised and requested he send someone to watch for us in Lynbrook Province.

When I move on to the second page, an inner gasp scratches my throat. One side of the paper is ripped, the page torn from its former home. The profile sketch of me is recent, not quite a year old. Mom does one for every birthday. Since we don't have a ton of pictures, this is her way of commemorating the milestones. She always drew the profile from my left side, my good side. Just another way she showed her love. Mom knew I'd hate to have my ugliness recorded.

My fingers tremor as I roll the papers together and hand them back to Gage.

He pockets the scroll and quirks a brow. "I must admit, I expected Commander Archer and Lieutenant David to accompany you."

I close my eyes, shielding tears. Shake my head.

"I see." Gage clears his throat. "This is Robyn. She'll take care of you from here. If you'll excuse me, I have business to attend." He lowers Ky, gives me a departing nod. They disappear below the crown of trees.

Robyn comes over and kneels. Her catlike hazel eyes examine me. "You're injured."

Nod. Wince. "Haman." Swallow. "He did something to—"

"Say no more." She holds up a hand. "Can you move at all?" Her voice is tender, pretty. The tonal quality suggests she'd make a lovely singer.

I lean forward. Bad idea. "Listen, my mom . . ."

Her hand warms my shoulder. "One moment." She vanishes beyond the landing. Moments later, a gorgeous Bengal tiger creeps forward, a bundle of clothes in its mouth. The animal is larger than a cub, but not fully grown either. What strikes me most is its teeth are flat, not at all menacing as they glisten dramatically in the sunlight. I hold perfectly, statuesquely still. What other option do I have? I can't even twitch, let alone move. Wait, that purple tuft of fur on one cheek, the wad of blue and cream cloth in its mouth. Robyn? Can she shape-shift too?

I drive rationality aside as the tiger approaches. She lowers her body, scooting toward me like a submissive pet. Her clawless paw touches my leg, and she jerks her head backward. The tiger wants to take me for a ride.

Weirder things have happened today.

I hunch over the throbbing in my stomach, biting my lip and closing my eyes. My crawl onto her silky back is slower than service at McDonald's in Times Square on New Year's. When I'm straddling her body, clutching her fur, Robyn walks to the platform's end and pad, pad, pads down a spiral staircase.

The scene below is a vision for homesick eyes. Tromes and cabins. Brick towers and cottages. Woven together along networks of paths and roads. Women, men, children, animals. How many of them can transform the way Wren and Robyn can? How many are merely wildlife? My questions could fill Carnegie Hall.

Robyn leaps from the last stair onto the soil, her shoulder bones peaking and sinking with each step.

I lift my head an inch. Earthy scents. One stands out. Basil. A very Manhattan sort of smell. I don't know why. It just is.

We head down a road. Multicolored storefronts cluster on either side, giving it a Chinatown feel. A woman with a baby attached to her hip by a wide piece of cloth sells eggs. We pass by and her green eyes expand, the corner of her mouth lifting.

A stranger just smiled at me. Definitely not New York.

Chop! An enormous fish head tumbles off a counter, plops into a basket on the ground. The butcher drops his cleaver, wraps the headless fish in brown paper, and hands it to an older man with a wheelbarrow. Their carefree exchange ascends on laughter and pleasantries. There's a vibe to this place, a distinctive quality of interconnection and community.

The style seems to be a mixture of medieval bohemian and not-so-distant-future dystopian. Unlike Wren, the girls and women wear long skirts and lengthy tops accented with knotted sashes. Braids and teased buns and makeshift twists for hairstyles, hand-made Uggs decorated with beads and feathers for shoes. The men sport boots and fabrics in muddied hues. Flannel shirts. Loose-fitting cargo pants. Casual. Farmer-esque.

A log cabin stands at the end of one lane, a garden to its right. Smoke rises from a chimney, and curtains the color of Robyn's skirt trim the windows. Some of Mom's earlier paintings featured mountain scenes. Cottage homes cozied up among thickets of trees. Did her inspiration transpire here?

Robyn walks up two steps, nudges the slightly open door with her nose, and enters.

The one-room cabin is larger than it first appears. My nostrils flare when the smells of aloe vera and ash intrude on my senses. A fire crackles in an ancient-looking wood-burning stove. Hammocks tied to wooden frames line the far wall, a curtain hiding one. A pair of boots peeks out where the hanging fabric ends. Subdued voices converse on the other side.

"I'm sorry, Wren. I won't be able to clear you until your ankle heals."

"What?" Wren's owl-like screech reminds me she's no ordinary human. "It's no big deal. I'm fine."

"You are *not* fine. That's a nasty sprain. You must have over-exerted it."

The curtain swishes open. Wren springs from a hammock and hobbles toward us. Her fury is a hot coal in my stomach. A lit match at my ear. "This is *your* fault."

The guy with the boots walks over and places a hand on her back. His weathered smile reaches his grandfatherly eyes, and surprise, surprise, a blue braid nestles behind his ear. "Go get some supper, Wren. You need your strength."

She shrugs him off with a blood-chilling scowl. Then she tromps away. Limp, shuffle, limp. *Slam!* The walls shake. Bottles on shelves rattle and clink.

The man scratches Robyn between her ears. "How can sisters be so different, kitten?" He strokes the underside of her chin and she purrs. "In a few years your Confine will lift. We'll see how tough Wren is once your fangs and claws come in, hmm? She won't be so ferocious with a full-grown tiger in our midst."

Robyn emits a shaky growl. Is she laughing?

"I'm Wade Song." He stoops to my level. "I see you've met my girls."

What did Ky call Wren? Song?

Wade lifts me off Robyn's back without pause and carries me to a hammock. Starchy fabric envelops me, drooping under my weight. Stiffness and fatigue press down. Kneading. Coaxing. The curtain closes. My eyelids sag.

Footsteps. A sigh.

"Is it bad?" Robyn must've morphed back into her human form.

Another sigh, long and exaggerated. "I won't know until I've examined her fully—"

"Don't lie to me, Papa. I know your ability to diagnose with a single look." Her argument isn't rude or disrespectful like her sister's. Instead her words carry genuine concern. I haven't even really met her, and already she cares more for me than Quinn ever did. "Now tell me. How bad is it?"

He clears his throat. Stalling? Shoes shuffle. Water gushes. "I'd know Haman's touch anywhere. The damage is beyond my ability to heal. I can make her comfortable, give her Illusoden, but that is all."

I don't know what Illusoden is, but I'm sure I want it. Now.

"No." Robyn sniffles. "No. There has to be something you can do for her. Did you see her face? That mark, it's—"

"I know. I know."

Seconds tick off in my head as I wait for him to continue. To give me some context as to why my cursed birthmark is so important. One, one thousand, two, one thousand, three . . .

"There . . . might be a way," Wade finally says.

The suspense is killing me. Literally.

"I can't heal her, but there's someone who can. He's the only Physic known to bring anyone back from something like this."

"Is there a way to get word to him? We at least have to try to bring him here."

Yes. Try. I have to save Mom.

"That's the problem. Nathaniel's been in hiding nearly two decades. The only person who might know his whereabouts is Makai, but he hasn't returned."

Nathaniel. I know that name. Why do I know that name?

Robyn asks the question for me. "Nathaniel? I've never heard of him."

"You wouldn't have. He's one of the oldest Physics. Worked for the king before the Revolution. Nathaniel Archer refused to side with Jasyn, but he wouldn't fight him either. Shame and fear sent him into hiding. He could be anywhere . . ."

Wade's voice trails off, not because he's stopped talking but because I've stopped listening. If I thought nothing else could surprise me, I was wrong. Of course Makai would have the information they need. Because Nathaniel Archer is none other than my not-as-dead-as-Mom-said-he-was grandfather.

And I might know exactly where he is.

TEN

sudden silence

They won't quit arguing. Do they think I'm deaf?

It's been hours since I told Wade and Robyn what I know about Nathaniel. Explained how I'm related to him and what happened to Mom. After that, Robyn made me comfortable. Set my soggy boots by the fire, gave me a pillow. Then Wade served me some sort of red liquid that tasted like fermented beets. My pain is gone. I'm fine. Never felt better. Let's get moving already.

I explained the urgency of the situation, but they don't seem to understand. Haman's probably reached the castle by now. I shudder to think how he plans to fulfill his vow to Isabeau. How can he even promise something like that?

Cringe. I'm coming, Mom. I'm coming.

"Consider what you're asking," a gruff voice scoffs from the cabin porch. The open window admits every word. "You want us to trust a foreign girl none of us have ever seen before? How would she know where this Physic Archer is anyway?"

I may not have any of Mom's sketchbooks with me, but I remember them well. Sketchbooks were my picture books. Fingertips stained with charcoal and lead, I'd sit for hours and study those renderings. Mom journaled between sketches, too, but I never read any of her entries. The pictures were what fascinated me. Back then I thought the drawings were random. Now I'm starting to wonder if they tell a story. Makai. The Second Reflection landscapes. And Nathaniel—my grandfather—standing in front of our brownstone, holding baby me in his arms.

Except something was different. Subtle variances I'd never considered until now. A planter we've never had. Ivy I've never seen. Square window frames rather than arched. Brick steps where cement ones should be. Come to find out, it wasn't our brownstone in the drawing. It was a reflection, a replica, a copy.

I described the building to Wade in detail. His expression shifted from shock to delight. "How could I have missed it? All this time he's been there, right under Jasyn's nose."

"Been where?" Robyn asked.

"Lisel Island. It's just ruins and rubble now, abandoned during the Revolution. No one in his right mind would've stayed there." Wade laughed. Shook his head. "But Nathaniel's never been in his right mind."

Wade excused himself to his work area and left Robyn to watch over me then. She's been urging me to rest, but I can't sleep. Not with all the activity happening within earshot. I lean forward, turn my ear toward the porch.

Gage speaks next. "She has the mark, plain as day. Makai's been secretive about his business in the Third all these years. I'd wager this girl—his niece, apparently—*was* his business. When he sent word he'd be bringing someone with him, he didn't mention the mark. I'm as stunned as you are, but Makai wouldn't deceive us without cause. He's obviously been hiding her from Crowe. Joshua's been helping him. It's the only explanation."

A sardonic, raspy laugh. "Why keep the rest of us in the dark then, if they've known of her existence all along? Perhaps Makai and Joshua are not as loyal to the Verity as we believed."

"Be careful, Saul. That's your commanding officer you've just insulted." Gage's voice wavers on the border of resolve and resentment. "Our men would never betray us or the Verity."

A pause. Creak, step, shuffle. Cough, grunt, murmur.

"Wouldn't they?" Sheesh. This Saul guy refuses to quit. Maybe he's related to Ky. "Need I remind you of Haman's betrayal, not to mention the dozens of others who've surrendered to the Void? Decent men and women we trusted. Our numbers are dwindling, Commander. And still we wait. Do you know how many mornings I've awakened and wondered if today would be the day the Verity might return? Anticipating its vessel would come forward and take back what Crowe stole from us? Our freedom. Our land. Our home. How can we be sure this girl's not a spy, a Soulless even? She was traveling with the traitor Kyaphus, no trace of Commander Archer or Lieutenant David. It all seems highly suspicious to me."

Robyn purses her lips, casts me a sidelong glance, and steps outside. "She's no Soulless. Her eyes and skin remain unaltered." My new friend's support salves my blistering uncertainty.

A harrumph wafts through the window.

"I do not believe she has reached her eighteenth year yet," Robyn adds. "The Void could not touch her if it tried."

"She has the mark." Gage again. "That's good enough for me. As for Commander Archer and Lieutenant David, they made their choices. You have made yours. Our oath as Guardians is 'To the Crown until Death.' I stand by my vow, just as Makai and Joshua do. We must hold out hope we'll see them again." Another creak, a few stomps. They're gone.

He misunderstood my silence earlier. Gage thinks his men are still alive. How can I tell him the truth?

At my side once more, Robyn urges me to lie back down, gives me a gentle shove. I obey but catch her wrist. "Tell me what they're talking about. Please?"

She smiles. "Shhh. You must rest now. The journey to Lisel Island will not be easy. The Illusoden is doing its job on your pain, but you are far from well."

I shake my head. My brain whooshes, Jell-O in my skull. "No. I need to know what's going on."

She tilts her chin. "How much have you been told?"

Finally. "This is a Reflection. There are seven in all. My birthmark is significant, but I have no clue why. A guy named Jasyn Crowe wants . . ." What *does* he want? It was never made clear. ". . . something from me." We're running out of time.

Robyn retreats, then returns with two steaming teacups. She passes one to me, then pulls over a stool. Its legs vibrate against the wood. She sits and cradles her teacup in her hand, breathing slowly as if preparing to perform a monologue. "I can only tell you what I know. The histories my parents shared with me as a child."

This is it. I sip my tea, suck in my cheeks. Bitter but warm. Comforting. I swallow, the tea coating my throat, and stare at the grainy, dark-spotted log ceiling. The hammock swings slightly.

Tracing her teacup's rim with one fingertip, Robyn begins, "Jasyn Crowe refers to himself as Sovereign, but he is a servant of the Void—the quintessence of all darkness and deception. With every year that passes under his rule, a little more of this Reflection becomes shadowed. If Jasyn remains on the throne, swaying more followers toward wickedness, the Second will cease to exist as we know it. Those of us who serve the Verity—the purest form of light imaginable—will not be able to stop it. We will be forced to abandon our homes or live out our days in darkness. Then this realm will no longer be a Reflection, but a Shadow World." Robyn pauses, lifts her teacup, and sips.

Chills spider-walk down my spine. Void and Verity? Darkness and light? This is crazy.

Yet I believe every word. I come from the Third Reflection. Where children are abandoned and trafficked and abused. Where those with power cheat and manipulate for their own gain. Where words such as *terrorism* and *shootings* have become commonplace on the evening news. That place becomes darker every minute. It's practically a Shadow World already.

"Why not leave?" I hold my breath as I sip the tea again. Makes the bitterness not so pungent. "If things are so bad here, what reason do you have to stay?"

"Because . . ." Robyn lowers her cup, the worry around her eyes softening. "This is our home. Running would serve no purpose. Jasyn Crowe won't stop until the Void's power reaches the ends of the Reflections." She leans forward, her top's drawstring caught in a swirl of steam. "But we are not without hope. Because before Jasyn seized the throne, there was another king, the last-known vessel of the Verity. King Aidan Henry."

Emotion corkscrews. Joshua. He mentioned King Aidan—right before he died. I swallow back the shards of my heart threatening to lodge in my throat. "What happened to him?"

"He and the queen had one desire—to have a child of their own. Papa remembers when the king and queen would walk along the streets, playing and laughing with the people."

"They had such a light in their eyes when they'd join the children in their games." Wade speaks.

I jolt. I'd forgotten he was still in the cabin.

He strides over and squeezes Robyn's shoulder.

Robyn beams at her father, and suddenly I'm an intruder. I taste bile but gulp it quickly. It's not her fault I never knew my dad.

Another second. She faces me again. "But the king and his queen remained childless. They grew old and the time was fast approaching when Aidan would pass and the Verity would inhabit a new vessel, someone good and worthy of the crown who served the Verity as he did. With this charge would come great power. Most assumed King Aidan's closest confidant would be chosen."

The fog lifts a hair. "Jasyn?"

Wade nods.

Robyn gazes into her teacup. *Tap, tap, taps* the porcelain with her fingernails. "He was forty-seven at the time. As Commander of the Guardians and the king's dearest friend, he did everything right. He seemed like the perfect candidate. He was noble. Kind. He had everyone fooled."

A frown draws Wade's entire face south. "None of us were prepared for what came to pass."

Neither of them speaks. Wade squeezes his daughter's shoulder again and then walks to the stove.

Robyn offers me a weak smile, communicating something private in her bright eyes. Wade loved King Aidan. No question about it.

I finish my tea in three long gulps, treating it like cough syrup instead of a beverage. "What happened?"

She retrieves my cup, rests it between her thighs, and exhales. "On the king's seventy-fifth birthday, the king and queen vanished." Silence. Another sip of tea.

Back turned toward us, Wade sniffs, fiddles with a pot on the stove. Robyn may be relaying these events, but Wade lived them. My heart aches for this man I hardly know. For the pain I so relate to.

This story is getting good. Or bad. I glance at what looks like vegetable stew. No beef chunks. It'd be perfect if I had an appetite. Instead the scent of veggie broth welcomes back the constant nausea I had after Mom disappeared. How can I eat when I'm already full of something else? Sorrow. Grief. Agony. Take your pick.

A tear slips. Then another. I'll never see Joshua again.

Robyn pats my hand, probably assuming my tears are story related and nothing more.

"Naturally, the king's second-in-command took charge. He sent out search parties, combed the Reflection for the rulers. When they weren't found, Jasyn declared a time of mourning across the provinces." A loose hair falls into Robyn's face and she tucks it away. Pulls her lips inward, then blows out a puff of air. "The few who encountered Jasyn Crowe during that period said he seemed . . . different. Despondent but crazed. He holed himself up, hardly left his chambers."

"It was nearly a year before he summoned anyone to court again." Wade returns, wooden bowl in hand. Steam rises from its heart. "I remember it so clearly. My wife, Lark, had stayed home with Wren, just an infant at the time. I stood in the throne room, fully expecting Jasyn to give the people answers. What had happened to the king and queen? Had they died? If so, what had become of the Verity?" Eyes glossed, he takes a deep breath before continuing. "But we received no such comfort. Jasyn proclaimed the Verity had vanished along with the king and queen, but not to worry, for he had access to another power—a greater power. Those were his exact words."

Robyn trades our teacups for the bowl in Wade's hands. *Clink, rattle.* "That was the day he released the Void from its prison." She places the bowl in my lap.

Eyes closed and brow creased, Wade lowers his hands to his sides. The last bit of tea from Robyn's cup *drip, drip, drips* onto the cabin floor. "I saw it even then. There was a darkness about him beyond anything I'd witnessed in my lifetime. He'd succumbed to the Void's power."

"The Void had been contained for hundreds of years," she explains. "Entombed in a secret prison. Supposedly, only the Verity's vessel knows where the prison is, for the Verity alone has the power to contain or unleash the Void."

"Then how did Jasyn release it?" I take a sip of the peppery broth. Wrong pipe. *Cough.*

Robyn leans forward. "That's the mystery, isn't it? It's possible Aidan told Jasyn of the prison. The king trusted the man, after all, kept him close all those years. But there is still the conundrum of how, even if Jasyn knew the Void's location, he was able to unleash it." She rubs little circles on my back. "Some speculate Jasyn is actually a Mirror."

I swallow the lump in my throat. Mom always used to rub my back this way when I was sick. "What's a Mirror?"

"A person containing all the Callings. The gifts and abilities we're given as children." Wade paces to the other side of the cabin, sets the teacups in what appears to be a washbasin.

Ky mentioned Callings. And Wren. These Callings—powers—must be why Ky can paralyze. Why Haman can injure. Why Wren and Robyn can transform. And why Nathaniel can heal me. What about Makai? Is that why he could disappear? And Joshua. He was from here. Did he have some special superpower as well?

A pang stabs my chest. Now I'll never know.

"But," Robyn adds, "Mirrors are a myth. No one should have that much access to the Callings. It's not natural." She shudders. "Which leaves us where we started. Wondering how Jasyn freed the Void in the first place."

"And so began the Era of Shadows," Wade says when he returns, "bringing with it a Revolution. Those who served the Verity against those who submitted to the Void. Jasyn closed trade with the other Reflections, cut power throughout the provinces. The castle is the only place in all of the Second that still has access to electricity."

I stare at my bowl, broth growing colder by the breath. Holy wow. This is the most epically tragic story I've ever heard. Suddenly my problems seem small in comparison.

But then Robyn smiles, teeth and all. Could this story have a happy ending?

"I always believed . . ." She swipes a stray tear with her knuckle and starts again. "I always believed he was lying, Papa. Even after Mother left, I still hoped."

Wade takes his daughter's hand. "I know, my girl. I know." He chokes on the words.

"Believed what? Who was lying?" I'm like a little kid, begging to be read one more page at bedtime.

"There is much left to conjecture," Wade answers. "We still have our Callings. That was our first clue Jasyn concealed the truth."

When I scrunch my brows, Robyn adds, "The Callings are sourced by the Verity, you see. If the Verity had truly vanished, our abilities should have gone with it. We always hoped Jasyn's claim was fabricated. Now we know for sure." Her gaze finds my right cheek.

Out of habit I dip my head and let my hair fall over my birthmark. "What do you mean?"

"The mark on your face. It's proof the Verity lives." Robyn's practically bouncing on her stool.

"How so?" I peek through my hair curtain.

"You are sixteen, seventeen maybe?" Wade's eyebrows arch.

"I'll be eighteen in three weeks." I've always resented looking younger than I am. Mom says I'll appreciate it someday.

"And you've always had that mark?" Wade asks.

"Since I was born."

"All of this took place two decades ago," Wade muses. "Before you even existed."

"So?"

"Sooo . . ." Robyn stands. "There is only one person who could've given you a mark like this one." She reaches out as if to brush the hair from my face, then seems to think better of it, her hand faltering.

This is a whole new kind of strange. Snickers and avoidance I'm used to, but someone looking at me with . . . awe? Wonder? I don't know how to react. I'm almost afraid to ask, but I can't help myself. "Who gave me this mark?"

Sudden silence, so tangible I can almost hear my blood pumping through my veins. They exchange grins, eyes alight where moments ago sadness lingered. It's Robyn who breathes, "The vessel of the Verity, of course."

sudden Heat

Whoa. Back up. Hold the phone. Take a number. "Excuse me?" I gape at them. "You're telling me . . . what are you telling me exactly?" I press my palm against my forehead.

They open their mouths at the same time and then a *knock, knock, knock* resounds from the door. Robyn moves toward it, but Wade gestures for her to stay put. She takes a seat on the stool again as Wade crosses the cabin and answers.

"Thirty minutes," someone says. "Have the girl ready." Wade blocks my view, but the voice undoubtedly belongs to Saul the Grouch. Not that I'd recognize him otherwise considering I haven't actually *seen* him yet.

"Very well." The door clicks closed. Rather than returning to story hour, Wade bustles about the cabin. Bottles clink. Cupboards open and close. He adds a log to the woodstove. *Crackle. Whine. Bang.*

I focus on Robyn. We don't have long. It's up to her to finish explaining.

Before I can ask, she swallows, clears her throat, and says, "Where was I?"

"The Verity. And my mark."

She offers a slow nod. Deliberate. As if choosing her next words. "What you must first understand is the very nature of the Verity. Humans have a tendency for darkness and light. To choose good or evil." Palms upturned, she mimics the movement of a scale. "But no such mixture exists for the Verity or the Void. The Void houses no light. The Verity embraces no darkness. So when the Verity seeks a new vessel, it always searches out the purest heart—the person least likely to be swayed by darkness. A heart so true has the capacity to love like no other. And a love like that? It changes a person."

"What does any of this have to do with me?" I shift. The hammock swings and creaks.

Reaching out, Robyn stills the hammock. Her gaze wanders. "Until now we've only hoped. Guessed. Waited blindly for the Verity's return. To save us all. It wasn't until you arrived that dream became a reality." Two espresso eyes lock on mine.

"I'm not following." Spit it out already.

"The mark on your face is proof the Verity lives—that Aidan lives. It's a phenomenon Papa claims he's seen only once before—on the queen herself. A mark appearing when one has been touched—loved—by the Verity's vessel. Only death can release the Verity from its current home. King Aidan must still be out there somewhere. If he'd died, if the Verity had found a new soul to reside within, that person would've come forward by now."

"Let me get this straight. You think the Verity's vessel—King Aidan—touched *me*? Loved *me*?" Sudden heat ignites my neck. My marked cheek. "How is that even possible? I've had this mark since I was a baby. If what you say is true, the king touched me as an infant. I'm almost eighteen. If he's your savior, where's he been all these years?"

Robyn shrugs. "Who knows? Perhaps he's afraid of what Jasyn's become. It's even possible the king and queen were imprisoned, hidden in the catacombs deep beneath the castle. But it doesn't matter now. Because we have you."

I turn my head to the side. Daylight wanes as shadows stretch across the cabin floor. "There must be some mistake. I'm nobody."

Freak. Ugly. Hideous. Deformed.

Worthless.

The names I've been called all my life flood my memory. Every one of them digs its way in, expounds on the definition of me.

My shoulders slump. *Don't feel. Don't care.*

Clasping my hand, Robyn rushes on, "There's no mistake. You are more important than you realize. The mark, it binds your soul to the vessel. Bound souls always find one another. Once you're healed, you can lead us to him. If he's locked away, we'll free him. Then the rightful king can return the Void to its prison."

"How am I supposed to lead you to your king?" This is so much more than I bargained for. All I want is to rescue Mom and get as far away from this place as possible. Is that what she wanted? Is it why she took me? Hid me away?

I can't blame her for never sharing any of this. I wouldn't have believed her. I would've thought it was her well-meaning way of making me feel like my birthmark was a blessing, not a curse. That my deformity served a purpose. Which is crazy. Look where this thing has gotten me.

Joshua is dead. Mom is in danger.

I'm dynamite. I should've stayed home. Holed up. Nonexistent. Invisible. I'm a danger to anyone who gets close.

At some point I'm going to explode.

Bang!

Robyn and I jump.

Wade bends, snatches a pot from the floor. "Apologies. Carry on."

"As I said, bound souls always find one another." She offers a knowing look. In this moment her eyes hold the wisdom of a woman well beyond her teenage years. Taking my still-full bowl, she retreats, her footsteps cat quiet. I feel the absence of her calming presence instantly.

I relax into the hammock, close my eyes, even if for just a

moment. Bound souls find one another? How? When? If I'm attached to King Aidan, wouldn't I feel . . . *something*? Anything? A nudge. A pull. A voice in a dream?

Instead I feel nothing.

"It's time."

I open my eyes. Funny how you never realize how tired you are until you need to sleep and can't. A dim lantern burns on the windowsill, twilight in full swing beyond the glass. Robyn and Wade stand by the door along with a figure who is unmistakably Gage.

"We've done all we can," Wade whispers. "It's up to you now."

"The team is ready." Gage doesn't bother hushing his response. "Five in all, including the girl. The smaller our caravan, the better our chance at success."

Pain-free, I sit, the Illusoden still working wonders.

Robyn joins me, my boots and a jacket identical to Wren's in hand. "These are pretty dry now, thanks to the fire." She sets the boots on the floor beneath my dangling feet. "This is my sister's. She won't miss it." With a wink she helps me shrug into the sleeves.

"Thanks." I slip on Mom's Uggs.

We walk out together, and Robyn gives me a small hug. Her touch is a sunbeam in the night. "Be careful. You may feel better now, but you aren't healed. Don't make any big movements to speed up the internal bleeding and absolutely no running." She hands me a tiny vial tied to a loop of string. "More Illusoden. It's all we have left. Don't take it unless you absolutely must."

I nod, sliding the string over my head like a necklace and tucking the vial beneath my shirt.

"These too." She hands me a bulgy satchel and a canteen. "Promise you'll eat a little something every hour. I will petition the Verity for a safe journey." Her hand palms her heart. "With any providence, you'll find Nathaniel and he'll heal you. I can't imagine he would refuse when he sees you are his granddaughter and the greatest hope for our people."

An internal groan. No pressure or anything. "Okay." I descend the porch steps and inhale, but compost and smoke taint the air, making the breath less satisfying. Three men stand several yards away dressed in clothing similar to Wren's. They all have a satchel or pack of some sort. The short, pudgy one carries a bow and quiver of arrows like Makai. I join them, then look back at the cabin. One last glimpse of the Physic and his kind daughter wedges a lump in my throat. I might never see them again.

Answering my heart's cry, Robyn waves. "We'll see you soon."

How can she be so optimistic?

Gage shakes Wade's hand. "We're traveling by land and sea. Not as fast, but safer. I don't dare risk having her moved by air again. If I thought we had time, I'd retrieve the Physic and bring him back to heal her. Taking her with us is our best option for a positive outcome on all counts."

Moonlight washes the forest floor, exposing Wade's worried frown. "She informed me she'll be eighteen in three weeks. That gives us a very small window—"

Our leader nods. "It'll be fine. Three weeks is plenty of time."

When Gage reaches me, I touch his arm. Swallow. "Gage? About my mom . . ."

"Wade filled me in. I'll do my best to form a rescue mission once you're well and safely returned to our hideout. I won't make any promises, but I will try."

I bite back my argument. She needs rescue sooner, not later. But what can I do? I'm bleeding internally. Gage's answer has to be good enough. For now.

Then we're leaving. Gage takes the lead and two others follow, one stout, the second massive. The last man, petite and boyish, falls in step behind me. This is a sandwich, and I'm the butcher's special.

I squint toward Wade and Robyn, standing huddled on the porch, watching us. My heart cinches. I was wrong. Because I do feel something. I gaze without seeing the back in front of me, dwelling on Robyn's gentle voice and Wade's warm smile.

For the first time today I wonder if maybe Mom's not the only person who needs saving.

TWELVE

Hearts Leap

Crunch, crunch, crunch. My entourage's monotonous march drones on. Like listening to Joshua eat Oreos.

I miss him so much. Has it only been half a day since he held me in the subway? Feels like decades. If I hadn't taken an involuntary bath in the Threshold, his scent might linger in my T-shirt. I lift my collar and sniff. Nothing but dirt and mildew. Not a trace of him remains.

"Everything I've done is because . . ."

Because you what, Joshua? Because you wanted to see King Aidan returned to the throne? Because you were doing your duty? *What* were you going to say?

I'll never know. I want to curl up in a ball and mourn him properly. I want to go back and kiss him before I was yanked away. I want to tell him I love him. I want him to say it too.

I want what I can't have. More time.

It's odd. My brain's aware my life is draining, but aside from a broken heart, my body feels fine. Better than fine, really. I feel eight-hours-of-sleep, don't-even-need-coffee good. What's in that Illusoden stuff anyway?

I finger the vial hanging from my neck.

"Don't take it unless you absolutely must."

The way I feel now, I doubt I'll need to.

The only person here I sort of know is Gage. No one else has

bothered introducing themselves. We're well past the populated
area. Storefronts and cottages with lantern-lit windows no longer
dot the path. No tromes either. Just boring, Third Reflection–type
trees. Still, there are oddities I'd never see at home. Spanish moss
dangling in copious swags from evergreens. Vibrant wild roses,
alive and thriving even in late autumn, carpeting fallen logs.
Shallow streams bustling with glowing purple fish, creating bright
runways for birds of prey. Mysterious. Beautiful. Clearly an area
not taken by the Void.

Yet.

When we finally halt, I almost run into the very tall and wide
Samoan-looking dude in front of me. Thankfully, I stop inches
before my face meets brawny muscle. I make room. Lean to the side.
Peer down the line. A cluster of boulders rises ahead. A cave yawns
at their center. No, not a cave. A tomb. Two statuesque guards stand
on either side of its mouth.

Gage strides away and enters the black den. The guards don't
bat an eye.

"What's he doing?"

"Grabbing some collateral." The unexpected female voice
approaches from behind.

I twirl. Face-to-face with a young woman not a day over twenty-
five. Boy-cut hair sticks out in every direction from her pixie-like
head. She's just the kind of girl they'd cast as Peter Pan on Broadway.
Petite. In the dark I assumed everyone here was male. Her face,
though, is anything but masculine.

"Collateral?"

"Gage has his reasons." Samoan Dude steps up beside me,
the reflection of the moonlight on his bald head a soft halo. Wow.
Those are the fleshiest lips I've ever seen.

A breeze picks up, sending the scents of peppermint and
tobacco my way. I cough, covering it up with the back of my arm.

"Move back a little, Kuna. You'll choke her to death." The woman laughs, then addresses me. "You'll have to excuse my husband. We all have our vices. Tobacco is his. He thinks he can hide it by rubbing peppermint leaves on his skin. I always say that makes the stink more pronounced."

Husband? These two are New Yorker and country bumpkin opposite.

"Appearances can deceive."

Ky's words haunt me. Why did I let him get to me?

"Sorry, Stormy." Kuna widens the gap.

Thank you. "No problem. I'm from a big city. I've smelled worse." The words flow free before I realize what I'm saying. I peek at him. Is he offended?

He hoots, bends over, and slaps his knee.

"Shhh," Stormy hushes through her own lightweight giggle.

Here it comes. I'm laughing. Not because anything is particularly funny, but because Stormy and Kuna's fit is viral. Ow, ow, ow. It hurts. I can't stop. I'm shaking so hard I'm crying. I can't see through my squinty eyes. Robyn's gonna kill me for not being careful. Any minute my insides could rip apart.

"What the crowe? Are you three looking to get us all killed?" The gruff voice from earlier hisses through the gloom. Saul.

We freeze, though Stormy lets out one last snicker.

I inhale deep, slow breaths. Man, my middle aches, but it was worth it. I haven't laughed that way in—

What am I doing? I shouldn't be laughing. It isn't right. Not when Joshua's death is so fresh.

I'm sorry, I think to no one.

"Watch your mouth, Preacher. We weren't that loud." Kuna's attempted whisper emits at a normal volume.

Saul—Preacher grits his teeth. With his knit cap and unkempt beard, he's a hobo's clone. "Crowe has scouts everywhere." He waves skyward. "You may be willing to put your life on the line. Do not be so careless with mine." He faces the tomb again, his body rigid against the bow and arrows on his back.

Stormy rolls her eyes and murmurs past her hand, "That's Saul Preacher, but most everyone calls him the latter. Don't mind him." She winks. "We're still within the Haven's boundaries. He's just paranoid."

"The Haven?" I lean in.

"That's what we call the island. From shoreline to shoreline is rebel territory. People who remain loyal to the Verity." Her eyes alight with passion. The same light Wade and Robyn carried when they spoke of King Aidan.

I'm about to ask more, but her eyes shift and her casual demeanor switches back to that of a silent soldier.

Gage returns, a young man walking in front of him. So these are the Crypts.

I clench my fists. What's Ky doing here?

My pulse accelerates when he looks at me.

Probably because I want to strangle him.

They pass Preacher and stand before Kuna. "Keep an eye on him." Gage clutches Ky's shoulder. "And you. No Dragon games. You'll find I hold no value for the life of a traitor."

I lean close to Stormy and whisper through the side of my mouth. "What are Dragon games?"

"It's an expression," she says under her breath. "Dragons are cunning tricksters. Never turn your back on a Dragon." She juts her chin toward Ky. "Or a traitor."

"Did you hear me, traitor?" Gage shakes Ky.

After another moment Ky nods, his face drawn. Black and blue shrouds his green eye on all sides. Blood trickles from his temple, stains his busted lip. Is this the same boy who held a knife to my side a mere day ago?

The caravan continues, everyone careful to avoid Ky's gaze.

Hands tied behind his back, he ambles between Preacher and Kuna. Any minute he'll turn the tables. He'll fight or run. But he doesn't. What, or who, broke him?

Before long we pause again. A dead-end wall of ivy looms. It stretches left and right, curving through the trees. "Does this border the entire island?"

"Yes," Stormy says. "One of the best façades I've ever seen."

Façades. Ky mentioned something about them. They're illusions, like the gap in the Broken Bridge.

Gage strides to the wall and . . . walks right through.

And the door at the Threshold beneath the subway. That must've been a façade too. One by one, we follow suit. When it's my turn I hold my breath, whirl when I reach the opposite side. Nothing but a wall of gray, ivyless rock. Weird.

"It looks so real," I say.

Stormy shoos me on. "That's because it is. The wall is perfectly solid, but there are chinks in the armor. Gaps for entering and exiting that only Guardians know about."

Wow. I take one final glance at the wall before shuffling forward. Salty air enters my lungs. The crunch of leaves dies, our footsteps muted.

We're near a beach. My heart does the arabesque my klutzy legs and arms never could. The forest thins. The ground changes from dark soil covered in twigs and needles, clover beds, and mushroom patches to soft shore. The rippling sand beckons a memory.

For my twelfth birthday Mom took me to Nantucket. Being November, it was freezing, the water stinging, salted ice against our naked shins. We got hot chocolate at this little mom-and-pop joint. I don't even remember its name, just the jar of M&M's by the register. The vase of yellow silk flowers in the window. The tinkling brass bell over the door. Despite our frostbitten toes and the bitter wind, I never had a better birthday.

I close my eyes and imagine kicking off my boots, burying my soles in the sand. I'm on that island again with Mom, our fingers interlocked as we run through floating foam. A breeze lifts my bangs. I can almost hear our hearts leap through peals of laughter—feel the warmth of the to-go cup against my palm.

The moment drifts as I open my eyes to reality. Mom's not here, and she won't be unless we hurry. At the water's edge a large rowboat awaits, Gage and Preacher already aboard. Ky climbs in next, and Stormy and I do the same.

The unsteady vessel rocks. I take the bench behind Ky. He doesn't look at me again.

Stormy straddles the rear seat as Kuna pushes us off and dives underwater. I whirl. "What's he doing?"

"You'll see." Stormy's fingers brush my arm, her brown eyes twinkling. Away from the shadow of the trees, the colored tips of her brown hair shine. They're flames of neon purple. Dancing. Licking the night air.

I could never pull that off.

When we're several yards out, a tumultuous splash pierces the tranquil sea. Kuna reverse-melts up from the water, shirtless, a tattoo identical to Wren's looks miniaturized on his exaggerated pec. He smiles, pearly whites and all. There's a secret in his eyes.

What?

He smiles wider, vanishing below the glassy waves. Another splash. A set of scaly green fins flicks. Slaps. Sends a cold shower our way.

I guffaw. This can't be real. Kuna is, he's a . . .

Merman?

Flying I can handle. Seasickness, not so much.

The waves chop and slice, manipulating the boat like a

sautéed vegetable. The taste of stomach acid fills my mouth. I guzzle it back on a flood of stale canteen water. Nasty.

Kuna shows up every now and then to give Stormy the thumbs-up, then returns to the world below when she mimics the gesture.

Wow. A merman. What next?

How long until we reach that sliver of land on the horizon? It might as well be a floating stick of gum. Thin and flat and far away. I can't see the Haven's shore anymore. Maybe we're going faster than I think.

Ky sits and sulks, his slumped back toward me.

Let him sulk. He deserves to feel guilt for what he's done. He's lucky I don't push him overboard. He did as much to Joshua.

"Is that how I raised you? To hurt the people who hurt you?"

Of course not, Mom. But where's the justice? The punishment for his crimes?

My middle churns again, and not because of the waves or constant undecided motion. Gage's disdain for Ky is no secret. I don't know much about him, but I know he wouldn't bring Ky along just for kicks.

Kuna must be pushing us from below because no one's rowing. I always thought of merpeople as dainty redheads in purple bikinis. If Disney only knew.

The boat tips too far to the right. I brace myself, eyes on the water. Any second Kuna's going to pop up, his potato-sized thumb pointing to the moon.

Come on, come on . . .

Ka-boom! Thunder. Close thunder. One, two . . . *flash!* Lightning surges. Droplets of rain pelt down, full and extravagant.

Stormy's eyes are locked on the sky. Without a glance she orders, "Get down."

I scoot to the left and jam myself into the hampered space

between benches. My hand slips, sending a splinter through the tip of my middle finger. I try to get it with my teeth. Futile. Never thought I'd miss Quinn, or rather, her purse. Tweezers would be nice to have right about now.

The bottom stinks of mildew. It's not far down. I sit with my knees to my chest, the sea still in full view. Rain gathers in the cracks between floorboards. I'm no sailor, but there must be a drain somewhere because we're not sinking.

Ky abandons his seat, too, fixes his gaze on me. "Untie me."

I recoil, refusing to look him in the eyes. "You think I'm going to help you after what you did to me? To Joshua?"

"I can help them."

"Why should I trust you? What reason have you given me?" I turn my head slightly.

He opens his mouth. Closes it. Opens it again. "Let me give you one now."

Around us the storm intensifies. We're rocking uncontrollably. I stiffen from a spike of pain. Is the Illusoden wearing off so soon?

"Hey." Ky draws my attention back to him. "You're bleeding."

The pain prickles and spreads, most pronounced on my right side. I press my hands to the warm, damp spot on my shirt. I don't have to look. Ky's right.

The others busily prepare defense.

Crud. This is a bad idea. "Fine," I hiss. "Don't make me regret this."

He turns, and I dig my fingers into the thick knots binding his wrists. The rope chafes my skin. It's too tight. I bend and work at it with my teeth, gnawing and pulling. There. Almost got it. It's loose!

Ky acts quickly. He removes his top layer, wrings it out, and then rips it down the middle, leaving only a black thermal clinging to his form. He slips his hands beneath my jacket, wraps his torn tee around my waist, cinching it snug. The others are so focused on what's happening outside the boat, they don't notice us.

"Ouch!" I will not take the Illusoden yet. I don't need it. I *don't*.

He pauses. "Does that hurt?"

"You think?"

His brows furrow, and his lips flatten into a thin line. "Didn't the Physic give you something for the pain?" Why should he care if I'm in pain or not?

"Illusoden." The word pants out of me.

"When did he give it to you?"

Does it matter? I shrug. Wince. "This afternoon."

Ky's lips move but no sound emerges. He closes his eyes, then opens them. They're hard and calculating. Then he shakes his head. The odd moment is over.

What was that about?

He knots the ripped T-shirt once, twice.

This must be what a corset feels like. I can barely breathe, but I'm alive.

He shakes as he stands, hugging the bench between his calves. Ky picks up the rope and wraps an end around each knuckle. Is he planning to strangle someone?

Did I make a mistake?

His focus remains seaward.

I sigh and take in the others. Stormy's gaze hasn't left the sky. Preacher watches the sea, a death wish in his glare, in the way he grips his weapon. Gage holds a pair of binoculars to his eyes, his head twisting from side to side. Nobody seems to notice or care their prisoner is free.

Splash! Kuna soars over the boat. Did he jump? Was he thrown? I've got a feeling I won't have to wait long to find out.

Is that . . . a head . . . in the distance? Coming closer. No way.

A little girl, no older than six or seven, swims toward us. She's wailing, "Mama! Mama!"

We have to help her. Whatever danger lies below the surface will go for her first. I push the pain aside and reach out.

Ky grips my wrist, shoves my arm down. "Don't. It's a ruse."

Isabeau's gorgeous face invades my thoughts. Was that her true form?

No. It wasn't.

My heart seizes. The girl cries louder, her squeal carried by the wind. Every instinct says rescue her. I cover my ears, trying to drown out the sound. I'm tired of this. Tired of fear.

The girl snakes into the air, towering high. Like a mermaid, the top half of her body is human. But the similarity ends there. Her bottom half is red, slender, and slimy. Serpentine.

Preacher nocks and shoots, nocks and shoots, his face twisted into wrinkled knobs.

The monster doesn't even twitch. Instead she opens her small mouth wide, exposing rows and rows of deadly-looking fangs. A Venus flytrap, hungry and ready to devour. Then, ever so slowly, she glides forward on the chopping waves.

Gage yanks an oar from the boat's bottom and rows, puffing determined breaths through puckered lips. Left, right, left, right.

"What's happening?"

"Leviathan," Ky answers. "The Dragon of the sea."

We're going to die. Right here, right now.

I rise, gripping the boat's smooth edge. If we're all goners, I'm going to stand. Face what's coming. I won't cower. My knees knock as water sloshes over the side.

"What are you doing? Get down." Preacher reprimands me like an insolent child caught with her hand in the cookie jar.

Ky brings the rope over my head and pulls back against my neck.

I claw at his hands. I love you, Mom.

He pulls tighter.

Gasp. No air. Joshua's face flashes across my blurred vision, calming me for the briefest, purest instant.

Stormy looks our way at the exact second the storm subsides.

Why doesn't Ky's stare affect her, or the others for that matter? If he wanted to, he could make them all go limp with one glance. Couldn't he?

"Let her go, Kyaphus," Gage commands.

The Leviathan shrieks.

The boat flips.

Smack!

We're all going to be fish food.

THIRTEEN

That Boy

My eyelids are fifty pounds too heavy. I'm waking, but I can't quite bring myself to full consciousness. These sheets are so not Second Reflection material. I roll my head from side to side. This pillow isn't either. Too . . . fluffy. Do I smell lavender and vanilla? Yes. Mom's burning candles again. We're home.

I open my eyes. Billows of white gossamer drape over and around me. I'm lying beneath a heavy gold-and-maroon damask comforter. Not home. Not even close.

The surroundings beyond the four-poster bed are, in a word, presidential. Persian rugs. Ceiling-high curtains. Soft-glowing lamps. Wingback chairs. A grand vanity mirror with intricate carvings in its frame. A tray piled with frosted pastries. A china tea set on a mahogany table. It's a scene straight from *A Little Princess*.

I sit. Ky's T-shirt bandage is gone, along with my clothes. A silky green robe swathes my naked body. My face flushes. Who undressed me?

Testing my strength, I lean forward, then side to side. Sore. Far from dying. I peel the comforter off, swinging my legs over. The mattress is as deep as it is wide. I have to hop to get down. The plush rug conforms to my feet. I walk to one corner where a fire crackles in the hearth. My Uggs rest beside it. Next to them my clothes are neatly folded on a chair, bra and underwear included. Who folds underwear? I pull my long-sleeved shirt from the middle of the pile. *Sniff.* Things are looking up. I'm not going to smell like a hobbit today.

With my back to the door, I dress locker-room-style, the robe draping my body. When I'm done, I toss it on the bed and glide my feet into the toasty, sand-flecked boots. I find a brush on a table and run it through my hair. Where knots should be, the bristles meet sleek locks. I set it down and smell my skin. Baby-powder fresh. Has someone been grooming and bathing me too?

Why do I feel as if I'm forgetting something? The Illusoden. I dig in my pockets, check under the chair. Nope. It's gone. Nothing I can do about it. Might as well eat.

I snatch a croissant from the pastry tray, tear off little pieces, and pop them in my mouth. The sweet, buttery flakes melt on my tongue. Steam rises from the teapot. I pour some, add cream and sugar, and sip with caution.

Earl Grey. Mom's favorite.

I meander around. The lamps are electric. If I'm still in the Second Reflection, there's only one place this could be. Jasyn's castle. Robyn said he's the only one who has access to electricity.

My insides seethe. Ky. It's the only explanation. I've no idea how, but I know he brought me here, the traitor. Why did I untie him? Stupid.

Another glance around and I scrunch my face. Wait. If I'm a prisoner, why am I in this luxurious suite instead of a dungeon?

I open what I think is a closet door and discover a master-sized bathroom complete with civilized plumbing. Guess I could've changed in there.

What now? No doubt those grand double doors are guarded. I pace to the covered window, push the velvety curtains aside. Night blankets the sky beyond the glass, pale moonlight doing little to illuminate the landscape. We're on a hill. The only other light provided is artificial, spilling from lampposts stationed around the hill's edge. Beyond that, the world is inky black.

I zero in my gaze on what I can make out. One story below me lies a courtyard, a Bethesda Fountain replica dominating its center. Where the *Angel of the Waters* statue should be stands a sculpture of a Dragon, a single, thorny rose nestled between its bared teeth. I press my face against the stained glass. Are those stables? How hard can it be to ride a horse? If this *is* Jasyn's castle, Mom's here somewhere. I'll find her and—

"You ought to be resting."

Crash! China shards and hot tea ring my feet. Good thing I put on my boots.

A man with a pragmatic expression and deep-set brown eyes stands by the bed. He's dressed in a suit and tie, his hands folded casually in front of him. "Please, do not be alarmed. I am not your enemy."

Liar. "Jasyn?"

He laughs. "I do not think I have ever heard my name spoken with such disdain. We have not even been properly introduced."

Scowling, I cross my arms. "Where. Is. My. Mom?" Each word is a spiraling dagger.

"Elizabeth is in her suite. She is resting now. You may visit with her later."

What's up with this guy? He's so coy and . . . nice. "Why all the dramatics? Healing me. Putting me up in a fancy room. Why not kill me now and get it over with?"

His eyebrows sink. "Kill you? What purpose would that serve?"

I drop my guard a fraction. What game is he playing?

He steps forward gingerly. "I can assure you, my dear grand-daughter, the last thing I want is your blood on my hands."

I convulse from top to bottom. "I'm not your granddaughter." No way. Not buying it.

"Come." He gestures toward the doors. "Let us go for a stroll in the rose garden."

❦

The courtyard's layout reminds me of Conservatory Garden. Paths broken up by plots of soil where flowers and grass should be. We amble over a flagstone walkway, sharp angles of broken rock pieced together like a mosaic. Sconces dangle from the castle walls, giving the courtyard a certain ambience. A waist-high, gray brick wall borders the brink of the leveled hilltop. When we reach it, I stand beneath a lamppost, let my eyes adjust to the dim light. Below, a black forest waits, and beyond that, a lake comes into view through a break in the trees. From this distance, it just looks like a great big puddle. The smallness reminds me of a landscape model Joshua built for school once.

Twinge. How am I supposed to let him go? Maybe I was his duty, but he meant so much more to me.

The water in the fountain at the courtyard's center is frozen. Our footsteps seem to whisper "shhh" as we round it in silence. If I thought the inside was grand, the outside is just as impressive. While the interior is sophisticated—The Plaza, The Ritz, and The Pierre all rolled into one—the exterior is magnificent. Belvedere Castle and background skyscrapers combined. A seamless blend of contemporary architecture and medieval charm. Walls made of granite. Cone-capped towers. And oh, for all the windows. High and low, arced and squared, wide and narrow. It's literally like gazing upon Fifth Avenue hotels at night, with some guests still awake, rooms illuminated. Others have long gone to bed, their lamps extinguished.

Joshua would have loved this.

Jasyn clears his throat. "Tell me. What have you been told?"

You're my enemy. You're a power-hungry soul-stealer. I alone can supposedly lead the people to their lost king. "Not much." My breath fogs. I shiver. How is he not cold?

"Ah." He grins. "You do not wish to tell me?"

"How about I ask *you* some questions?" He wants to talk, let's talk.

"All right." He veers from the fountain and heads down a hedge-lined path. The leaves have all fallen and died, the bare branches stretching, unashamed at their nakedness. This is his rose garden?

I glance again at the night sky. The naked rosebushes. The black forest. Joshua mentioned Shadow Territory. This has to be it. Maybe it's not even night at all. What if it's always night here?

I trail Jasyn's course. The hedges are a maze, weaving out from the courtyard and back in again. "How did you heal me?"

"I did not simply heal you, my dear. I brought you back from the dead."

"Impossible."

"Is it?"

He's lying. No one is that powerful.

"I have access to many rare remedies. One of the many perks of being king."

You're no king. "How long have I been here?"

"Two full nights."

I count backward in my head. It's Wednesday. Three days since Joshua died.

Since I died.

"Who undressed me? Brushed my hair? Bathed me?"

"One of my female servants."

Phew. *If* he's telling the truth.

"Where did you get your fancy suit?" He looks as if he stepped out of an Armani catalog, nothing like the other residents I've seen.

"I have the means to conduct commerce with some of the other Reflections. My favorite is yours, the Third. So much luxury and frivolity there. I send my personal assistant, and she brings me back whatever I request. If you like, I can have some peanut butter M&M's sent to your room. I know they are your favorite."

How did he—? "No, thank you." Don't fall into his traps. Move

on. "Haman promised Isabeau he would give her my mom's . . ."
Gah, how do I say this? "He promised something of my mom's."
Is hers one of the lit windows? Is she looking down on me now?

He frowns. "Haman said what he had to in order to get past
the Troll."

"He seemed serious. Made some kind of weird, hand-kissing
vow." When Jasyn shows no sign of concern, I add, "I don't want
that night crawler anywhere near her."

Waving me off, he says, "Do not worry about Haman. I have
made it explicitly clear to all my servants no harm is to come to
you or my daughter."

I stop, cup my hands on my hips. "Well, harm did come. Haman
and Ky killed Joshua, and they almost killed me. If you're my grandfather, as you claim, how could you let those things happen?"

Jasyn pivots, inclining his head. "Tell me more about Joshua.
He was your Guardian, correct? You two were close?"

My arms relax, and I march past him. "It's none of your business." How does he know so much about my life? "You're avoiding
my question. If you're my—?"

"My business is whatever I choose." He falls in step beside me.
"Were you in love with him?"

"How did Ky get me here? We were in the middle of the sea,
about to be eaten by a Leviathan."

"The girl works for me, of course. She brought you and
Kyaphus here."

That was no girl.

"The Leviathan brought you up the Stae River, which borders
Gnol Island on one side and the Forest of Night on the other." He
extends a hand toward the shadowed trees. His explanation comes
out like a speech. Formal. Professorish. No way I'm related to this
guy.

We reach the courtyard again. A crow caws and lands on the
fountain's lip, then pecks at the ice and shudders before it takes

flight once more. Jasyn sits on a marble bench, crosses his legs, and smiles wide.

I don't sit next to him. His friendly act won't work. "If you don't want to kill me, what *do* you want?"

"You get straight to the point. I admire that."

What is this, an interview? Enough patronization. "You didn't answer my question."

"In time I will. For now, let us enjoy getting to know one another."

I want nothing to do with you. I need to see Mom. "I'm actually kind of tired. I'd like to go to my room." So I can formulate a plan of escape.

Jasyn lifts one eyebrow. "Certainly."

He escorts me back inside without any further attempts to get me chatting. We walk a different route than before. Beautiful paintings, some portraits, some scenery, adorn the white-walled halls. One rendering in particular stops me, turns my blood reptilian. It's a teenage girl portrayed from empire waist up. She's lovely, with curls like chocolate shavings heaped high and bonbon eyes to match. I'd know her anywhere.

It's true. He wasn't lying.

"Your mother the day she turned sixteen." His voice falters a bar. "I was not present for this particular birthday." Was he freeing the Void at the time? "It was a time of distress for our people." The Revolution? "By the time I gained a handle on things, I was quite grieved to learn she had run away." He casts a sidelong glance. "Now I know why." He picks up his pace.

I linger by the painting. Run my fingertips along the custom-gilded frame. It's all coming together like a dress rehearsal the day before a show opens. Mom was sixteen when she had me. Jasyn didn't know Mom was pregnant because he was too busy playing tyrant.

When I catch up to him and enter my suite, Jasyn shuts the door. He doesn't say good-bye. *Click.*

I jiggle the handle. Locked. So I *am* a prisoner.

Knock, knock, knock.

The sound doesn't come from the door.

Knock, knock, knock.

The second set is louder. Where? I do a 360. Wait for it. The knocks play again. I inch toward my bed. Again. I'm getting warmer. There they are. The wall behind the headboard. I rush over and press my ear against it, pounding back in response.

"Hello? Is someone there?" The voice is faint, muffled, but distinctly male.

"I'm here. Who are you?"

"It isn't real."

"What do you mean?" I press my ear harder. I can barely hear him, whoever he is.

He's saying something.

I don't understand. "What?"

"The mirror. Look in the mirror." *Cough. Hack. Wheeze.*

The vanity across the room. I took care to avoid it when walking by. Like most opportunities to gaze upon my reflection, I simply turned it down.

I take hesitant steps across the room and place myself directly before the mirror.

A gasp escapes me. That girl isn't me. She's beautiful with frizzless hair and airbrushed skin. No birthmark mars her porcelain face, no red vines crawl along her cheek. But her eyes, a warm, hot-cocoa brown. Mom's eyes. My eyes.

And Jasyn's.

I stumble backward, my heel catching on the lip of a rug. I reach out and grab the bedpost before I land on my rear. I can't look away. That can't be me. I wish it was.

At the wall I yell, "Are you there? What's happening? I don't know how, but my reflection—"

"Look again." He sounds tired, old. "Not with your eyes, though. See with your heart."

How am I supposed to do that? I try anyway. I stand before the mirror again and gawk at the beauty reflected there.

See with your heart.

I close my eyes. No matter how much I want it to be true, the beautiful girl with her unblemished face isn't me. I know how I look, and it doesn't come close to her.

My eyelashes flutter open. I swallow, taking in the full measure of the transformed image. The birthmark is back. But that's not what has me quivering, sweating, my jaw plummeting to my collarbone.

I whirl, taking in my new surroundings.

The lavish, kingly bed is gone, replaced by a toddler-sized cot with brown stains on the sheetless mattress. All the furniture has vanished, too, aside from a low stool in one corner. There's no door leading off to a bathroom, just a bucket against a wall where the door used to be. I don't even want to think about what the bucket is for. Sick.

My regard returns to the mirror. No more than a tall shard of glass leaning against grimy stone. No fire. No rugs. No cascading curtains. The window is a simple barred rectangle. I jog to it, fit my face between the two middle bars.

I'm not on a high floor. This is a basement—a dungeon. The familiar odor of horse doo forces me back. I hold my breath and press my face forward, wanting the full picture to sink in.

Whinny, neigh.

My prison is below a stable, not near one. That dirty, rotten, no-good—I didn't want to let him fool me, but he did. He called me granddaughter, with a term of endearment. I actually believed he was going to let me see Mom.

I turn my back to the wall, sink to the cold floor, and hug my knees. I'm starving, exhausted, crying yet again. I should've eaten more when I thought the tray of stale rolls was a mountain of baker's goods. There's no hope of escape or rescue. As Jasyn's guest, I really believed it might be as simple as sneaking Mom out after everyone went to bed. How could I have been so naive?

The stranger doesn't call to me again. Just as well. I'm not in the mood to talk.

I could shout out the window for help, but what's the point? Even if I could lead the people to their king, what chance would an old, incarcerated man and the cast of *Les Mis* have against Jasyn and the Void? He's Javert to their Jean Valjean. Except this time, the villain wins. The people of the Haven dress in rags and carry outdated weapons. Jasyn's men have blades and guns and possess the ability to paralyze with a look or injure with a snap. He has electricity—power. What other weapons and resources does he have up his custom-tailored sleeves?

My blood boils and burns, drying my tears. This is all King Aidan's fault. I pity the people of the Haven and their useless, dangerous hope. Aidan and his queen didn't vanish, they left, but everyone is too blind to admit it. Too afraid of the truth. The rulers must've sensed mutiny was on the horizon. If they hadn't given up, the Void might still be imprisoned. Joshua might still be alive. Mom would probably be working on her first winter sketch right now.

Jasyn Crowe might be a horrible, evil man, but King Aidan was worse. He abandoned his people, left them with nothing.

Clang. Crreeeaaakkk.

My head snaps up. I did it again. I fell asleep.

The cell door fans open. In the fractals of lamplight bleeding through the window bars, only a shadow is visible.

"Go away, Jasyn. The jig is up."

He steps into the cell and closes the door. He doesn't speak. Slinks toward me, keeping to the shadows.

My heart stampedes. This isn't Jasyn Crowe. I get up, pressing my back against the stone. If whoever it is plans to try something, I won't go down without a fight. I'll kick and shriek, making it as difficult as possible for him to get what he wants.

Closer, closer. I open my mouth to scream and then . . . then the stranger steps into view. He flashes a crooked smile, his mismatched gaze exuding arrogance. Beneath the moonlight his tussock of cowlicks is the color of warm honey, caramel streaks melted in here and there.

What am I thinking? Nothing about him is warm. He will always be *that* boy—the one who took everything from me.

Arms crossed he says, "Are you going to stand there all day, or are we getting out of here?"

Anger flares. Three, two, one. Breathe.

"Ky."

FOURTEEN

DON'T DREAM

I've never punched anyone before. First time for everything, I
guess.

Charging, I reel my right arm back. Swing.

Ky blocks the blow easily, catching my clenched fist in his palm.
"I'd love to stay and teach you a thing or two about self-defense.
But I'm afraid we'll have to reschedule." He's clad in black, a knife
sheathed at his hip. Black boots. Black leather jacket. Black. Black.
Black. Could it be any more obvious he's one of the bad guys?

I rip my fist from his grasp. "I'm not going anywhere with
you." My knee jerks up.

He dodges my attempt. "Did you really think that would work
a second time?" He shakes his head, blond tendrils brushing his
eyelashes. "Nice try, princess. Let's go."

Feet planted, I lift my chin and glare.

"Don't make me carry you out over my shoulder."

Gaze narrowed and teeth gritted, I hiss, "Go ahead and try."

And he does.

"Hey! Put me down." I pound his back with my fists. Pointless.
We're out the door and into a new-to-me sconce-lit hall. How did
Jasyn do that? Not only did he lead me to believe I was in a suite,
but he made me see white-walled halls and paintings and fancy
carpet. Was it one of those façade things Stormy mentioned?

Two guards lie crumpled in a heap on the floor. Ky steps over them, hoisting my body and tightening his hold. The guards are dressed in the same pirate garb my captor wears. My brow knits. Ky's dressed the same, but he had to knock the guards out to get to me. What game is Jasyn playing?

When we head up a spiral stone staircase, I stop fighting.

Ky sets me down on the step above his. "Can I trust you to behave? Once we're out of the dungeon, we'll have new problems."

"You really expect me to believe you're rescuing me? After all you've done to prove where your loyalties lie?"

An orange glow washes his face, a grin lifting his cheeks. "Consider this. How do you think your mother escaped the castle the night I kidnapped you?" When I don't answer he says, "I freed her so she could help you, genius." His eyebrows arch.

Makai said Mom had someone on the inside. But it couldn't be Ky. Could it?

My guard lowers a fraction.

"If David and Archer had arrived at the Pond sooner," Ky continues, "Haman wouldn't have involved himself. Then you, them, your mom—you'd all be safe right now."

Guard back up. How dare he blame this on Joshua and Makai. "What a load of manure." I move to walk past him. I'd rather be back in my cell than listen to this garbage.

He grabs my shoulder. "Stop. I can prove I'm telling the truth. Just give me a chance."

Ugh. I face him. We're on the same step now. So close. Too close. "Why kidnap me in the first place then? If you're so bent on helping the rebels?"

"I never wanted to aid Crowe, but I had my reasons for making him believe I served the Void." A pause. He stares at the wall past my shoulder. Clenches and unclenches his fists. "Those reasons are no longer valid."

This oughta be good. "Do tell."

He flattens his lips. "Look, all you need to know is before I delivered you to Crowe, I couldn't let him know I helped the rebels in secret. Now it doesn't matter. I don't care if he finds out."

"Why not?"

His shoulders sink. "Because I have nothing left to lose."

"So your 'poor me' act at the Haven. That was . . . ?"

"I thought if you felt sorry for me it'd be easier to get you to trust me."

"I don't believe this. " I fling my arms in the air, then let them collapse at my sides. "You're admitting you deceived me and expect me to go with you now?"

"Actually, yes." He thumbs his chest. "I just incapacitated two of Crowe's men, guys I know, to get you out. Why would I do that if this wasn't really a jailbreak?"

"Some warped version of capture the flag?"

Thud, thud, thud.

Ky grips his knife's hilt with one hand and presses me against the curving stone with the other. His pulse throbs through his wrist.

"Find them. Don't let them escape!"

That honeyed voice. *No.* Not him. Anyone but Haman.

I take in Ky's nervous stance. The way he hides from a man who's supposedly on his team. Maybe he is being genuine this time. Only one way to find out. "We have to find my mom." I tug on his leather sleeve. "She's somewhere in the castle. Jasyn said she's safe, but I don't believe him." Sweat seeps into my shirt. So much for clean clothes.

"I know where she is." He doesn't look at me, his gaze attending the commotion above.

"And there was a prisoner. A man. He spoke to me. He sounded ill. We should go back and free him."

"I'm sorry, there's no time. You're my priority."

"But—"

"No."

I don't argue. We wait, our heartbeats a single percussion instrument. A drum roll ushering in the big finale.

Silence. Ky creeps forward.

I move in harmony with him, the distance to the next floor brief. The steps continue to ascend, but we exit and enter a smoky hall. *Sizzle, clang.* A greasy bacon odor gusts toward us. Barf. How can anyone stand the artery-clogging muck?

A rounded door looms at the hall's end, open archways running toward it on either side. Ten feet ahead, a plump woman wearing a gravy-splattered apron waddles across, a wooden bowl in her dough-caked hands.

If I'm ever going to have a heart attack . . .

She bends over a flour sack and scoops some into the bowl. A strand of hair falls into her eyes. She swipes it away, straightening and arching her back. Her gaze trains on us.

We're doomed.

Ky rolls his shoulders, throws my hand aside, and strides forward. He walks with all the pomp and confidence of a rock 'n' roll legend taking the stage for the thousandth time.

I trail him, head down.

"Master Kyaphus." The woman bows her head.

Master Kyaphus?

"Ophelia." He nods in her direction. "Our security has been breached. His Sovereignty instructed me to transfer the girl to a more secure location. Please, do not let us interrupt your work. Carry on."

We saunter straight past as she stares. She doesn't protest, but my heart batters violently until we're free.

When the door moans closed, I lean against the outside wall. "Which way to my mom?"

"Follow me."

We circumvent a turret, relying on sparse shadows to conceal us from the guards above. The stables I saw—and smelled—lie just

ahead. A long brick building with a sloping roof and several archways punched out of its face.

"This way!" Haman shouts.

Double snap.

Ky drags me forward, practically catapulting me behind a
stack of hay bales. The spiky straw bites my palms.

"Rhyen?" Venom drips from Haman's tone as he nears. "I was
not aware you were on the patrol schedule this evening."

Ky leans against the side of the bale stack, props an elbow on
the hay, and shifts his body, shadowing me even more. "Switched
with Carmichael." He crosses one leg over the other, adding to his
casual front. "Thornson authorized it."

"You know very well all shift changes are to be approved by
me. Only. Me."

I hold my breath, but I can't do anything about my very audible,
hammering pulse.

"I didn't think you'd mind, Haman. After all, I'm the only reason
His Sovereignty has forgiven you for losing the girl at the bridge."

I have to hand it to him. He's got guts.

Pause. Scuffle. "Be very careful, Kyaphus." I can almost see
Haman's leer, cruel and condescending. "Or you might find yourself without a soul one of these days." More scuffling. Retreating
footsteps.

My lungs free a breath. If I doubted Ky was truly rescuing me
before, I don't now.

He comes around the bales and crouches. "Shall we?"

I nod.

He helps me up and we rush through an arch into the stables'
shelter. It's quiet aside from the horses' heavy breathing. I inhale
the stale air. Choke. My eyes water from the manure odor. I pull
my shirt collar over my nose like a medical mask. We continue
forward, our footsteps muted by the hay-clumped earth.

Ky stops. Scoops something off the ground. *Click.* A flashlight beam illuminates his face. He shoulders a tan leather pack. Opens a door. "In here."

I'm shoved into what appears to be a supply closet. Push broom. Saddle. Coils of rope. "What are you doing? Where's my mom?"

Ky steps into the closet. The space is cramped, hardly big enough for two people. His chest presses against my arm.

I shrink into myself. This is a little too close for comfort.

"Ready?" Ky says.

"For what?"

The door snaps closed. First comes a chugging whine, like cogs turning, metal grinding. I cover my ears. The back wall swings out. A staircase. Ky shoves past me, points the flashlight down the steps. "Come on."

We descend, dust motes floating on the shafts of light preceding us. The passage narrows the farther we go. Great. I just love small, cramped spaces.

At the bottom I stop. "Where. Is. My. Mom?"

"Don't worry." He moves along what appears to be an underground tunnel. The flashlight beam only illuminates the space a few feet in front of him. "We're nearly there."

My hesitant heart twists.

"He rescued you. Give him a chance."

Sigh. Okay, Mom. I trail Ky.

"You still don't trust me," he muses over his shoulder.

Thank you, Captain Obvious. "What other choice do I have?"

"There's always a choice."

Easy for you to say. "I guess."

We continue on in silence. Time becomes obsolete. How much farther? At one point the path slopes upward. Thirty minutes? An hour? Finally, Ky climbs another set of stairs, then shoves a door open. Two sore calves and a sweat-soaked shirt later, I emerge from a cave into the night.

I whirl. We're in the middle of a forest. "Where are we?" Panic presses in, cramping my middle, constricting my throat.

"The Forest of Night." His flashlight-carrying hand waves me forward. "We have to keep moving. I don't want to be in Shadow Territory any longer than necessary."

I stalk toward him, matching his determined stride. "I thought we were going to get my mom." My arm flings in the direction we came from.

"Keep it down," he whisper-yells. "And I never said that. I believe what I said was that *you* were my priority."

My boots slip on loose gravel as I come to a heartbreaking halt. "You said you know where she is." I hug my stomach. "You lied to me." All the hate and fury and rage I had for him before doubles. Quadruples. "Again."

"I didn't lie. I do know where she is. But after her escape the other night, Crowe increased her security detail. I didn't have time to deal with that and get you out."

No. No, no, no, *no*. I whip around, hair snapping my face, and march back to the tunnel's exit. But where I thought there was a door stands nothing but solid rock. I press a hand to it, hoping it'll be a façade like the exit at the Haven. It's not.

Ky comes up behind me. "The tunnels are emergency exits only. The doors lock from the inside." He takes my elbow. "Come on. We have to keep moving." When I don't budge, he adds, "She'll be okay. Crowe won't hurt her."

"You weasel," I seethe. Sob. "It's not Jasyn I'm worried about." Tears burn my cheeks. I swipe at them with so much force I poke myself in the eye. "Haman said—"

"Haman's a conniving snake and a liar. He had no authority to promise Isabeau your mom's baby."

"She's not even pregnant, blockhead." I push Ky once. Twice. "What if Haman . . . ?" I can't finish my question. The thought is beyond unbearable. Mom can hold her own, but Haman isn't just some guy off the street.

"He's always had a silver tongue. Haman can't touch her. Crowe won't allow it." Ky's hatred for Pirate Grease-Head is no secret. It's apparent in the twitch of his mouth. In the growl underlying his words.

"But—"

"Do you really think Crowe would search for his daughter all these years just to let some guard have his way with her?"

Ky's forward question stops me. Jasyn did seem sentimental when we stood before Mom's painting. He's deluded himself into believing he's king. Does that make Mom a princess? Is this why Ky keeps calling *me* princess?

"She's going to be fine," he presses, looking over his shoulder, then back at me.

I stare him down, waiting for a sign of deception to give him away. But it doesn't come. "I'll never forgive you for this." My elbow finds Ky's ribs.

He flinches, not blocking my jab this time. "The best thing you can do for your mom is assist the rebels. Let me take you back to the Haven. You'll help them find their long-lost king. He'll defeat Crowe, recapture the Void. Everybody wins."

I nod. *Don't hope. Don't dream. It will only lead to more heartache.*

We enter a forest far different from the Haven, or even the one in Lynbrook Province. Ky's flashlight beam leads the way as gravel-covered ground grates beneath our footsteps. Blackened vines wind up charred tree trunks. Near the tops, the bark color changes to deep white, extending into porous awnings of black and gray leaves. Abandoned tromes seem to jeer at us, their filthy windows like dead, unseeing eyes. The ajar doors make no sound, inching in and out, in and out. No birdsong or babbling brooks. Eerie quiet. Like the sound right after a major car wreck when even the sirens are drowned out for a moment.

Like the last day I spent with Mom. The world faded away. Just us. No one else. Or that's how I remember it. It was the kind of day that makes me wish time travel were viable. Eating roasted peanuts bought from our favorite vendor. Throwing bread crumbs to the ducks in Central Park. People-watching at Grand Central Station. We were natives acting as tourists, a pristine, untainted memory.

"Oh no. Now what?"

Ky's voice draws my gaze from the ground. I wasn't even paying attention. How long were we walking?

He shoves me inside the nearest trome. Leaves stomped like bottom-of-the-bag chips dust the stoop. I step inside a room half as wide as our brownstone. Breathe the sour, musty air. When was the last time anyone opened the windows? Ky clicks off his flashlight, yanks us down to the floor.

My ankle twists. Ouch. "What the—?"

He claps his hand over my mouth. "Don't move." One, two, three breaths. "Someone's coming."

fifteen

TOO far

My heart hammers. A smile haunts my lips. I must be crazy.

It's not like I want Crowe to get his way. But if someone is here to capture me, to take me back to the castle, maybe I can find a means to save Mom. If we can just be together, we'll figure this out. She always knows what to do.

Always.

"Not always, brave girl."

Fine. Most of the time then.

"I saw something over here," someone familiar grunts. The sound is muffled. Distant. Bearlike.

"Preacher." The word is a whisper. Never thought I'd be relieved to hear his voice. Standing, I dust off my bottom. Ky attempts to pull me back, but I'm too quick. I'm out the door and out of reach.

Outside, six figures walk in a horizontal line as if raking the area for a dead body. They all carry flashlights or lanterns. As they close in, each one becomes easier to identify. Stormy's neon-purple hair. Kuna's coffee skin and hulking frame. Preacher's scowl embedded beneath his wiry beard. Gage's proud walk, head always erect. And . . . and . . .

No. Way.

I break into a run. Squint. This can't be real. It's a mirage. A delusion I've concocted to fill the emptiness inside. Fifty feet. Twenty. My heart is yards ahead of my body. *Please let this be real, please let this be real . . .*

He's wearing the last thing I saw him in. Flannel shirt. Jeans. Coat. Boots. The entire group has ceased their march. All except him. He drops his flashlight. *Thud.* Then he's tripping over himself to get to me. It's the first time I've seen him so completely uncoordinated.

"El?" He freezes two feet away. Disheveled, with dark circles under his eyes and a shadow lining his jaw. Brow scalloped and lips pursed, his expression seems pained. Is that fear in his eyes? Suspicion?

My heart is shattered and put back together in a single moment. And then I can't stop crying. I've held so much in these past days. Reunited and ripped apart from Mom in one breath. Loving Joshua. Losing Joshua. Trying to be brave. To survive. Refusing to acknowledge reality. Because if I accepted what really happened, I might've died from the pain. It's only now, in my ugly, uncontrollable sobbing, I realize the truth.

I was already dead.

"Joshua." His name tastes like a first breath after drowning for days. "Joshua David." I grab the collar of his jacket in both hands, afraid if I don't hold on he may vanish.

"El." He smooths my hair with shaking hands, examines me. "Are you hurt?"

"I'm fine." My sobs transform into laughter. "You're alive. How is this possible?"

A throat clears behind me. "I hate to break up this little reunion," Ky says. Funny. He doesn't sound sorry at all. "But we really need to move farther south."

Joshua lifts his head. He reaches past me and shakes Ky's hand. "Kyaphus. I assume you're responsible for keeping her safe. I can't thank you enough—"

"Thank him?" Preacher scratches his beard. "For what? He nearly turned us into sushi." With each word his tone rises in volume.

"Who's the loud one *now*, Preacher?" Stormy smirks, arms crossed and hip popped. "And in Shadow Territory, no less. Why not invite an entire army of Soulless to our rendezvous?"

Lip curled and teeth bared, Preacher gives Stormy the most shudder-worthy stink eye I've ever seen.

"Now, Preacher. Give the boy a chance to explain. I certainly owe him *my* life."

This is too good to be true. "Makai?"

My very-much-alive uncle steps forward and stands shoulder to shoulder with Joshua. His right arm hangs in a sling made out of what looks like a potato sack. "Eliyana." Makai dips his head. "I apologize for the delay. We—"

I clash with him, wrapping my arms around his trench-coated frame.

He stumbles back a little. Hasn't he ever been hugged? Slowly, he envelops me with one arm, wincing.

I pull away. "Sorry. Is it your shoulder?"

He nods. "Just a scratch. It'll heal. Kyaphus knew what he was doing."

Guilt pricks my chest. Maybe I was too hard on Ky earlier. "What do you mean?"

"Kyaphus stabbed me, but the wound wasn't fatal. When he pulled his knife out, the gash closed up. My shoulder is sore, and I have to be careful not to strain it. Which reminds me"—Makai draws the glass dagger from the pocket of his trench coat and hands it to Ky—"I believe this belongs to you."

No ordinary blade.

Ky flips the knife over once in his hand. Trades it for the plain steel blade sheathed at his hip. Next he secures the excess weapon with a strap at his ankle. "Thanks."

"It's made from mirrorglass, is that right?" Makai strokes his chin.

"Yes, sir." Ky shifts beside me. What is he, nervous? Afraid he's gonna get his toy confiscated by Gage who, to my surprise, has yet to say a word?

"A rare commodity, that one," Makai says. "I had an arrow tipped with mirrorglass once. My father gave it to me back in my Guardian training days. Such a shame to lose it."

Not that I wouldn't love to know what in the Reflections mirrorglass is, but there are more pressing questions on my mind, such as, "I understand how Makai is here, but . . ." I fix my gaze on Joshua. "How are you here? I saw you die."

He opens his mouth, but it's Ky who answers. "Because he's an Ever."

Joshua works his jaw, then says, "How long have you known?"

"You're not as mysterious as you think, David. During my Guardian training I heard the stories. How you were fast. Strong. Always walked away from sparring matches without a scrape. I put two and two together."

"I see." Joshua scratches the back of his head.

I reel on Ky. "Do you mean to tell me you've known he was alive this . . . *pant* . . . whole . . . *pant* . . . time?"

Palms up surrender-style, Ky backs away. "Easy now, princess. I thought you knew."

"Like the Void you thought I knew. You saw how destroyed I was after passing through the Threshold." Twigs snap beneath my livid steps.

Ky backs against a tree. "I thought it was an act. Evers are very secretive about their Calling. I just assumed you were trying to protect him from Haman. Ever blood is even more rare and valuable than mirrorglass."

I lift my hand. He deserves a good smack in the face. Even if he did rescue me and has apparently been on our side from the beginning. "Fine." My hand lowers. I pivot and march back toward the others, kicking dirt and gravel in my wake. "Who wants to explain to me what an Ever is?"

With a light touch to my elbow, Joshua pulls me aside. "Can we talk?"

He knows me so well. My need to get away from the group. Have a moment to breathe. To process. "Sure."

"You two go ahead," Makai says. "It will give the rest of us time to figure out our next move." He passes Joshua his flashlight.

"Wait." I pull my uncle aside, relaying under my breath the vow Haman made to Isabeau.

His gaze darkens and he nods, easing my anxiety a fraction. Makai won't let us leave Mom behind. He'll tell the others we have to go back for her. I know it.

We shuffle away, Joshua's fingers somehow sending tingles through my jacket sleeve. The trome seems as good a place as any for some privacy. Once inside, I let my eyes adjust and ascend a stepladder leading to an opening in the low ceiling. Flashlight in hand, Joshua follows close behind.

The second floor houses a library. Shelves line the curving walls, all cluttered with toppled, unevenly stacked leather-bounds. Mom would have a field day in here. She always had to have books organized by genre, then size. If she saw this, she wouldn't stop until every last volume was in its proper place. A regular Snow White.

I climb the next stepladder to a third floor. A twin-bed-sized bench adorned with faded green cushions sits to the left, a round wicker table and two matching chairs to the right. A window waits behind the bench. Four square panes invite patches of moonlight. The floorboards need a good sweeping. The large square rug is so dirty I have no idea what color it is. It should just be thrown out.

"Should we . . . ?" He gestures with the light toward the bench.

I shrug. "Okay." My answer may be casual, but butterflies have gone rampant beneath my skin.

I cross to the bench and sit, dust clouds rising when I do. A cough escapes, and I wave my hand to clear the air. The flashlight beam illuminates every mote and bunny.

"I'm going to see if I can find us a snack. You must be starving." Flashlight tucked beneath one arm, Joshua climbs to the next floor. His leg muscles flex beneath the fitted, but not too tight, jeans. Does he have a clue how good he looks?

Thud. Something heavy sounding rolls across the floor above. *Stomp, stomp, stomp.* Whoever lived here must've had a terrible time sleeping whenever someone was upstairs. Every echo and squeak is audible, pronounced.

Like home. The sound of Mom in her art studio above my room lulled me to sleep like nothing else could—aside from Joshua's guitar playing.

He returns with a jar and a grin, though it doesn't reach his eyes. "Breakfast." He hops off the last step and holds up what appears to be pie filling. It's yellow and liquid and has flecks of brown—cinnamon maybe—in it. He unscrews the lid and takes a whiff, then passes it to me.

I inhale through my nose, and the sweet scent of peach nectar almost satisfies my appetite by itself. Almost. "Don't you mean dinner?"

"It's easy to get confused in a place without day." He plops down beside me, sets the flashlight between us, and kicks off his boots, toes wiggling in his socks. "But I assure you, it's breakfast. Drink. I couldn't find any spoons."

I let the Uggs fall off my feet and sit cross-legged. Lifting the lip of the jar, I open my mouth and drink. A tender chunk of peach flesh falls out, and I swallow it whole. Mmmm. It is cinnamon. And honey too. I take another gulp, then pass the jar to Joshua. We sit this way for a while, drinking pie filling and smacking our lips in silence. When only sticky goo remains, he slides two fingers in and starts scooping.

"You're such a guy." The tease feels so natural. The way it used to be.

He stiffens.

Did I say something wrong? Let's try again. "I missed you."

"Kyaphus appears to have changed sides." Is it really so difficult for him to say he missed me too?

"Um, yeah. I guess." I relay Ky's story, trying to include every detail despite my distractedness. When I finish I ask, "So, what's an Ever?" I trace the corners of my mouth with my finger, wiping away the pasty residue.

"Has anyone explained to you about the Callings yet?"

"I know they're special abilities. And they're sourced by the Verity."

"Correct. There are seven Callings—abilities—each one unique to the soul that carries it. When a child is born they're given water from a Threshold. Once the water is consumed, a safeguard is bestowed on the child's soul until they come of age. Sometimes the water's power works beyond mere protection, and a Calling manifests as well. It affects everyone in different ways. During childhood the Calling is limited, never reaching its full potential until adulthood." He sets the nearly clean jar on the floor. "Then, at the age of eighteen, what we refer to as a Confine lifts."

Wade mentioned the Confine. Is that why Robyn's teeth were flat and her paws clawless?

"The child is then an adult," he says. "Their soul is no longer guarded. At that point they have a choice. It's always a war between the two—between serving the Verity and the Void. Even before Crowe released the Void, there were those who believed it was the power worthier of allegiance."

Whoa. I explain what I've learned about Jasyn and King Aidan, the Verity and the Void, all of it. When I get to the part concerning my birthmark, my face flames. ". . . which means my soul is bound to the Verity's vessel—er, King Aidan." So weird. Saying it aloud feels like a confession. Do I believe it's true?

I'm still not sure.

Joshua folds his hands and lets them hang in the gutter between his knees. "I see. We've been apart longer than I care to admit." He shakes his head. Pounds a fist against his knee. "What good is being an Ever? I couldn't protect you. I can't." Anger peppers his tone.

I toe the floor. My hands long to hold his. To assure him it's no big deal because we're together now. Instead I refrain. Wait.

He exhales. Finger-combs his hair. "My Calling is in my blood. I heal almost instantly, and very few things can kill me. A single drop of my blood could cure even the most fatal wound."

Lightbulb moment. "Could Jasyn have used Ever blood on me? He claimed he brought me back from the dead."

"I suppose it's possible, though I don't know where he would've gotten it. Evers are very private. Most don't even trust those closest to them with the knowledge of their gift. Years ago, Ever blood was sold for a high price on the black market. People would drain Evers of their blood over and over and over again. Since it reproduces at a rapid rate, an Ever wouldn't have died from the process, but it still would have been excruciating." He shudders. "We experience pain like everyone else." His last words are guarded. Is there another meaning beyond the surface?

"Joshua, I—"

"I failed you, El." He clears his throat before continuing. "I have this rare gift, and still I couldn't stop what happened. I've been such an idiot. It was immature and selfish to think I could handle this." He rises. "Which is why I'm recommending Ky be reinstated as a Guardian. *Your* Guardian. Under the circumstances I don't see why Makai wouldn't approve the request."

"Are you . . . ?" I swallow the lump wedged in my throat. "Are you ditching me?" Not this again. Why is he always looking for a way out? Every time he takes a step toward me, he takes five more giant leaps back.

Don't feel. Don't care. Don't love. Isn't that what I promised myself? So things like this wouldn't destroy me anymore?

"Eliyana." Joshua sets a hand on my shoulder. His touch is a roller coaster. Thrilling. Turning me upside down. "You're better off without me. Ky will make a fine Guardian. He already has."

This is a nightmare. Mom's still a prisoner. I just got Joshua back and he already wants to leave? "No." I spring to my feet. "I don't want anyone else." Especially not Ky. Never. He's cocky and sarcastic and impulsive and everything Joshua is not.

"I can't guard you anymore. I've let things go too far. I've made mistakes with you I never would have before. Sloppy decisions. Poor judgment calls. It's been a long time coming. I probably should've done it sooner."

I don't believe this. Not only does Joshua not want to be around me but he's forcing me to be around someone I barely tolerate. "Fine. I just won't have a Guardian then. If I can't have you, I don't want anyone."

"It doesn't work that way." He looks out the window. A spider scuttles up the filmy glass, oblivious to the dilemma just beyond its reach. "It is imperative you have a Guardian."

"Why? Do *you* have one? Does Ky? Once we're back at the Haven, I'll be plenty safe. I don't need a shadow following me around all the time." I hate to give Ky credit, but he said so himself. "There's always a choice."

"You're different. Special." His gaze is a thief, stealing this moment as he caresses my least favorite cheek with his thumb.

I turn my head into his palm and close my eyes, memorizing the scent of his skin. Why does this feel like a good-bye? "I wish everyone would stop saying that."

Joshua tilts my chin up. I stare into cerulean eyes like glass, begging me to know what's behind them. "When you turn eighteen, this will all be over."

Wade and Gage. Their whispered conversation about my upcoming birthday. I'd forgotten it. Too worried about dying and grieving and Mom and simply surviving.

"What will be over?" And how does my birthday fit into the equation?

He remains stark still. Reactionless. Not a flinch or a blink to let me in on what he's thinking.

"Tell me." I close the space between our faces, stopping just before our lips meet. He can kiss me if he wants. Right here. Right now.

"This." An exhale escapes his lips, warming my face. "Is." His hands find mine, lowering them to our sides. "Over." He releases me, backs away. Resolve chisels his features as he dons his boots and departs the way we came.

I wait a dozen breaths before following. Shoulders squared and cheeks dry, I slip into Mom's Uggs, snatch the flashlight, and head outside. Because Joshua is *alive*. This changes everything. We have a chance I never thought we'd get again. I'm not going to be so easy to push away this time.

It isn't over until it's over.

SIXTEEN

don't lose sight

Something's not right. My fingers drum my thigh. One, two, three, four, five, six . . .

Makai. Where's Makai?

Joshua's already joined the group, his back turned toward me. They stand in a circle, emitting hushed tones like white noise. Except for Ky. He's off to the side, his too-cool attitude grating my nerves.

Stormy's the first to spot me. She sets her lantern down, flits over, and hugs me a little too tightly, her bony arms digging into mine. "Everything's going to be okay now." She tugs me toward the others.

"Thanks." I can't match her enthusiasm. Not when Mom isn't here.

Once we complete the circle, it's Gage who speaks. I don't hear him. Rise on my toes. Lean past Stormy. Where's my uncle? Why am I the only one who seems to notice his absence?

"Girl, are you listening?" Preacher's crotchety voice wrenches me from my search.

"Huh?" I blink twice.

He's a handbreadth away, nostrils flaring. "The Commander is speaking to you. Have some respect." Is his face permanently scrunched?

"Commander?"

Preacher hitches a thumb at Gage and then backs away, though I can still smell his rank breath.

"That would be me." Gage flashes a bristled look at Preacher who is, of course, not paying attention. The guy couldn't catch a hint if it bit him on his mushroom-shaped nose.

"Be nice."

Sorry, Mom. He's just so hostile, like he has it out for me.

"Your enemies are the ones who need love most."

Not my problem. Let someone else bring out the teddy bear in this porcupine.

"Makai thought it would be best to name me acting commander for now," Gage explains. "In case something happens."

Dread surges, accelerates my pulse. "Happens?"

"Oh, come on." Ky shoves off the tree he's been leaning against. "Stop placating her. She's been through more in the past week than most people have endured their entire lives. She can handle it."

Why is he suddenly my defender? I don't need him to stick up for me. It will only make Joshua more confident in his decision to name Ky my Guardian. "Handle what?"

"Makai continued north. He's gone for your mother." The way Gage breaks the news, so cautious and tempered, turns my stomach sour.

He must be joking. "We can't let him go for her alone."

"He'll be fine." Stormy pats my back, ever the optimist. "He's the only one of us who can enter the castle undetected."

The invisibility thing. Right. Even so, "He's injured. So what if he can get *in*? How's he supposed to get them both *out*? I don't suppose my mom can become invisible as well?"

Only Ky's head shakes, confirming my fear. At least he's honest. Why does everyone else keep treating me like a crystal vase, about to break with the lightest flick?

"It's a three-day journey back to the Haven." Gage wastes no time, acting as if our discussion is finished. "I'd like to at least be out of Shadow Territory before nightfall."

"We can't go on without them." I thrust a hand in what I think is the castle's direction. "What if they get hurt?" I don't care what Ky said. Mom's in danger. No one is going to convince me otherwise.

Gage hands his lantern to Kuna, kneels, scoops up some of the sandpaper earth, and rubs it between his palms. "Makai would die before he'd let something happen to your mother. Isn't that right, Joshua?"

He nods.

How comforting. *Not.*

"Listen." Gage stands, unsheathing his snakeskin-handled dagger and flipping it once, twice in his hand. "I understand, really. But your mother and Makai forfeited their well-being for yours. Don't lose sight of the bigger picture. Allow us to take you to the Haven. Then you have my word, on my honor as a Guardian, if Makai has not returned with your mother in tow by then I will put together a rescue operation. Lead it myself." He sheathes his weapon.

"It could be too late by then!"

A murder of crows startles, flapping their wings and taking flight from a patch of tall weeds.

Gage's expression hardens. "I don't wish to discuss this further."

I press my lips, widening my eyes at Joshua.

He avoids my gaze. Is he just going to stand there? "I'm not taking one step farther away from my mom and Makai."

Gage exhales. He steps closer, glares down at me. "You have no intention of coming willingly?"

"Careful now."

It's fine, Mom. I've got this. "No."

"Then you leave me no alternative." He lists his head. "Kyaphus, how would you like a chance to earn my trust?"

"Depends." Ky has resumed lounging against the tree, fingers laced behind his head. "What do you want?"

"Eliyana is refusing to cooperate." Gage's words are for Ky, but his unblinking glower belongs to me alone.

I glare right back. Does he think a staring contest will scare me into submission?

"Yeah." Ky laughs, a hollow sound. "I got that."

"Let's see you put your Calling to good use for a change."

"You can't be serious," Ky scoffs. "How is paralyzing her now any different from what Crowe had me do?"

"So you won't use your Calling on her? Even if it would earn my full and complete confidence?"

"What makes you think that's something I want?"

"Very well." Gage withdraws a section of coiled rope from his cargo pocket, then confiscates my flashlight and places it in Stormy's palm. Next he takes me by the shoulder and spins my back toward him. Finally he binds my wrists, not too tightly, just enough so I can't pull free. Loose or not, the rough threads chafe.

"Is that really necessary?" Ky, not Joshua, comes to my defense. Again. He moves toward me, as if he's going to do something about it, but Kuna blocks his path.

"Yes." Joshua? He can't be supporting this. He's supposed to be on my side.

Tears burn, and I gaze at my blurred boots. These guys are no better than Jasyn. Why would Joshua do this? It's out of character.

Or maybe it's not. Maybe New York was his act and this is who he is in real life. I stare at him, silently begging him for help. Pleading with him to show me who he really is.

For the briefest moment a grieved look flashes across his expression. His mouth turns down, his hands clench. Then he seizes the extra flashlight from Stormy and . . .

Walks. Away.

Coward.

"I'm sorry." Gage turns me to face him again. It's obvious he's trying to be as gentle as possible. Doesn't matter. "It's for your own good. We can't have another mishap like we did at sea." He shoots a glare toward Ky. "Keep an eye on him, Kuna. I couldn't care less if his alibis check out. I still don't trust him." Gage strides in the opposite direction, no hesitancy in his gait. Gentle or not, this is wrong. And I'm betting he knows it too.

Stormy links her arm through mine, carrying her lantern like a handbag on the other. Just what I need, a personal babysitter. "Come on. I've been dying for some girl time. These lugs can be such a drag." How can she act like we're friends, as if I don't have my hands tied behind my back?

As she leads me I peek at Joshua. He and Gage are already twenty paces ahead, skulls bent together. Are they talking about me? About Ky taking Joshua's place? I stifle a groan as Stormy relays the past couple of days in detail, leaving no hashtag or topic unturned. How surprised they were to run into Commander Archer and Lieutenant David. How they had no idea what Jasyn had planned for me. Would he kill me? Use me to bait the rebels?

I nod along, trying to keep up.

Preacher takes position as the loner, behind Joshua and Gage but in front of us girls. Ky and Kuna compose the caboose of our little train. I glance over my shoulder. Ky's two-tone eyes fix on mine. His shoulder lifts, and the corner of his lips quirk. "*Sorry*," he mouths.

I break eye contact swiftly. We're not friends. He may have helped me, but he abandoned Mom. If I knew she wouldn't be with us, I never would've left the castle.

We near where the crows gathered. I breathe through my mouth. A rotting animal carcass lies half eaten beneath thorny, berryless brambles. The body is mangled and shrouded by shadows. I can't tell what it used to be. A deer? A horse? A mythical creature I've yet to encounter? Stormy just chatters on. Either she's too self-focused to notice the roadkill, or she's turning a blind eye—and nose.

The rope twists into my skin as I adjust my wrists. That'll leave a mark.

We amble through the woods, and I try to focus on her words. She's saying something about how much she hates sleeping on the ground, about . . . I can't help it. Joshua's right there, completely ignoring me, behaving as if the last three years never happened. Like we haven't spent time together nearly every day, growing close and, for me, falling in love. How can he let them do this to me?

I'm a fool. He cares about one thing and one thing alone—his oh-so-precious duty.

I've never resented my birthmark more.

who you are

A nd then Preacher landed right in a huge pile of manure."
Stormy laughs. The other night it was impossible not to be
infected by her contagious trill, but after hours on end—the sound
is a dying smoke detector. *Beep. Beep. Beeeeep* . . .

I don't bother faking amusement. I'm a captive now. No need
to pretend I'm anything more to her than a means to an end.

"Hey, are you okay?" For the first time in miles, she actually
takes a breath.

Is she serious? "I've had better days." I don't attempt to hide my
sarcasm.

"Gage means well." She gives my arm a light squeeze.

"Right. Because tying me up like a slave is totally under-
standable." I roll my eyes. Just try to sugarcoat this.

She frowns. "It's not as if you gave him a choice."

"There's always a choice."

Ky snickers behind me.

My cheeks burn. Great. Now he's heard me quote him. He'll
never let me live this down.

Stormy must get the hint because she goes quiet. She keeps our
arms linked, most likely to prevent me from falling.

My feet ache despite the cushioning in Mom's Uggs. Today's
Thursday. Nearly a week since her funeral, since I thought she was

dead. It's almost worse *not* knowing. The unrelenting worry curdles my stomach. An ulcer probably formed from all of this. Some Illusoden would be good about now. Too bad Jasyn took it, the same way he rips everything from me.

The endless night continues, making it impossible to tell the time. It's not too cold, the trees insulating what little warmth there is. Wren's jacket is tight and uncomfortable and hard to move in. I'd ask Stormy to untie me so I can take it off, but she'd never agree, thinking I was just trying to escape. It might be true in part, but at this point, we've made so many turns I would never find my way back to the castle on my own.

A bubbling trickle reaches my ears, like rainwater rushing along a gutter. Faint at first, then escalating to a decent volume. We ascend a hill. When we reach its crest, I freeze. Daylight. There, just down the hill and beyond a stream. While night's never-ending overture blankets this shore, day's finale illuminates the opposite one. Finally.

I dig my feet in as I shuffle down the slope. For a second I'm glad for Stormy's presence. Without my hands to catch me, a fall would probably end in a broken nose. Rocky earth changes to overgrown crabgrass and tufts of white clovers. Gray morning glory blossoms pop up at random, begging not to be choked out by its vines. On the stream's opposite side, the flora and fauna are painted in shades of white and gray. The tree trunks are the color of ash, their leaves a mixture of butter and cream. Was it once lush and vibrant like the Haven? Robyn said eventually the Second Reflection will become a Shadow World. How much longer until the infinite night reaches its claws across the stream?

"This is the border to Wichgreen Province and the end of the Forest of Night and Shadow Territory. Everything between here and the sea is neutral ground, belonging to neither the Void nor the Verity. We won't be completely safe until we reach the Haven, so keep your guard up." Stormy helps me sit on the damp grass, the three men ahead of us advancing to the water. Dew seeps through my jeans. "I'm going to gather some food. Stay here." She follows the guys, leaving me to sulk.

I scoot back and lean against a tree trunk. The uneven bark bites my spine. A headache lingers between my eyebrows. Should've asked Stormy to bring me some water.

"Need a hand? How about two?" Ky squats beside me, sets his flashlight on the ground between us. "I'll untie you, but only if you ask nicely."

"I'm fine. I don't need your help." I shift and squirm, attempting to get comfortable. Joshua hasn't bothered checking on me. He stands by the stream. I study him as he takes off his boots, rolls up his pants, and wades into the water. His legs are paler than his arms but much hairier. He bends, letting the mini river flow like silk over his hands. In the next moment he straightens, a wriggling fish in his grasp.

So he's a fisherman too? What else don't I know about him?

He tosses the fish to Preacher on the shore, who catches it with ease and sets it on a wet rock. He draws a knife and slices down the slimy middle, cleaning out the guts and muck. I've never seen anyone enjoy killing a living thing the way Preacher does now. It's the happiest he's appeared in the brief time I've unfortunately known him.

If anyone thinks I'm eating that poor, murdered creature, they're seriously mistaken.

My wrists are suddenly unbound. I whip my head left. Ky grasps the sliced rope in his fist. How did he do that? I didn't feel a thing. "You're welcome." He tosses the rope into the grass, and it disappears with a hiss.

I roll and rub my wrists, unable to deny how good freedom feels. "I didn't ask for your help."

"But you got it, Ember." Ky rocks back on his heels and sits, knees bent.

"Don't call me by my last name. I'm not some linebacker for the New York Giants."

"No. You are definitely not that." His eyes comb my body. Looking. Observing. Not the way Blake did at the party. Ky isn't rude or gross about it. He's just . . . watching.

"Where's Kuna anyway?" I pick at the grass, letting my hair fall to conceal the discomfort blossoming on my cheeks. "Isn't he supposed to be keeping an eye on you?"

"He went back there to hunt." Ky points the way we came, then cocks his head. "I think I *will* call you Ember. I've decided it suits you better than your first name."

"And why exactly?"

"Because an ember is neither fire nor ash. Smoldering but not truly alive. That describes you perfectly. It's who you are. Someone must've burned you bad. Hasn't anyone told you anger is unbecoming?"

The pleasure he's apparently getting out of this sends a blaze up my arm. One of these days I'm going to punch him. And I'm *not* going to miss. "You tricked me into thinking we were rescuing my mom. The only person I'm angry at is *you*."

"You're a horrible liar."

"Don't act as if you know me." I will Joshua to look at me, to care. He doesn't. By now he's caught three fish. Preacher has them cleaned and lined up in a neat, disgusting row.

"I get it, believe me. No one understands holding a grudge more than I do." Ky reels my attention back in. Why is it so difficult to ignore him?

Stormy joins Preacher by his fish rock, holding her now-stained shirt out like a basket, a cluster of what looks to be berries resting inside. Good. At least there'll be something edible on the menu. Joshua sloshes back to shore, two more fish in his closed fingers and a lopsided grin on his face. He used to smile at me that way.

"Forget about it, Ember. David's a jerk. You two just aren't meant to be."

I cast a scowl Ky's way. Why's he still here? "Knock it off. I'd rather you call me princess, like before. Even if Jasyn's not a real king."

"You think I call you princess because of your relation to Crowe? You really are clueless, aren't you?" He lets loose a mocking guffaw.

Not what I was expecting, but okay. Take two. "Isn't it?"

He shakes his head. "No, but I'm not sure you'd believe me if I told you." An elbow to my ribs.

I elbow him back. While his gesture was playful, mine has enough force behind it to make him rub his side. "Why don't you tell me, then I'll decide if you're lying or not."

"Suit yourself." Ky crosses his legs, pulls a yellow apple from his pack. He slices it with his knife, then hands me a large chunk.

I'm too hungry to refuse him. I stuff the whole piece in my mouth. Not too crunchy or mushy. Exactly ripe.

"That mark on your face—" He points to my birthmark with the tip of his blade, and I lean away. "It has more meaning than what they're letting on." A quiet crunching emits from his mouth. Juice oozes onto his chin. I reach up and swipe it with my thumb, jerking away almost as quickly.

Oh my word, what am I doing? I blame Mom. Her maternal instinct has apparently rubbed off on me. I ignore Ky's slack jaw and questioning eyes. He almost looks like just another teenage boy.

But he isn't. He's dangerous. A few rights don't erase his wrongs.

"How would you know?" Conversation back on track. I clasp my hands in my lap, sentencing them to solitary confinement.

"I'd wager they've explained the basics. Your connection to the Verity's vessel? How you're the *only* one who can lead them to him?" Ky scoots closer. His patronizing tone makes me feel like a student in a class way too advanced for my knowledge. "Am I close?" He pulls something else from his pack. A canteen. He sips, then offers it to me.

I hesitate. We're sharing drinks now? What next?

He sets the canteen in my lap. I don't have to give him the satisfaction of an answer. His know-it-all expression gives him away. Crud. He knows he's right. "You think these people are your friends." A flippant gesture toward the stream. "But I'd be careful who you trust. Crowe isn't the only one with an agenda."

I snatch the canteen and take a swig, giving myself time to process what he's implying. The cool liquid has a slight sweetness to it, as if he added honey or something. But I can't enjoy it. Not when my mouth has already turned bitter. Does he really expect I'd believe him over them? Over Joshua?

"I changed my mind," I say. "I'm not interested in listening to your conspiracy theories."

Ky wipes his knife on his pants and tosses the apple core toward the stream. It bounces and rolls, covered in dirt once it reaches the bank. "I'm just trying to help you. Do you really hate me so much you'd refuse to see what's right in front of you?"

"I don't want your help. I didn't ask for it. So just stop, okay?" Taking no care whatsoever, I toss him the canteen. Water sloshes and soaks the front of his shirt and pants.

Nostrils flaring, Ky screws the cap on the canteen, stashes it, and then rubs both hands on his thighs. Dirt streaks his pants like tire tracks. "Have it your way." He moves to stand. "If you won't listen to me, at least consider asking your precious David why he's fighting so hard to protect you. Why they all are. You might be surprised to find what dirty little secrets they've been hiding."

I shoot him a stone-cold glare.

His mismatched eyes lock on mine. "One last thing." He slides his hand into his pack, withdraws a familiar leather tome. "This is yours." He tosses it to me.

My gaze widens. "Mom's sketchbook." Emotion swells, lodging in my throat, pressing against the backs of my eyes. "How—?"

"You dropped it. The night I followed you." He kneels and double knots his bootlaces. "I held on to it."

Is this some sort of game? Another trick to earn my trust and gratitude? "Why would you do that?" The words sound more like an accusation than a question.

He shrugs. "After this delightful conversation, I have no idea, to be honest."

His transparency unnerves me. I hug the book to my chest. "Thank you." Swallow. Does he have any idea how much this means? To have this piece of Mom when I'm not sure I'll see her again?

A nod. "You're welcome."

He grabs his flashlight and tromps off down the hill, leaving me adrift between suspicion and uncertainty. I inhale Mom's pencil and paper scent, the familiarity easing my headache. Part of me is aware this is his strategy to gain my confidence.

But there's another part, small and fragile and insecure, wondering if his words hold even a modicum of truth.

"Crowe isn't the only one with an agenda."

To the Crown until Death.

My breath hitches. Not to me, to the crown. But what does that mean, exactly? Would the Guardians go to any lengths necessary to see their king returned to the throne? I stare at my red-ringed wrists. Everyone supported Gage's decision to tie me up.

Everyone. Except Ky.

A warning bell pings in the recesses of my mind, its context obscure. Is the alarm for Ky or something else? Ugh. I draw my knees to my chest, rest my chin in the space between them. The only person I can count on is Mom, and she's not here.

Scrape, scrape. Gage kneels beside a teepee of twigs, a nest of dry grass situated beneath. He's striking his knife against something black and shiny. Flint? Sparks fly. Flames burst. Gage cups his hands around his mouth and blows. Soon a small fire crackles, smoke rising from its center.

Ky's relaxed against a tree down the hill, eyes closed, hands clasped behind his head. He's with the others, but he's not, always maintaining his distance.

My own eyelids droop as I tune out everything but the stream's mollifying babble. Can I trust him? I hug the book more tightly against my chest, clinging to the lifeline Ky's given me. He didn't have to save Mom's sketchbook, but he did. Knots form in my stomach. I can't let my guard down. Ky's peace offering isn't enough. Not yet.

Not until Mom is safe. Not until we're home.

might have been

I'm going to hurl. *Chew, smack, swallow. Chew, smack, swallow.* How long does it take one tiny person to finish a meal?

Stormy strolls alongside me, nibbling a chicken leg. It took Kuna all of thirty minutes to catch, kill, pluck, and clean the thing. He roasted it section by section over Gage's small fire, then everyone took a piece to go. Except me. How can anyone eat something that once had eyeballs? Disgusting.

"Want some?" She waves the meat in my face, bits of torn flesh dangling like loose threads.

My nose scrunches at the wood smoke fumes. I shrink away. "Gross."

She shrugs, shredding off another rodent-sized bite. "If you keep eating meals meant for birds, you're going to starve."

I roll my eyes. I'll die before I eat body parts that once moved. So far, the food here is a mixture, some familiar, some not so much. The berries Stormy picked had a raspberry look and feel, but a strawberry taste. Sour and not at all juicy, but I can't be too particular.

Kuna belches behind us, the resonance closer to a roar than a man-sized burp.

Stormy giggles as if this is the most endearing thing in the world.

Oh brother.

Now that we're beyond Shadow Territory, keeping track of time is less daunting. Gray fades to indigo as twilight bruises the day. When we crossed the stream, leaving the Forest of Night behind, the trees began to thin, the foliage spreading farther and farther apart. The ashy hues faded to actual colors, a black-and-white film remastered frame by frame.

As the sun sets we tramp across rocky terrain, which Stormy informs me is Pireem Valley. To the east stands the tallest mountain I've ever seen, and to the west tall rocks and tree clusters block our view of what's beyond. Despite the desert landscape, the depth of color awes me. Red rock and glittering sand and tulips! Tons of them, shooting from the hard earth. Total misfits yet the perfect addition to the otherwise bland valley.

At the valley's edge we pass beneath a stone arch. Knee-high foliage and arcing sycamores greet us on the other side. We take care with our steps, trying not to trample the undergrowth completely. I look over my shoulder. Ky straightens every bent weed and vine with meticulous effort. Kuna causes the biggest trail, but even his steps will be untraceable because of Ky.

Distracted, I trip over a thick, unearthed root and stumble forward. Thankfully, Stormy let me continue our trek unbound. My hands reach out, free to stop my face from joining with the earth. Something thorny sinks into my left palm, stinging. Stormy pulls me upright, and I dust my hands on my thighs. A red line stains my jeans, and I turn my palm skyward.

I'm bleeding. Again. I squeeze my fingers into the inch-wide wound and keep going. No big deal. Just a scrape. Might as well be a paper cut. I wince and hiss through my teeth. Okay, maybe a tad worse than a paper cut, but even so, it doesn't sting as much as Joshua's failure to notice my fall.

The flourishing verdure thins and spreads. A fern here. A shrub there. I walk easier, no longer inhibited by weedy fingers of grass and vine. The branches seem to shift up the more the vegetation disperses, a trodden path materializing ahead. A tall hedge wall forms a dead end at the path's conclusion, untrimmed branches sticking out like Ky's cowlicks.

We near the rectangular bushes, their true formation sliding into focus. Not a dead end, but actually two overlapping walls, the barricade an illusion. Gage sidesteps into the opening and leads our group into a maze of green. Right, left. Right, left. I can't help but think of the labyrinth scene in *Harry Potter and the Goblet of Fire*. A Portkey would be great about now. I'd rather be anywhere but here.

The maze exits into a courtyard, a dry fountain as wide around as a trampoline at its heart. The knee-high bordering wall encircles a bronze statue of a serious-looking man with a book tucked between his forearm and chest. Unkempt hair brushes the back of his gladiator-style battle garb. As we near, I squint at the words engraved on a rusted plaque beneath him. "In sincere memory of Lancaster Rhyen—Wichgreen Province prince and founder of the League of Guardians."

Lancaster Rhyen? As in Ky Rhyen?

We skirt the fountain, three to the left, four to the right. Ivy and wisteria crawl over its lip, and moss blankets the stony, hollowed-out belly. An iron gate, run over with more tangled wisteria vines, looms just beyond.

"Why are we stopping?" Ky shoves past me and Stormy.

Gage ignores the interruption, steps up to the gate, and rings a brass bell protruding from the vines.

Ky turns to Joshua. "We have to keep moving. A village is way too obvious. The Maple Mines would be less conspicuous. There's an entrance just a couple more hours south—"

"Get back in line, traitor." Gage darts to Ky, snatches a fistful of his jacket collar, and lifts him off his feet. "I have been lenient with your past discrepancies to this point. Do not try my patience or you may find yourself back in the Crypts where you belong." He sets Ky down, bristling as he faces the gate once more.

Ky rolls his shoulders and resumes his position at the rear with Kuna. Kuna doesn't say a word, merely shakes from silent laughter, apparently finding Ky's attempt to undermine Gage humorous.

And Joshua? Joshua says nothing.

My shoulders tense and my toes curl in my boots. Fear creeps its way up my spine, raising the hairs on my neck. The feeling is irrational. Despite his caveman methods of bringing me here, Gage wouldn't put our entire group in danger. If he feels this is a safe place to rest for the night, who is Ky to argue otherwise?

Right?

An owl soars overhead, hooting hello. A few moments lapse before a haggard, hunchbacked woman hobbles to the gate. Her walking stick *tap, tap, taps* in rhythm with her meander. When she smiles, she bares half a mouthful of missing teeth and spreads lips so cracked and flaky I expect them to fall off. "Welcome, my friends." She opens the gate, and it whines in dispute, offsetting her cool, deep voice.

We file through, a cobbled path extending on the opposite side.

Once the gate closes with an ominous *bang*, the woman shuffles to the head of our line. "Come," she coos.

On either side of the path, quaint cottages take refuge beneath the golden wings of maples. Walkways well kept. Weeds plucked. Stoops swept. A curtain in one window flutters, five little fingers curled around its hem.

I gasp. "There's a child in there."

Stormy just nods.

"Families live here? Shouldn't they be at the Haven?"

"The Haven is for rebels only, people organized in the ongoing Revolution against Crowe and the Void. Many didn't agree with his actions, but not all resolved to fight him. We're in neutral territory now. The people here hold no loyalty to either side. Careful what you say. If Lark"—Stormy inclines her head toward the old woman who teeters as she leads—"gets the slightest notion of trouble, we'll be sleeping in the woods."

Lark? Why does the name ring a bell?

I glance back at the window. The curtain is still, the fingers gone. Stormy's explanation only serves to deepen my anxiety. Is it really the best idea to stay in a place where the residents would surrender us should Crowe's men come looking? Why is no one besides Ky questioning Gage's decision?

The farther we walk, the more my thoughts battle. Majority rules, right? Besides, the others have done nothing to deserve my mistrust. Ky, on the other hand . . .

That settles it. The doubt stops here. I have to at least try to put my faith in those who have risked their lives for mine. Otherwise I'll make myself sick with worry. What has Mom always said?

"Distressing about the future only serves to make us miserable in the present."

When the path ends, it opens into a quaint square. Businesses bearing awnings and wooden signs line the perimeter, giving it a turn-of-the-century, small-town feel. A butcher shop with raw meat draped like tapestries beyond the glass. A bakery with bushels of bread and rolls on display. A library with a slanted welcome sign on its door. It's a scene straight out of *The Music Man*. All this place needs is a building marked Billiards, and Professor Harold Hill would feel right at home.

Lark ushers our group to a two-story brick structure at the northernmost corner. Two weathered Adirondack chairs face outward from the porch, and a calico cat sleeps on a paint-chipped windowsill behind them. The sign above the door reads Wichgreen Village Inn, the letters bleeding gold. Whoever fashioned it didn't wait for the paint to dry. Lark walks in, and we follow her into an inviting, bed-and-breakfast-type atmosphere.

A lemony scent settles around us. Whitewashed furniture dots a sitting room, and lonely vases rest on empty surfaces. I imagine in the spring they're filled with flower arrangements. A chest-high counter stands close to the back wall, a balding man with deep dimples and rosy cheeks positioned behind. He's got a book in one hand, his mouth agape as he reads by lamplight through a pair of spectacles.

Lark clears her throat.

Baldy doesn't budge.

She *ahems* a second time, an overacted sound.

The man starts, as if he didn't hear us come through the creaking door or walk over the moaning floorboards. His eyes fill with light. "Visitors? Visitors here?" He stretches up on his toes.

"So it would seem." Lark gives him a nod and then directs her attention to us. "May I introduce Master Thomas Grizzly, innkeeper and librarian of Wichgreen Village."

Thomas circumvents the counter, his distended belly squishing against the wall as he squeezes through to greet us. "Welcome, welcome. Pleasure, pleasure." He shakes each of our hands in turn. "I'm Grizz, just call me Grizz. No need for formalities, no need at all."

Grizz steps back, puffing out his chest and rubbing circles on his stomach. He lets out a soft whistle. "My, my. What a fine group of guests, a satisfactory lot of patrons indeed."

Lark purses her lips. "They are in need of accommodations for the evening. I trust you can take care of them from here?"

"Will do, Mistress Lark. Will do." Grizz produces a grand bow, waving a hand and bending low.

She lists her head and exits, closing the door behind her.

"Please, please, come in, come in." Grizz claps twice.

Joshua approaches him, uttering the first words I've heard leave his mouth since he stood by and watched Gage tie me up. "Thank you. If you'll point the way, I'll show everyone to their rooms. Gage here will discuss the matter of payment." His voice is milk on a sour stomach. Why can't I stay mad at him, especially when he deserves it?

Grizz brushes his hands together, chuckling, his potbelly

jiggling. "Yes, yes. Very good, very good. It's just up the stairs, right that way." He waves to our left. "Every room is vacant. No sir, not a single one is occupied. You are my first guests in quite some time, yes, in some time."

Joshua navigates the narrow stairway. Preacher, Stormy, Kuna, Ky, and I shadow him while Gage remains in the lobby. Poor guy. I feel sort of bad for the Commander, forced to endure more of Grizz's irksome redundancies. A song track set on never-ending repeat.

The shadow of a grin haunts my lips. Okay, maybe I don't feel *so* bad for Gage's discomfort.

A short hall spreads from the top of the steps, a floor-to-ceiling window at the end. Four white doors, each with a brass numeral nailed to its front, wait. Two to the left and two to the right. Joshua opens each one, peeking in, then moving to the next. After viewing every room, he faces us. "There are only four beds. Kuna and Stormy, you'll of course room together. I'll bunk with Gage and, Preacher, you can have your own." He hesitates, letting the obvious sink in. He exhales. "Kyaphus, you'll share with Eliyana. I'm assigning you as her full-time Guardian from this point forward. You'll sleep on the floor. Lock the door. The rest of us will keep watch in shifts. I'll take the first two hours. Once everyone has had a couple hours of sleep, we'll move on." He strides by.

I touch his shoulder. "Can we talk?"

He shrugs me off. "It's probably best if, from now on, we don't engage. Ky is your Guardian now, which means you and I have no real reason to converse. If you have any concerns, take them to Gage." Joshua clomps down the stairs.

My incredulous gaze follows his form until he rounds the corner at the bottom. If his goal is to hurt me, he's aiming for the high score. But I won't give up. He can't avoid me forever.

Ky opens the first door to the left but doesn't enter. "After you."

I pad past him. Is this how it'll be from now on? Never a moment of privacy, always being watched?

So much for invisibility. I'm the Statue of Liberty. I represent freedom. Independence to these people. All eyes are on me.

All. The. Time.

The door clicks closed, and Ky slides the bolt in place. He walks to a stool, a lamp and a matchbox resting on top.

When a ball of gentle, yellow light cha-chas with the wall, I plop down on the bed. Its mattress gives beneath my curve without a sound. The blanket is soft knit, a rainbow of woven hues. A minute ago I wasn't tired, my anger and confusion served as shots of espresso. But now, sitting here, long-awaited sleep is the only thing on my mind.

Ky sits in the rocking chair in one corner. Rests his elbows on the arms. Leans his head back and lets his shoulders slump. "You should keep your clothes on. Shoes too. If we have to make a hasty getaway, we won't want anything to slow us."

I glower. "And what makes you think I'd even consider getting undressed with you sitting five feet away?"

He laughs, palms up in defense. "Calm down, Ember. Just trying to do my job."

Ugh, I'm so fed up with being a job to everyone. Is that how Mom thinks of me too? As someone she had to protect for the good of the Reflection?

How could I think such a thing? Mom loves me. She's probably the only one who ever has. Ever will.

"Sorry." I scoot back on the bed, half lying, half sitting against an embroidered pillow mountain. "I'm just tired, I guess." Did I just apologize to Ky? The exhaustion must be wearing on me.

He rocks slowly. Back and forth. Back and forth. "Don't let David get to you. From what I hear, he's always been that way. Standoffish. A loner."

"You don't know him like I do. We were close before all this happened."

"Or so you think. Did it ever occur to you his nice-guy act might have been exactly that? An act?"

Of course it's occurred to me. A lot. "Just leave me alone. I don't have the energy to fight with someone who wouldn't know love if it punched him in the gut." Fabulous. I've just admitted to Ky I'm in love with Joshua. How's he gonna use this one against me?

"You're wrong." The words are a whisper, as though coming from far away. "I know exactly what it feels like to care for someone so much, the very thought of their pain cripples you."

Ky's transparency stops me. Knocks on the barrier surrounding my heart. I cross my arms loosely over my stomach, loathing this person I've become. Mean and angry and bitter. Saying things to someone else I'd hate to have said to me. Even if that someone else is Ky. Mom would be ashamed.

I turn my head and stare out the slender window behind the lamp. A starless sky goes on forever, an evening fog settling low to the ground. "Who was she? The girl who broke your heart."

Ky drums his fingers on the wood. "It doesn't matter."

I slide off the bed and cross to the window. "For what it's worth, I'm sorry." And I mean it. I finger-comb my hair, pulling it off my neck. I've never liked ponytails, preferring to keep my face as hidden as possible. Now, in the grand scheme of things, the action seems pointless and shallow. I press my left palm against the window, flinching at the pressure against my cut.

Ky rises, meets me where I stand, and takes my hand in his. "Did this happen when you fell? Why didn't you say something?"

"It's nothing, just a scrape." I start to pull away but stop midway. No reason to flip out. It's not as if he's making a move.

"It'll get infected if you don't clean it." He takes off his pack and lifts the flap, removes his canteen. "Sit." I relax against the edge of the bed, and Ky kneels before me. "Hold your hand out." I do. With brows pinched and jaw set, he pours water onto the wound. Dirt and dried blood thin and separate. Dark liquid drips onto the floor. Next, he withdraws a small vial hanging from a loop of string.

The Illusoden! "Where did you get that?"

He empties a few drops onto the scratch, and the sting vanishes. "Took it before Crowe could. Thought we might need it." Finally, Ky pulls out a wad of gauzy material. Tears off a section with his teeth. Wraps it around my hand. His fingers linger there. After a moment he withdraws and repacks his first-aid kit.

I relax my hand, the warmth of his kind touch still present. "Thank you."

He smiles. "That's twice in one day you've thanked me, Ember. Never thought that would happen."

Me either.

Ky moves to his place on the rocker, and I curl up on the bed, tucking my feet to my thighs. I withdraw Mom's sketchbook from the inside pocket of Wren's jacket and thumb through the pages. My eyelids droop, but I force them open. Mom's drawings and scribbled words make me feel as if she's here with me. I glance at Ky. Smile. For the first time in two weeks, I feel safe. Protected.

Not alone.

soften the ache

Fourteenth Day, First Month, Thirty-Fifth Year of Aidan's Reign

Officer Archer spoke to me today. I was walking to the library when it happened. We passed each other in the hall. Normally he acknowledges me with a simple nod. But not today. Today he smiled and said, "Good day, Lady Elizabeth." Oh, that smile. My blush could've rivaled the queen's rose garden.

I hope I see him again tomorrow. Maybe I will even learn his first name.

Wow. Never pictured Mom as the swoony type. Learn something new every day.

Regina usually accompanies me, insisting a thirteen-year-old girl should not wander the castle without a chaperone. But today she was needed in the kitchens. The entire staff is preparing for the king's seventy-fifth birthday party tomorrow . . .

Holy Verity, this entry was written the day before Aidan and his queen disappeared.

I flip the page. Inhale. Let the discovery sink in. The lamplight is nearly extinguished. Ky sleeps on the rocker, legs stretched before him. One hand splays across his stomach while the other clasps the hilt of his dagger. His breaths are extended, slow. The deep circles under his eyes remind me he's exhausted too. What is it about seeing a person asleep that makes him seem so vulnerable? Likable even.

I roll over onto my back and hold the sketchbook up, trying to catch the last morsel of light. Mom's entries have me hooked. Why have I never read them before? When I was young and first discovered her sketchbook-slash-journals, the calligraphic cursive was too hard to read. As I grew older I never thought much about them. I can't believe what I've been missing. Just one more page. One more, and then I'll go to sleep.

> . . . but parties are the last thing on my mind. Because I've decided, someday, I'm going to marry Officer Archer. He is only seven years my senior, and what are seven years between adults? Regina insists my feelings are a "crush," whatever that is. She is always using strange Third Reflection terms since that's where she grew up.
>
> Father would never approve of me wedding a Guardian, believes it is below our station. Why can't I have a normal life? A simple life far away from Father's critical eye. All I want is a small cottage some-where. Dewesti Province is so lovely . . .

A sharp, papery sound ensues as I flip to the next page. Ky stirs and I wince. I'll have to be more quiet.

Like something from a storybook, a sketch of a quaint cottage stares back at me. A stone chimney peeks out of the thatched roof, smoke rising in wispy spirals. The fence isn't a fence at all, but a hedge of rosebushes. A break in the bushes opens to a winding path that leads to a front door framed in ivy. The caption on the drawing simply reads: *Someday . . .*

I've always loved this drawing. But seeing it now, in the con-text of Mom's words, it's like an entirely different picture. This was Mom's dream house. Small and simple and oh so very country. Was she disappointed with our life in the city? Living in a home where we could hear our neighbors singing show tunes in the shower if they belted loud enough?

Yawn. I stretch and flip onto my stomach. Close my eyes. Why didn't she share any of this with me? Or maybe she tried and I didn't listen. Her entire life was about me. She never dated, never asked for anything. Did I ever once stop to think about her happiness apart from my own?

Another yawn. I turn the open book upside down on the bed to save my place, fold my arms beneath my head. A few minutes of shut-eye won't hurt. Mom's sketchbook isn't going anywhere . . .

My eyelids burst open. The lamplight has died. A hand clamps over my mouth. Stormy's wild-eyed face hovers above mine. "Shhh."

I nod, and she removes her hand. "What's the matter?" I glance at Ky, still asleep. Beyond the window brilliant stars salt the sky, and the moon illuminates the night. "What time is it?" I rub my eyes.

Stormy grabs my hand, drags me out of bed. "Late. Hurry. We have to go."

Something's wrong. She's acting . . . panicked? Nervous? "I'll wake Ky."

She shakes her head. "No time." We exit the room, spilling into the shadow-shrouded hall.

"What about everyone else?"

"They're waiting at the gate. Come *on*." Stormy leads me down the stairs. Out the door. Into the square.

Crickets perform their cacophonous song as our feet plod stone. My hyperventilating breaths release in clouds, the night's chill washing my hot face. At the abandoned gate we stop. Stormy stares through the bars, focused and unblinking.

What's that noise? Moving water. I peer through the bars. The fountain. It's working, filling. Glowing green and churning like a whirlpool. "Stormy, what's happened? Where are the others?"

Her hands shake. Voice cracks. "A-asleep. I . . . slipped them all something. Had to be sure they'd doze until morning." She doesn't look at me.

Why won't she look at me? "Why would—?"

"You have to understand." Her fingers curl around iron. "I don't have a choice in this. Please understand . . ." She whimpers, wedging her face between two bars.

No, this can't be happening. I retreat, backing toward the inn. "Stormy—"

"I made a promise." She opens the gate a crack. "If I don't do this, I'll die and then he'll kill Kuna."

My boot snags on cobblestone, and I fall. Pain slices through my tailbone. "What? You're not making sense. Who—?"

"Gage," she says, her voice deadpan. "Gage will kill him if I fail to uphold my vow."

I feel around the ground for a stone, a stick, anything to use as a weapon. I don't want to hurt Stormy, but I have to defend myself. If it comes down to it, I could take her. I inch away. Her back is still toward me. Maybe she won't notice if I—

Oh. Snap.

The interim commander towers over me, a section of coiled rope in his left hand. His face is rigid. And then, then he smiles, baring two rows of toothpaste-ad teeth. "Going somewhere?" He stoops and grabs my ankle with Herculean strength. I kick at him, but I might as well try to escape an iron shackle. For the second time in one day, Gage captures my wrists, binds them. He doesn't bother to be gentle this time. My skin is still raw from earlier. This doesn't help.

He straightens. "A word of advice, girl. Don't ever give someone a Kiss of Accord unless you're prepared to bear the full weight of your bargain." His sneer fixes on Stormy.

Kiss of Accord? What nonsense is he babbling about?

"Don't do this, Gage," Stormy sobs, eyes still fixed on the

fountain. "I'll find another way to repay you, but please, don't make me do this."

Her desperate pleas chisel at my core. What in the Reflections have I walked into?

"Oh, but you *will* repay me." Gage steps over me, stands behind Stormy. He caresses her shoulder and she shudders. "You'll do as I say until I'm satisfied your debt is paid in full."

I think I'm going to be sick. Ky was right all along. His disdain and distrust for Gage were justified. I attempt to separate my wrists, fighting against the rope. Useless. Stall. "You'll never get away with this." With my peripheral vision I search for anything to help me out of this maelstrom.

A sigh escapes Gage's lips as he begins to pace. "Oh, but I already have. When Kyaphus took you to Crowe, I worried my opportunity had passed. Imagine my delight when you showed up in the Forest of Night, alive and unscathed. Healed even. Then all I had to do was get rid of Archer, which turned out to be easier than I foresaw. When I suggested he continue on for your mother, he didn't hesitate. It's obvious he's in love with her." Is that disgust in his voice? "Why else would one of the most talented Guardians of our generation spend nearly eighteen years as your invisible babysitter? Pathetic."

Makai in love with Mom? It's insane considering the position I'm in, but my heart does a little flip. Mom deserves to be happy. Does she feel the same about my uncle? Is it because of me they've never made their feelings known? Because of my dad?

"With Archer out of the way, carrying out the rest of my plan was a breeze. I even found myself glad for Rhyen's presence. His defiance made my decisions all the more grounded. Who were the others going to trust? A former traitor or their loyal ally and friend?"

What's that, glinting just below Gage's pant hem? The point of a knife. Bull's-eye.

Gage cups his hands under my shoulders, lifting me as if I weigh no more than a sack of feathers.

I keep my eyes downcast, zeroing in on my target. Timing is key. Otherwise it won't work. "What are you going to do with me? Send me back to Jasyn? I escaped once." With Ky's help, but still. "I can find a way to do it again."

"You insult me." His fingers lock around my forearm. "Crowe is a blip on the map. His vision is too tapered. What I have devised far surpasses that numskull's plans."

I struggle, and he tightens his grasp. My knees lock, and my soles skid across the ground. Not yet. "Gage, why are you doing this?"

We're at the gate now. A wolf howls in the distance. An owl hoots from a nearby tree. If only the owl was another shape-shifter, maybe then it could sound an alarm.

Gage propels me past Stormy and through the opening in the gate. "Because I'm tired of standing in someone else's shadow." His top lip curls. "A high price has been placed on your head. In exchange for you, Mistress Isabeau has promised me something very valuable indeed."

Isabeau? As in crazy-lady-who-wants-Mom's-nonexistent-baby? I'm so not playing slave to that wicked witch. I inch my foot next to Gage's. If I distract him just long enough . . . "What could possibly be worth this? Betraying your friends? The Verity? When the king takes the throne—"

"Don't you get it?" He grabs my biceps, his voice a desperate rasp.

I lift my foot off the ground, keeping my intent gaze locked with his frantic one.

"There *is* no king."

My boot touches stone. The knife will have to wait. "What?"

"You heard me. If King Aidan is alive, where's he been? You believe you're so special because of your wretched little mark. The truth is, no one needs you to find the vessel of the Verity. The king probably died a long time ago. No one with that much goodness living inside him would stand for what Crowe's done."

"Even if King Aidan died, the Verity would've found a new vessel. It finds the purest heart." Robyn's words seemed like a tale at the time, something unfathomable and out of reach. But saying them aloud now, I know they must be true.

"You stupid, naive child." Gage's hands shake. "No such thing exists anymore. Consider this. Have you ever met anyone selfless enough he'd give his life for yours?"

Yes. Mom. Joshua. Makai. All of them have put my needs before their own.

"Everyone has an agenda. *Everyone.* You may think those close to you love you unconditionally, but take it from me, there's always another reason behind their actions. *Always.*"

Oh my word. Ky was right. Gage's behavior tonight proves it. Why did I let my stupid pride get in the way?

Hoot. Hoot. I search for the owl. Are its calls meant for me? No. I'm delusional. If the nocturnal bird is a disguised human, what's it waiting for?

Stormy plunges to her knees, still clutching the gate's bars. "I'm sorry, Eliyana. Please forgive me. I have to do this. For Kuna." Her grief is a black hole.

"I understand." And I do. Because I'd do the same for Mom. Gage is wrong. If Stormy's willing to risk everything to save Kuna, there has to be a vessel of the Verity.

"See what love gets you?" Gage leers. Is he taking pleasure in Stormy's sorrow? "If you weren't so desperate to keep your dirty little secret from your oblivious husband, you wouldn't be in this position now."

Dirty little secret? Stormy? Now I've heard everything.

"You made an oath, Gage. We all did. 'To the Crown until Death,' remember? I didn't think you'd actually go through with this."

"Oh, please. Of course you did. What good is an oath when there is no crown to bind it? And don't feign innocence for the girl's sake. You knew exactly what I was doing when I brought that traitor along on our little excursion across the sea." He faces me again, his superior smirk pleading to be smacked off. "It took a good beating, but Kyaphus eventually spilled about your encounter with the Troll. How she seemed to think you'd make a fine slave. Everything was falling into place. We'd take you to the Physic. Once you were healed, we'd ditch the others and trade you to Isabeau."

"We? Are you saying Ky was . . . he was *helping* you?" No way. He said his brokenness was an act. A ruse to earn my trust.

"Don't get me wrong, the little weasel was reluctant. But when I told him his precious baby sister's life was at stake, I knew he'd do anything to protect her. Even if it meant aiding me."

"I know exactly what it feels like to care for someone so much, the very thought of their pain cripples you."

Oh, Ky.

"And then my entire plan went to the Void. Kyaphus saw through my lie. He figured out there was no possible way for me to get near his sister, so he double-crossed me." Gage releases me, darts to Stormy. "And *you*. Did you really believe summoning the squall would slow me down? That somehow drowning me would let you off the hook?"

She swipes at her dripping nose. "It didn't hurt to try." The disdain in her eyes is like nothing I've witnessed.

"Lucky for me the Leviathan came along." Knife in hand, he stalks to me. "All Kyaphus did by taking you to Crowe was make my job a whole lot easier. When we found you, I knew his tune had changed. He wouldn't have released you if his sister was still alive."

"Those reasons are no longer valid."

Ky's story becomes clearer by the minute. The reason he worked for Crowe. His sudden switch of sides. His refusal to use his Calling to force me into submission. Did something happen to his sister?

"I have nothing left to lose."

I know the answer. Because I'd do anything for Mom. If I lost her, I'd feel the same way.

"Which brings us here." He withdraws a small vial from his jacket pocket. "I swiped this Slumbrosia from Wade's stock. A couple drops below the nose, one inhale, and you'll sleep for hours. Joshua was more difficult. Had to sneak up behind him."

"Some nerve you have calling Ky a traitor when you've been one all along." I spit in his face.

He blinks, then closes his Hulk-strong fingers around my neck. "Stormy, is the Threshold ready?"

Threshold? Where are we going?

Without lifting her head she whispers, "Yes."

Just when I'm about to be soaked by the now-full fountain, the owl's hooting grows louder. It swoops down, digging its talons into Gage's hair. He swats at it, and I scramble away. The owl pecks, unrelenting, at his skull. I can't look away. I'm the rubbernecker I always criticized.

He stabs the air with his knife. Steel connects with the bird's wing, and it screeches, taking flight.

Blood flows down Gage's face as he lunges in my direction. I avoid him easily, running back through the gate and slamming it behind me.

He removes his shirt and mops the blood away, smearing it so his skin looks stained. And his torso . . . his arms . . . every vein is visible. Blackened as if burned. Winding and twisting, reaching straight for his heart. "You think a little iron's going to stop me?"

Before I can answer, a voice behind me bellows, "No. I am."

I spin as Ky flings his mirrorglass dagger past me. A flawless throw, spiraling straight through two bars and into Gage's stomach.

He staggers back.

Ky sprints past me, bursts through the gate, seizes Gage by

his biceps. And looks him directly . . . in . . . the . . . eyes. "Come near her again and you'll wish this blade was made of steel." He yanks the knife out, wipes the bloody blade on his pants, sheathes it. "Leave. Now."

Gage's face turns white. He tumbles over the fountain's edge and lands in the water with a deafening splash.

He's gone. Stormy falls backward, bawling. Whether from relief or terror, I can't tell.

Ky could've paralyzed Gage and let him drown. But he didn't. He showed mercy. Maybe I was wrong to jump to conclusions. There's more to Ky than meets the eye.

He releases heavy breaths as he comes to me and unties my wrists with care. "This would make the third time I've saved you, Ember."

I don't argue. Instead, my current level of flip-out causes me to do something against all previous resolve. I slam into him, crushing my face against his shoulder and clutching him so tightly I can hardly breathe. My entire frame trembles, but not for long. His warmth permeates my shakes, dispels them. He smells like fresh-cut grass and earth. If I close my eyes I can almost imagine I'm standing in Mom's sketch, breathing in the scent surrounding the life she always wanted.

Arms stiff and body rigid, Ky just stands there for a moment. But then his muscles relax. As if in slow motion, he drops the rope and enfolds me, softening the ache inside. Ever so gently, he strokes my back, his pulse thunderous.

Somehow I don't mind.

TWENTY

Reality

What now?

Is this wrong?

Doesn't feel wrong. Doesn't feel right either.

He's not Joshua. No one will ever be Joshua.

Except . . .

Joshua's touch is otherworldly, like a fairy tale. Perfect, but forever unattainable.

But this . . .

This is real. Ky's holding me, and he's not changing his mind or pushing me away.

Maybe a little too real. I clear my throat. Slip from his hold. "Ky, how did you . . . ? Gage said she gave everyone some sort of sleeping potion." Did that really happen? If Gage was a traitor, who else might be?

Ky links his thumbs through his belt loops, jerks his head to get the hair out of his eyes. "Apparently Commander Cretin forgot to pack his brain. Everyone knows Shields are immune to medicines of any kind."

Before I can ask what a Shield is, the owl dives, circles our heads, and then lands with grace at our feet. Two black-and-yellow marble eyes blink up at me as the owl cocks its head in a very humanlike gesture. Then it morphs, growing, stretching. Brown-and-white feathers smooth into sun-kissed skin. The eyes and beak shrink inward, and a woman's face takes shape. Just like Wren, Owl Woman is naked.

Ky, as usual, doesn't react. At this point he's probably used to seeing animals transform into naked girls.

The woman's lips camber into a mischievous grin. "I do apologize for not swooping in sooner, but I thought it might be useful to hear what the Guardian's plans were. May I borrow this?" She tugs on my jacket sleeve. Her voice is lovely, clear and deep.

"Lark?" I balk, shrugging out of Wren's jacket and handing it to her. Blood seeps from a cut on her arm. She's tall, with soft, bell-shaped curves and waist-length, coffee-colored hair. I'd peg her at age forty, much younger than the woman who welcomed us earlier. But what astonishes me most is the confidence she exudes, not a trace of embarrassment in her almond eyes.

"Yes." Lark slips her arms through the sleeves and pinches the front flaps closed. It cinches, barely covering her. "I take it you've never met a Mask with three states of being?" Her dark eyebrows arch, a prideful air resting on her squared shoulders.

"She has," Ky says. When did his tone become so soft? Can this be the same boy who pressed his knife into my side four days ago? "She just didn't know it at the time." He turns to me. "Isabeau has three forms like Lark here. Woman, Troll, and animal."

If the wench changed into a bug I'd squash her. "What animal?"

"No one knows." Lark's shoulders rise, the jacket opening slightly.

I can't help but notice Ky's gaze doesn't fall to her abundant cleavage.

"I do believe Isabeau prefers it that way."

Could the Troll's secret have something to do with Haman's fear of her?

Lark abandons our huddle and approaches Stormy, who's clutching her knees to her chest, rocking back and forth in silent agony. Is she grieving Gage or her betrayal?

"Come on, dear. Let's get you inside." Lark helps Stormy to her feet, wraps an arm around her. As they pass, she offers me a weak smile while Stormy stares with vacant eyes at the ground.

Now that Ky and I are alone, what am I supposed to say? I shift from foot to foot, my shoulders elevating to my ears. What did the hug mean to him?

What did it mean to me?

I push my frigid fingers into my shallow jean pockets and bounce on the balls of my feet, shivering. The crickets' song dwindles to a gentle hum, reminiscent of a skipping CD player.

Ky widens his eyes as he takes in my shuddering. He removes his leather jacket. Hands it to me. "Here. What kind of Guardian would I be if I let you freeze to death?"

I survey Ky's form. His black, long-sleeved T-shirt clings to him, outlining the curve of his biceps, the width of his chest. He's not football-player beefy or bodybuilder buff. He's simply solid. Strong. I can't believe I called him skinny before. Even so, this isn't what captures all the air from my lungs. There's a sadness in his eyes that stills me, forces me to fix my gaze. How did I fail to notice it before?

Because this is the first time I've trusted him enough not to look away. Because I know he won't hurt me.

"Because you're beginning to see with more than your eyes. You're seeing with your heart."

Will I ever see *you* again, Mom?

Silence.

The thick leather wards off the cold when I slip into it. It's baggy like my favorite sweatshirt, the sleeves reaching past my fingertips. The slippery material, still warm from hugging Ky's body, carries the distinct after-scent of boy. I suppress the urge to inhale the alluring smell more deeply. When I look up at him to express my gratitude, he's staring at me.

Warning. Danger ahead. Maybe he won't paralyze me, but a

new threat presents itself in his focused stare. I break eye contact. "So . . . that fountain's a Threshold?"

His gaze bores into me. Impossible not to feel something so intense. "An old one. Hasn't run in years. Stormy must have used her Calling to summon the water. Did Gage let on where he was taking you?"

"To Isabeau. He said she possesses something he wants. He was planning to trade me for it."

Ky growls. "This is my fault. I never should have told him what happened at the bridge. The water"—he gestures toward the fountain—"was probably from the Threshold in Lynbrook Province. It would've taken you right to her door."

"Ky." My fingers twiddle, itching to touch him, to show I understand. Instead I curl them into my palms. "Why didn't you tell me about your sister?"

"Would it have mattered?" He inhales a rickety breath. Steps closer. His chest rises and falls. He's so close, the heat emanating from his body warms me. How is he not cold?

"I'm sorry. I've been so awful to you." My own breathing quickens. I inch backward, looking at the gate, the trees, anything but Ky's purposeful gaze.

"Don't be." He shrugs one shoulder. "I didn't exactly give you the best first impression."

"What happened to her?"

He breathes one word. *"Crowe."*

Hatred bubbles for the man who rips families apart without a second thought.

"Come on." Ky jerks his head toward the inn. "We don't have to worry about Gage anymore tonight. The fountain is already draining. Even Magnets have their limits. Unless Stormy stands there, focusing only on the water, it can't remain."

"Could you explain this whole Calling thing to me? I'm getting a little confused."

"We've got hours until the others wake. Might as well. What do you know?"

I relay what I've learned from Joshua, Robyn, and Wade. I stride beside Ky, keeping a respectful distance, our pace unhurried. The cottages are dark. It's a ghost town, minus the gunslingers and saloons. Even before night fell, the Village was dead. Is this how these people live? In constant fear? The Haven is large, but it's still a prison. No matter the breadth between, walls are still walls.

"So, David explained about Evers?"

I nod, my conversation with Joshua seeming Reflections away.

"How about Shields?"

I shake my head.

"We'll start there then. As you know, there are seven Callings, all unique to each person. I'm a Shield, but so are Makai and Haman. I can paralyze my enemies with a look, yet I can't inflict internal wounds or render myself invisible."

Makai seemed to disappear the night I followed him. And when Ky attacked him—he definitely vanished then. What did Gage call my uncle? An invisible babysitter?

"Shields are defenders, making them ideal Guardians. Their ability can be offensive, defensive, or both, but all stem from the mind. A Shield cannot harm a human in an alternate form, such as Lark's owl. And most importantly, they are unaffected by others of their kind. I can see Makai, even when no one else can, and Haman can't injure me without the use of physical contact."

Ky's using a knife on my uncle makes sense now, but, "If you could see Makai, why would he turn invisible in the subway?"

"Who knows? He was probably trying to spare you from seeing him struggle." He kicks a rock and it *click, clack, clicks* across the cobblestone, lands in someone's lawn.

Wow. My uncle really does care for me. "So you've always been a Shield?"

"It's different for everyone." His shoulders slump. "Children are given Threshold water as infants, but it's not known if they have a Calling until several years later. If one doesn't manifest by the time they turn eighteen, it never will. I was seven when mine revealed itself. I'd really hoped to be a Physic, like my mother. Though the Callings aren't genetic, they usually reflect an ability of a parent or close relative. Probably because we share similar attributes with those near to us. I just hoped I was more like my mother than my father." His fists clench. "Apparently not." Halting, he tugs his shirt collar down to reveal his shoulder blade.

My breath ceases. I can't help but run my fingers along the crimson-inked tattoo no larger than a tennis ball, a banner fashioned of foliage and vine. And at the banner's center, a rose blossom framed in thorns.

No words form. The tattoo is . . . beautiful. I draw my hand away, touch my right cheek. The image almost reminds me of—

No. I lower my hand, concealing it in the jacket's sleeve. That's crazy. My birthmark isn't beautiful.

Ky adjusts his shirt, and we resume our lackadaisical pace. A weather vane on one cottage sways, squeaking as the breeze kisses its ends. In a yard, two lawn gnomes smile merrily, their painted rosy cheeks puffing out, chipped in places. Some things here are so familiarly American, I can almost imagine I'm on vacation upstate. Then Kuna turns into a merman or Joshua comes back from the dead, reminding me I'm nowhere near home. If only I could click my heels three times and be back in my own bed. Then again, without Mom, New York isn't home at all.

"The rose represents power and protection," Ky says, drawing my attention back. "A sight to behold, but get too close to its thorns . . ." An exhale clouds the night air. "When the mark surfaced during my seventh year, my father was thrilled. I would be a Shield, just like him." His last words exit through clenched teeth.

I say nothing. Whatever transpired between Ky and his father, the wound is still fresh.

"The day after the rose appeared, my training began. I hated it. Father took me away from my mother. He said if I was going to be a soldier in Crowe's army, I had better start young. I tried to be everything he wanted, but I was never good enough. When I didn't meet his expectations, he'd punish me."

Ky doesn't elaborate, leaving me to imagine the cruelties his father inflicted. How could someone be so horrible to a child? No wonder this Reflection is becoming a Shadow World.

"When I was ten, my sister was born, and Mother feared for her life. To my father, having a daughter was the epitome of failures. He wanted a son."

"But he already had you." Just hearing about the guy makes me want to pummel him.

"Not good enough." He kicks another pebble, and it pings a lawn gnome's pointed hat. "I was adopted. My father wanted a son of his own flesh and blood. Just another of the many ways I was a disappointment to him."

Sheesh. And the Worst Dad of the Year Award goes to . . .

"The Void had its claws in him," Ky says. "At that point he was unrecognizable, veins blacker than night from skull to toe, eyes masked in fog."

"Her eyes and skin remain unaltered." Robyn's words. Realization dawns. "Your father was Soulless?"

A nod. "Think of the Void like a disease—one afflicting the soul. One to which only children are immune. Just as a Threshold sourced by the Verity empowers the Callings and guards young souls, so a Threshold contaminated by the Void has its own influence. To my father, his Shield Calling wasn't enough. So he drank from Midnight Lake, the Threshold within Shadow Territory, hoping the Void would give him something the Verity hadn't."

"Did it?"

"Yes. It was like a drug to him. He could no longer feel pain. Or love. The more he consumed, the sicker he became. The illness fed on his cruelty until there was nothing left but a numb shell of the person he once was . . ." His voice trails.

Does the memory of his Soulless father haunt him?

"So my mother took me and my sister, and we fled to her childhood home in the Third. We had to keep our Callings hidden, as most people in the Third hold no belief in the Verity, the Void, or the Callings. Some do, but they conceal their abilities well, opting for a quiet life rather than becoming a science experiment in some test facility. It's a completely different world, the Third. But I'm sure you know that."

I do. Ky's understanding of my Third Reflection references come to light. He grew up there. Just like me. "But eventually you returned to the Second, right? What brought you back?"

"The only thing that could have—my father. He found us, or rather, he found my mother and sister."

I almost don't want to hear what happened next. From the murderous expression tensing Ky's face, it can't be good.

Eyebrows cinched, he says, "We lived in a small town off the coast of Maine. I was eighteen and had secured a job unloading freight at the docks. It wasn't the most fulfilling work, but it helped my mother pay the bills. I came home one day to find her crumpled at the bottom of the stairs and my sister gone." Voice catching, he quiets.

My throat constricts. For all the sorrow I've had to bear, Ky's is ten times worse.

"He did it. He killed my defenseless mother, kidnapped my eight-year-old sister. I should've been there. I'm a Shield. I could've done something." He kicks at nothing. Grabs fistfuls of hair.

I place a tentative hand on his shoulder. I've never known what to say in these situations. When I thought Mom died, I preferred when people said nothing at all.

"I swore on my mother's grave I would make my father pay for what he'd done. I found him at the Threshold that had become his demise. He was forcing my sister to drink the water with him. Though it couldn't touch her young soul, it still made her physically ill. My father wouldn't stop, insisting she drink more. More. More . . . I still remember his eyes. That's when I understood why they call it the Void. There was no life in him. He was a black hole of malice and hatred."

"What did you do?" I'm on the edge of my seat, fear and awe battling for center stage.

"I attacked him. He was so much stronger than me. Even if we weren't both Shields it wouldn't have mattered. I can't control a Soulless any more than I can control one of my own kind. I was sure he would kill us right there, drown us in the Threshold and then drown himself. Our fight ended with him holding a knife to my sister's neck. He said he'd release her on one condition. If I drank from the Threshold myself."

A twist in my gut tells me this story doesn't have a happy ending.

"I knew if I did I would always want more. But what choice did I have? I couldn't let my sister die. So I cupped my hands and drank. In an instant I felt something snap inside of me. I no longer had anything holding me back, no conscience to keep me from doing what needed to be done. My father must've seen the change, too, because he was wild-eyed. *Don't you feel it?*' he taunted. *The surge of power?*' And I did. He released my sister. Then I took his knife. He just smiled at me, said he was going to die anyway. He was raving mad. So I killed him." Not a hint of remorse is present in his words.

"I'd finally protected someone I loved, but at the same time I sensed my own humanity slipping away. After that I swore I'd never take another life, no matter how much the Void wanted me to. I would defend myself, do what was necessary to guard my sister, but I wouldn't kill. It's why I went to such great lengths to find a mirrorblade." His hand rests on the dagger's hilt.

Biting my lip, I consider his tale. Would I have had the strength to drink the Void's water for Mom's sake? "But you're not Soulless. Which means you're okay, right?" My own question startles me. And I realize . . . I *do* care what happens to him.

He removes his shirt and I gasp. Black veins like Gage's run along Ky's right arm, from his wrist to his bicep. "It's like an addiction, one I battle every day."

"The Void? Ky—"

"It appeared at first drink. I was becoming the very thing I feared—my father's son. I wanted to be as far away from that Threshold as possible. I swore I'd never take another sip, no matter how crazy it made me. No matter how much it called to me. Resisting became easier with time. I needed an outlet, some way to expel the anger within. So I joined the Guardians. Gage trained me. It was easy to take my ire out on him because he was always such a thorn. When he sent me on my first mission, I felt as if I was finally doing something to make my mother proud. Until Haman captured me."

Hesitating, he stoops and plucks a blade of grass, spins it between his thumb and forefinger. "Crowe had a proposition for me. He knew about my sister, compliments of my father's loose tongue before he died. He'd been indebted to Crowe, for what I don't know. I had a choice. I could either serve Crowe and pay off my father's debt, or he'd take away the only person I had left in the seven Reflections."

And there it is. The reason behind Ky's betrayal. How can I hold it against him? I would've done the same for Mom.

"Are you . . . ?" I swallow. Did my ability to form coherent thoughts take a sick day?

"Don't worry about me. I've got it under control. I drink from a Verity-sourced Threshold as often as I can, which keeps my craving for the Void at bay. It's not a cure, but it helps. At least, it seems to. The Void has never spread past my arm." He slips his shirt back on. Clears his throat. "Enough sob stories. You wanted to know about the Callings."

I do, but I have one last question. One that's been nibbling at me since Ky mentioned his adoption. "Your father, what was his name?"

Three, two, one . . .

"Tiernan," he says. "Tiernan Archer."

I'm frozen. Stranded on my own reality show with no hope of being voted off.

"I think he was Makai's brother," Ky says. "Though I'd never met him until a few days ago." Right. Because my uncle was in the Third protecting me. "From what I can tell, they're nothing alike. I took my mother's maiden name, Rhyen. I wanted no association with the man who called himself my father."

Could Ky possibly comprehend the atomic bomb he's dropped? I can't see how.

The man who raised him, the one who killed his mother and kidnapped his sister . . . *my* half-sister if she wasn't also adopted . . . that man is—was—my father.

It takes everything in me to contain my shock. Hurt. Anger. Curiosity. Emotions war. I always wondered about my dad. Mom said he left us. No more. No less. How could she have fallen for such a cruel man? Was he always so heartless? So easily swayed by the Void? What does that mean for me? I used to wonder if I was like my dad, since I seemed to be nothing like Mom. My soul aches at the thought.

He didn't want a daughter.

He didn't want *me*.

Ky may not know what Tiernan's debt was, but it's not too difficult to figure out. According to Mom's journal entry, Jasyn never would've approved of Mom falling for a Guardian. But she did, and obviously became pregnant with me. Ky said Tiernan didn't want a daughter. Maybe Mom wasn't only escaping Jasyn when she left. Could she also have been running from Tiernan, just as Ky's mother did?

If so, the reason Ky sided with Jasyn, the debt he had to pay for his sister's sake . . .

That debt is because of me.

TWENTY-ONE

He chose

I should tell him.

I can't tell him.

He'll hate me. We were just starting to get along.

I have . . . had a half sister. And now she's gone.

My father raised Ky. I have so many questions. I don't dare ask.

"Magnets, such as Stormy, can summon things. Their symbol is a moon."

I blink. What's Ky saying?

"Like Shields, all Magnets hold different strengths."

The Callings. Right.

"Stormy is a water Magnet. Her ability is linked to that particular element alone. Other Magnets might control fire, wind, or earth. Still some have no connection to the elements at all, their gifts lying with matter or energy. Whatever their specialty, this Calling takes great focus and exertion. The summoned thing can remain only as long as the Magnet wills it."

It all comes together. The storm. The Threshold water. Stormy is one talented Magnet. I wonder if she'd let me see her tattoo.

"Then there are Masks. Lark, Kuna, Isabeau, Wren, Robyn—they all have alternate forms. It's a more common Calling than you'd think. They're represented by a butterfly, the simplest and most beautiful example of transformation."

Hard to picture Kuna with a butterfly on his back. "And

Physics?" Act natural. Don't let him see all I can think about is Tiernan and how he connects us.

We've reached the square, and Ky sits on an iron bench across from the inn. Two empty flowerpots flank it. The cat from the windowsill curls up on one end, its orange-tipped tale tapping.

Ky stretches his lean legs out in front of him. "Physics come in all shapes and sizes. Organic Physics, like my mother or Physic Song, have a knack for mixing medicines. They use remedies concocted from nature. Illusoden, for example, was invented by Lancaster Rhyen, my mother's grandfather."

As in the dude they made a statue of? "A Physic founded the League of Guardians?"

"Don't sound so surprised. A Physic is more than a white coat and a fancy title. There are some Physics who guard their Calling with more ferocity than an Ever. A mere touch from such a Physic could cure even the deepest wound, which is why a Physic's mark is a handprint."

Nathaniel. Is his touch that powerful? Must be. Why else would Wade put so much faith in the man? Does Ky know my grandfather is his adoptive grandfather? Part of me hopes he never finds out.

"No matter what," Ky adds, "if someone is already meant to die, if it's their time, nothing can change that. Not a touch from a Physic or a drop of Ever blood. Death is a Calling all its own." He scratches the cat's neck, and it purrs in satisfaction.

I join him on the bench, trying not to sit too close. Otherwise he might hear my thundering heart, see the sweat forming at my hairline.

He scoots over so our thighs touch. Ky hesitates a second before raising his arm and wrapping it around me in one fluid motion. He's just protecting me. Doing his job. The big brother I always wanted.

Moan. He has no clue how technically true that is.

As he continues his explanation, the hand resting on my shoulder lifts animatedly every so often. "Finally there are Scribs and Amulets. Scribs, like Grizz, have excellent memories and are talented in reading, writing, or drawing—sometimes a mixture of all three. They're responsible for recording anything and everything regarding Reflection history. Genealogies. Events. Even legends. They can be a bit insufferable because of their brilliance. Think of them as the savants of the Called. Scribs are always correcting you, and some have compulsive tendencies. Many are able to read something once and never forget it. It should be no surprise a Scrib's symbol is a quill."

Compulsive tendencies, huh? Grizz in an eighth note.

"Amulets have the gift of illusion." An unexpected chill sends a tremor through my body. Ky rubs my arm with his palm. "They're meant to be secret keepers, their purpose to conceal anything an enemy might desire. Amulets are generally attractive and easy to like. Their symbol is a lock and key. Crowe, as you may have guessed, is an Amulet."

I consider my time with Jasyn. His kind demeanor and calming voice. He almost had me fooled. "Amulets are responsible for the façades, aren't they?"

"Yes. The trick is to look for tells. No matter how strong the façade, there are always glitches—signs that what you're seeing isn't real." Such as my nonexistent porcelain skin? "If an Amulet can't fool you, the façade is useless."

"So the façades at the Haven and subway Threshold, at the Broken Bridge, an Amulet created those?" My eyelids droop and I stifle a yawn.

"Many Amulets, actually." Ky yawns too. We'll never make it to the Haven if we can't stand up in the morning. Still, I can't bring myself to move. "The ones on our side act like sentinels, assuring certain protections remain in place. I've no idea who constructed the façade at the Broken Bridge for Isabeau. But the Threshold beneath the subway, the Haven entrance, and many other gateways have an Amulet ally assigned to them. Every so often the façade has to be strengthened, reconstructed, or even moved, should its location be jeopardized. The Guardians have a good team, though I've yet to see an Amulet as talented as Crowe."

So much to take in. Not just the Callings, but their unique aspects as well. And the tattoos. I can't get them off my mind. But there's this other thing, too, something Robyn mentioned. "What about Mirrors?"

Ky stiffens. "Mirrors?"

"Back at the Haven, Robyn said something about a person who could have all the Callings."

"Mirrors don't exist. No one is that perfect."

"Perfect?"

Another stretch. Another yawn. "The Verity augments your greatest strength." His words have that slow, falling-asleep pace. "For me, it was my desperate need to defend those I love. For my mother, it was her innate desire to help people. Crowe was probably good at keeping secrets as a child, a talent he's obviously abused since then. But for someone to possess a quality strong enough to hone all seven Callings in some form or another? Such a person might as well be the vessel of the Verity himself."

Mirrors don't exist. Got it. "What about me?"

"What about you?" He knocks his knuckle against my shoulder. Is he teasing me?

I squirm. Flush. Maybe it's a stupid question. "Do you think my mom gave me Threshold water when I was born?" Yep. Saying it aloud does sound childish. I just escaped playing the lead role in *Close Encounters of the Troll Kind*, and I'm worried about auditioning for a part in *X-Men: Days of Future Called*? Priorities, anyone?

"If she loves you as much as you appear to love her, I wouldn't doubt it."

I make a mental pros-and-cons list. My soul is guarded until

I turn eighteen: pro. If a Calling hasn't manifested yet, I probably don't have one: con. Sigh.

The cat crawls onto Ky's lap, a purr rumbling its back. He doesn't seem to mind, stroking the feline with his long fingers. "I know what you're thinking. You've still got some time. You don't turn eighteen for a couple weeks, right?"

"Yeah."

"So a Calling could still be in there somewhere. And if not"—he shrugs—"be glad you won't have to carry the burden. Plenty of people don't have Callings. Gage, Preacher—" His mouth snaps closed, as if realizing comparing me to those guys probably isn't the most encouraging thing he could say. "Don't worry. I have a good feeling about you."

Better. "Thanks." Goose bumps sprout along my arms, despite my layers. Could I possibly have a Calling somewhere deep inside? Does Mom have one I never knew about? I rack my brain trying to picture her bare shoulder. The image doesn't surface. She never was the tank top–wearing type.

"So, we've spent this entire time talking about me. Your turn. Tell me something about you."

Me? What's to tell? "I wear a size eight shoe." Gah, that was lame. Now I'm thankful for the cold. Otherwise my cheeks would ignite, turn my skin to ash.

"While I appreciate that imperative piece of information, it's not quite what I had in mind. Try again, this time make it real."

Real?

Real.

I've never spent much time trying to get to know myself. I'd actually avoid myself, if it were physically possible. Except, there is this one thing . . . "I love music." My heart contracts. I *miss* music. "Singing actually, though I do play a couple instruments. It's kind of like my outlet. My way of expressing emotion? When I'm sad or lonely or scared, and I find the perfect piece to describe that feeling, it's like the artist climbed inside my head and wrote the song for me. Or when I don't know what to say, I sometimes find it easier to reference a particular lyric." I twist the hem of my shirt. This is the most anyone has talked. Ever. "Dumb, huh?" I tuck a stray hair behind my ear. My right leg jiggles. *Stop fidgeting, will you?*

"You are many things, Ember, but dumb is not one of them." Ky slouches against the bench. Tilts his head back. Closes his eyes. "Sing to me," he croons.

My heart stops beating. Literally. His reference to one of my favorite songs ever catches me so completely off guard, gives me déjà vu like he wouldn't believe.

"Well?" He taps his toe.

"What, you mean now?" Breathe in, breath out. Let it go.

"I'm sorry, was there another time you had in mind?"

He's so infuriatingly sarcastic, it's almost endearing. "What do you want to hear?"

"Singer's choice."

Out of habit I begin humming the melody to one of Joshua's favorites, one we played often during our afternoon jam sessions. But the sound falls flat, a generic cover of my past life. Nothing's ever as good as the original.

Or maybe it's not the song. Perhaps I need to change my tune. Joshua always picked the playlist. It didn't really bother me, mostly because it meant I didn't have to make a decision. They were always made for me. Whatever he chose, I sang.

But not tonight.

I clear my throat, start again, this time choosing an oldie Mom used to sing when I was little. I still remember the first time I heard "Smile" by Charlie Chaplin. It was the first day of kindergarten. I didn't want to go, didn't understand why I had to be separated from Mom for four whole hours. Then she started singing.

"I want you to remember these words," she said. *"Sing them until you can't remember why you were sad to begin with."*

And I did. Mom couldn't get me to stop singing after that.

My voice shakes a little during the first verse since I haven't warmed up, but when I reach the chorus, the melody comes easily. I'd almost forgotten how much I love this. I close my eyes, letting the lyrics flow, thinking only of Mom and how I'd give anything to see her smile again.

The thought forces my own lips to curve.

On the final note I open my eyes.

My grin fades, and all air flees my lungs.

Joshua is standing on the inn's porch. Teeth clenched. His gaze acid. It's almost as if my eyes float out of my body, watching from above, taking in the whole scene. Ky's arm around my shoulder. Me wearing his jacket and singing to him, a pastime Joshua and I shared. Something special and so very much our own.

Oh no. He's got the wrong idea. I reach out, but Joshua turns his back, strides into the inn's shadows, and slams the door. The sign rattles on its hinges, echoing the shake of anger beginning to rise in me. What's his problem? He made it clear he wants nothing to do with me. I just sit there, staring where he stood. I control my urge to move. Maybe I was wrong. Maybe it *is* over. It's better this way. Easier.

Don't feel. Don't care. Don't—

I close my eyes, clamping my lashes against inevitable tears. If it's easier, why does it feel as if I've just attended another funeral?

wishing

The turning point came two years and seven months after we met. Or, I should say, *my* turning point. It surged up on me, a stealth wave sweeping me away.

"We're going to get in trouble," I hiss through nervous laughter. "We could be arrested for breaking and entering."

Screech. Bark. Clang.

I start. Even the everyday hits on Manhattan's playlist make me jump.

Joshua smirks. As if doing a magic trick, he waves his hand. With a flourish, a shiny key appears between his thumb and forefinger. "Not if we didn't *break* in."

I gape. No way. "Where'd you get that?"

He swings his arms and knocks his fists together, mock innocence lighting his face. "Let's just say I know a guy who knows a guy who just so happens to be the stage manager." He releases a hot breath onto the key and rubs it against his plaid shirt. He flips it in the air as if performing the coin toss at the Super Bowl, then catches it on the back of his hand.

Show-off.

I quirk one eyebrow and plant my hands on my hips. "Seriously?"

"It's the truth." He's a horrible liar. "But if you don't want to go inside—"

"Oh, I'm going, but if we get caught—"

"*If* we get caught, which we won't, I'll take full blame as the responsible adult." Joshua stands at attention, raising three fingers in the air, an overgrown Boy Scout.

I give him a light shove. How does he make it so easy to be myself around him? "You call breaking into the Gershwin on a school night responsible?"

His expression turns serious. Is he going to say something about the touch? I've been hinting since my seventeenth birthday, trying to show him I want more, that I'm no longer a kid. He never responds to my prodding. Is he ignoring the obvious, or is he just the average clueless guy?

"You're on spring break," he says. "It's not a school night for *you*."

He's always teasing. Was it ever not this way? I can't remember the last time I felt awkward around him. "But *you* have finals coming up. Shouldn't you be studying?"

"It can wait." One more mischievous grin, and he ducks around the corner, consumed by the alley.

I take half a step. Pause. Breathe. What will tonight bring? Could I finally get my very first kiss? I look around, absorbing every inch of my surroundings. I don't want to forget a single thing.

A woman in outrageously tall wedge-heels drops a cigarette butt, then stomps it out with her clunky toe. She hails a cab and ducks into it, her miniskirt riding up her bronze thigh before she closes the door. I still taste the smoke on the air after she's gone.

On the corner two teenagers walk so close together they look like conjoined twins. The boy stops and pulls the girl into him for a spontaneous kiss. I stare unabashedly, replacing the girl's face with mine, only without the birthmark. I imagine the boy is Joshua, his lips soft, tender. He opens my mouth with his—

"El, are you coming or not?" Joshua pops his head around the corner.

Thank goodness it's dark and he won't see how my temperature's changed, how my blood has rushed to my head. "Yeah."

The alley is the same as any other, stinking of sewage and alcohol. Half a dozen cigarette butts lie in a pile by a metal door. Joshua sticks the key in the lock, turns it, and pushes down the chrome handle. The door swings toward him.

A burst of conditioned air batters my face. I hesitate only a second before entering.

He follows. Tugs the door closed silently.

"I can't see anything," I whisper.

Click. A flashlight illuminates our path. "Always be prepared." Joshua steps in front and leads the way.

Everything is black. Black floor. Black walls. We pass two rolling racks stuffed full of colorful costumes. In one corner a web of cords and wires spills from a box. A mirror leans against one wall, along with a cart containing everything from makeup palettes to eyedrops.

When we reach the stage, I stop. This is it. Am I really standing here?

Joshua thrusts the flashlight into my palm. "Wait here. I'll be right back." His voice is low, his breath hot in my ear.

The lyrics to "Kiss the Girl" scream across my brain.

His footsteps dwindle as he flees into darkness.

I take light steps, angling the flashlight in different directions, exploring this very off-limits first date venue.

Wait. Is this a date?

Technically, yes. He picked me up at my door, bought me a tofu dog, and took me to my favorite place in the city, aside from Central Park. Sounds like a date to me.

Above, a catwalk hovers. Ropes, lights, and metal poles surround it. I shine the beam downstage, toward the orchestra. Surreal. I half expect the Phantom of the Opera to leap from the curtains and whisk me away.

Flick, flick, flick.

Blue, purple, and green channels of cool light inundate the stage. I squint against the luster, blinking, letting my eyes adjust. Row upon row of empty cushioned seats slide into focus. They slope upward, the mezzanine leaning over them like an anxious onlooker awaiting a climactic scene. I twirl in slow motion, breathing in the once-in-a-lifetime atmosphere. The stage. The lights. Broadway.

A backdrop of a giant Ozian clock all green and towering gives me the illusion I'm floating, defying gravity. Sold out within hours, we couldn't get tickets to the one-night reunion of the original cast of *Wicked*, but this is so much better. I continue revolving, living in the moment, imagining hundreds of people applauding, begging for an encore.

When I face downstage again, I spot Joshua, sitting front and center, beaming. Even from this distance, his cerulean eyes invoke a soft gasp from my lips. Has he been watching me this whole time?

"Sing to me." His melodic voice echoes. Rises to the rafters.

I inhale, unable to shroud the chagrin expanding to my ears. I trace a circle on the floor with the toe of my Converse sneaker. "Okay, but on one condition."

Joshua laughs, full and deep. "Anything."

We both share a passion for music and quickly connected on that note. The roof of my brownstone has become our personal haven. We go up there afternoons and weekends, sharing an iPod, a pair of earbuds connecting us. He teaches me guitar chords, and we practice singing harmonies. Mom always said we sounded like we were born to sing together.

"Sing with me?" I ask. At his hesitation, I add, "Come on. It's just like on the roof. Just us." He brings out a confidence in me I've never known.

He runs his fingers through his recently cut hair, scratches the back of his head. "I can't say no to you." He ascends the stairs two at a time and meets me center stage. "What should we sing?"

I gesture toward the backdrop. "What else?"

He rolls his eyes. "Should've known. I guess all those times you forced me to listen to the *Wicked* soundtrack are going to pay off." He takes the flashlight. Sticks it in his back pocket.

I smile. "Guess so." I withdraw my iPhone. When I tap the screen, a candid shot of Mom stares up at me. I scroll until I find the duet. The haunting melody drifts through the tinny speaker, and I begin to sway.

As I start the first verse to "As Long as You're Mine," my cocoon falls away. I spread my vocal wings, testing their strength, belting the notes. I'm no longer the ugly girl from the Upper West Side. I'm the bold and tenacious Elphaba of Oz—and I'm flying.

Joshua hits his cue flawlessly. He's the perfect Fiyero. Charming. Funny. Handsome. He holds my gaze, his eyes alight. For a moment I forget we're only acting. The way he's looking at me . . . it's as if he wrote those lines himself. Words meant for my ears alone.

Our voices intertwine, meld into one. Mom's right. We do sound like we were born to sing together. And that's when I know. This boy who moved next door three years ago is more than just a friend.

So. Much. More.

Somewhere between our first encounter and becoming friends, he stole my heart. No. Scratch that. I gave it to him.

And then the magic ends. Poof. I'm out of breath. Gravity triumphs, hauling me to earth.

"Thank you." I slip my phone away.

He's quiet. I've never known him to be speechless. His mouth twitches as his gaze flutters below my nose. Is he looking at my lips? Is he going to—?

"Hey, you!" A man with a napkin tucked into his white undershirt jogs toward us from the rear of the theater. His overshirt is white, too, unbuttoned, with some sort of patch on the right breast.

Looks like the security guard isn't too happy we interrupted his break.

We bolt for our exit, my heart nearly pulverizing my sternum from the thrill. We don't stop running until we're two blocks away, safe within a streetlamp's yellow blush.

I bend over, breathing deep, reining in my hysterics. I can hardly see through my tears of laughter. When I straighten, Joshua's wiping his own eyes, stretching his jaw. One look at each other and the snickers start all over again, lasting the entire cab ride home. The cabbie probably thought we were drunk.

Best. Night. Ever.

Once we're climbing the steps to my front door, the mood shifts. The air grows heavier, the way it gets just before it rains. I hold my breath in hopes of calming the *boom, boom, boom* resounding from my chest.

I turn to him, fumbling with my house key like in the movies.

His Adam's apple bobs, and he rubs the side of his scruffy cheek.

"I had so much fun." Insecurity crawls over my arms, spiraling up to my face. Not now.

"Me too." He coughs, moves his left foot down a step.

I shove my key in the lock, flip it. The dull tick of the dead bolt counts another second closer to our evening's end.

"So . . ." I turn the knob, crack the door.

"So . . . good night." He jogs down my steps and then crosses to his own. Before he goes inside, he gives me one last crooked smile. Then, as is his custom, he's gone.

"I found snacks." Ky's voice wrenches me from the memory—dream.

I suck in a breath, open my eyes. My head rests on a pillow, and little wet spots pepper my sleeve. Did I cry myself to sleep? I roll my neck. Ack. Knots. How did I get back to our room?

Oh. Right. Ramped up from the nonmoment with Joshua, I

stormed inside. Ky must've sensed my irritation because he was more than happy to give me some space. I paced the tiny room until my energy drained. Then I curled up on the mattress and waited. And cried. And dreamt.

The bed gives beneath Ky's weight. "I found rolls and cheese. It's not much, but it'll do till morning."

I sit up. He passes me a cheese sandwich, and I bite into it. Yeasty bread almost evaporates on my tongue, the sharp cheese sticking to my teeth. My taste buds throw a party as the much-needed sustenance jives around my mouth. I inhale the thing in two more bites, and before I can ask, Ky hands me another. We eat three each, and by then I'm already full. Funny. I used to eat three monstrous slices of New York pizza and still want more. Did my stomach shrink? I couldn't handle another nibble now if I tried.

Ky burps, raps his chest with his fist. "If you're still hungry—"

I shake my head, my bangs making my eyelids itch. They've grown too long. Need a trim. "I'm so stuffed. All I want is sleep."

He stands, and crumbs tumble from his lap in a mini rockslide. Then he crosses to the rocker and drags it along the floor toward the bed.

"What are you doing?"

"What's it look like?" He sits on the rocker, leans back, and props his feet up, boots and all, on the mattress. "Guarding you. In case you didn't notice, sitting on the opposite end of the room didn't quite cut it last time."

I scoot over, slip off my boots, and slide beneath the blanket. "Just don't kick me in the face with your big feet, okay?" Yesterday the comment would've been meant as a jab. Tonight it feels more like a joke from one friend to another.

Friends? Maybe.

"I make no promises." Without another word he closes his eyes.

I turn on my side and study him, Joshua's opposite. Joshua always has a clean and finished look about him, even when he needs a shave, which is most of the time. Ky, on the other hand, is a mess with his blond hair curling out at his car-door ears, dirt caked underneath his fingernails, myriad pimples dotting his skin. There's something so relatable and real about him. I can't look away.

Long after his breathing slows, I'm still wide awake. I can feel him, smell him. I touch the bandage wrapped around my palm, unravel it. There's a scar but no pain. Ky did that.

The ache of Joshua's rejection is an open sore yet to heal. I've spent so much time wishing for something more with him. Maybe it's time I stop wishing, start healing. Then, someday, there'll be nothing left but a scar like the one on my palm.

A scar. But no pain.

wounds

Second Day, Third Month, Third year of ~~Father's~~ Jasyn's Reign

It has been just over three years since the king and queen disappeared. Guardians have searched the provinces over, and still no sign of Aidan or his bride. My heart hurts to imagine them in pain. Or worse, dead. At first Father seemed to hurt for them too. For an entire year after the disappearance he rarely came out of his room. Refused to converse with anyone. Now a thirst for control consumes him. He cares only for the Void and its power. Thank the Verity I have found comfort in a companion.

Thank the Verity for Tiernan Archer.

The day of the disappearance, Tiernan found me weeping in the library. He offered me his handkerchief. I realized then that I loved him before I knew his name, I loved him more with each kind word he spoke. With every beat of my heart growing louder as he gazed at me with understanding eyes. We have remained friends these three years. But today . . . today will be different. Because today I turn sixteen. I am no longer a girl but a woman. Today I will tell him how I truly feel . . .

I stir. Shiver. Did I kick the covers off? I blink awake. Must've dozed off while reading when I couldn't get to sleep. Where's the journal? I search for it with my free hand.

My *free* hand?

First I feel it. Skin on skin. Callused fingers curled over my smooth ones. Then I peek across the bed at the still-sleeping boy. So peaceful. Innocent. An unexpected stint of hesitation. Ky's hand is warm, and I don't want to let go.

Move.

I . . .

Get up.

I force myself to pull away, the fire of Ky's touch lingering on my skin when I do. He's still in the rocker, back arched, arms and head resting on the bed's edge. Somehow, as we slept, my hand found his. Or did his find mine? I can't ask him. He's still asleep, oblivious to my dilemma.

I flex my bandaged hand. It's sore, but I won't need the Illusoden again, probably didn't need it last night. The stuff wears off too quickly anyway. Better save it for an emergency.

Beyond the window pink streaks an indigo sky, ushering in the dawn and melting into the mountain we passed on our journey. I roll over. The journal lies akimbo on the floor, half of it hidden beneath the bed. I leave it. Don my boots. Creep out the door. Resolve pushes me forward. Joshua's going to listen to what I have to say. Here goes nothing.

Muffled voices waft up from the first floor. I breathe on my palm, then inhale. Cheese breath. Nice. I'm in desperate need of a mint. And a shower. Please let there be a shower.

At the bottom of the stairs, I find Lark in her youthful form whispering to Grizz. They halt the moment they notice me. Lark stiffens. Grizz clears his throat, then stares with intent at the open book on the counter. No echoed greetings today. Is he using his Calling now, committing to memory every word on those pages?

"Good morning." Lark smiles, takes me gently by the arm, and leads me down the hall to a quaint washroom complete with indoor plumbing and fresh towels.

Bingo.

"You'll find everything you need in here. Hot, pressurized water from the spring and clean clothes. Just leave your old ones on the floor and I'll get them washed. Feel free to use anything in those bottles and holler if you need something else." She blinks. A sliver of yellow surrounds her blue irises. Funny how those little things are easier to pick up on after knowing someone's secret.

I nod a silent thank-you. Step inside. Lock the door. A small window over the claw-foot tub admits the morning light. I draw the embroidered curtains and sit on the tub's edge. My brain is worse than my locker at school, all unorganized emotions and unfinished thoughts. I shuffle through the piles, selecting what I'm certain of.

Mom. My top priority, all things aside.

Joshua. Wrong. *Certain* is the last word I'd use to describe him. Try nine letters, a synonym for *enigma*. *Conundrum*. Mom, the ultimate crossword junkie, would be so proud.

Ky. Not as perplexing as Joshua, but still an ambiguity. He saved my life. Three times. He's proven I can trust him, but is it really so easy for us to switch from enemies to friends in such a short period?

Guess I'll find out.

I peel away my clothes piece by piece, the layers of me. Ky's jacket, smelling like him, a scent I'm growing more accustomed to. *Fall*. My shirt, the one I wore the first time Joshua held my hand in the subway. *Flutter*. Mom's Uggs, the ones she may never wear again. *Thud*. My jeans, the ones Mom bought me even though they were way too expensive. *Drop*. Every article represents something, a significant moment, a fraction of my heart.

A mirror on the back of the door confirms my fears. My hair is a tragedy, dry, the ends splitting. Without a flat iron or product, it cascades from my unconditioned scalp in kinked waves. My face is plain aside from the birthmark, my brown eyes lost without shadow or liner. I just stare at myself. This is me. Deal with it.

After I bathe, smelling of lavender and rosemary, I survey the clothes Lark set out. They remind me of Robyn. A long-sleeved, cream-colored peasant top and a knee-length eggplant pinafore dress. Between the folds rests a braided leather tie. At the bottom of the stack, a pair of gray knit leggings and a cardigan made from the same material. A bra and underwear, plain white, thin, complete the ensemble. The bra is one piece, with no clasps or underwire. I slip it on. It's so light I feel as if I'm wearing nothing at all. The rest of the outfit hangs off my frame. Too long. Too baggy. At least I'll be comfortable.

Next I turn to the sink, a mini version of the tub. A twig with its top bark peeled away to reveal strings of softer sapwood lies on the counter. A toothbrush? I lift the faucet and wet the bristles, then scrub my teeth from back to front. Brush, spit, rinse. Brush, spit, rinse. I dab a bit of the peppermint oil from the basket on my tongue for good measure. I suck a breath through my teeth. Strong.

Before I leave this momentary haven and brave an encounter with Joshua, I glance in the mirror once more. What do I do with my hair? I scan the tiny bathroom and spot a wooden brush. I run it through my tangles, then fashion a diagonal French braid, securing it with the leather tie. Quinn showed me how to do it once, insisting I stop wearing my hair in my face. It's a really pretty style on her. On me, it just looks as if I'm posing.

Lark waits in the front room, her lips a flat line. "Breakfast is on the porch." She nods toward the door. "You two have a lot to discuss."

I gulp and head outside. She can only mean Joshua. How does she know we need to talk? Did he say something to her?

He's waiting for me, sitting on one of the Adirondack chairs, silent as a musical rest. When he sees me, his eyes widen.

I bite my lower lip. What's he thinking? Is he finally realizing how ugly I am with my hair pulled off my face?

Crud. Thinking I could confront him was easy in the shallows of the bathroom. So much harder in the ocean of his eyes.

"El." His voice rasps. He coughs.

I fiddle with a button on my sweater. It comes loose and falls to the porch. *Tick.* "Joshua."

"You look . . . different."

Great. He's speaking in guy-code. "Er, thanks." I guess.

He leans forward. He's looking at me but in an unseeing way. "We should talk."

Wait, wasn't talking my idea? "I agree." I take the chair across from him.

A tray on a low table between us holds a continental-style breakfast. Rolls like the ones Ky and I shared last night, muffins, berries, pine nuts, boiled eggs, a bowl of granola. A pitcher of milk and a steaming teakettle wing the spread. I grab a muffin and pick at the top, the best part. Mmm, like bran, but sweeter and not as mealy.

In the square, down the cobbled lane, life emerges. A woman in an apron beats a rug outside the notions shop. A boy and girl play tag, zigzagging around her. The butcher turns the sign in his window to the *Open* side, and the baker holds his door for an elderly man, the aromas of butter and yeast floating past their smiling faces. And I thought no one here ever came outside.

"Eliyana," Joshua starts, tearing at a roll, "what happened last night . . . with Kyaphus . . . it can't go any further. Do you understand?" He shreds the bread, crumbs falling to his feet scrap by scrap. Anyone else might think a bird pecked it to death.

I narrow my eyes. "What exactly are you accusing me of? Ky saved me, which is more than I can say for you." But it's not Joshua's fault Ky is immune to Slumbrosia. My anger doesn't appear to influence him.

"As an Ever I'm susceptible to being drugged. But the effects don't last long on me. I left the moment it wore off, but then I saw you two . . . *together*."

"I was cold. He gave me his jacket, put his arm around me. It didn't mean anything." Does he think I'm some ninny, flitting from one guy to the next? Unbelievable.

Every muscle in his face hardens, a chiseled sculpture. "I know it meant nothing to *him*. I'm concerned it meant something to *you*."

Right. Because no guy could possibly be attracted to me in that way. "No." Pause. "Of course not."

He drops the last bit of roll to the ground, brushes his hands on his thighs. "Guardians are trained to do whatever it takes to protect their charges. Lie. Cheat. Kill. Anything really." His tone is Novocain. He almost sounds like . . .

Jasyn.

This isn't happening. "I don't believe you." My hand trembles. Vision blurs. I clench my fist, my nails digging into my cut. This is so not going as planned. *Keep it together.* "You're lying now. You can't stand the idea of me being with someone besides you." I test the words, relishing the way they sound, the sense they make.

His voice remains even. "I'm sorry if I led you to believe—"

I shoot from the chair, nearly knocking over the table when I bump it with my shin. That'll leave a bruise. "You care about me. You can't stand there and tell me the past three years meant nothing. Even if it was your job, I know what I felt between us. No one is that good an actor."

The remainder of my muffin crumbles to the ground. I'm pacing now, trying desperately to believe my own rebuttal. "I heard Makai. He said he thought you'd fallen for me. I couldn't believe it then, couldn't fathom you might actually want to be with me. But you know what?" I point a finger in his emotionless face. "Now I'm starting to think he was right. You act one way with me and another around everyone else. This hot-and-cold act isn't you. The Joshua I fell in love with isn't a liar, no matter how well trained he might be to do so. You feel something for me, too, but you're scared, of what, I don't know."

My emotions hyperventilate. I just told Joshua I love him. I search his face for a reaction. A sign my admission has an effect. Instead I receive a patronizing stare. Nothing to indicate he heard me or understands the epicness of what I've said. The amount of courage it took to do so.

"El, calm down." He stands, too, touches my elbow. "You don't know what you're saying. You are not in love with me."

I flinch away as if burned. People are staring at us now, stopped to watch our soap-opera exchange. "Yes." No turning back now. "I am."

"Listen," he says, words hushed, eyes unapologetic. "Everything I've done is because . . ." Here it is. He's finally going to admit it. ". . . I swore to protect you. I *have* to protect you, and if that hurts your feelings, I'm sorry, but it's the way it has to be."

"Why? Why does it *have* to be that way?"

He thrusts his hands in his pockets. "I took an oath, 'To the Crown until Death.' I had to get close to you to keep you safe. That meant getting you to trust me. It was obvious you had a crush on me. The best friend bit seemed the easiest route to take." He doesn't even blink. The way he's looking at me, as if he pities me, makes my blood roil. "When you tried to kiss me after your mom . . . I knew I'd gone too far. A kiss would've destroyed everything." He clears his throat.

"Oh, don't stop. Let me know how you really feel." My pulse thunders in my ears. Black and red spots dart past my eyes.

Joshua's mouth goes slack. "I *am* telling you."

Blink. Breathe. Get ahold of yourself. "Does this have something to do with my connection to the Verity's vessel?"

"No." His eyebrows arch high, rippling his forehead. "It has *everything* to do with it. I thought you said your bond was explained."

"It was." Or so I thought. "Our souls are connected. Bound souls always find each other. I'm the only one who can find him."

He exhales, leans against a wooden beam. "And how are you planning to do that?"

"I don't know. I thought it would be something that just . . . happened." Sounds stupid now, saying it aloud. Why didn't I ask more questions? Oh right, I was practically on my deathbed when Robyn and Wade relayed their tale.

"You are not going to find the vessel."

"Oh? And why not?"

"Because he doesn't want to be found. Think about it. What's keeping him from standing against Crowe? From taking what's rightfully his?"

I open my mouth. Close it. Open it again and say, "I—I don't know."

"The vessel linked himself to *you*." He points a finger. "Not the other way around. It's where the mark came from, why everyone believes you will lead them to their savior. Everything you feel, the vessel feels. Pain. Sorrow. Love. He's given up everything for you. So long as he stays hidden, Crowe won't try to kill you."

"Why?"

"Because Crowe knows if he kills you, the vessel will die. Then the Verity will find a new soul to cling to. Crowe doesn't want that. His plan is to capture the Verity when it leaves its current home. Then he can imprison it just as the Void had been before Crowe released it."

Holy Verity, I need to sit down. I reach out, grab the arm of the Adirondack chair, lock my elbow. "So what you're saying is . . . all this time the rebels have been in hiding, while more people become Soulless and this Reflection is shrouded in shadows, it's all because of . . . of me?"

No, no, no, no. Mom's capture. Ky's debt to Crowe. Now this? How much blame can one person take? "Because the vessel of the Verity has been protecting . . . me?" Impossible. "Why would anyone do that? Why sacrifice so much to be linked to one person? Who is that saving?" My shrill voice scratches. I pour myself a glass of milk and drink, the fresh liquid coating my throat.

Joshua blinks twice. "You. It's saving you."

I set the glass down, dab my mouth with a napkin. "I thought you said if I die, the vessel dies." Make up your mind.

"I did. But if that happens, you will live."

Now he's lost me. I lower myself into the chair, palm my forehead. "In what Reflection does what you just said make sense?"

"When the vessel linked his soul to yours, he was choosing your life over his own." Joshua paces, boots clunking over the creaky porch. "Think of him as a replacement, a substitute, a second chance, a get-out-of-death-free card." He stops. "His life would be taken in place of yours." Resumes pacing. "Crowe is no fool. He won't harm you until his enemy is captured."

"I never asked for this." I cross my arms, look away.

He faces me. "I know." The resignation in his tone is all too familiar. "Soon it will be over."

There's that word again. *Over.*

"There's a loophole."

My ears perk.

"The bond can be broken. The connection was made with your child's soul, not your adult one . . . two very different things. If the tie isn't made whole, the vow is annulled when you come of age. As long as you don't return what's been given, your connection with the vessel will break when you turn eighteen. His life will no longer be in danger on threat of yours."

"Return what's been given?"

His lips twitch. "A Kiss of Infinity, or more commonly known to you as 'the kiss of true love.'"

Okay, Ursula. I roll my eyes.

"Kisses hold their own power. They create a bond between

two people no matter their age. Children, adults—a kiss is a kiss, because love doesn't change. It matures and grows, but it's one of those constant things that can't be explained. It just is. The kiss that gave you the mark was the rarest and most powerful of kisses, more potent than a Kiss of Accord—"

"Whoa, back up."

"Don't ever give someone a Kiss of Accord unless you're prepared to bear the full weight of your bargain."

"Gage said something about a Kiss of Accord last night. What is it?"

"There are different kinds of kisses, some stronger than others. The Kiss of Accord creates a physical tie. One only death can break. It's a contract. If you seal a promise with a Kiss of Accord, a life link is forged. Break the promise and you die."

Stormy's pleas make sense now. She must've given Gage a Kiss of Accord. Why else would she betray us? And Haman. Is that what he gave Isabeau? If so, Mom's in more danger than I thought.

From the corner of my vision, I spy the road leading out of the Village. Will Makai know where to find us? Has he gone ahead of us to the Haven? "And the Kiss of Infinity?"

"A kiss as rare as it is powerful." Reverence coats his tone. "Rare because very few people have the capacity to love that deeply, with no regard for their own life or well-being. Powerful because it binds two souls on such an intimate level, they become indistinguishable from one another—but only if the link is complete."

"So as long as I don't give the king a Kiss of Infinity before my birthday, I'll be free to leave?"

"Yes."

"And Mom and I can go home?"

His teeth grind. "Yes."

It's what I've wanted from the beginning, isn't it? But Joshua's confirmation adds finality. Can I really move on, live a normal life in the Third after everything I've witnessed?

"But until then you must be on your guard. If you give a Kiss of Accord or Infinity before your eighteenth birthday, you'll place the vessel in danger. He made a promise—his life for yours."

His life for mine? I can't understand this. My own father didn't want me. Joshua—*inhale*—doesn't want me. But the one person who can save the Second from Crowe and the Void is the same person who would die so I can live? Why? There must be some ulterior motive. Something the vessel gains. It can't simply come down to love. No way.

"If you link your life to another," Joshua continues, "and they die, you would die. And if you die—"

"—the vessel dies." So I was right. I *am* dynamite. A death trap for anyone who comes too close.

Joshua squeezes his eyes shut. "You belong to him." Opens them. "To him and no one else. For now, at least. My hope is this won't be the case much longer."

The words sink deep. Ky's term for me is clear. If I belong to the true king, I really am a princess.

"Which is why you can't just go throwing yourself at anyone who gives you attention."

His chastisement stings. Is this really what he thinks of me? "If a Kiss of Infinity is as rare as you claim, I wouldn't worry. And no way am I giving anyone a Kiss of Accord after what happened last night with Stormy."

"You don't understand." He glances left. Right. Lowers his voice. "Unlike a Kiss of Accord, a Kiss of Infinity isn't something you decide to bestow. It comes from the deepest part of your soul. Stems from desires and emotions you may not even be aware you possess."

I bite my lower lip. I know exactly what I desire. "The only person I want to be with is you."

He doesn't hesitate a breath before he says, "No."

Ouch. "Why not? You said after I turn eighteen I'll be free."

"You will be free. I will not."

"But—"

"Don't do this, Eliyana." He shakes his head, stares at the sky. "What you're asking, it isn't possible." A curl of hair by his ear catches the light. Dark, dark blue, almost black, blending with his natural color. How did I miss that before?

"I need to hear you say it, Joshua." I step closer, crossing the force field he's constructed around himself these days. The same one I put up after I thought Mom died. It's as if Joshua and I have switched places.

"My duty is to the Verity and its vessel. To the people. The rightful king. That means ensuring your safety until your birthday. Nothing more." His dynamic tenor is gone, replaced by an unrecognizable, droning lament.

Why won't he look at me? It can't all have been a lie. Our afternoons on the roof. That night on Broadway's stage. The way he held me in the subway. "Say it." My teeth grind so hard my jaw pops.

He takes a lengthy breath. With shoulders straight and head erect, he looks me square in the eyes. "I. Do. *Not*. Love. You." Joshua holds my stunned stare, chin high.

"What wounds the heart only serves to make it stronger."

If Mom's words are true, I'll be Hercules after this.

I step back, dizzy, the landscape tilting sluggishly. It's as if this is a scene in a movie playing in slow motion. If this were a montage, the music would be dark, depressing, falling like forever rain. I force myself not to lose it. Steady now. "If that's how you feel, I guess this is good-bye." I hold out my hand, waiting.

He takes it. "Good-bye, Eliyana." Our hands fall away. Separating. Dividing. Creating a permanent chasm that can't be bridged.

"One last thing," I say. "How do you know so much about this?"

He flattens his lips. "I have my sources." He moves to go, then pauses when we're shoulder to shoulder. "Gather your things—we're leaving within the hour. We've been here too long. Kyaphus was right. We should've gone straight to the Maple Mines last night." He walks back inside. The door clicks closed. The end.

This is it then. I have to let him go. I'll do what I must, return to the Haven, and hide out until my birthday. What's two more weeks? Mom is the only thing that matters, my final goal.

Joshua is nothing more than a memory now. "Somebody That I Used to Know."

❧

I wait the full hour until I head inside. Joshua, Kuna, Stormy, and Lark converse quietly in the sitting room to the right. I pass them, aiming for the stairs. The front desk is vacant, Grizz nowhere to be seen. Ky tromps down the steps, carrying two packs. One is his, made of fading brown leather. The other appears to be—

"Ky," I gasp. "Are those my jeans?"

He grins. Hands me the denim pack. There's a heart-shaped pocket on either side, the remainder of the seat of my jeans. Sloppy and uneven stitches bind the sides, but a tug proves my new purse won't be falling apart anytime soon.

"Did you make this?" I turn it over, tracing the seams, then thread an arm through the straps on the back. I should be furious. He cut up my favorite pair of faded blues without even asking me first.

"You need your own pack. You can't expect me to be your carrier boy forever. Open it."

I lift the top flap, crafted from the end of one pant leg, and peer inside. My Third Reflection shirt and underthings rest at the bottom. I blush, picturing Ky holding my bra and underwear. Moving on. Besides my clothes it contains the vial of Illusoden, a canteen, the hair and tooth brushes from the washroom, Mom's sketchbook-slash-journal, and my cracked, lifeless phone.

"You grabbed my cell from the gutter?"

"I wanted David to be able to track you to the Pond. Wasn't sure if you'd want it back."

Ky has no idea my treble-clef necklace was the real tracker. I'd give anything to have it back. Still, I appreciate the gesture, so I say, "Thanks."

"There's something else too."

I move my phone aside. Is that . . . ? The copper jean button bearing an engraved rose is tied to braided cords.

I should be fuming. Instead, a lump forms in my throat.

"Don't worry." Ky's cheeks redden. He can stare at a buck-naked girl without blinking, and *this* he blushes at? "Stormy collected your things from the washroom and packed them. I just added the stuff on top."

He reaches into the bag and withdraws the button necklace. He brings the homemade jewelry to my neck, a bandage wrapped around one of his fingers. Did he prick himself as he sewed? He leans in to tie the cord at the back, and I inhale his earthy scent. The button tilts to one side at my collarbone.

"There." Ky draws back, but his touch lingers on my skin a second longer than necessary. "I know how upset you were when you lost your other necklace at the Threshold. I figured you needed a replacement. It's one of a kind. Like you."

Heart. Beats. Fast. If Christina Perri only knew.

My birthday isn't for another two weeks. Afterward I'll be free to start over. Move on. Not anytime soon, but . . . someday.

I touch the rose button, a near mirror image of Ky's Shield tattoo. When I turn eighteen, my spell will break. Like the Beast in my favorite fairy tale, could I also learn to love again?

ACT III

something
There

unsure

We've been back at the Haven for most of the day. We had zero trouble on our journey south. The recesses of my abdomen churn. Shouldn't Mom and Makai have joined us by now? Our delay at Wichgreen Village would've given them time to catch up. And what about Jasyn? Why hasn't he sent his men after me? Something's rotten, and it's not the undigested beets we ate for breakfast.

It took us five days to make it to the island by way of the Maple Mines. Five days of worrying and wondering if I'll ever see Mom again.

What's taking Makai so long?

Stormy and I are on friendish terms now. I was right. She did give Gage a Kiss of Accord. Kuna still has no idea what transpired, only that Gage is a traitor and Ky proved he is not.

"It happened a long time ago," she shared.

It was our second night in the mines and her shift to keep watch. I couldn't sleep, anxiety crazing my thoughts. So I just lay there and listened, staring up at the root and dirt ceiling.

"Kuna and I have always been sweethearts. We married young, trained as Guardians together. He's my best friend. I *love* him." She paused then, as if wanting that piece of information to sink in. As if needing me to believe its truth. "When I met Gage, there was something different about him. He had this magnetic kind of attraction, you know? I fooled myself into thinking friendship was the only thing between us. That spending time with Gage didn't hurt anyone." She hung her head. "I was wrong."

"A few months back I tried to end things with him," she continued. "At first he seemed to understand, but several days later he came to me in a rage." Stormy lifted her right hand to her cheek and shuddered. "He . . ." She sobbed. Shut her eyes. "He begged me to come away with him. When I refused, he threatened to kill Kuna and tell everyone how I'd been unfaithful. I couldn't bear it . . ."

"So you made a promise sealed with a Kiss of Accord."

She opened her eyes then. Nodded as she stared with a blank expression at nothing. "He'd keep our secret and wouldn't touch Kuna in exchange for three favors. Anything he asked I'd have to do until my debt was paid. The other night in Wichgreen Village was favor number one."

With the burden her words carried and the sorrow weighing her tone, I knew her cries the night at the Village didn't stem from guilt alone. Part of her cared for Gage. As much as it hurt her to keep her promise to him, I think it also caused her pain to see him go.

It makes no sense, and yet it does. Which is why I have to talk to Joshua again. As clear as he's made his feelings and as much as it hurts to be near him, I can't leave things this way. We have too much history to end on sour terms. My birthday is just over a week away. Once Makai returns with Mom—and he *will* return with her—we'll be free to go the moment I leave childhood behind. I may never see Joshua again. If I'm going to move on, I need a proper good-bye, not one hanging on the end of an argument.

Robyn helped me hitch a ride to Joshua's trome while I avoided her dozens of questions about the Verity's vessel.

"Do you feel anything? Does the king's soul call to you? Do you think you'll find him soon?"

How could I tell her all these years her savior's been hidden, refusing to come forward because of me?

Joshua hasn't spoken a word to me since we arrived at the Haven's border this morning. Scratch that. He hasn't spoken to *me* at all since we left the Village, relaying messages through Ky as if I've suddenly gained my uncle's invisibility.

Ky, on the other hand, has hardly left my side. By day he's been the perfect Guardian. Alert. Professional. But by night, shadows and moonlight performing their close-knit tango around us, he's become more than my protector. He's sweet and kind. My friend. I urged him to get some rest. He's exhausted, hardly allowing himself an ounce of sleep since we left the Village.

"We're safe inside the Haven now," I insisted. "What could possibly happen?"

He eyed me but finally relented, agreeing to get a few hours' sleep as long as I promised not to go far.

Now I ride along the gravel-paved road in the bed of a horse-drawn cart, leaving the Haven's "inner city" and entering what Robyn calls the Fringes. The late-afternoon sun blinks at me between the branches. The Haven is grander than it appeared on my first encounter. From above, the Second Reflection skyline looked so much like home. But the more I explore this strange land, the more I realize how truly different it is. In the Third, New York is merely a city, a dot on the map. In the Second, it's as if Mom's painting is the entire world. Haven Island could be its own state. A Rhode Island or a Maryland, but a state just the same.

Hopefully Ky won't consider a visit to the Fringes "far."

I pull out Mom's journal to pass the time. Find the dog-eared page where I left off last night.

Twenty-Eighth Day, Eleventh Month, Third Year of Jasyn's Reign

I suck in a breath. If the Second's months match up with the Third's, this entry was penned in November. The day after my birthday. Nine months after Mom turned sixteen.

*My sweet baby girl sleeps between my bent knees. It has become
impossible to stop staring at her. This love is beyond anything I
have experienced. It hurts and brings joy in the same breath. It's all-
consuming. For the first time, I am at a loss for words.*

My throat closes. Eyes water. I trace her cursive with the tip of
my finger. *I love you, Mom.*

*Tiernan's ~~rejection~~ absence is painful, but I cannot focus on my heart-
break. ~~Our~~ My daughter needs me. And I need her. We have each other.
Even if I never see Tiernan again, my heart will mend.*

A list of names embellishes the bottom of the page, along with
a tiny sketch of a baby's face. *My* face, birthmark free. Which means
the king hadn't kissed me yet. When did Mom meet him, and where?

I add the questions to my mental save-for-later list and peruse
the names. Almost every one is crossed out. Some are circled and
then scribbled over. The only name without an *X* is mine. I smile.
Thank goodness she decided against Peartree. I never would have
lived that down in school.

I stash the journal just as the cart drops me at the brink of
a long row of colorful dwellings. Cottages, tromes, cabins, huts.
Each unique. The perfect subject for one of Mom's paintings. Her
life was orderly, structured, everything in its labeled drawer. But
not her artwork. On canvas she showed who she wanted to be.
Free and fun. Living in splashes of color and freehand lines.

I shoulder my pack and meander down the peaceful dirt lane.
The quiet fits Joshua, really. I love the city, the lights, the noise.
Joshua was never into it. He took every opportunity to escape the
crowds. Now I see why. He's a country boy in the truest sense.

I pause at the trome with a faded blue door at the path's end.
It's just as Robyn described it. If this were Manhattan, Joshua's
trome would be an East Side high-rise.

I take a breath, stalling. Unsure. No reason to be nervous. This is Joshua. He was my next-door neighbor for three years. I will not let him intimidate me.

Rap, rap.

Movement inside. *Shuffle. Creak.*

The door swings inward. Really? He couldn't have taken two seconds to put his shirt on before answering? I've never seen him this way. Not even when we took a mini road trip to the Jersey shore last summer. I didn't question it. I'm not the bikini-wearing type, and I just assumed a preference for modesty was something we had in common. Now I know. He was hiding the sword and arrow Guardian tattoo. Just another of the many secrets he's withheld. I can't see his back, but I'm betting he has a mark there, too, one it's more important he keep concealed. What is an Ever's symbol? Ky never said.

The line between his eyebrows gullies deep. He removes the black shirt slung over one shoulder, shakes it out, and slips it on. "What are you doing here?"

I step inside without waiting for an invitation. "Hello to you too."

He shuts the door, and I crane my neck, looking up into the hollowed-out, windowless tree. Rather than separate floors as in other tromes I've visited, Joshua's houses a single spiral staircase, coiling to an opening in the fifty-foot ceiling. Did he build this himself? Was his love for architecture real? I grasp the thread of truth. Maybe he's not completely lost to me.

He clears his throat. "El, you aren't supposed to be here. Where's Kyaphus?"

I brush my fingers along the slick, varnished stair rail. "Resting." I cross my arms. Force myself to look at him, to act normal. "Have you heard anything from Lark?"

"If I had you would've been the first to know."

Apparently Lark is a rebel hiding out in neutral territory. It's why she attacked Gage. Joshua says she's the eyes and ears—and wings—connecting the Haven to the goings-on in the castle. She even had proof, revealing a wispy violet tendril curling at the nape of her neck. Turns out a blue or purple strand of hair marks those who remain loyal to the Verity. What about Grizz or the rest of the Village? Are they on our side too?

When we left, Lark offered to fly to the castle and see if she could spot Mom and Makai on their way. It helped ease my growing concern, but not much. "What's taking so long?"

Joshua closes his eyes, opens them. "This isn't a video game, El. I can't just skip a level, hop through the secret door, defeat the bad guy, and rescue your mom. This is the real world."

A half laugh, half cry spurts from my lips. "Ha. The real world? Trolls and sea monsters? Castles and kings? This place is nothing but a figment of some Grimm brother's imagination."

He narrows his eyes. "Which do you think came first? The Second or the Third?"

"You tell me."

He exhales, and his stiff posture slackens. "Come on. I want to show you something." Joshua passes me and ascends the stairs.

I follow. When we reach the opening, I climb out onto a circular platform nestled within the tree's crown. Massive branches curve out, up, and over, forming a perforated canopy. Rows of empty planter boxes spread before me. But my awe is not drawn by the everyday rooftop garden. What's above the platform stills me, parts my lips.

Another stairway, this one carved right into a wide branch, leads to a higher landing. Joshua continues the climb, and again I shadow him. A railing borders the entire space, and a huge unmade bed dominates the open room, too large for just one person.

I falter. Does Joshua have a girl here? Is she the reason he said he's not free? I cross to the trunk at the bed's foot and sit, running my trembling hands over my lap. "This is amazing. Do you live here alone?" Be obvious, why don't you?

"I do."

So it isn't a girl. Hope falters. Guess he really doesn't love me.

"Before I met you this was my home. It's strange to return after so long." He laughs. "It's exactly as I left it." Joshua turns, climbs another set of carved-out steps.

I rise and trail him, taking in every inch of his surrounding creation. The intricately detailed bedposts. The care he took to carve each step, to design every inch of the layout.

When I reach the third and final floor, my breath snags. Hollowed logs turned on their ends edge this platform. Shelf upon shelf bursting with books fit inside. Instead of the natural branch-and-leaf canopy like the two floors below, a glass roof covers this space. I walk alongside the shelves, scanning the volumes. *Peter Pan. The Hobbit. Pride and Prejudice. Anne of Green Gables. The Catcher in the Rye.* My eyes widen at the familiar titles.

"Where did you get these?" I pull out *La Belle et la Bête*—the original French version of *Beauty and the Beast*. I always wondered what would've happened if the Beast hadn't transformed. Would Belle have loved him anyway? I like to think so.

"All the most imaginative minds from your Reflection lived in mine first. For example, C. S. Lewis was a Scrib's apprentice before the young author ventured into other Reflections. It was in the Third where he met another Scrib, one who was also born here but lived in a different province. Ultimately the two became very close due to their mutual origins."

I lose a breath. "J. R. R. Tolkien."

Joshua nods.

I almost laugh, but how can I? Of course men who traveled through a portal, such as a Threshold, or experienced the wonder of the Callings would write fantasy novels featuring magical wardrobes and powerful rings.

Joshua withdraws a tattered journal from a high shelf. Hands it to me.

I return *Beauty and the Beast* to its home and examine the other book, tracing the familiar cursive on the flimsy leather cover. *The Reflection Chronicles*, First Account, E. K. C.

I don't believe it. The initials on Makai's handkerchief. I didn't know who they represented before, but now it's clear. E. K. C. Elizabeth. Katherine. Crowe. She must've changed her last name to Ember in the Third to keep us hidden.

"This is my mom's handwriting."

"I know."

I blink once, twice. "Where did you get this?"

"I never knew my parents. My mother died during child-birth . . ." There's a tinge in his voice, a bitterness. Is this what Haman was referring to when he called Joshua a murderer? Does Joshua blame himself for his mother's death?

He clears his throat, his Adam's apple dipping. "I'm told my father was so heartbroken he died soon thereafter."

I've never seen him so vulnerable. A sudden inkling rises inside me. I should go to him, hold him the way he held me after I lost Mom the first time. But I can't. He'd never let me.

"Your grandfather, Nathaniel Archer, delivered and raised me. Makai is like an older brother." Joshua has never spoken of his life before moving to Manhattan. "Nathaniel and Makai helped your mother escape with you to the Third. You were supposed to remain there, none the wiser to the significance of your mark or your eighteenth birthday. Crowe's discovery of you changed all that, of course.

"Your mother left this with Nathaniel when she fled." He gestures toward the journal I'm now clutching like treasure. "Once I was old enough to leave his care, he gave me this volume. I came here, to the Haven, to train with the Guardians. But it wasn't until I joined Makai in the Third that I found my niche in combat."

His comment strikes me, and I realize I've never seen him fight. Is he an archer like Makai and Preacher? A knife fighter like Ky?

"All I ever wanted was to serve the Verity, to see its vessel put on the throne. When Makai assigned me to you, I had no idea what to expect. Then I saw you that first day, and I knew who you were. It was then I realized just how important my task was."

He tells of our first encounter as if reminiscing with an old friend. Is he as fond of the memory as I am?

"Anyway." He leans on a bookcase, crossing his legs. "I'd like you to take it. Elizabeth would want you to have it."

I lift the book to my nose. Inhale. "She's a Scrib, isn't she?"

Joshua nods.

All this time I never knew. I picture Mom. This Reflection depicted—no, recorded—in her artwork. Her crossword puzzles and piles upon piles of sketchbooks. Urging me to write down her adages. Repeating them to me over and over and over again.

I slide the book into my pack, careful not to tear the curling pages. "Thanks." I want to add I miss him. That I hate this weird thing we've become. Instead I let it be. This moment—it's the perfect way to say good-bye. "I'll see you around?"

He nods but doesn't smile. "See you."

I hold out my hand.

One long inhale, and then he takes it.

Unlike our curt handshake at the Village, rushed and forced, this one feels like a true ending. Sad but real. Then the mood between us shifts. He doesn't let go, and neither do I. Joshua strokes the inside of my wrist with his thumb. It's a brief thing, but the infinitesimal gesture says so much, reminds me—

His eyes flick to a spot below my chin. "What's that?"

Huh? Oh . . . My fingers graze the button necklace at my collarbone. "Ky made it for me." I've been wearing it since we left the Village. Is he just now noticing?

"What happened to the one I gave you?"

Does he have any idea how much it broke my heart when I lost his gift? If he did, would he care? "I lost it."

Joshua's eyes darken. "Probably for the best. Once you return to the Third, I won't need to track you anymore." He stiffens and pulls away. "If I hear anything from Lark, I'll let you know." He turns around, a cue my welcome is worn.

I nod even though he's not looking at me, our perfect good-bye now ruined. I creep down the steps and leave the way I came.

Unsure.

⤫

The cart driver waited for me, something no cabbie would do without guaranteed payment. He drops me at the Physic's cabin, but Robyn and Wade aren't here. And where's Ky? He was crashing on one of the hammocks. Now all are vacant.

The road of shops, bustling with activity only hours ago, is now void of life. Where is everyone? Panic swells. This is bad.

Pop, pop, pop.

I'm running, tripping, hauling my way through streets, only stopping to breathe when I can't stand not to.

And then I see them. A crowd gathered in a clearing just ahead. Someone's shouting. Another is wailing. What in the—?

A hand fastens over my mouth, dragging me back, down to the ground. I kick and claw. But then my captor comes around and faces me. *Breathe. It's only Ky.*

He lifts his hand. Puts a finger to his lips.

I nod, afraid to as much as blink.

Ky clutches my hand like a lifeline, and together we slink under the cover of the trees, keeping a wide berth between us and the mob. He leads me to an outcropping of boulders.

I peer through a crevice at the horror scene ten feet away. Soulless dot the area, weapons in their possession ranging from swords and machetes to shotguns and crossbows. One guard restrains Wade, presses a jagged knife to his throat with a black-veined hand. Wade's arms are pulled tight around his back, his contorted face an agonized version of his former persona.

Beyond him Haman stands with his back toward us, a handgun aimed at the ground. No, not at the ground. At an owl.

Lark.

"I will execute one rebel every hour until you relinquish the girl. Do not think His Sovereignty will be fooled. Once we have her, you will be free to live in peace."

The crowd falls silent. My heart aches. These people don't even know me, yet they would die before they'd turn me in to Haman?

But it's not really me they're protecting, it's their king. How could I forget?

I train my eyes on Lark. She's just lying there, unmoving. Is she already dead? I squint, zeroing in on her middle. *Up, down. Up, down.* She's breathing. Not dead. Yet.

Haman's particular Shield Calling didn't work on Wren when she rescued us from the bridge. What did Ky say? Shields can only affect someone in human form? Must be the reason for so many guns—to compensate for the limits on the Callings. Did Jasyn send his assistant into the Third for the modern weaponry? I remember Haman having a gun, but this—

Ka-chick. He cocks the gun.

No. This is happening too fast. We need more time.

"One!"

I lunge forward, but Ky wrestles me back, wraps his arms around me, locking me in place.

"Two!"

"Use your Calling," I beg Ky. "Paralyze him! Make him stop!"

"I can't. Shields can't affect other Shields, remember?"

"Your knife then."

"No. I won't jeopardize our position."

I cover my mouth to stifle sobs.

Before Haman reaches three, a section of the crowd parts. Robyn in tiger form bolts into the clearing, charges Haman.

He re-angles his gun just as she pounces. "Three."

An earsplitting growl. *Thud.*

Robyn's blood stains the ground.

TWENTY-FIVE

I Didn't See It

Tears. Snot. Spittle. Bodily fluids seep from my eyes, my nose, my mouth. I suck them back. Only blood is missing. The blood I should've shed. The blood Robyn didn't deserve to.

That murderous, good-for-nothing—I'll kill him. I don't know how or when, but somehow I'll find a way.

"Revenge looks sweet on the outside, but its center is full of worms."

Enough with the adages, Mom. Silly little sayings won't bring Robyn back. I have to do something. No one else can be harmed because of me.

Cursed birthmark. Haven't you caused enough trouble? Mom. Joshua. Ky's sister. Did you have to take Robyn too?

I squirm and Ky squeezes tighter. He puts his mouth to my ear. "We have to go, Ember. She's gone. You can't save her."

How can he be rational? A girl just died for Verity's sake!

The Soulless holding Wade releases him. The Physic stumbles to Robyn's side. She's transformed back into her human self, no longer alive to retain her feline state. Wade removes his jacket. Drapes it over her naked, lifeless body.

My stomach clenches into a fist. I can't watch this. I twist, pressing my face into Ky's shoulder.

"I'm sorry, Em." He whispers the shortened version of his nickname for me with more tenderness than I've ever heard him use. "But we have to go."

I pull back. Golden flecks I never noticed before dance in his green eye. I shake my head, hysterics rising. "We have . . . *sob* . . . to get . . . *sob* . . . Joshua." I inhale, exhale, bite my lower lip. "His blood . . . *sniff* . . . can save . . . *sniff* . . . her." And what about the others? Lark, Kuna, Preacher, Stormy?

Ky's mouth turns down as he rubs little circles on my back. "If David revealed his Calling, Haman would know what he is, and we couldn't place a worse weapon in Crowe's hands right now."

My knees buckle. Ky holds me up, the rock I so desperately need. "We have to at least warn him."

"David can take care of himself." Ky looks past me, eyes scanning, the Guardian in him shifting to full throttle. "He would want me to get you to safety."

Safety? Wasn't the Haven supposed to be safe? "But Haman could hurt him."

"If he gets the chance, but David's not stupid. He'll figure something out."

A scream severs the blip in this tragedy's reel.

I whip my head around. Through the boulders I see the human Wren wailing. She's on her knees, hovering protectively over her sister's form.

Lark transforms into her human self, takes Robyn's limp hand.

Wren scowls, pushes Lark away. "No, Mother. You do not get to mourn her."

Mother? Oh my—that's why Lark's name sounded familiar. Wade mentioned her. Robyn said she'd left.

Wade lifts his tunic over his head and lays it across Lark's shoulders. He helps her to her feet, holds her as if she never left.

Wren rises, a pillar of hatred and fury. "Where is she?" Wren screams. "Who's hiding her?"

My heart shrinks to my spine.

Haman chuckles.

The people lower their heads, not one meeting Wren's fiery glare.

She spins, her braid lashing her face like a whip. "How long before another innocent dies?" Her shoulders heave with each seethed word.

Two Soulless, weapons drawn, converge and shield Haman. Morons. As if he needs their protection.

Haman parts the guards as if opening a sliding glass door. He strokes his chin, steeples his long, bony fingers. "I do love a good revenge scene." His upper lip curls, revealing his silver tooth. "I'll strike a bargain with you, girl. You have one day to seek the girl and return her to me. During those twenty-four hours, I swear I shall not so much as snap my fingers near a rebel."

Captain Hook's voice echoes Haman's words in my mind. *"I have given me word not to lay a finger, or a hook, on Peter Pan."* Yeah. Right.

"Fine." Wren offers her hand. "I bind you to your vow."

Haman leans down and kisses the heel of her palm, just as he did with Isabeau. "By a kiss I am bound."

A Kiss of Accord. Has to be. But what could Haman possibly stand to gain from such a bargain? At least I know the rebels are safe for another day. If Haman breaks his promise, he'll die.

Soulless comb the streets, raid houses. Doors fly open and wood splits. Children cry. How long before the Haven becomes part of the endless night?

We duck behind trome trunks and crouch near cabin porches, two fugitives escaping arrest. I maneuver with ease, grateful for the Guardian uniform Stormy lent me. The pants are a little snug, the jacket a bit short. Still, it's better than a dress.

At one point Ky and I lie low in a patch of wild sumac. I can only hope it isn't poisonous. Our bodies press against earth as a Soulless passes just feet away. Ky tosses a stone against a tree to divert the guard, and we flee, twilight's shadows camouflaging our escape.

I don't know how long it takes to reach the wall enclosing the island. The wall built to protect. To keep. To guard. It's nothing but a farce. An elaborate trick constructed to make the people feel safe. How did Haman find it? The Haven is covered by trees, and the door is hidden—

Moan. We were followed. No wonder we didn't have trouble on our way here. Jasyn wanted us to succeed, to lead his men straight into the rebels' hideout.

When we finally stop, I hug my cramped middle with one arm and reach for the vine-infested wall with the other. "What's the plan?"

Ky kneels and knots his bootlaces, yanks the cuffs of his brown pants down to his heels. "You tell me. You're the one who's supposed to find the vessel. We could really use him right about now."

Crud. He doesn't know. What am I supposed to do now? Joshua would want me to hide, but it's obvious Mom isn't on her way. How can I cower when I know she needs rescuing?

Ky rises and gives me a sidelong glance, feeling around for the secret door in the wall. "Any inkling as to where the vessel might be?"

Should I tell Ky the truth?

"Em, did you hear me?"

"What's it going to be, brave girl? Time to choose for yourself the path you will take."

"Em?"

"I need to go back to the castle. Is there a faster way to get there? What about the Leviathan—Via? Can you get her to take us?" Cringe. My request sounds ridiculous.

He widens his stance. "She works for Crowe. He knows I

betrayed him. The only place Via would take us is the dungeons."
He folds his arms across his chest. "Want to tell me why you need
to return to the place I busted my butt to rescue you from?"

"My mom—"

"No way." Ky pounds his fist against the wall, smashing ivy
into stone. "*Crowe.* We'll be lucky to make it off the island. I guarantee Soulless swarm the beach on the other side. They'll kill me
without a thought. Take you straight to the castle, which is apparently what you want anyway. My Calling doesn't work on Soulless.
I can't control them any more than I could control Robyn's dead
body." He flattens his palm and rests his forehead on the back of
his hand. "I'm sorry. I know she was your friend."

Robyn's name stings like swallowed salt water, adding to the
helplessness curling over me like a tidal wave. I hardly knew her,
but yes, she was more of a friend to me than most.

Sigh. What now? We have no weapons, no defense. Ky has the
mirrorglass blade, but how much damage can that do?

I sit cross-legged, grabbing at my hair, picking out pieces of
leaf and twig.

"*Brave girl . . .*"

I'm sorry, Mom. I'm useless.

"*Peer beyond the surface.*"

Another of Mom's sayings, a tender kiss brushing the lip of
my soul.

I withdraw the book Joshua gave me from my pack, along with
the flashlight Ky stashed there a few days ago. I click it on and
begin thumbing through the pages. The beam dim, the batteries
dying. I'll have to speed-read.

Ky pauses his search for the door. Leaves crunch under his
boots as he shifts closer to me. "Is that a volume of *The Reflection
Chronicles*?"

"Yes."

"Whose account—?"

"My mom's." I bend into the old volume, willing my eyes to read faster than the light wanes.

The pages crinkle with each turn. *Flip. Flap. Flit.* I peruse the entries written in Mom's signature cursive. Yep. She was a Scrib all right. One chapter includes drawings and descriptions of poisonous versus safe-to-eat vegetation. Another lists the chronology of our ancestry five generations back. Still another records detailed descriptions of the Callings, paired with sketches of the tattoos. The space beside *Evers* is blank. I guess Joshua's kind really do keep themselves hidden. Even Mom doesn't know their symbol.

Come on. There has to be something in here we can use.

Ky moves down the wall a few feet, resuming his hunt.

Flip. Scan. Turn. When I reach the final entry, my breath catches. It's written on a loose slip of parchment, the handwriting smudged and sloppy, as if it were stuffed into the tome at the last minute. The top of the page reads "Mirror Theory." Beneath the title, a four-line poem is printed, followed by several paragraphs beginning on the front and concluding on the back. I study the words quickly, phrases popping out like flickers of light.

And there, at the end of the entry, is a drawing.

No. Way.

I read the paragraph three times over, trace the illustration with my fingertips. It's . . . beautiful. I didn't see it, but now—if this works, Ky and I could escape unscathed. I smile.

Thanks, Mom.

Ky rushes over. He must take in my sudden demeanor change because he asks, "What is it? What did you find?"

I clutch the pages to my chest. "Our ticket out of here."

⌀⌀

We were at the wrong part of the wall. The exit is another mile down. I see it now. Just looks like a big gap.

"Are you sure about this?" Ky hesitates at the façade.

"Yes." Brackish air fills my lungs. Before our sea monster encounter, the scent would've drawn me forward. Now I pause, wary. Do I really believe Mom's theory?

I guess I'm going to find out.

Ky heads through the opening first, then pulls me through.

Crud. Just as he predicted. Soulless camp where the tree line ends, about the length of a New York block away.

He intertwines our fingers and squeezes my hand. "We could go back, try to find a way around."

I draw a deep breath. Exhale with a shudder. "No. That'll take too long."

We move forward, staying undercover as much as possible as we head onto the beach. The tide has receded, the lapping waves a seemingly unattainable goal.

What am I doing? This is beyond stupid.

No. I'd trust Mom with my life. Which is exactly what I'm about to do.

We go unnoticed through the camp, hopping from tent to tent, sticking to the shadows. Several of Jasyn's men laze around a bonfire while others set up tiki torches at intervals, washing the beach in a ruddy glow.

My flesh crawls at the sight of them. It's like a horror movie, all charred veins and deadened stares. Some don't seem to be completely turned, like Gage. Their eyes normal, their skin still visible beneath the black vines.

Beyond the camp a massive ship fresh off the pages of a J. M. Barrie novel looms just offshore. Sea foam gathers where wood curves into water. *Hiss, spray, whoosh.* What are we doing? We can't steal a pirate ship. Even if the plan works—

Ky releases my hand.

I freeze.

"And where do you two think you're going?" a guard deadpans.

I face him, trying to mask my shock as I absorb the sight before me. I've never looked into Soulless eyes. I wish I wasn't now. They're completely clouded. The haze glassing them moves and swirls, as if permanent fog resides there.

Ky draws his knife, uses his body as a barricade, backing us away from the guard. "Anytime now, Ember."

I fumble with Mom's book in my sweating palms, shaking as I read the page again.

I lift my head and start to sing. My voice wavers, cold and cracking.

The guard halts his pursuit.

It's working. My melody grows stronger, surer.

He drops to his knees.

Other guards begin to notice and pursue. I keep at it. Sing as loud as I can manage, my alto hitting its range limit. We walk backward up the ship's ramp. I stop singing. Catch my breath.

"Do you have any idea how to drive a ship like this?"

"Drive? You don't drive a ship."

"I'll take that as a yes."

He shakes his head. "We don't have a crew. We're better off taking one of the lifeboats. Climb in and keep singing. I'll handle the rest."

One by one, Jasyn's army ignores us, acts as if we aren't here. I begin my song again. My throat begs for mercy, but I thrust the lyrics through. It seems like forever before the rowboat breaks water. Ky rows, and I sing until I can't see the sand anymore. I feel like a siren, but instead of drawing sailors to their death, I'm saving us from ours.

When I finally collapse onto a bench, I gaze at the stars overhead, brilliant in a new moon sky. How is it possible this Reflection holds the same constellations as my own? Yet another conundrum to add to the list.

"I don't believe it." Ky slows his rowing, hunches forward.

"Me either." I laugh, giddiness competing with sanity. If I wasn't afraid of capsizing, I would literally jump up and down.

Splash, slosh, splash. Ky works the boat forward, staring at me. "I've heard the legends." Ky ceases once more and raises the oars. *Drip, drip, drip.* Water trickles from wood to sea. "I always thought they were just stories. Fables my mother told to help me fall asleep." He resembles a country kid visiting New York for the first time. Awestruck. Eyes as wide as cymbals. "How did you know?"

I dig *The Reflection Chronicles* from my pack, flip to the last page, and raise it. "Because of this." I tap my finger against the sketch on the back.

Ky laughs. "I guess we need to change the name." He resumes rowing, his biceps flexing with each stroke.

"The name?" I pull my canteen from my pack and drink, the cool liquid coating my dry throat. I offer some to Ky.

"*Birthmark* is the wrong term." He raises the canteen into the air as if preparing to give a toast. "*Mirrormark* is more like it."

when we touched

M irror Theory. *Seventh Day, First Month, Fifth Year of Aidan's Reign . . .'* The *fifth* year of Aidan's reign?" I flip open Mom's sketchbook-slash-journal, scan the entries. Aha! There. She was thirteen in Aidan's thirty-fifth year as king. She couldn't have written this. It explains the torn page, the dissimilar texture of the paper. On first glance I assumed this had been written in haste, the handwriting simply not as tidy. But no. This cursive is different. The slant and formation. The loop on the capital *O*, the tail on the *y*. Even the *t* is crossed with a unique swish.

"Em, don't leave me hanging. Keep reading." Ky nudges my shin with the toe of his boot. He's stopped rowing, reclining on the boat's opposite end, knees bent and elbows propped on the bench behind him.

Licking my lips and taking a breath, I readjust my flashlight and continue to the poem.

"'Once upon a time is ne'er what it seems. And happily ever after oft a mere device of dreams. What wicked snares are vines, and thorns cause many throes. But peer beyond the surface; you may there find a rose. E. G. A.'"

"E. G. A.? Who's that? I thought the initials on your mom's book were E. K. C."

"They are." I pass him the paper, now slightly damp. The sea is serene, the shimmery surface lapping, flowing, swaying. Like a ballet, the water seems to have its own choreographed cadence. The waves glissade. The sea foam chassés.

"'Mirror [n. 'mir r]: 1. *One who possesses the seven Callings as previously defined in* The Reflection Chronicles, *Eighth Account, Dimitri Gérard.*'" Ky's voice is deep, his brows high. He reads with all the pomp and circumstance of Professor Henry Higgins from *My Fair Lady.*

"Give me that." I attempt to snatch it back.

He plays keep-away, dangling the paper over the boat's edge.

"Don't you dare." I try to sound serious, but my warning releases through a grin.

Straightening his shoulders and clearing his throat, Ky snaps the paper before his face and reads, "'*Origin: Unknown.*'" He peers over the sheet at me. "Well, that's helpful."

Eye roll. "Just keep reading."

"'Hypothesis: When bestowed by the Verity's vessel, a Kiss of Infinity imposes an unusual outcome upon the subject's soul. As always, two souls are bound either wholly or in part, depending upon the mutuality of said kiss. However, an additional change occurs due to the unique pairing of the Verity and the Kiss of Infinity, producing an entirely new Calling.'"

He lowers the paper again. "Whoa."

Whoa is right.

"Sounds like your bond with the vessel did more than guard your life. I can't believe you're really a Mirror."

My shoulders scrunch. "Maybe."

"What, maybe? Did you see that display on the beach? Because I did, and let me tell you, it was awesome."

"I know, it's just . . ."

"Just what, Em?" His tone flips from jocular to serious.

I rub my temples. "Why would Joshua keep this detail from me?"

The boat rocks as Ky climbs over the benches separating us and sits on the one opposite mine. Our bent knees touch. Our eyes meet. "I know you don't want to hear this, but I tried to tell you, Crowe isn't the only one with an agenda." When I don't respond, he adds, "But hey. Maybe David just didn't know."

"He knew." I bristle, clutch the board beneath me. "He's the one who gave me this book."

"Doesn't mean he read it." Ky shrugs. Places the "Mirror Theory" in my lap.

I smooth it flat and continue reading in silence, studying every word and syllable I missed on my quick perusal back at the Haven. Ky leans in, probably reading upside down. His hair tickles my forehead and our breaths mingle.

One, two, three, *breathe*, two, three, *focus*, two three . . .

Indications:

⇠ Conveys traits relating to, but not necessarily identical to, the other seven Callings. Strengths may manifest all at once or over time. May seem coincidental in the early stages, i.e., ability to defend oneself with no previous training (Shield), ability to recall past events in great detail (Scrib), etc.

This is the paragraph that first caught my attention. I recall kneeing Ky's groin, how it happened so fast, as if I didn't realize I was doing it. Then there are the memories of Mom's sayings playing over and over in my mind.

⇠ Quick-healing; medicinal remedies may wear off sooner than normal or be ineffective altogether.

The Illusoden. Is that why it didn't last very long?

Additional qualities:

⚘ Ability to employ any reflective surface as a Threshold, i.e.,
   water, glass, etc.

That's cool. I file the tidbit away.

⚘ Ability to perceive façades earlier than most with consistent
   practice.

Also cool. I flip the page over. Here we go.

Restrictions:

⚘ Only one Mirror may exist at any given time.
⚘ Mirrors can be affected by every other Calling, i.e., can be
   harmed by a Shield despite their own Shield ability.
⚘ May only pass through a reflective surface to a location
   previously seen.
⚘ May only transport one person at a time through reflective
   surface. Skin-to-skin contact required during transport.
⚘ May retain Calling so long as the connected vessel remains in
   possession of the Verity. Should the Verity transfer to a new
   vessel, the current Mirror will be bereaved of all abilities as
   expounded upon above. Should the soul bond break, the Mirror
   will be bereaved of all abilities.

Holy Verity, that's a lot to swallow. Sounds like my newfound
gift won't last much longer. When my bond with the vessel breaks,
I'll be average. Normal. Nothing special.

Seal:

❧ What is perhaps most fascinating about the Mirror Calling is the unique symbol in correlation with it. Unlike other Callings, this symbol is located on the face instead of the shoulder, relating directly to the force that drives a Mirror's abilities—song. A Mirror's song is by far her most powerful asset, not only igniting her strengths, but working as its own weapon. When honed properly, a Mirror's song could bring an entire legion to its knees.

An exact replica of my birthmark curves and winds at the entry's end. This is what sold me before confronting the Soulless. Seeing it here, with its delicate lines and strokes, the image is clear. I always gazed upon the mirrored, backward version in my reflection. Now I see it for what it is—a song. Note after miniature note weaves in and out of vine-like staff, jumbled, disorganized. On the beach I did my best to "ahh" the few bars I could make sense of. How much more powerful will this melody be when I decipher the pattern, learn the entire piece by heart?

I tuck my hair behind my ears. Stow the paper and Mom's books in my pack.

Ky returns to his side of the boat and my body relaxes. He grabs the oars. "What now?"

Great question. Can I really use any reflective surface as a Threshold? If so, I have a door to anywhere. I could jump ship, enter the castle, rescue Mom. We could go straight home. Be done with this place forever.

Except nowhere does E. G. A. give instructions on how exactly to do that. Do I simply start swimming, hoping I'll end up in the castle the farther I dive? Does my touch alter the surface? My mind? My song? A combination of all three?

Determination riding on my recent high, I ask, "How far to Lisel Island?"

❧

We're going to see my grandfather. Nathaniel gave this book to Joshua. Perhaps he can elaborate on E. G. A.'s theory. He's one of the oldest Physics alive according to Wade. If anyone can shed some light on this subject, Nathaniel's the one to do it.

I pass the time by perusing Mom's journal again. The next entry is dated nearly two months after her last one.

> *Twenty-second Day, First Month, Fourth Year of Jasyn's Reign*
>
> *Tiernan has changed. He rarely comes around since Eliyana's birth, but when he does he is distant. He refuses to hold his daughter, hardly glances in her direction. His behavior is unsettling. Tiernan talks of nothing but gaining a son—an heir. And when he does look at my sweet girl, there is a madness in his eyes. This is not the man I fell in love with . . .*

Ky still doesn't know how Tiernan connects us. Is Nathaniel aware of my father's adopted son? What will Ky's reaction be if he finds out?

> *. . . He is so easily angered now. Accuses me of giving all my attention to Eliyana instead of to him. He yells and screams. Sometimes he hits me, though, thank the Verity, he's yet to lay a finger on Eliyana. He says if I won't give him a son, he'll find one on his own . . .*

Ky. I glance at him beneath my lashes as he rows. Mom's journal only confirms what I feared. Tiernan's anger began with my birth. Mom wrote he was sweet and kind to her up until the day I came into this Reflection. If I had been a boy, he wouldn't have adopted Ky. If I had been a boy, Ky might've had a completely different childhood. A good and loving family. A life free of the pain he's endured.

What happens when Mom and I go home? Will I ever see Ky again? Is he just another character I'll have to kill off? One more number to cut when my link to the king breaks?

A new possibility forms, meek and fragile.

What if we stayed?

. . . *We have to leave. I must get Eliyana as far from her father as possible before Tiernan hurts her too.*

Once the boat stabilizes, I snap the book shut. Ky arches his back, interlocks his fingers, and stretches his arms over his head, palms facing the sky and knuckles popping. He makes a noise like brakes squeaking and says, "All ashore who's going ashore."

I scan the coast. Rocks jut at sharp angles like bayonets, ready to impale anyone who might be dumb enough to get too close. High above them, snowcapped trees similar to evergreens stand as soldiers at attention.

Ky starts toward the rocky slope. "Any idea where your grandfather lives?"

My knotted arms loosen, replaced by spiraling guilt. I omitted Nathaniel's last name on purpose. All Ky knows is I believe my grandfather can help me use my newfound Calling to find the vessel.

And save my mom.

"We're looking for a brownstone." I remove Mom's sketchbook-slash-journal from my pack. I flip to the page featuring Nathaniel, purposefully keeping my thumb over the caption bearing his last name.

Ky's brows scallop.

"What is it?"

He leans closer. "I think . . . I've seen this place before."

Oh, crud. He knows.

He shakes his head. "Weird. It kind of looks like your house."

"Yeah." I bite the inside of my cheek. "It does."

"Probably why it seems familiar, eh?" His tone is light, teasing. Like Mom when she's keeping a secret. The way she sounded the night she gave me my eighteenth-birthday cupcake. She told me to make a wish.

It did not come true.

I stow the book and exit the boat. Amendment. I *try* to exit the boat. Clumsy as ever, I catch my ankle on the lip and soar toward mud and murk.

Mr. Catlike Reflexes catches me by my hips, tows me into a hug. A briny aroma masks his natural scent. Water spots soak his shirt. It's similar to when we touched after he saved me from Gage, but also different. Other.

My vision clouds, my brain conjuring an alternate future. We stay. Make a home here in the Second. Mom and Makai can finally be together, unhindered by their need to protect the vessel. And me? I open up my heart to someone new.

I shake away the premonition. Focus. My top rides up my middle an inch. Ky's fingers graze the skin on my lower back, yanking me into the now. Heat floods my cheeks. Goose bumps freckle my arms. His breath grazes my forehead. His pulse thuds against my ear.

Before I can dissect and analyze these foreign feelings, he pushes me away. Not in the way Joshua does, as if I might bite. Ky's gesture is more . . . cautionary.

I repress another blush. Tug my shirt down.

"Let's get moving." He offers his hand, and I take it without hesitation.

We begin climbing the jagged mountainside, our boots slipping on slick stone. Ky assists me at the difficult points, but the higher I climb, the less help I need. I'm stronger than ever since crossing the Threshold. The initial ache following my overdue workout has worn off. My body has adapted to a life where everything isn't a short walk or subway ride away.

A few summers ago, the Central Park Conservancy held a youth event at the North Meadow Rec Center. They had free food, relay races, and to top off the festivities, a climbing wall. Mom thought it might be fun to go, and after much protesting, I finally agreed. She was right for the most part. I mean, who says no to free funnel cakes? But my joy over fried batter crowned in a mountain of powdered sugar and whipped cream didn't last when she insisted we scale the rock wall. It was awful. I kept losing my footing, and my hands developed blisters.

What a spoiled, sheltered life I had. Mom gave me everything. Did I ever thank her? Will I get another chance?

Ky reaches the summit first and lugs me up next to him.

I lean over. Laugh through deep breaths. I did it.

"Invigorating, isn't it?" He holds his arms to his sides, closes his eyes, and inclines his head back. He's more king of the world right now than Leo could ever be.

I straighten, brush my sweaty bangs off my forehead despite the glacial temperature. "I can't believe I've lived my whole life without experiencing that."

He lowers his arms and looks at me, laugh lines lifting his cheeks. "That's nothing. One day I'll take you to Pireem Mountain. Show you what a real climb feels like." He points northeast, and I'm surprised I know the direction. Guess I'm more oriented with this new Reflection than I thought.

Though it's dark, I can make out the faint outline of a distant summit. "I seem to recall you being afraid of heights."

"Nah."

I raise an eyebrow.

"Okay, flying maybe. A little. But a climb is different. You'll see. It'll take your breath away."

My smile fades. Ky's does too. Unanswered questions fester. What if I leave? What if I stay? Does Ky feel the shift taking place between us? The prospect of something more? Then again, I was wrong about Joshua. Maybe Ky is just acting, doing whatever he has to in order to give me a sense of safety, protection, love.

No. I refuse to let Joshua's actions dictate my emotions. At some point I have to learn to trust again. "Where to?"

He nods toward the forest. "Seems a good place to start."

Coniferous trees stack before us like fence planks. We weave through their labyrinth, scooting sideways between the slots separating the ebony trunks. Bark and needles grab my clothes, my hair. It's almost as if these trees were planted close together on purpose—a natural obstacle course discouraging hikers from breeching its border.

Sappy oxygen opens my airways. The forest isn't deep, but it takes extra time to maneuver because of its thickness. When we emerge from the brief pine infestation, a lone three-story brick home rises amidst heaps of ash and rubble. I swallow air. Hiccups emerge. There it is. So similar to home, yet so very far away.

Packed snow crunches beneath our steps as we creep forward. Our boots leave muddy grooves, marking where we've been. The brownstone looms over us. Dead ivy climbs the front and sides, coiling around the boarded windows like anacondas. The front door hangs off its hinges, a black abyss looming beyond.

Does Nathaniel really live here?

Ky takes the lead, withdraws his flashlight from his pack. I mirror the action, and we click our lights on at the same time. We mount the stairs, avoiding the wide cracks and debris, and step inside.

Cobwebs dangle from every corner. The unswept floorboards creak. Overturned furniture creates a maze, the path obscured by shredded cushions and broken bottles. Crooked picture frames hang at odd angles, like arrows pointing this way or that.

"Place looks deserted to me." Ky steps lightly, his boots crushing glass.

Never one for haunted houses, I stick close to his side. *Creepy* doesn't even begin to describe the eeriness of this place. "Let's search the house." Why am I whispering? No one's here. "Maybe we'll find something."

Ky snorts. "Yeah, like a dead body maybe?"

I slap his arm. "Not funny."

The floor plan is nearly identical to our house in New York, with only a few minor adjustments. A table where the open kitchen bar should be. A wood-burning stove instead of a fireplace in the sunroom. The wall separating the sunroom from the stairs and foyer is at least three times as thick as the one back home. In the hall, wallpaper and wainscoting replace brick, and the stairs are spiral instead of a straight shot to the upper floors. We meander through the house, each room filthier and more disheveled than the next.

When we reach the attic, I pause on the final step.

Ky keeps moving, seemingly unaware of my momentary hesitation. But then he stops. Turns around. Shines the flashlight in my face. "Everything okay?"

I shield my eyes and he repositions the beam lower. "Back home, this floor houses my mom's studio. It's just a little weird, that's all." Two deep breaths, a cough follows. Man, this place is musty. I will my feet to move and join Ky in a room crowded with old knickknacks and random antiques. A shadeless lamp. Rolled rugs. Shelves with rows and rows of snow globes, which should really be renamed dust globes for all the dirt settled on them.

We split apart, exploring the space like a couple of Goonies on a treasure hunt. I clutch my pack tight against my shoulder, cover a couple more allergy-induced coughs. I can hear Ky somewhere at the other end of the room, moving furniture and riffling through what sound like pots and pans.

When I reach the corner where Mom's art desk would be, I pause. A boarded window sits beyond the vacant space, an empty flowerpot resting on its sill. Beside the window is a tall object with an old sheet draped over it. I reach and the sheet floats to the floor, sending dust airborne in wafting clouds. I wave it away with my hand, blink a few times, and lift the collar of my jacket over my mouth and nose.

The object is a human-sized painting set in a gilded frame. Wait, no. Is that—?

My pulse is dead to me. I do a 360.

An elderly man wearing spectacles and a ratty bathrobe towers over me. His bulbous nose protrudes as if detached from his face, and his wiry alabaster hair sticks up at electrocuted angles.

I back away, nearly knocking over the mirror.

"Well, are you coming in or aren't you?" The British-accented man pivots and shuffles away. He pauses before a cushionless armchair acting as a bookshelf. Bending over, he lifts the chair to reveal a square hole in the floor.

Without pretense he steps into the hole and disappears into darkness.

TWENTY-SEVEN

IT CAN'T BE

L et me just say, following strange old dudes through holes in the floor is not my thing. Kids, don't try this at home.

Ky scrambles to my side, tripping over the corner of a half-rolled rug. "Was that him?"

I shine the flashlight into the opening. "Guess we'll find out."

We tread lightly down a narrow stairway, Ky in front and me behind. The steps are unfinished, the boards warped. Bent nails and splinters stick out like booby traps. At the bottom an ajar door waits, soft light leaking through its cracks. Ky places a finger to his lips, gestures for me to stay.

He approaches the door and peers inside.

I rise on my toes, leaning over his shoulder to get a better view.

On the other side is a narrow room with a high ceiling, a meager fire crackling in a mini hearth. After prodding blackened logs with an iron pole, the man occupies a damask armchair. "Well, what are you two lollygaggers standing around for? Either sit or don't, but do not be all evening about it, please."

I mouth, *"Lollygaggers?"* and Ky responds with a half smirk, half shrug.

"Where are we supposed to sit?" The man inhabits the only piece of furniture in the cramped space.

He shifts in his seat, eyes me over his half-moons. "You are your mother's daughter. Elizabeth had just as much tactlessness at your age. If the floor is not good enough for your royal rear ends, I suppose I could relinquish my chair."

My mother? He knows me? He must be Nathaniel. I move deeper into the room and sit cross-legged on a circular rug at his feet. Ky remains standing, holding up the wall behind me.

Nathaniel faces the fire again, and his shoulders slump. "What brings you to my door at this hour?" His voice is winter and fog, hibernating beneath years of solitude.

"We're here because of this." I retrieve the loose-leaf paper from Mom's book, pass it to my grandfather. I have so many questions for this man. About my father. About Mom. But none of those are important right now. "I was hoping you could explain how the Threshold thing works."

Orange embers spit onto the rug. Nathaniel stomps them out with a slippered foot and snatches the paper, examines it over the bridge of his nose. "Where did you get this?"

I produce Mom's account of *The Reflection Chronicles*.

He leans forward, the fire's radiance washing his wrinkled face in ginger light. "I can tell you one thing. That book and this entry were not penned by the same author."

I was right. He can help me. "Who's E. G. A?"

He removes an antique pocket watch from his robe. The heirloom is tarnished, in need of a good shine. He flips it open and rotates it toward me. One side contains a clock face, frozen where it last ticked. But the other half bears a silver dollar–sized photo of a cinnamon-haired beauty with a constellation of freckles and passionate blue eyes. And there, winding up the right side of her face in crimson tendrils, is what we have affectionately dubbed the mirrormark.

Aidan's queen. Has to be. Robyn said she had a mark like mine, one that linked her to the king as I am linked to him. Was she a Mirror as well? If so, what happened to her? The theory says only one Mirror can exist at a time.

Nathaniel snaps the watch closed, returns it to his robe, pats the spot where it rests. Bracing a hand on his knee, he cranes his neck. "I would know Queen Ember's handwriting anywhere."

"Queen *Ember*?"

Nathaniel reveals he has the ability to smile. "Your mother felt she needed a pseudonym if she was to hide from her father." A pause. "And yours."

I feel Ky's presence behind me. Please don't bring up Tiernan. Not here. Not now. Change the subject.

"So . . . ," Nathaniel continues, "Elizabeth donned dear Ember's first name as her last in hopes it would conceal her true identity."

I swallow, relief sliding to my core. "You speak as if you knew her personally."

He removes his glasses, then blows a hot breath on each lens. "Indeed. She was my student before she was ever my queen." He wipes the lenses with a corner of his robe. "After they moved from England to the States, my parents turned their home in New York into a boardinghouse of sorts." His spectacles return to their perch. "By then I was already grown and living in the Second with my wife and two boys."

Tiernan and Makai. My family history is coming together, shard by broken shard. Another peek at Ky. All Nathaniel has to do is say his sons' names, and then Ky will connect the dots. *Please don't say their names, please—*

"I'm getting ahead of myself. How I came to be here is a story for another time. Where was I?" Nathaniel taps his temple. "Ah yes. My parents. Originally from the Second, they sustained a deep reverence for the Verity and the Callings. When Ember came into their home, she was fourteen. No parents, no family to speak of. She even adopted our surname, Archer. Ember worked for them in exchange for room and board. I visited the Third often and got to know her. She had a sharp wit and a keen sense of intuition. No use lying to the girl. She would call you on it every time." He laughs at that, as if reliving a private memory.

A ghost of a smile haunts my lips. Despite the circumstances, I feel as if I'm getting a sense of who my grandfather is. Serious, yes. But also someone who cares for those closest to him. Maybe when this is all over, we might have a relationship. Family has always been singular to me—Mom. Perhaps it has the chance to be more.

"My parents and I taught Ember of the Reflections, the Callings," Nathaniel continues. "Rather than scoff at them or call them insane, she welcomed the knowledge. At sixteen she drank Threshold water, but a Calling never manifested. Still, she was eager to learn everything she could about the worlds beyond her own. Ember was twenty-five when my parents passed. It was the first time I brought her into the Second—the day I introduced her to Aidan."

A love story? My stomach flutters. I'm the sick kid from *The Princess Bride*. In the past I would've groaned at the mention of romance, knowing all too well it wasn't in my future. But now? Now I don't mind so much.

"Aidan had only just become the Verity's vessel," Nathaniel explains. "He was thirty and busied himself with matters of the Reflection—keeping the Void imprisoned his top priority. But when Aidan saw Ember, I knew something in him had changed." Is that a twinkle in his gray eyes? "When they kissed and Ember's mark appeared, I began my research. As I'm sure you may have guessed, there was little information regarding such a mark. The vessel preceding Aidan never found true love. There was, however, an account recording the stipulations of a Kiss of Infinity."

"E. G. A.'s—Ember's reference to Dimitri Gérard's account of *The Reflection Chronicles*." I twirl my shoelace around one finger, twisting until my circulation cuts off.

"The very same." He coughs but doesn't bother to cover his mouth.

So this is where Joshua learned everything—the source he mentioned. Nathaniel taught him about the kisses, the mirror-mark, all of it. Except I still don't understand what would motivate Joshua to conceal my gift from me. It makes no sense.

I wish he were here so I could ask him. Is he okay? Did he make it out of the Haven unseen? And what about the others? For the first time I realize I'm worried about more than just Mom and me. I do want the vessel to succeed in defeating Jasyn and the Void. Then my friends can stop hiding. Then the Second will be free.

"Yes." Nathaniel coughs, drawing me from my internal epiphany. Leaning forward, he folds his hands between his knees. "We soon developed the 'Mirror Theory' as is recorded on this page." He raises it to the light. "I must say, I thought you would have sought me sooner. After Ember passed, I tore this entry from her diary, stowed it in your mother's book. I thought it might help her prepare you for the path ahead. Of course, she wanted nothing to do with it, left the tome here and never looked back."

I switch positions, tuck my legs and feet beneath me. "So you gave it to Joshua?"

"He was your Guardian, was he not? I presumed if your mother refused to help you hone your gift, perhaps Joshua would. Unfortunately, he, too, was of the mind-set it would be better for you to remain ignorant. I doubt he even opened the blasted thing." Nathaniel harrumphs and crosses his legs. "Why I bother, I do not know. No one listens to an old man."

Lies. Too many to count. Joshua is one thing, but Mom?

"I'm sorry. I was wrong. I never should have kept—"

I hear her apology as if she's already given it. Kept what, Mom? The fact that my soul is the only thing detaining the savior of this Reflection from doing his job? Or how about the colossal detail I have this special gift, one I could've used to rescue you, had I actually known about it?

I retrieve Ember's theory from Nathaniel, resolve lifting me to my feet. No more hiding. No more fear. "Well, *I'm* listening. So how about you fill me in on how I can use that mirror up there as a Threshold?" I plant my hands on my hips. Enough wasting time. Enough wandering around, waiting for someone to dictate my next move.

Fingers steepled and gaze regarding the fire, Nathaniel says, "To understand the purpose of a Mirror, you must first understand the function of each Calling. Shields to defend. Physics to restore. Scribs to teach. Masks to serve. Magnets to provide. Amulets to keep. Evers to save." He taps out the list on his fingers.

Evers to save. Even though I know Robyn is gone, I can't help but hold a candle of hope Joshua was able to save her. She didn't deserve to die.

"What then is the purpose of one who possesses all the Callings?" My grandfather gestures to me, like a professor singling out an unsuspecting student.

Um . . . Mouth agape, I let my hands fall to my sides.

"I will pose another question. When did you begin to notice signs of the talents you possess? You have borne the mark since infancy, yet only now are seeking answers."

I bite my lip, consider his insight. When *did* I begin to notice a change? Shutting my eyes, I run the events of the past few weeks over in my mind. Mom's fabricated death. Joshua's rejection. My lashes flutter as I glance up at Ky. "When you followed me the night we met. I never thought I was capable of defending myself like that."

Ky crosses his ankles. "You definitely threw me off guard."

Wince. I shrink inwardly. "Sorry."

"There were other things too." Ky paces behind me. "I para-lyzed you with my Shield Calling, but the effect wore off within minutes. You survived Haman's gift much longer than I antici-pated. And the Illusoden. It didn't last. Then there was your display on the beach. It's as if you carry fragments, pieces of each gift that grow stronger each day." His tone smiles and sprints, his face becoming more animated with each word. "I'll bet when you turn eighteen and your Confine lifts, you'll be unstoppable."

Except I won't. Because my link will break on my birthday. Then this amazing gift I've only just discovered will be gone.

Nathaniel considers him. "What did you say your name was, boy?"

"I didn't."

I roll my eyes. "Ky. His name is Ky."

"Not much of a name," Nathaniel muses, adjusting his spectacles. "Short for something, perhaps?"

What is the point of this? I jut my chin at Ky, waiting for him to give Nathaniel the answer he wants so we can move on.

But Ky, with his arrogant smirk and popped brow, is getting a rise out of flustering someone, as usual.

I fling my arms toward the ceiling. "Ugh. His name is Kyaphus Rhyen. Can we continue, please?"

Nathaniel nods, seemingly satisfied with my answer. "The Verity feeds off your innermost strengths, just as the Void feeds off your weaknesses. Your desires mold your powers, so you must ask yourself—what do you crave most in the seven Reflections?"

I fold the paper once, twice, pressing the creases with my thumbnail and sliding the square between the pages of *The Reflection Chronicles*. My go-to answer is always Mom. I want her back. But it must delve deeper, right? Ky's story kisses my memory. How his Shield Calling stemmed from his need to protect others. What *do* I want? What have I *always* wanted?

It can't be so simple. Can it?

"Love." The single word is a confession. I've refused to admit it, tried my hardest to suppress it. But there it is, plain as the notes on my face.

"That," Nathaniel says, "is the right answer."

꧁ ∞ ꧂

My grandfather traces the mirror's carved frame. "I cannot tell you everything about the unique Calling you've been given, Eliyana. But somewhere deep inside you, distinctive aspects of each Calling reside. You must wait, see how they unfold."

Ky moves beside me, the attic floorboards groaning beneath him. He's been so silent. Patient. I could never repay him for his kindness.

"One day," Nathaniel says, "while still living in the Third, Ember wanted to see Aidan. They were engaged, but she had not yet moved from my parents' home. By then she had been given the mark and was only beginning to learn of its indications. It was her love for Aidan that made him appear in her reflection. That day, Ember stepped through the mirror."

Whoa. A real-life Alice in Wonderland.

"After they married, the castle became her home, but she still missed her old one terribly. The king would have done anything to make her happy, so he had a replica built, a whole row of them. He thought it would be more authentic. As you saw upon entering, mine is the only one left standing."

We have more than our Calling in common. Queen Ember caught homesickness too.

"They spent summers here. Ember loved this house." Nathaniel's mouth turns down. "This is where she died."

My heart hurts for him. His pain has been my own. "How?"

"Natural causes." He sighs, doesn't elaborate. "A part of Aidan died that day as well. He couldn't bear to be in a house where every nook and cranny reminded him of her. He left me in charge of it, along with her estate in the Third." Is this why the king vanished? Because he loved his queen so? "The home belonging to my parents. The one I assume you were raised in?" His eyebrow quirks.

I nod. So Mom had been telling the truth on that note. My grandfather really did leave us the brownstone.

He inclines his head in return. "This has been my home ever since. After the Revolution, the other residents burned their homes to the ground and fled, erasing all evidence of their former lives. Only I remained, but I couldn't very well stay out in the open with Crowe sniffing around for more people to add to his Soulless collection. Joshua and Makai have seen to it I am provided for. The hidden room has been my personal sanctuary for many years."

"Why didn't you go to the Haven with everyone else?" Ky asks.

Nathaniel eyes him. "I have my reasons. Which bring us back to the mirrors." He beckons me closer. "This is ordinary-looking glass to me, to your friend, but to you it is a gateway. As a Mirror, just like Ember, you have the ability to pass through any reflective surface and enter through another by merely thinking of it. Love empowers you. However, you will only be able to bring one person back with you. As you appear to have a new Guardian"—he inclines his head toward Ky—"is it safe to assume your previous Guardians are otherwise occupied?"

Sweat beads. Stomach knots. "Joshua is still at the Haven." I fidget with the strap on my pack. "But your—Makai . . ." A glance at the boy beside me. ". . . went to the castle in an attempt to rescue my mom." Breathe. "He never came out."

"That boy . . ." He shakes his head, mumbling under his breath. Straining to hear, I lean closer.

". . . has loved your mother since the day he helped her escape this Reflection eighteen years ago." His fingers twiddle against his cracked lips. "But with Elizabeth free, Makai should be able to use his Calling, become invisible. He shouldn't have trouble escaping once he knows she is safe."

Thank the Verity Nathaniel doesn't continue. Could he possibly know who Ky is? What Tiernan did to him?

I don't have time to ponder because Ky blurts out, "It's too dangerous." He brushes my arm with his fingers, traces all the way down to my hand. He takes it in earnest, turning me toward him. "As your Guardian, I cannot allow you to go into the castle alone."

"No." Nausea rears. "I can only bring one person through at a time. Getting Mom out will be tricky enough. I'm not risking leaving you behind." My protectiveness of him raises an alarm. Was it only last week I wanted nothing to do with him? "I'll be okay."

"What if you get caught?" He moves between me and the mirror, as if I might leave without him otherwise. "What then?"

"Jasyn won't hurt me. You *have* to let me do this. I need to make my life count for something." And to make up for all the times it didn't.

His lips press. Eyes narrow. Five droning beats. And then, "Not returning is a risk I'm willing to take. Either I go with you, or you don't go at all." His arms cross, his stance widens. Final answer.

I sigh. No time for arguing. "Fine."

"I knew you'd see it my way." He squeezes my hand.

Operation Save Mom has finally begun.

never Looked

So how does it work?" I flatten my palm on the mirror. Solid. Cold.

Nathaniel steps away, giving us room. "As I said, your desire will become your strength. Let the love you have for your mother empower you."

Without an utterance Ky unsnaps the sheath at his belt, offers it to me. "We should each carry a weapon."

"Ky, I can't take your mirrorglass knife."

"You can and you will."

"No. Give me the steel one—"

"Absolutely not. You've never stabbed anyone before." He grabs my hand, closes my fingers around the knife's hilt. "If you need to defend yourself, I will not have you second-guessing. The mirrorglass will ensure you follow through. Any wound you inflict will heal as long as you withdraw the blade. Don't hesitate."

"But your vow to never kill again—you can't use the steel blade."

"I'll be fine." He rolls his shoulders and faces the mirror. Conversation over.

"Thank you." I hook it at my side. The weighty addition is confidence and security. Next I pull my hair off my face, secure it with the leather tie around my wrist.

Now I'm ready.

"Don't thank me yet. We may be walking to our executions."

Uncertainty keeps my feet glued in place. If things don't go our way, I may not have a chance to explain about Tiernan. I want to say I'm sorry on my father's behalf. But I also want to know more about him. To ask if there was ever any good in him. From Mom's journal entries, it seems so. Could Ky have any positive memories of the man who raised him? No one can be all bad. Right?

But the questions expire before they reach my throat. With a deep exhale I face the soon-to-be Threshold. Close my eyes. Love is my strength.

My palm levels with the glass. I picture Mom, inhale through my nose. Let the notes flow free. Press.

Nothing.

Teeth clenched, I try again. Imagining the castle, its windows and doors. The courtyard and stables. The scent and the night and Jasyn's pitiful rose garden. The fountain frozen in time.

The mirror remains a mirror.

My song dies. "It's not working." Frustration bubbles. I let my hand fall, clenching it against my thigh.

"You must dig deep inside," Nathaniel instructs, waving his hand as if he's the conductor of this little experiment. "You cannot simply think it. You have to *feel* the music inside you." His fist covers his heart.

Feel it? "I *am* feeling it." Aren't I?

Ky puts his mouth close to my ear.

Can't. Breathe.

"Remember what you told me at the Village?" he whispers. "How lyrics are your way of expressing emotions?"

Since when did Ky begin to know me better than I know myself?

I swallow. Can he hear my heart rate switch cadence? "Yes."

"So sing your heart out." He returns my personal space.

My lungs expand. He's right. The perfect lyrics are everything. With one palm kissing the mirror and the other linked with

Ky's, I gaze into the reflection I've never truly looked at until now. Mom lives there. And Joshua. Ky, by my side now, found a place too. I'd do anything for them. How did I miss it? This entire time I've been closing myself off from love, but it's been the solution all along. I've built walls at every turn. No more. As with Queen Ember, drawn to her king from another Reflection, it isn't song alone that ignites my Calling, but love. True, unblemished love.

Now I sing for them. The words tumble forth as I pair them with my melody.

> *"Ashamed of the outside, I've never belonged.*
> *Hidden in shadows, I locked my heart away.*
> *But inside I was fading. Breaking. Dying.*
> *Now I'm a flame. My soul is igniting.*
> *Love is a fire. Burning. Refining.*
> *Its blaze lights the way. I am no longer afraid."*

The mirror shimmers. More than a song, these lyrics are a confession. I've changed. I'm not the girl who left Manhattan. No more hiding. No more fear. I am the rose beyond the thorns.

On the final line, the glass melts to liquid beneath my touch. And then I step through.

⁕

A cold burst of air pelts my skin as I drop to a hard floor. Hailstone-like tingles shoot through my hands, pinging my arms, my neck and shoulders. I flex my fingers. Look to the ceiling, spring to my feet, and whirl. Hyperventilated breaths labor my abs and lighten my head. To my right, an arched window no wider than my arm from elbow to wrist.

Oh my soul, I did it. I turned the mirror into a Threshold.

Ky rises beside me. "That was weird." He brushes off his pants, checks for the blade at his ankle, tightens his bootlaces. "Like being sucked through a vortex or down a drain."

Impossible to suppress my grin. It really was. What a rush.

Beyond the window night capes a villainous sky. I press my face to the glass. It's the castle all right. There's the Forest of Night. But where in the castle are we, exactly? This tower is similar to the dungeon stairwell, stone curving along spiral steps. We're high, at least three stories aboveground. A maze of thorny hedges twists and turns directly below—Jasyn's rose garden. "Which way?"

"Let me see."

I move aside, allowing Ky to glimpse the view. "We're in the eastern wing, but this tower doesn't open onto her floor. She isn't far. We just need to move deeper into the main part of the wing." Gripping my hand, he leads me down the stairwell. At once this feels familiar and yet far removed from the night he rescued me. So much has changed since then.

With reserved breath I trail him, our hastened footsteps echoing off the walls. At the stairwell's end, a door blocks our path. Breathe in, breathe out. One thing at a time.

He presses his ear against the wood.

I hear nothing aside from my intensified pulse. No hint as to what waits on the other side.

Ky nods, touches a finger to his lips. Three. Two. One. He turns the knob, pulls.

An empty hall stretches before us, ends in a T at a balcony overlooking a magnificent throne room with arched windows and marble columns. The path splits right, then left, forming a rectangle all the way around and joining at the other end where a grand staircase fans to a shiny hardwood floor. A set of double doors waits adjacent to the staircase, probably leading outside. I look up, down. Two floors above and two below.

"This way." Ky tugs me left. "Stay close. It's late. Aside from the night-shift guards, everyone will be asleep."

Doors and windows deck the balconies framing the throne room below. We pass door after door. I keep one hand on the weapon at my hip and an eye on the periphery the entire time. When Ky opens a door leading to a new set of serpentine stairs, we duck inside and climb to the next floor.

The moment we exit onto the new level, Ky shoves me into an alcove, presses me against the wall. He ducks his head, shielding me with his black-clad self. Our breaths become one. His thigh presses against my hip.

What is it with guys always smelling good no matter the circumstance? Why can't he smell like garbage or sewer or left-over Chinese food? Why am I inhaling so deeply, attempting to memorize—?

Footsteps. Whistling. *Click.* Someone's coming.

Five seconds, ten. I'm just tall enough to see over Ky's shoulder. A beam of light bounces over the floor and balcony railing, getting smaller, closer.

I hold my breath. Will my pulse to quiet.

The guard walks right by.

One, one thousand, two, one thousand, three . . . A full minute passes before Ky's rigid stance relaxes. He leans over me, propping his forearm against the wall over my head. "Listen, Elizabeth's door is just around the corner, situated in another alcove like this one. She will have at least two guards at this hour, maybe three. I'll lure them away, then you sneak in and transport her out. I'll circle back in time for you to take me through too."

Sounds like a decent plan. The *only* plan. But what if it doesn't work? What if Ky gets left behind?

No. Think happy thoughts. Find Mom.

"Wait for my signal." He leans away, cranes his neck, gaze focused beyond our shadowed refuge. "When I whistle, it means the door is clear."

"And if you don't whistle?"

He fixes mismatched eyes to mine. "Then find the nearest window and get out of here. Do not come back for me, understand?"

I nod, though my emotions stage a protest. I'll scale that obstacle when I come to it.

"Don't die." Ky draws the knife at my hip and thrusts it into my palm. Then he's gone.

Alone I wait, heart hammering, temples throbbing. The knife slips in my sweaty hand. I wipe my palm, clutch the hilt until I'm sure a blister will form. Feels like hours before I hear it. A distant, high-pitched whistle.

"This way," someone calls.

I peer around the wall. Two guards jog across the balcony on the other side. I watch them turn a corner, delay until I hear nothing but the sound of my pulse in my ears.

I exit the alcove and creep against the wall. Five yards. Ten. When I reach the next alcove, I freeze at its edge. It isn't vacant. Someone is breathing only a few feet away.

Double-crud, what now?

I back up a few feet, reach into my pack, withdraw my cracked phone. Good-bye, old girl, you've been good to me. Then I chuck it. Hard. It bounces off the railing, descends to the throne room floor.

Wait for it . . .

Smack!

If it wasn't broken before, it sure as crowe is now.

The lone guard does just as I'd hoped. I shrink against the wall as he abandons his post and walks in the opposite direction, back turned toward me.

Here's my chance. I jet into the alcove, open the door, and click it closed behind me.

"Eliyana?"

TWENTY-NINE

could be

M om is a yard away, sitting at a small table in a replica of the
room Jasyn duped me into seeing. Except no windows. No
mirror. A four-poster bed at the center, a fireplace, Persian rugs,
silver and silk.

Mom's forehead pleats. Her chin tips up. Again, she appears
older. Warier. The pigment of her cheeks is no longer dawn pink,
but overcast gray. And . . . has she gained weight? I count a full
minute before her expression turns silken. She sits, resumes her
previous activity—drinking tea. Wearing an emerald-green
mermaid-style gown, she's drinking her regularly scheduled cup
as if all is right with the Reflections.

A consternating chill wraps around me. I flip the lock. "Mom."
What's the matter? Why is she just sitting there?

She doesn't look up, though her temple muscles tremor the
way they always do when something irks her. "Go away, Father."

My breath escapes in a *whoosh*. She thinks I'm Jasyn come to
toy with her sanity. I can't blame her. This might be harder than I
anticipated.

"It's really me. Eliyana."

"Nice try. Next time you should have your assistant conduct
her research more thoroughly. If you knew anything about *my*
Eliyana, you'd know she doesn't wear her hair off her face. You

might as well advertise your farce right there." Mom stares into her teacup, steam moistening her cheeks. Or are those tears?

I twirl a loose strand around my finger. It hadn't even crossed my mind how different I might appear. And not just my ponytail, but my clothes, the way I've begun to carry myself lately. I go to her, kneel by her side. "Mom." I circle my arms around her waist, savoring her warmth and forever-fabric-softener scent. Haman didn't get to her. Jasyn hasn't hurt her.

She peels my arms off one by one as if they're leeches. Rising, Mom turns, lifts her rustling skirt, and moves toward the room's opposite end. An unfinished painting of a black-and-white Second Reflection rests on an easel in one corner. She lifts a brush, dabs it in a puddle of gray on her palette. "Just go," she says, her tone bitter.

"Mom, I—"

She twirls, her French-twisted hair loosening, cascading past her symmetrical shoulders. "Enough, Father! I have already agreed to your terms. What more do you want from me?"

The bottom-dwelling cockroach. Jasyn's messed with her mind so much, she doesn't even recognize her own daughter. Mom's back turns to me again. How can I prove my authenticity?

I inspect the area, scouring for an idea. My Aéropostale sweatshirt, the one Mom took at the Pond, is folded on a nightstand. I slip my pack off, shrug out of my jacket, and don the fleece-lined hoodie. *Zip.* Fits like a glove.

Mom peeks over her shoulder. "What are you doing? Please, don't touch that."

Shouldering my pack, I ask, "Why not? It's mine, and I want it back." Could this work? Any other time I wouldn't be so snarky, but it's imperative to convince her I'm really me.

"No."

"Remember when you bought this for me? Right after I spilled red slushy all over my old one, two summers ago at Coney Island? It was my favorite sweatshirt. I think you called every Aéropostale in the Tri-State Area trying to find this exact one." I only meant the memory to show her I'm not a mirage, but it invites a sense of nostalgia anyway.

Her cheeks perk, brows pucker. "Eliyana?" She hurries to me, snatches my shoulders. "Is it really you?"

"The one and only."

Mom hugs me a little too snugly, then draws back, her eyes alight. "How did you—?"

"I'll explain everything, but once we're safe." Now I sound like Joshua. "Is Makai here?" I don't know why, but somehow I sense my uncle's presence. As if I'm being watched. It's a feeling I've always had.

She sighs. "You can come out now."

Makai appears beside the bed. He's been here all long, invisible but never leaving Mom's side. My uncle joins us and drapes his good arm around her, the other still residing in a sling. His bow and quiver are slung over his back. When will his arm heal enough to use them again? "I thought I'd give you two a moment."

Pink tints Mom's cheeks. She's never looked happier.

I give them the abridged recap of the last days. Haman at the Haven. Robyn's murder. The Soulless on the beach. Queen Ember's—*my*—Calling. Nathaniel and the mirrors and Ky.

"And Joshua?" Makai and Mom ask in unison.

Oh. Right. Joshua. Like a little brother to Makai. Mom took a while to warm up to him, but eventually she got used to the idea he wasn't going anywhere. Of course they want to know if he's okay. "He was at the Haven last time I saw him." I look to Makai. "Haman and the Soulless infiltrated the wall." I cross to the door. "Come on. He gave Wren twenty-four hours to find me before he kills again. We have to get you both to safety so I can go back and help them. If the king won't intervene, I will." The words escape without warning, igniting my fury, energizing my bones. I'm a part of this now. No turning back.

They look at each other, at me again.

Makai's peppery brows furrow. "Joshua isn't with you?"

Why would he be?

Oh.

So much has happened since I last saw these two. "Ky—er, Kyaphus is my Guardian now." I relay Gage's betrayal, how Joshua stepped up as acting commander. I know they want the full monty, but the longer we stay here, the smaller our window of escape becomes. Maybe it's already gone.

Their expressions shift from puzzled to disbelieving.

"You're here alone?" Mom's question borders on reproachful.

"Ky's with me, but I'm only able to take one person through my reflection at a time. Makai can slip out unseen, but we have to get you to a window or a mirror so I can come back for Ky."

Mom's eyes widen. She rounds on Makai. "This is exactly what I was trying to avoid. She can't be here. Do you think my father has figured it out?"

"We can only hope—"

"What are you talking about? Jasyn already knows about my link to the king." I glance at the door. Come on, Ky, come *on*. "As long as Jasyn doesn't have the Verity's vessel, he won't hurt me."

Makai approaches. "Did you have any trouble getting into the castle? Discovering this room?"

"Not really." I lick my dry lips. "There were a few guards, but we distracted them." Uneasiness ferments in my stomach. Drat.

Footsteps echo outside the door.

Makai takes a protective step in front of Mom, who grabs my arm and pushes me behind them both.

I peruse the room. My gaze settles on the bathroom door. I sprint over, glance inside. No mirrors. Think. There must be a way out.

The doorknob rattles.

I'm a Mirror. I can protect us. Not that I've had a ton of time to practice, but—

Knock, knock.

I raise Ky's knife. Brilliant. As if I know anything about hand-to-hand combat.

"I love you," Makai whispers to Mom, temporarily freeing me from my panic attack.

She rises on her toes. "I love you."

He leans down and kisses her, long and deep. Is this their first kiss? Could it be a Kiss of Infinity even?

I avert my eyes, not wanting to intrude. The mirrorglass blade reflects the soft lamplight, sending bursts of rainbow dancing on the ceiling and wall. Epiphany! It could work. I hope.

Mom clings to Makai. He separates himself from her, takes a giant step back. "I'll hold them off."

Grabbing Mom's hand I say, "We have to go."

"I won't leave you." She clings to Makai, then turns to me. "Go, brave girl."

"Lizzie . . . if you're going to choose this moment to exhibit your stubborn side, so help me, I'll never speak to you again."

Mom opens her mouth in protest.

"Get her out of here," Makai roars, then disappears.

I tug on Mom's hand. *"Mom, he'll be fine. Pleeease . . ."*

She hesitates only a moment before relenting.

The door vibrates. A man shouts.

I lift Ky's blade over our heads, my love for Mom drawing a reprise of "the song" from my lips.

Thud, rattle, bang! Bellow, yell, holler!

Just as I arc the blade toward us, the door bursts open.

Terror grips my soul, drains the blood from my skull.

Soulless guards flank Ky, restraining him. His lip is busted open, his green eye red and swelling.

"Go!" he bellows. One of the guards knees him, and he doubles over. "Don't come back! Don't you dare come back for me, Em."

My heart hits the floor. Not Ky. Please, not Ky.

I lose sight of him as Mom and I melt into the mirrorglass, shrinking and expanding, defying the laws of physics.

Time slows. We fall into the attic. *Our* attic. The one in New York.

I release Mom's hand. She's safe. Finally.

She's on her knees. Smiles, but it doesn't last. Her brows scrunch.

I'm still holding Ky's knife, hand trembling.

"Eliyana." Mom's mouth turns down. She has that look she used to give me when I was a kid. Warning. Danger. Stop. "Wait," she says.

I want to stay. I have to go. "I can't leave him." Not when the only reason he's there is because of me. I won't be the cause of anyone else's pain. Not anymore.

She nods. "I never should have kept you from all of this. I thought I was protecting you. But you don't need protecting anymore, do you?"

I don't have an answer. My only goal has been to save her—the one person I've always needed most in the world. Now that I have, I find I want more. Not because I don't love her. Because I've learned she's not the only person who could ever love me.

"I love you, Mom."

"I know." She smiles. "Go now. We'll see each other soon."

My heart breaks into a million pieces as I sob my song once more, these lyrics for Ky alone. Because I want the chance to know him. Because if I don't go back, I'll always wonder what would've happened if I did.

The blade wavers. I draw it down over my head and brace myself for the impact.

I smash into the floor of Mom's suite, tumble, and roll. The knife flies, clatters. My pack slaps my spine. I push myself up, pins and needles pinging my palms. The room is empty. Except for Ky. He's facedown on the rug. I scramble to him. Fall to my knees. Turn him over.

Blood. Smearing his skin. Soaking his shirt.

Chip. Crack. Shatter. The ice within is breaking. Melting. I cover my mouth. Then I reach for the knife at his ankle. Gone. Drat. With all the force I can muster, I rip open his shirt.

Oh. My. Soul.

The blackened veins are no longer secluded to his right arm. They're crawling across his broken body, creeping beneath his bleeding skin like dozens of venomous asps. Infecting him. Killing him.

He coughs and gags. Opens his eyes. "Em, you idiot." The insult is quarter-hearted.

My hands hover over him. I throw off my pack, remove my hoodie, and dab at the blood trickling from his lip and brow. "What do I do? How do I stop it? I'm a Mirror. There must be some way I can—"

"You can't." Eyelids fluttering, his body convulses and he hisses in pain. "It's the Void," he rasps. "They injected me with something, sent it straight into my bloodstream. I've never seen anything like it. It feels as if . . . it's feeding off me. The more I fight it, the faster it spreads. I'm—my soul. I don't have much time. You should go. I don't know what kind of monster I'll become when the Void takes over."

"No." My lip quivers. I shove childish tears away. "I don't want to lose you."

"Never." Ky's gaze holds mine as he lifts a shaky hand and sweeps my bangs to the side, fingertips tickling the skin above my right brow.

The Void is spreading up his neck now. Over his face. It will be over soon. His soul will belong to darkness.

His arm falls away, hand limp at his side.

I close my eyes, tears cascading down my cheeks in a sticky mess. "Don't leave," I sing against his cheek. "Don't give up. Stay with me." And then I press my lips to his, kissing him before he's gone. Begging the good in him to fight against the Void. Reminding him he has something left to live for.

At once I feel a whooshing sensation, like breath expelled on a summer wind. I'm floating ten feet aboveground and drowning in my own tears. This moment is everything and nothing and I can't explain why I feel as if I've found life and death, beginning and end, all in one kiss.

"A Kiss of Infinity isn't something you decide to bestow. It comes from the deepest part of your soul. Stems from desires and emotions you may not even be aware you possess."

Ky's lips come to life, move against my own. His kiss carries all the force of butterfly wings. Soft. Tender.

I lift my head, blinking. The Void is retracting, slithering away, the color returning to Ky's beaten face. But not only that, his wounds are closing, his broken skin healing before my eyes.

Did my kiss save him? Impossible.

He gulps a breath. Opens his eyes. Touches two fingers to his swollen lips. "Em, what did you do?"

"I . . . don't know." Except I do. "I didn't want to lose you." If I gave Ky a Kiss of Infinity, we're both linked to the king now. For another week at least. I grab his hand. No time to analyze the implications. "We have to go. We have to—"

Clap. Clap. Clap.

My head jerks up.

A girl with icy-blonde hair stands in the doorframe. A ruthless smile, reminiscent of a Troll I once met, curls the corners of her lips. "My, my, my, Ky Rhyen. You have been a busy boy."

Quinn?

THIRTY

TRUE

I can't believe I thought for one second she was my friend. Is everyone in my life a token in some Verity versus Void rivalry?

The doorframe around Quinn shimmers like a hologram. Was it always made of marble?

"The trick is to look for tells. No matter how strong the façade, there are always glitches—signs that what you're seeing isn't real."

Oh. Crud.

Quinn retreats as if whisked backward on a moving sidewalk. The suite transforms, lengthening, widening. Carpet converts to cherrywood. Staggered quartzite bricks protrude from papered walls. Arching windows cut through as if hole punched. Marble columns support five tiers of balconied floors.

We're centered in the throne room. Jasyn commands the marble dais before us, a high-backed chair upholstered with burgundy fabric directly behind him. A majestic celling-to-floor tapestry, featuring a Second Reflection atlas in vibrant hues, flows beyond the dais. My emotions blaze as I peer at the threads detailing every province and landmark. Blood pumps, head whirs, eyes water. This is my world now. I've claimed it. No turning back.

Jasyn stands there, hands folded in front of him, every bit as he was the last, and first, time I saw him—pressed suit, kind eyes, and all the arrogance of a Wall Street big shot. "Bravo, granddaughter. Marvelous performance, really. So tender. So heartfelt."

I gawk at Ky.

He shakes his head, and his eyes go wide.

The mirrorglass blade. Where is it? I scan my periphery.

"I must say." Jasyn descends the dais stairs, his dress shoes clapping against marble as if applauding his cleverness. "When I allowed Kyaphus to release you from the dungeon, I expected him to fall for you." He halts on the last step. "What I did not anticipate was that you would also become so attached to him."

We scramble to stand, Ky helping me up, placing his body protectively in front of mine. "What are you rambling on about, Crowe?" he spits, arm locked and tendered like a sword.

"Only that I needed someone to keep an eye on the girl until I was ready for her." His attention rests on Ky. Doesn't he know what Ky's capable of? Why is Jasyn making eye contact without an ounce of hesitation? "Who better than one of my own to complete the task?"

And why is he talking about me in third person as if I'm not here?

"By the way," Jasyn says with a leer, "your darling Khloe sends her regards."

Khloe? Ky's sister. Must be. I grasp Ky's bicep, my vise grip begging him not to do something stupid. Like get himself killed.

His body is a pillar of energy, vehemence vibrating his being from bared teeth to pounce-ready stance. "Don't you dare speak her name, murderer."

"Now, now. Let us speak in a civil manner, hmm? Khloe is . . ." Jasyn pauses, as if we need the dramatic effect. ". . . just fine. I am fully aware her life has been my greatest bargaining chip when it comes to you, Kyaphus." His gaze falls to me. "Until now."

"Where is she? I want to see her." Veins pop beneath the skin on Ky's neck, on the back of his clenched hand.

"I am afraid that is not possible, but I assure you, she is being well cared for." When Ky doesn't relax or lower his arm, Jasyn adds, "I never do anything without cause, my boy. What purpose would killing your sister serve? When the Confine on her Calling lifts one day, I do believe she will make a fine addition to my collection. She has potential, does she not?"

One, two, three drawn-out pulses in my ear. And then . . .

Ky. Lowers. His. Arm.

There. Something glints beside a marble column twenty paces to my left. But how to reach it? I've had no practice. No reason to believe the Magnet within is strong enough to summon Ky's special knife. Not sure if a knife is something I'm capable of summoning. What if I have a connection with water like Stormy, or one of the other elements Ky mentioned? Even so, I have to try. Focus. Play the notes in my mind. See them. Will the weapon into my hand. Adrenaline courses through me, pumping, rushing, surging.

The blade doesn't budge.

Why didn't I inquire more about Stormy's Calling?

"What . . . do . . . you . . . want?" Ky seizes a breath between each word.

"Only exactly what you have given me. The key to the vessel's undoing."

Me. My train of thought temporarily derails. "If you kill me, the Verity will leave King Aidan and find another vessel." I duck beneath Ky's arm.

"First, would you stop insisting I want to kill you? It is becoming redundant. And second, who said anything about King Aidan?"

"You can't win this, Jasyn." I press on, ignore questions. "No matter what you do, the Verity will always be out there. And one day it *will* imprison the Void." I relish the words, feel their truth seep through my pores.

Jasyn flicks a thread of lint from his suit. "Do you truly believe I am so oblivious to the happenings and history of my own Reflection?" He tilts his head, eyeing me so penetratingly I have no choice but to look away.

Creepy.

"Take the rebels' hiding place, for instance." He faces the tapestry, extends an arm toward the Haven. "The vermin think they are so clever, hiding out on that hole of an island, a place that has been their prison all these years." He folds his hands in front of him, Grinch-like smile unfurling. "The truth is, I have allowed them to remain there. They cause me no trouble, and I in turn let them live their lives, weeding them out one by one. Much less hassle to maintain them that way, would you not agree?"

"Need I remind you of Haman's betrayal, not to mention the dozens of others who've surrendered to the Void? Decent men and women we trusted. Our numbers are dwindling . . ."

Preacher's words float across my memory, the Scrib in me recalling his argument syllable for syllable. Jasyn has known of the Haven all this time? "Then why did Haman and the Soulless attack? Why now? He killed"—I swallow, forcing composure—"he killed someone." Robyn. A pinch in my chest.

"Yes, well, I needed the rebels to know they are no match for me. I am keeping them right where I want them—fearful and in hiding. You have given them hope, and that is a dangerous thing. I am afraid casualties are inevitable."

Robyn a casualty? Why, you mouth-breathing son-of-a-troll.

"But let us start from the beginning." He ascends the steps once more, resuming his place five strides above. "Shall we commence with your mother?"

Despite the resident fear slinking up my spine, I can't help but expel a relieved breath. Mom is safe. No matter what else happens, I've done what I came for.

Jasyn sits on the throne, rests his elbow on the chair's arm, and leans his head against his extended thumb and forefinger. "I have searched for the vessel of the Verity for twenty-one years. But I have sought someone else too."

Mom. My jaw goes slack. I don't like where this is going.

Jasyn catches my eye with an iceberg glare. "Do not look so surprised. I am not the heartless villain everyone makes me out to be. When Elizabeth disappeared, I put every effort into finding her. If I thought the vessel was an enigma, Elizabeth was even more the conundrum. Where had she gone and why? I never harmed her. Never gave any indication I would do so."

I spy the knife out of the corner of my eye. Slide my foot left an inch. All I need is a window. If I can't summon the stubborn thing, I'll have to get it the old-fashioned way. Then I can transport us out of here.

"It was actually your father who finally shed some light on the matter."

Wince. Focus deterred—again. Please don't say—

"Tiernan Archer's only loyalty was to himself." Jasyn speaks with all the enthusiasm of the cow from *Into the Woods.* "It took very little coaxing to get it out of him. A few hallucinations, a bit of torture. I do not believe I have ever encountered a weaker human being."

Ky shifts. "Why would my father know anything about her mother?"

I turn to Ky. He should hear this from me.

Jasyn beats me to it. "No, no, no." He chuckles. "Not *your* father. *Her* father." He must take in Ky's confused expression because he adds, "Do you mean to tell me you two have not been formally introduced?"

My head grows light. I sit on the bottom dais step to keep from toppling. This is not how this was supposed to go.

"Well then, allow me to do the honors. Kyaphus, may I introduce Tiernan Archer's second child."

Second child? What did I miss?

Cocking his head and narrowing his eyes, Ky moves toward me. "You're Tiernan's other daughter?"

Other? Does he mean Khloe?

"Did you know about this?" He crouches to my level. "Why didn't you tell me?"

"I couldn't." I press a clammy palm to my damp bangs, smash them against my forehead. "It was my fault he became so angry. He adopted you because I was born a girl. His debt to Jasyn, the one *you* had to pay, was because of me. Tiernan was the reason my mom fled the Second. I thought if you knew you'd—"

"What, Em? That I'd hate you? Your opinion of me must still be pretty poor." The hurt in his voice arrests my heart. "Do you really see me as the kind of man who would blame someone for their parents' mistakes?"

I blink. He's right. He's *so* right. "No." I reach out to him. "I don't."

He straightens. Steps away. "I thought you knew me better than that." Turning his back on me, he adds, "I guess I was wrong."

I rise. Take two steps. "Ky—"

"Give it a rest, El."

My regard switches to the grand staircase.

Quinn descends the steps, fingers caressing the glossy rail. *Click-clack, click-clack.*

My insides knot, knot, knot.

When she plants her peep-toed feet on the throne room floor, Quinn transforms. Goth clothing remains, from lacy headband to fishnet tights, but the body beneath changes. Cascading yellow tresses shrink to her shoulders, darkening to deep cocoa. Her oval face rounds into a heart shape, and her eyes shift from ice-queen blue to ganache brown. Aside from her still-perfect skin, she could be my—

"Eliyana," Jasyn announces, "may I introduce Ebony Archer . . ."

No. It can't be true.

". . . your half sister."

prince charming

I have a sister?

I have a sister.

Two sisters if Khloe is Tiernan's biological child as well.

"You should see the look on your face, El," Quinn—Ebony—says. "It's the same one you made that time Blake dunked your backpack in the toilet. Classic." She approaches Ky. Places a possessive hand on his arm.

He turns his head to the side and shrugs her off.

At least we can agree on one thing. Quinn—Ebony—is no one's friend.

Seemingly unbothered by his rejection, she meets me at the dais steps. "Let me spin a tale for you, baby sis." She twirls a finger in the air, taps me on the nose. "One in which the only happy ending belongs to me." Her hand flutters to her chest.

I recoil. Clamber backward up the steps. I trip, fall. My hand slips, my wrist twists—crowe, that hurts.

Hips swaying, Ebony joins Jasyn on the dais and begins, "Once upon a time . . ."

Is ne'er what it seems. You had that right, Queen Ember.

". . . there was a little girl who loved her father very much."

A Cinderella story, huh? Bet I can guess which of us is the ugly stepsister in this scenario.

"Her father was often away. To be a Guardian in the king's

army was a high honor. One of the most talented Shields of his generation, Tiernan Archer was not a man to be trifled with."

So I've heard. I peer at Ky, still ignoring me. What kills me is that he's not angry Tiernan is—was my dad. No, the blame falls to me alone. Because I didn't trust him enough to share the truth.

I wish he could read my mind.

I'm sorry, Ky. I'm so, so sorry.

He twitches, swivels his head a fraction of an inch.

What the—No way he actually heard what I was thinking. Right?

"When his wife, Isabeau, could not conceive a second child—a son to carry on the family name—Tiernan made his bed elsewhere."

Isabeau?

Isabeau.

Her desire for Mom's unborn child becomes clear. Mom was Tiernan's mistress.

I think I'm going to be sick.

Drawing my attention back, Ebony struts across the dais as if it's her personal runway. "While Isabeau was nearly thirty, Tiernan was younger. Wilder. He was twenty when he left. I was three."

I blink, my heart softening. I almost feel bad for Ebony. If I had a mother like hers, I'd be bitter too.

"Your whore of a mother seduced my father."

Never mind the softening part. "If anyone seduced anyone, it was Tiernan. My mom would never take another woman's husband." I rise and cradle my wrist, uncertainty wobbling my knees. Mom didn't refer to this in any of her journal entries. She couldn't have known Tiernan was married.

"He left my mother. Left me." The steadiness in Ebony's cool tone wavers. "When he learned your mother was with child, he hoped to gain the heir he so desired. And then *you* were born." A pause. A sneer. "Funny how things work out, isn't it?"

Jasyn watches her, glee lighting his brown eyes. Is that genuine affection I see? "For so many years I wondered what I had done to compel my Elizabeth to run." He stands beside Ebony. They make quite the pair. His arm wraps her shoulders. "When all along it was Tiernan who scared her off, not me."

I hate that I have no rebuttal. Mom's journal mentioned nothing about Jasyn aside from his obsession with the Void. She never said he harmed her, or even that he tried to turn her Soulless. Tiernan truly was the reason for Mom's disappearance.

"It did not take long for me to connect the dots," Jasyn says. "I had no knowledge of Elizabeth's pregnancy until Tiernan confessed a few years ago. Naturally, I planned to have him executed for treason. How dare he, a meager Guardian, touch my daughter, only sixteen at the time. However, I was not required to lift a finger. Kyaphus disposed of him for me."

Ky bristles. The side of his face is visible, the bulge in his jaw clear. I can't imagine how difficult it is for him to stay calm as Jasyn speaks. Are his efforts to protect Khloe? And me? The timeline falls into place. Ky defending his sister. Killing his adoptive father. How long had Ky been a rebel Guardian before Jasyn dug his claws in?

"Once I found Elizabeth," Jasyn continues, "she confirmed what I could only speculate. Strong willed, your mother. It was much more difficult to extract information from her than it had been with Tiernan. She had many years of practice, of course, defending her mind against my façades. But I was able to draw it from her eventually."

So Jasyn isn't as all-powerful as he appears. The stronger the mind, the harder it is for him to fool his victims. I file the note away, storing it for later. Poor Mom. No wonder she didn't know what to believe when I rescued her. Jasyn *had* been playing with her head.

"She believed Tiernan would kill you, so she fled, sought a man named Nathaniel Archer. Does the name ring a bell?"

I clench my jaw. I solemnly swear to tell nothing, and nothing but nothing.

"Unfortunately, that is where her trail ended. Try as I might, I could not breach the wall surrounding her memory after that. Even I am no match for a Kiss of Accord."

Mom made a promise sealed with a kiss? To whom? "I don't understand. How did you find us in the first place?"

"Have you not figured it out yet?"

Duh.

"As providence would have it, Elizabeth's photo turned up in a newspaper a few months back. What is it called, my dear?" He flashes a sweet smile at Ebony.

She flips her hair over one shoulder, a classic Quinn move. *The New York Times.*

"Ah yes." Jasyn beams. "That is the one."

No. All those years Mom insisted on privacy. Her no-photo policy. Her rule I stay off social media. It was all because, "The picture for the art contest. That's how you found us."

"Indeed," Jasyn says. "It was easy to trace her whereabouts then. A few simple phone calls made by my darling assistant"—he squeezes Ebony's shoulder—"and Elizabeth's coordinates were made known. I did not act right away, of course. Delicate situations require patience. It was not until two months later that I finally brought Elizabeth home. Meanwhile, Ebony watched over you both."

Quinn was his assistant. No wonder he knew—knows so much about me. The constant questions from Quinn when we met. I thought she was trying to get close to me. Because that's what friends do. I was so blind.

"However, there was another surprise waiting for me. I knew of your existence but had no idea just how valuable you would turn out to be."

I touch my marked cheek. I might as well have "I'm connected to the Verity's vessel" written in neon across my face. My head spins. I press the heels of my palms to my eyes. This is all my fault.

If I hadn't entered Mom in that contest, maybe none of this would have happened. We'd be in New York. Joshua and I might not have this chasm between us.

Except, even if I hadn't been dragged here kicking and screaming, the rebels would still be trapped, waiting for their hero to swoop in and save the day. If Jasyn never discovered us, my birthday would have passed without a hitch, but then I never would have known another world—another Reflection—existed. I never would have met Ky. My life would be normal, but it would also be a lie.

And Joshua. After my birthday he'd have no reason to stay in New York and guard me. What then? I'd spend my life wondering why he left, what had become of him. At least here I know he's okay. Even if he doesn't love me, that's enough.

I drag my hands down the sides of my face, let them rest at my thighs. The pain in my injured wrist becomes more pronounced by the minute. I don't care. My left hand opens, rotates toward the wall. *Come here, you stupid blade.* The words form a melody in my head.

"I always wondered"—Jasyn straightens his tie—"what was the Verity's vessel waiting for exactly? Why allow me to unleash the Void and rule all this time? But when Ebony described your mark to me, I thought to myself, ah"—he lifts one finger—"here is the reason." Extends a palm to me.

Scrape. Is it working? Is the knife moving?

"Ironic how these things work out." My grandfather descends the steps, crosses to the marble column, and scoops up Ky's knife. "Aidan and Ember have been dead these twenty-one years. If Aidan lived, I never would have been able to release the Void from its prison. He was the one keeping the Void at bay, you see." He holds the weapon up to the light.

They died? So the king and queen aren't locked away. They really did vanish. Which means . . .

"Once I understood your importance, I also knew precisely where the Verity's new vessel had gone." He strides to me, stands so close I can smell his hoity-toity cologne. "I merely had to bide my time." He places the hilt in my open palm. What kind of game is this? "According to Ebony, the vessel hardly let you out of his sight. I had to wonder then if he would ever confront me."

My fingers curl around the weapon, but I can't bring myself to raise it. Impossible to breathe.

"So I decided to test a theory." Jasyn extends a hand toward the grand staircase.

I turn to find Long John Silver taking the steps one by one as if performing a dance. But he isn't alone, a slumped Makai at his side. He lugs my uncle, who surpasses the skinny pirate in both height and weight, step after painstaking step. Heave, rest. Heave, rest. When they reach the dais, Haman drops him, brushing his hands in rhythm with my uncle's achy groan.

"Makai," I croak, moving toward him.

Ky stops me where I step. Hand on my shoulder, he still won't look at me.

Jasyn clears his throat. "Along with Ebony, I assigned the task to Haman. I wanted to see exactly what the vessel would do, how he would react to the events surrounding you. First came your mother's fabricated death. It seemed the pain you bore belonged to him. It was obvious in the way he looked at you."

"How could you possibly know that?" Remain calm. He's trying to get to me.

"I told him."

I whip toward the dais at the sound of Lincoln Cooper's lurid falsetto. Apparently, Ebony not only can skip from form to form at the bat of her fake eyelashes but she can change her clothes as well. I would never know it was her in Lincoln's salmon-colored shirt, skinny jeans, and oak blazer.

My entire body jerks. "What are you, a Mask?"

"Shield actually." Well, that explains a lot. Why Ky won't—can't harm her. "I take after our dear departed father." I wouldn't brag about that. "Masks have two forms, three at the most, and they can only change their own matter. I, on the other hand, have the unique ability to camouflage myself. I'm limited to the human alias, of course, but you don't see me complaining."

"That's why you weren't at Mom's funeral. You came as Lincoln." No wonder I always thought the guy was such an insensitive jerk. "I don't get it. Why go through so much trouble to sell Mom's paintings?"

"All part of my cover." Ebony reverts to herself. Her manicured hand hovers over a yawn. "I needed to keep an eye on her. On both of you, until His Sovereignty decided his next move."

His Sovereignty? Gag me.

Haman glides by, dragging a bow-and-arrow-free Makai along. Captain Creepy drops my uncle at the foot of the dais and climbs the steps. He stands beside the tapestry. Pulls a cord.

Like a curtain, the atlas whooshes aside, fanning my face and revealing a stone wall.

I leave Ky and kneel beside my uncle. He waves me away. Says nothing.

"As I was saying . . ." Retreating, Jasyn joins his team, taking center stage. "The vessel's reaction was exactly as I predicted. He cared for your safety, but there was something else too. A sense of caution. And fear. When I allowed Elizabeth to escape the night of your kidnapping, my suspicions were all the more confirmed. He would go the distance to keep you from me. When Haman killed him, I had my answer." Jasyn waves his hand as if brandishing a wand.

Haman types a code into a small keypad, and the wall beyond the throne revolves. Stone grates against stone as the opposite side emerges, ushering with it three very familiar figures—two Soulless supporting a beaten and battered man.

"May I present the hero of our tale." Sweeping an arm toward the trio, Jasyn croons, "Prince Charming himself."

My heart palpitates as if separate from my chest. The blade clatters to the floor. I'm not going anywhere.

Joshua. Is. Here.

ACT IV

for good

THIRTY-TWO

Limited

The day I met Joshua is one I've relived a thousand times.

I burst through the front door. Slam it behind me. The light fixture rocks and rattles above our foyer.

"Mom?" I call up the stairs.

No answer.

I toss my backpack on the sunroom couch as I move toward the kitchen. I lean over the bar. "Mom?"

Silence. What day is it? Tuesday. Mom's drawing caricatures in Central Park.

I cut across the kitchen and exit through the back door. Backyards in Manhattan are a rare enigma. Too small to be considered a yard, but too large to be called a porch. We have lovingly dubbed it the "rear sidewalk."

September stinks. Do I really have to endure three more years of this? Of the homework and grades. The whispers and taunting. Stinkin' prep kids and their high-and-mighty attitudes. Stinkin' Blake and his band of brainless oafs. Name-calling is so third grade. What a bunch of juveniles.

I plod down the metal steps, *klunk, klunk, klunk,* and drop onto the glider swing. Tuck one foot under my thigh and let the other dangle free. My toe pushes off the ground, keeping the swing in motion.

Buzz. I draw my phone from my pocket. Text message from Mom. *Tap*, zoom.

I'll be home soon. Do you want pizza from Caesar's?

Even in a text, Mom doesn't lax on spelling and grammar. I tap out a hasty reply.

sure. c u soon. <3

Music. I need music. It'll get my mind off a rotten first day. Scroll, *tap*. Scroll, *tap*.

I sing a duet with Christina Perri about being "human." I let my head loll back against the swing cushion as words that could be my melodic memoir emerge. Fake smiles. Forced laughs. Falling apart. This, pathetically, is me. I sing past the heartache. My soul bleeds the lyrics. Is this it? Will anything ever change?

Crash!

I nearly crack my head on cement as I tumble forward. Cause of almost-death? Induced heart attack. I crane my neck, searching for the interruption's source.

A guy peeks over the western wall of my yard—er, rear sidewalk. He's older. Seventeen, eighteen maybe. Short stubble shades his strong jaw, and those eyes, a piercing cerulean blue.

I scramble to my feet, lurch for the stairs. Please don't let him see my face. I can't suffer further humiliation today. If only invisibility was an option.

"Wait!" His fetching tenor stops me midescape.

My pulse tap-dances on my eardrums.

Blue Eyes swings over the wall in an Olympic-worthy move. Pretty bold to enter a stranger's yard uninvited. This is New York. I could be a serial killer for all he knows. For all I know, so could he.

I smooth my hair. Study my charcoal Chuck Taylors. Maybe he won't notice the birthmark.

Ha. Good one.

"Please don't stop. That was . . . you have the most beautiful voice."

Beautiful? Nice try, Prince Eric. The only person who's ever linked that term to me is Mom, and she doesn't count.

"Thanks." I can't bring myself to make eye contact. I'm not ready for him to run away screaming yet.

"With a voice like that you could do anything." Does he realize how close he's standing? He smells different from other boys. Natural. Axe spray not required.

I lift my head gradually. Here it comes . . .

He flashes a crooked smile. "I'm Joshua David."

Why doesn't he look shocked or appalled? Is he blind?

"Um . . . Eliyana? Ember." Genius. Now he's going to think I'm—what's the word Blake uses?—"special."

"I just moved in next door. I'm sorry I startled you. I was trying to replace the bulb on my porch light. Then I heard your voice and . . ." Joshua scratches the back of his dark-haired head and shrugs. "I guess you know what happened next. Anyway, I just started at Columbia. One of my professors is letting me live here practically rent-free as long as I fix the place up."

Weird. I've never actually seen the guy who lives next door. He's kind of a hermit. It might be nice to have a friendly neighbor for a change.

"Pays to be the teacher's favorite, I guess." His smile evens.

I wouldn't know. "Cool."

He's going to leave now. His politeness meter is maxed out.

So why is he still standing here? No, not just standing here. He's acting as if he doesn't want to leave.

He rocks back on his heels. "So you like music. Do you play any instruments?"

"Yeah." What was the question?

"Which ones?"

"Which ones what?" Deer in the headlights. That's me.

"Instruments." He laughs, but for some reason I don't feel as if he's laughing *at* me. He just seems . . . happy.

"Oh." I twist a split-ended lock around my finger. "Um, piano?" Really? I'm asking this gorgeous guy if *I* play piano? Bury me now. "But I always wanted to learn how to play guitar."

"Wait here." He winks. "I'll be right back." He's over the wall and out of sight before I can give a coherent response.

He's kind of weird.

I like him.

When he returns, he lifts a beautiful, Ibanez electric-acoustic over the wall. I take it while he boosts himself back over. "I'll show you some chords if you want."

He's kidding. "I'm sure you have better things to do right now than teach me how to play guitar." Please say you don't.

He makes a face, as if seriously contemplating the concept. "Nope. Can't think of anything." Joshua reclines on the swing. He rests his guitar on one knee and strums with his thumb. "The song you were singing was really depressing."

Shrug.

"I've got a better one if you're up for it."

"Okay." I join him, noting our proximity once again.

He still isn't running, still is looking at me as if I'm no different from anyone else.

Joshua starts strumming, singing "Daydream Believer" better than any Monkee ever could. His tanned fingers pick the strings in fluid repetition. I survey him. The way he rocks in sync with the rhythm. How the corner of his mouth twitches between lyrics.

Moments ago my chest was torn and hemorrhaging. But now—now I'm the girl in the song my new neighbor sings.

"Your turn." He passes me the guitar and proceeds to place my fingers where they belong, officially making him the first boy who's ever touched me.

My heart capers. Cheer up, indeed.

⁓⧖⁓

Every seemingly random event from my life replays on my mind's silver screen. Each one scrambles, falls in order, the plot finally making sense. Cut a scene here and splice it in there and voilà—a coherent mystery flick. And I'm the star.

Stop. Rewind. Play.

The next-door neighbor I never saw. Code name: Joshua's "professor." A.k.a. Makai.

Fast-forward. Pause.

Joshua moves in. Seems odd he has nothing better to do than spend time with me. Mom hates him too. Until she doesn't.

Skip, two, three.

Mom's upset. Her picture is in the paper. She's acting panicked, not like herself.

New frame. Freeze.

Quinn sits beside me on the first day of senior year. She wants to hang out, despite what it would do to her social status.

Next scene. Hold it right there.

Mom "dies." I go to Joshua for comfort. He's distant. Almost mean. But he doesn't stay that way. I can't keep track of his emotions. He's warm one minute and glacial the next.

Blinking away the memories, I zoom in on the new members of our gathering. The guard on the left of Joshua, stout and bearded, is unmistakably Preacher. Odd to see him minus the scowl. On the right, bald and dark-skinned, is Kuna. His infectious smile vanquished, the frown painful to look upon. Both men have lost the light and color from their eyes, replaced by the swirling fog of the Soulless. Every inch of exposed flesh reveals midnight veins, twisting and winding and reaching.

But nothing, not Preacher's missing glower or Kuna's absent joy, strikes my core as much as the sight of the pale man between them. He's shirtless, a wide bandage encompassing his torso, the black Guardian tattoo peeking from beneath. Fresh, still-bleeding cuts mar his forehead, his cheeks, his neck, his arms. Even so, he remains himself, eyes blue as ever. Bruises and road rash–like burns splotch his skin, but it's still *his* skin—not a charred vein in sight.

Joshua gazes at me with a fierceness that starts an earthquake in my bones. He struggles against his captors. They release him, and he staggers forward.

I scramble up the steps. We fall to our knees. We're the only two people in the room. "Joshua," I whisper. "What have they done to you?"

He shakes his head, wincing at the minor movement. "I'm sorry," he croaks. "I should've told you." He hangs his head. Closes his eyes.

His brokenness might kill me.

"Do you wish to tell her now?" Jasyn's cello-deep voice intrudes. "Or shall I?"

Joshua's jaw works. He opens his eyes but doesn't meet mine. "I'll do it."

I brace myself.

"Twenty-one years ago, my parents died. Their names were Aidan David Henry and Ember Gabrielle Archer."

Joshua David.

"They were older, and I'm told there were complications with the pregnancy. My father wanted my mother at peace. The less stress she endured, the better chances the birth would come without difficulties. So he sent her away from the public eye, away from the responsibilities that come with being queen. He was an Ever but never took his Calling for granted. Mother would live with a Physic, a man my parents knew and trusted, where she would finish out her term and give birth."

"Nathaniel." Natural causes, he'd said. Ember's death . . . oh no.

He nods. "No one knew she was pregnant aside from my father, Nathaniel, and his two sons." Makai and Tiernan. "All were sworn to secrecy, sealed with a Kiss of Accord. My father covered every base. He wanted nothing interfering with my birth."

"He said he was going to die anyway. He was raving mad."

My father did this. He broke his vow. "When Tiernan told Jasyn about Mom, he also mentioned Ember's pregnancy." If my father wasn't already dead, I might kill him myself.

"Well done, granddaughter," Jasyn says. "As I have said, I am unable to get around a Kiss of Accord. But if the promise is broken of one's own free will, that is a different matter. Tiernan wanted to die. The Void had become too much for him."

I refuse to acknowledge my grandfather's presence. These may be my final moments with Joshua. I'm not going to waste them.

Combing stained fingers through my hair, Joshua continues, "I already told you my mother died in childbirth. But what you don't know is her death was directly linked to my father's."

"Of course it was." I smooth my thumbs over his stubble. He doesn't stop me. This is the first time I've touched him like this. It may also be the last. "Aidan was the vessel and Ember was his love. The Kiss of Infinity bound them, heart and soul."

Joshua shakes his head. Gathers my hands in his. "No. Aidan was an Ever, like me. Only one thing can kill an Ever." Our interlaced fingers rest in the crevice between our knees.

I watch his thumbs stroke my skin. Back and forth. Back and forth. "I don't understand."

He draws a labored breath, slumped shoulders quaking. I can almost see the peak of a tattoo behind his shoulder. The mark of an Ever? "Aidan passed the same night Ember did—the night I was born. The Kiss of Infinity connected them. When Ember died, Aidan's life should've replaced hers. Then his Ever blood would've generated new life within him, saving him too."

I intake a sharp breath. "Jasyn didn't save me. You did. The link created by the Kiss of Infinity—it's how he discovered you're an Ever. Your life replaced mine. Then your blood brought you back."

Joshua nods.

Jasyn titters.

Must he stand so close? "But if Aidan was an Ever, too, how did Ember die? How did they *both* die?"

Joshua's hands clench in mine. "Death is not easily explained. When it comes for you, when it's your time, there's nothing that can deter it from taking a life. If not yours, then someone else's. Death is the only Threshold into the First Reflection."

"Death is a Calling all its own."

"My mother died giving birth to me. When my father saw she'd passed, that not even he could bring her back, he didn't last long. His heart broke, and he died too."

Nathaniel was wrong. A *part* of Aidan didn't die that night. All of him did. Ember's death was his poison. He was a true Romeo. *"For never was a story of more woe . . ."*

"El," Joshua says. "The only thing that can kill an Ever is—"

"A broken heart." Jasyn pops our bubble, circling us like an incessant reprise. His voice boomerangs the space around us back to real time. "Touching story, I must say." He pulls us apart, forcing me to stand, to face him. "Have you solved the puzzle yet, dear granddaughter?"

I wrench away, my eyes wide. "Aidan was the Verity's vessel. Only death can release the Verity. It finds the purest heart." My gaze rests on Joshua. "You."

His eyes close. Head bobs.

Everyone is staring at us. Ebony with eyes gleaming and arms crossed. Kuna and Preacher with their nowhere-stare. Haman and Jasyn, two rotten apples fallen from the same tree.

And Ky. Ky who has finally brought himself to match my gaze. Ky who, in this moment, I can't bring myself to see.

I turn away, angling my body just enough so I can pretend he isn't here. "My mom went to Nathaniel when she fled. Nathaniel raised you. We didn't meet in my backyard the autumn I turned fifteen. We've met before."

Joshua gives another nod, so discreet I almost don't catch it.

I press my palm to my right cheek. "You gave me this mark."

"A Kiss of Infinity comes from the deepest part of your soul."

"You bound your soul—your life—to mine."

"When bestowed by the Verity's vessel, a Kiss of Infinity imposes an unusual outcome upon the subject's soul."

"You made me a Mirror."

"El," he interjects.

But I can't stop the realizations spilling from my brain and forming words on my lips. No time to breathe. No time to do anything but say, "Except you're an Ever, so even if I die while we're linked, you won't. Because you know I'll survive, which will keep your heart from breaking. Because my life is yours. Because—" Oh. My. Soul. Do I dare say it? "Because you love me."

His Adam's apple dips. He looks petrified. Limited to the next words that release from his mouth. "El, *please*. Don't."

But he doesn't have to say it. Because I know. The world stops. Colors fade to gray, then burst back to life, more vibrant and beautiful than before. This is the best and worst feeling I've ever had. And there is no song fitting for this moment, there are no lyrics to describe my myriad emotions.

Because Joshua loves me.

And this love will destroy him.

# of us

The truth smashes into me like a thousand falling stars, igniting my core, punching crater after crater into my already damaged heart.

How can I survive the impact?

"You were never going to come forward, were you?" Lies. Lies. Lies. "You were never going to stand against Jasyn and the Void."

"It isn't like that." Joshua struggles to stand, arm supporting his middle. "Nathaniel spent his life preparing me for this—my destiny. I always knew one day I'd have to capture the Void, imprison it. But I always felt a pull toward . . . something. I would feel sad for no reason, get excited over nothing." One step toward me. Two. "He finally confessed about my connection with you, and worse, what that connection meant."

Worse?

"I knew I had to find you, had to see for myself this person I'd always known but couldn't remember. The person who would help me save the people." He's directly in front of me now, eyes searching. "It was three years ago last September." Hands cupping my face, he exhales, "The day I met you was the day I found the piece of my soul that had always been missing."

Every glance. Every night out and afternoon in. All the plays and musicals, baseball games and museum trips. Every song and lyric and note and chord.

It was all for me.

My lips part. "You told Makai you wanted this to be over." Breath catches. "You said—"

"I *do* want this to be over. I've fought my feelings for you because our ending is your beginning. When our bond breaks on your eighteenth birthday, I can only hope my love for you will vanish as well. That somehow the link is the only reason I feel so close to you." He traces my right cheek. "My love for you can't be real. I won't allow it."

I press my face into his palm. He smells like dirt and rust. "Why not?"

"Because if I truly love you, even with the link gone, you will become a slave." Our noses are an eighth note apart. "But if I don't, you will be free to go. Saving this Reflection is my burden. I don't want it to be yours too."

Sob. Blink. "You're not making sense." I swipe at my nose. "I still don't understand why you won't recapture the Void." Swallow. "Take the throne from Crowe." Lick the salt from my chapped lips. "He's right here." I fling my arm toward my grandfather. "You should fulfill your destiny now."

"Don't you understand? I can't! Not until you turn eighteen and our bond breaks. It's the best chance you have. It's why I couldn't let you kiss me the night of your mom's disappearance. The risk was too great you'd complete the link, binding us forever." His desperate tenor echoes around the throne room. Rattling the windows. Climbing the stairs and sliding down the banisters. Extending to the painted domed ceiling.

I back away, nearly bumping into Ebony. She responds with an annoyed click of her traitorous tongue.

"And if you do love me after my birthday, link or no link? What then?"

Joshua catches my hand. "You don't need to worry about that. I won't let my heart get in the way. I can control it. I *will* control it." He's clutching my hand so tightly it stings almost as much as his words.

"And here is the twist in our tale. Do you mind? This is my favorite part." Jasyn steps between us, coming so close I can almost feel the wickedness emanating from his soul. "As you can see, the Verity's vessel is limited, love his greatest weakness. My theory is he does truly love you, but only time will tell." My grandfather *tsks*. "The Void can be imprisoned, oh yes. I have been its prison for quite some time, in fact."

Of course he has. I stare out one of the arched windows to the forever night beyond. Why didn't I see it? The Void's prison isn't a place. It's a person.

"I felt it when Aidan died. Sensed his passing in the deepest part of my charred soul. The Verity's vessel alone is able to imprison the Void. And with each new vessel, a new prison must be created— the one the vessel cares for more than any other."

I don't respond. I have no words.

"For the person closest to the Verity's vessel is also kind and good, another pure soul nearly equal to the vessel himself." Jasyn circles me now, my head spinning with each one of his egotistical steps. "It is meant as a fail-safe, you see. Such a soul is strong enough to fight against the Void within. With the help of the vessel who captured it, the Void can be controlled for quite some time. It is the sacrifice the Verity's vessel must make in order to maintain the delicate balance between good and evil."

And there's the hook. The true reason Joshua hopes his love for me is merely an illusion created by our childhood bond. The thing Mom's been keeping from me. The tidbit she worried Jasyn had figured out.

I am the one who will be the people's savior.

The Void's new prison is me.

"The Verity and the Void must always have living vessels," Jasyn says. "It is the only way the Verity can subdue the Void, contain it." Jasyn descends the dais, hands clasped behind him. He steps on Makai's hand at the bottom. My uncle doesn't move or react, too injured to get up and fight, but not so much he'd give Jasyn the pleasure of seeing his pain.

Thank the Verity Mom's not here. If she saw him like this it would kill her. It's killing me.

Jasyn rounds on Ky. Pauses behind him. Rests a hand on his neck. Ky is taller but their ranking is clear. Jasyn is in charge here.

Terror chills my face and ears. Discos before my eyes. This is why I can't leave. The reason it's not as simple as snatching the dropped blade and cakewalking it out of here. Because I'd have to choose who to take with me. My uncle. Joshua. Ky.

"But the Void isn't contained." I move toward them. "The Soulless. The Threshold. Shadow Territory. If you are the Void's prison, how do those things exist?"

Jasyn's fingers squeeze Ky's neck ever so slightly. I can almost feel the pressure against my own skin. My grandfather slips his hand into his blazer pocket, brandishes a syringe.

"They injected me with something, sent it directly into my bloodstream."

My own blood curdles at the memory of Ky's words.

"That is because . . ." The silver needle glints as Jasyn showcases it by Ky's left ear. ". . . I am accountable to no one. Aidan imprisoned the Void inside my soul. I was the one closest to him long before he met Ember. I felt it when he died, when I no longer had the Void's captor to control my actions. No Verity's vessel to help quell the darkness within." Jasyn removes his jacket. Loosens his tie and slips it over his head. Next comes his shirt, button by button. He folds the trio in half, laying one over the other. "I began to forget why I had allowed myself to become Aidan's servant in the first place. The more my humanity slipped away, the more I hungered for what Aidan never allowed me to have—power."

As if knowing what's expected of her, my half sister parades down the stairs and gathers Jasyn's unwanted layers.

I cross my arms. Assistant indeed. Does Meryl Streep know about her? Ebony brings new meaning to the phrase *The Devil Wears Prada*.

"It was quite the burden, really," Jasyn continues. "Battling the Void as it insisted on taking over my soul. So I discovered a way to expel it. To remain in control of myself while building an army. The Threshold was one thing, but not as quick as I would have preferred. Veins travel to the heart. With a mere injection I had a ready-made Soulless. Someone I could command and manipulate with a mere thought." He inserts the needle into his arm. Draws the plunger out slowly. Purposefully.

Unbidden nausea rises.

Blood does not fill the syringe's barrel. Instead a murky, smoke-like substance occupies the empty space. "I lay in wait, expecting the new vessel of the Verity to challenge me. But alas, he never came." A cutting glare toward Joshua.

I compel myself to keep my gaze trained on Ky. He does the same with me. His puckered brow and wild eyes issue a warning. Stop. Don't come any closer.

"And so." Jasyn levels the syringe with Ky's shoulder, needle pointed directly at his taut neck. "I win. If my theory is indeed correct, and Aidan's pathetic son loves you even after your bond breaks, I have no reason to fear. He will not kill me and release the Void, allowing it to latch onto your soul. It is the reason he waits for your birthday. If he captured the Void now, it would enter you but remain dormant until the protection on your soul lifts next week." His syringe hand remains rock steady. Ky remains frozen.

"Waiting, at the very least, offers the miniscule chance you will not be the one the Void enters."

Wait. Pause. Back up. I pivot toward Joshua. "If you don't love me after my birthday, who will the Void inhabit when you imprison it?"

His gaze flits to my uncle. Back to me. "Makai has already agreed. He's prepared to take on the Void for the good of the people. He's strong enough to fight it."

"And I'm not?" It's not as if I *want* to become the Void's prison, but does Joshua really believe I couldn't handle it?

He averts his eyes.

I whirl on Jasyn. Descend one step. Two. "So what now?" The words are rushed. Difficult to hide my panic when the needle is so near to Ky.

"I am nothing if not fair," Jasyn says. "I will give the Ever an opportunity to fulfill his responsibility. I suggest a celebration. You will be eighteen in a week's time. I wish to hold a ball in your honor. The entire Reflection will be obligated to attend. I am sure your rebel friends will not resist the invitation. They merely require a little extra convincing."

Haman fingers his gun. Blows on his snapping fingers as if they're made of precious metal.

Convincing? Attend or die is more like it. "Is this some sort of sick game to you?"

"I only desire an audience when I reveal the Verity's vessel. For every soul to witness his cowardice when he is unable to sacrifice you, an insignificant girl, for them."

There it is. The real reason for his party. Does he have to make such a show of everything?

"It will be quite the memorable evening. An exhibit of true power. Here I am, a mere Amulet, yet the rare and nearly indestructible Verity's vessel, an Ever no less, will not be able to touch me."

"You're wrong," I say through clenched teeth. "Whatever happens on my birthday, Joshua *will* capture the Void. If that means I become its prison, so be it." For Ky. And Mom and Makai. I glance at the Second Reflection tapestry once more.

For all of them.

"Allow me to prove you wrong," Jasyn says. "I believe his love for you goes deeper than he will admit. Which means, when it comes down to it, he will not be able to send the Void inside you. An Ever's blood heals, yet their emotions are their downfall. I could stab Aidan's son one hundred times over, and he still would not die. But if I so much as break your skin, he weakens, folds like a poorly played hand of cards."

Oh, crowe. Where's he going with this?

Lips curled back, he reveals two straight rows of pearly whites. "Except now I have another weapon, something far more interesting than splicing your pretty little neck, my own flesh and blood."

I'm dizzy and I can't feel my hands or feet. I glance from Ky to Joshua to Ky and back again. This is bad.

Jasyn grabs Ky's chin with his free hand, forces his face skyward. "I am able to keep my enemy weak simply by doing this." He plunges the needle into Ky's neck, pulls it out in rapid succession.

I feel it. Like a string connecting my soul to his, I sense the darkness pulling, yanking, drawing me in. I cry out. Clutch my chest. Fall to my knees.

Ky collapses, too, but he makes no sound. His veins are doing that thing again, crawling and darkening and . . . retracting just as quickly.

Three, two, one. It's over. The tightness above my ribs relents. The intangible connection between us loosens. I look over my shoulder at Joshua. His questioning expression says he felt it, too, the Void trying to take Ky's soul. The soul I saved with a kiss, linking the three of us for seven more days.

With a look of sheer disgust, Jasyn kicks Ky in the side.

Grunting, Ky doubles over.

"Please." I can barely get the word out. I close my eyes. "Don't hurt him."

"What was that, granddaughter? Speak up so all in attendance may hear."

I blow a breath through my nose, grind my teeth, and fume, "I said don't hurt him. This isn't his fight. You have what you want. Me. The Verity's vessel. But let Ky go."

"Oh, I beg to differ," Jasyn says. "It is very much Kyaphus's fight. You made it so when you bound your soul to his with a Kiss of Infinity."

"El, no." Joshua's voice is drenched in grief.

As if in slow motion, I turn toward him.

Fresh blood dampens the bandage around his middle, but it's the agony in his compressed expression that acts as my personal wound.

My chin quivers. I can't look at him, envisioning what I might find. Anger. Grief.

"How sweet," Jasyn blusters. "The Ever who would do anything for his beloved, and the girl who kissed a traitor. Which leaves us with the Shield who, despite his shady past, allowed himself to fall in love. This is quite the complicated triangle, indeed."

"You're wrong," Ky grunts, speaking for the first time in what seems like hours. He rises, rolling his shoulders, taking on the same manner he had the night we met. Cold. Cruel. "I am not in love with her. As always, I remain loyal to you, my liege."

My body goes rigid.

He faces my grandfather and—bows?

No. Flippin'. Way.

"Master," Ky appeals.

It's a ruse. Has to be.

Jasyn lists his head. Amused? Suspicious? I can't tell. "What can you offer as a token of your loyalty?"

Ky lifts his head. "What did you have in mind?" A smile lilts his voice, and a slant of his head oozes cunning. Well, well, the boy from the party returns.

Jasyn's eyes glint. "I am sure you can come up with something." He clasps Ky's shoulder in a fatherly gesture.

Rounding on me, Ky pauses a sniff away. The contours of his face harden further, if possible.

I shut my eyes. Oh no you don't—you're not using your Calling on me.

He leans down, places his lips next to my ear. "Would you rather it be me or Haman?"

Eyes narrowed, I face him.

His regard snatches mine with ferocity, and I can't look away. Numbness travels through my veins, my organs, rendering every part below my neck immovable.

Snap!

No feeling, no pain, but the deafening note triggers an awareness. I glance down. My hand hangs limply from my wrist. Contorted. Swelling. Broken.

Ky scoops me into his arms and carries me away as Jasyn steps up beside Joshua, leers down at him.

Joshua's face contorts. He clasps his wrist. Unlike me, he is not numb to the ache Ky caused.

But there's a greater ache there, something that splices me open, emotions bleeding onto the pristine floor. The broken wrist is trivial compared to the true agony he endures, far worse than any broken bone.

If he feels what I feel, it's not the physical pain that renders him immovable. It's the knowledge that I was able to give Ky a Kiss of Infinity. I still don't understand it, but one question rises to the surface above all the others.

If I'm linked to Ky, heart and soul, what does that mean for him if I become the Void's new prison?

THIRTY-FOUR

Before we part

Ky hasn't said a word since we left the throne room.

My head throbs, a headache setting up camp between my eyebrows. I glance up.

Ky's face is a portcullis. He has yet to meet my gaze. Away from the tiered balconies, down enclosed halls and corridors he carries me. Ignores me.

I stare at the ceiling. Cradled. Helpless.

When we're some distance from the throne room, he sidesteps into an alcove. Peeks over his shoulder. Then his face lowers, a mere hair away from mine. When his lips part, I inhale his breath, stare at him, will my concentration not to falter and find his mouth. Our kiss was so fleeting. Why can't I expel it from my mind?

"Why did you do it?" he asks.

He doesn't have to elaborate. I know what he means. I don't have an explanation. I kissed him because I wanted to. Because I thought I was saying good-bye.

When I give no answer, he continues, "You do know even when your link with David breaks, you are still bound to me. Forever. I'm over eighteen. You chose me. And I—"

My insides mush. "You what?"

"Never mind." He straightens, steps into the hall, and continues in silence.

Two more corridors and a spiraling stairwell later, Ky enters a circular room—a sort of attic-slash-tower. The accommodations are modest. A low cot with a hay mattress and faded quilt. A single wooden chair, a matching bowl resting on its seat and bucket beneath it. Straight ahead, a barred window emits the meager moonlight. Better than the stinky dungeon, at least.

He lays me on the cot. The hay rustles beneath my weight. "This is the Captive's Tower. Nobody will bother you here." He brushes my bangs from my eyes, then crouches and begins digging through his pack. His shoulder muscles flex against his taut jacket.

I find a cobweb hanging from the coned ceiling and ogle it.

A long while passes before either of us speaks again. I don't feel a thing, but I assume he's tending the bone he broke, something he learned from his Physic mother, no doubt.

"I'm done." His low, throaty tone further contorts my dilemma.

When I look at my wrist, it's splinted, wrapped in a bandage. I almost thank him but refrain. He only fixed what he fractured in the first place.

In slow motion, as if making sure I'm watching, he leans down and kisses the top of my dressed hand.

Again, I don't feel it, but the action sets off a siren in my brain's warning station. The heat between us is undeniable, energizing the atmosphere like a twister waiting to funnel. The slightest shift in the air and *whoosh!* Ky is a tornado—exciting and unpredictable. If I don't ground myself, he'll carry me away.

Since I can't extract my hand, I ignore him, acting as if the kiss doesn't affect me one bit.

"The numbness will wear off soon since my Calling doesn't affect you the way it does others." He rises, stretches his arms above his head. "Your wrist will hurt before David's connection heals it. I'm sorry."

He backs away, sits on the floor, and crosses his legs, tucking his feet beneath him. He looks so boyish and innocent, picking at the fibers in the dusty rug at the room's center. I imagine knowing him at a younger, more innocent age. If I met him before Jasyn got ahold of him, would his life have turned out differently? Would mine? And what about Joshua? If he hadn't bound our souls, would he have already captured the Void?

My pulse quiets. The possibilities are endless. But we're here now. Time to stop wondering and prepare myself for what's to come. I can't let Makai take on the Void. Mom deserves some happiness for once in her life. Which means I have to figure out how to convince Joshua he truly loves me. To persuade him to stop fighting it.

When Ky finally stands, he shoulders his pack. "I'll bring you some food in a bit. Is there anything else you need?"

My eyelids droop. "Nothing."

"I'll be back." Ky crosses to the door. He gives me one last apologetic look before slipping into the stairwell. The click of the lock preludes his fading footsteps.

I allow my eyes to close completely then, dreaming of my birthday and the nightmare it might bring.

I chew my nails, peering through the barred window as the final round of onlookers file—are herded—into the castle. For the past week people from all over have trickled in—Jasyn's welcomed guests.

More like involuntary spectators.

Ky was able to snag my pack from the throne room and smuggle it up here. Since then, I've pored over Ember's theory, over the drawing of the composition. But I still can't complete the arrangement. I've written and erased and crumpled and started again. What I have down, penned on one of the blank pages from *The Reflection Chronicles*, is broken, incomplete. But it will have to be enough.

A faint reflection considers me from the frosty glass beyond the bars. I slip my hand between them and rest my palm against the window, my skin chilling the way it does when I go ice-skating at Rockefeller Center and forget to wear gloves. My breath covers my reflected nose in fog, expanding, then shrinking. I wipe away the moisture, staring at what I expected to vanish at midnight.

My birthmark.

Since it's still here, does this mean Joshua truly loves me? That his feelings transcend the broken link, allowing my mirror-mark and Calling to remain? I cradle my head against the bars. Ember's theory provides nothing on the matter, probably because this is the first time something like this has happened. I should be disappointed, knowing what this means. Instead, a fire ignites inside me.

I'm ready.

Ky has visited me every day over the past seven. Bringing me food. Water. Clean clothes. He even brought me some purple dye at my request. The process was a mess but worth it. My blonde ends are now the color of eggplant, a symbol I stand with the Verity.

Last night Ky delivered a little something extra alongside my dinner. I wait in the most gorgeous gown I've ever had the pleasure of touching. Cornflower-blue chiffon cut into an A-line, a lace appliqué scoop neck embellishing the ensemble.

The lock clicks. The door whines. I twist.

Jaw limp, Ky leans against the doorframe. He's decked in black from vest and tie to slacks and formal shoes. His hair is combed off his forehead, and his face is clean shaven. Strange. When I first met him I thought him unattractive. The acne. How cruel he seemed when he kidnapped me. Now I see who he is beyond the surface. Kind and good. Brave.

He's never looked so handsome.

I shift. "What?" Why is he just staring? I twirl a curl between my fingers. "What is it?"

He blinks, snaps his mouth closed. "Nothing. You look"—
cough—"are you ready?"

Was he going to say beautiful? I almost wish he did. I'm almost
relieved he didn't.

"What's with the fancy digs?" I do a little pirouette, the gown's
delicate fabric swirling around my legs.

"Crowe likes his show, remember? He requested I make sure
you look your very best." Ky does a little bow, a smirk lifting his lips.

I tuck the curl in place and swallow the *thrum, thrum, thrum* in
my throat before meeting him at the door.

The corner of his mouth twitches as he inhales. Before we
part I want to say everything and nothing. To escape with him
and never look back. To run down the stairs, far away from his
complex gaze. To explain that even though my mirrormark—the
one Joshua gave me—remains, I still care for Ky.

My traitorous thoughts are bandits. Stealing my oxygen.
Robbing my resolve.

His throat throbs. My pulse speeds. How did we get so close?
Our fingertips brush. His breath caresses my face. Will he try to
kiss me? If he does, will I let him?

His expression ticks to serious. He crouches, withdrawing his
mirrorglass blade from the back of his pants. Then he lifts my dress
just enough so my ankle shows.

Tingles. Everywhere.

He removes the strap from his own ankle. Next he attaches it
and the knife to mine with care.

His fingers are hot, melting my skin.

Without a word he rises and ushers me downstairs. I'm a prisoner and he's the warden. Silence festers, the knife at my ankle like
a shackle. If he thinks I need a weapon, Jasyn's plan is more than
he let on.

As we near the party, a murmuring hum floats outward,
accompanied by the soothing strings of a *Swan Lake* pas de trois.

The music sweeps me up, and I can't help but sway as I walk. Once we reach the tiered balconies, gads of bodies pelt my sight. They lean against railings, huddle in groups against walls. Their chatter a jumbled whir, undecipherable. I stare straight ahead, attempting to ignore their sidelong glances. Their confused expressions. Everyone is thinking the same thing.

Why are we here?

The throne room has been transformed. White globe lights and tulle wrap marble columns and drape window ledges, where beyond a lazy snow falls from the night sky. Tea light candles glow dimly, decorating tall tables adorned with freshly cut fir branches. And . . . is that the scent of chocolate? Too bad I have zero appetite.

Everyone is dressed in their best. Even the Soulless guards scattered throughout model sport coats and ties. A string quartet to the right of the dais transitions into a gentle waltz, though nobody dances. It's a nice picture, but the people's fearful faces suggest anything but merriment. Jasyn is nowhere to be seen, probably planning a majestic entrance.

Ky leads me down the grand staircase and toward the dais. Light bounces off a painted, domed ceiling featuring Mom's handiwork. I'd know those broad strokes and swirling colors anywhere. The chandelier is brilliant, thousands of crystals sparkling and tinkling. Straight ahead, the throne waits. Chairs have been added to either side of it. And there, occupying one of them, is Mom.

I rush toward her, and she embraces me.

"Mom." Her name is an exhale of shock and relief. "What are you doing here?"

"When you didn't return, I knew I had to come back." She smooths her black evening dress when I draw away. "Even if I wasn't bound by a Kiss of Accord, I would've returned for you." She leans up and kisses my cheek.

"What do you mean?" I sit in the chair beside her. Ky has

already taken his station at the bottom of the grand staircase, acting the guard he's supposed to be.

She places one hand on her stomach. "I am with child," she breathes. "Just a couple months along."

Every inch of me wants to regurgitate. "Did Haman—?"

"No, my darling." A glance over her shoulder. "We, Makai and I—we went to the courthouse last year. Married in secret. I wanted to tell you, but I couldn't. How would I explain myself?" The pink in her cheeks is embarrassment and excitement. The glass over her eyes sorrow and wonder.

What does this mean? Isabeau. And Haman. I cup my hand over my mouth. He meant his promise. He's going to try to take Mom's baby.

"Jasyn found out," my invisible uncle whispers from somewhere behind. "He's promised not to harm us—the child, you, me—as long as your mother serves him forever. The terms became binding with a Kiss of Accord." He nocks each word, letting them soar like arrows.

"I have already agreed to your terms."

"Mom. How could you do this?" I can't decide who I'm angrier with. Jasyn for his sick, twisted bargain. Or Mom for agreeing to it. "If you'd just waited a little while longer, my rescue would've been your ticket out. You could've taken the baby and disappeared."

She blinks back tears. "I'm tired of running. What I saw in you before you returned for the boy, it ignited something within me. I've spent eighteen years hiding, cowering, always looking over my shoulder. No more. If you can be brave, so can I."

Covering my hand with hers, she faces forward. I want to tell her it will be over soon. Jasyn will be dead, the Void captured, and her agreement will no longer matter. But I can't. My burdens do not belong to anyone else but me.

The quartet stops, and a hush swathes the crowd.

Movement along the first balcony demands my attention.

Every few feet a Soulless steps forward, brandishing a trumpet and raising it to his lips.

In unison, the trumpets blast a brief overture, encored by an echoing silence.

"Get ready," Mom says. "He's here."

so much of me

S howtime.

Two tuxedoed Soulless roll a red carpet from the top of the grand staircase all the way to the throne. The edge flushes with its feet.

Jasyn steps to the room's summit, dressed to the nines in a 1920s-style tux complete with tails and white gloves. He descends, surveying the crowd, taking his time as if wanting everyone to catch a glimpse of his splendor.

Get over yourself already.

Once atop the dais he rotates and spreads his arms wide. "My people," he bellows with bravado. "I am so glad you could join us."

No applause. Nothing aside from the frightened expressions of a community that spent years under this man's oppression.

"Please help yourselves to the hors d'oeuvres making their way around the room. The entertainment will begin soon." I have a good guess his entertainment is just another word for torture. "For now, I invite you all to join me in a celebratory dance to commence this momentous occasion." *Clap, clap.*

An up-tempo waltz straight out of a Jane Austen film leaps from the quartet's strings.

Nobody moves.

"Feeling shy, are we?" Jasyn asks. "Please, I insist." Pause for dramatic effect. *"Dance."* He waves a hand and Soulless come out of the woodwork, withdrawing weapons and coaxing couples into submission. Men and women join hands across the dance floor, one-two-three to the music in perfect, synchronized time. Nobody protests, either too afraid to use their Callings in defense or unable to. Ky said he can't control Soulless. Does that mean none of the Callings are effective on the creatures once they've turned to the Void completely?

Except . . . mine was. On the beach. Transitioned or in limbo, every soldier halted pursuit when I began my song.

I scan the crowd for Joshua. Where *is* he?

My grandfather turns, smiles at Mom and me. "I must say, I was delighted to hear you had returned. I knew you would, of course." He offers a gloved hand to Mom. "It would give me great pleasure if you would accompany me in this first dance, Elizabeth."

Who does he think he's fooling?

Mom folds her arms and avoids his gaze, scowling. "I'd rather be torched by Dragon's breath."

I stifle a snort. Okay, I shouldn't be laughing, but Mom is awesome.

His jaw twitches. "That can be arranged."

I rise and lay my hand in his. "I'll dance with you. After today I probably won't make it to senior prom." Though the décor does remind me of last year's winter formal.

I didn't have a date—no surprise there—but Mom insisted I go for the experience. Joshua said he'd take me, but as soon as we got into the cab, he hijacked the outing. Whisked me off to Sardi's for dinner, a reservation he'd apparently made weeks in advance. Afterward we ended up at the Angelika in SoHo, butter greasing our fingertips as we snickered our way through a marathon of the most cringe-worthy movie musicals ever created, including but not limited to *Dr. Horrible's Sing-Along Blog* and *Xanadu*.

I'd welcome another night of laugh-induced tears and stitching side aches over a stuffy dance any day.

Regaining his composure, Jasyn eyes me, one brow peaked. "All right."

Together we walk to the center of the floor. Taking the lead, my grandfather sets a hand on my waist and lifts our joined hands in the air. *Blech.* Did he pour an entire bottle of cologne on himself this time?

I reach up and place my fingers on his shoulder, trying to maintain as little contact as possible. He twirls us and, to my awe, I don't trip or fumble. Much.

I scan the crowd. Still no sign of Joshua. Is he okay? Has he spent the past week agonizing over what has transpired? Is Jasyn waiting until the proper moment to reveal him?

"What is distracting you so?" Jasyn dips me back.

"I was just wondering where Joshua is." Might as well be honest. "I was hoping to dance with him before—"

"Before I reveal the true coward he is?"

I scowl. "He's no coward. He *will* capture the Void."

"We shall see." He ceases our waltz. "I will grant your wish, but only if you bestow mine."

Uh-oh. "Which is?"

He withdraws, brushing off his lapel. "I want to see you dance with someone else first. You did bind your life to his, did you not?"

Jasyn wants me to dance with Ky for his own perverse amusement? I should refuse, tell him where he can shove his sardonic wish. "Fine."

"Very good." He beckons Ky.

"Yes, Your Sovereignty?" He bows.

"Dance with the birthday girl, will you? I am going to have a chat with my daughter." Jasyn takes his perch on the throne.

Haman stands beside it now, bodyguard and torment commissioner rolled into one. Ebony's there, too, decked in a ruby miniskirt, a strapless sequined top, and a black leather jacket that halts at her waist. She sits, ankles crossed, in the chair farthest from Mom. When Ebony catches my eye, a haughty grin curls the corners of her mouth.

Is she really so bent on revenge? Can't she see what Jasyn's doing? He has no limits. At some point he'll inject her with the Void too.

Ky and I join hands and hips, our legs brushing as we swirl amidst the other couples. He's actually a good dancer, something I never would've surmised from our back-and-forth sway at Blake's party. The music slows, and our bodies match its cadence. My skin electrifies beneath Jasyn's gaze. I ignore it. He's getting his show, but I'm getting something too.

A good-bye.

After today it will be over. My intact birthmark proves Joshua loves me. I will become the Void's new prison.

Things will never be the same.

Ky pulls me close, his hand on the small of my back, his mouth at my ear. "Tell me why." He tilts my chin so our lips are angled toward one another.

Butterflies emerge from the cocoon in the recesses of my stomach. Flit to my lungs. I exhale their wings.

I've been telling myself our kiss was a fluke. Some unexplainable phenomenon that stemmed from sheer desperation. But a part of me knows it's not entirely true. Because a Kiss of Infinity is rare. Which means this thing between us is more than I'm allowing it to be.

I slip away, unable to handle the ache ushered in by the end. "I'm sorry, Ky. I can't."

"Don't give me that, Em." His wounded tone is almost enough to draw me back into his arms. "If you're going to choose him, have the decency to say the words."

Get it together. "It's not about that. I'm not choosing him over you." I stare at my feet. Can't look at him. "I'm not choosing anybody." Because I'm choosing everybody. Everybody but me.

He takes my hand. Tugs.

I look up.

His expression softens, churning my heart to butter along with it. "You think he really loves you. You expect to take on the Void." Not questions. Realizations.

I withdraw farther, eye the floor again. *Slam.* I whirl.

Joshua. He's here.

"Going somewhere?" His question is for me but his glare darts to Ky.

Say something. "No." Twisting fingers. "Nowhere."

Ky storms past, bumping Joshua's shoulder as he goes. He's misunderstood my reaction. Doesn't matter. He's better off without me.

Unfazed, Joshua takes me in his arms and leads me in our first dance ever. When we touch, relief washes my body. The music transitions again, this time into a *Sleeping Beauty* waltz. We move effortlessly despite my two left feet. I've seen him in dress clothes plenty of times, but somehow he's managed to deprive my breath once again. He's sporting a blue-and-white pinstriped shirt beneath a light gray vest and matching tie. The contrast brings out his eyes—eyes secured on me.

The world blurs, leaving us alone in the vast space. The music strips away too. "Happy birthday," he says, towing me from my trance. He doesn't smile.

"Now it is." I steamroll a grin over the rubble inside. Wait for the moment. It will come. I spy the dais. Jasyn is in deep conversation with Haman. "Can we go someplace? Alone?"

He stops. Exhales. I almost think he'll turn me down, but then he glances left. Right. Over my shoulder. He resumes our dance, ever so stealthily leading us away from the floor's center. It takes the length of two waltzes to inch through the crowd without drawing attention to ourselves. Once at the wall, we creep along and back, seeking shelter in a cramped, shadowy alcove beneath the stairs.

Joshua bumps his head on the low, curved ceiling. *"I think we're alone now,"* he sings, doing his best Tommy James impersonation.

The unexpected tune throws me off, and I emit a nervous laugh. The last thing I expected to find beneath these stairs is the easygoing, music-loving boy I fell in love with.

So much of me wants to respond in melody, but I can't. "Joshua—"

"I care for you." He angles away from me. Combs his fingers through his hair. "That I can't deny." His hands are trembling. "But, I'm sorry, I don't love you." He hangs his head. "Makai will take on the Void. I wanted to tell you before I do it. I needed you to hear it from me."

I touch his shoulder, nudge him to face me. "No. You love me. Don't you see?" I take his hand and bring it to my right cheek. "My birthmark—mirrormark—it didn't vanish. It has to mean something. That your love for me goes deep beneath the surface."

He lifts his head, eyes searching. "It didn't vanish?"

My brows knit. "You didn't notice?"

"Well, no." He scratches the back of his head. A smile plays on his lips. "I could never see it."

My breath hitches. He can't see it? Could *never* see it? What does this mean?

Our gazes lock, as if we're figuring out something we should've known all along. Me realizing how Joshua sees me. Him understanding I never knew what he saw—didn't see.

As if in slow motion, he draws me in. "It wasn't supposed to happen this way. You were supposed to have a way out. A chance to have a choice."

"This *is* my choice. It has to be me. You. And me. The Verity and the Void." I half laugh, half cry at that.

"I don't think—" He clears his throat. "I don't think I can do that to you."

"I'm strong enough," I promise, hoping the words sound true.

"Maybe," he breathes. "But I am not. How can I make you the vessel of the Void? What kind of love would that be?"

"The greatest kind of all." His heart *beat, beat, beats* against our hands. "The kind of love that will save this Reflection." *Don't cry. I need to get this out.* "The kind of love . . ." *Keep going. Almost there.* ". . . that happily ever after lives for."

His nose brushes my cheek. Fingers intertwine with mine. He gives no answer, careful as ever not to kiss me.

"Love me, Joshua. Love me enough to let me go. Let me help you give the people the happy ending they've been waiting for."

One, two, three breaths. And then . . .

His mouth pursues mine, and I'm melting, nearly forgetting myself. My chest constricts. Flutters. Despite what must come afterward, this is real. For a moment, I'm going to enjoy it.

In the beginning it's soft and hesitant, the way a first kiss should be. We keep our mouths closed, our bodies stiff and distant.

But that doesn't last.

Joshua slides his fingers from mine, finding my cheek with one hand and my waist with the other. He separates my lips with his, and I curve into him as he reaches around and cradles the back of my head with his palm.

I rise on demi-pointe, exploring the craters and contours of him. The line of his hair. The swell of his shoulder. The dip of his lower back. So strange to know a person one way for so long and still feel as if I'm meeting him for the first time. The newness of it sends little sparking thrills through every nerve ending. My right cheek burns as if ignited. He kisses me and kisses me and kisses me again, as if making up for all the times he's wanted to and held back.

This has to end. I want more.

When Joshua's mouth leaves mine, it's too soon. His breaths release in heavy waves, hot on my face. "I love you," he admits at last.

Then the shadows take me away.

THIRTY-SIX

MY HEART

"*She believed Tiernan would kill you, so she fled, sought a man named Nathaniel Archer.*" Jasyn's words drift across my heart as I fly through the night.

I'm bouncing, my arms and legs wrapped in something soft. A blanket? An icy chill pings my ears, and I stir. The jarring movement ceases, and the blanket is tugged around my ears, over my forehead. I feel small. So small.

Flying? No. I'm being carried.

Thump, thump, thump. My carrier's heartbeat races, pounding against my ear as the jolting continues. Judging from her higher-pitched breaths, she's a woman. Her feet slap the ground. She's running. Her arms cinch around me. Mmmm, cozy.

Thud! Thud! Thud!

Click. Creak.

"Are you Nathaniel Archer?" Mom's voice vibrates into me, muffled slightly by the fabric covering my ears.

My eyelids flutter. A helpless cry escapes without warning.

Mom's face hovers above me. She sways, a soothing motion.

Something in my mouth. Mom's finger? I suck vigorously, calming.

"Who wants to know?" Nathaniel asks in a gruff voice.

This isn't a dream. It's a memory. I'm a baby, remembering something impossible for me to recall. I will myself to focus.

"And if I refuse?" Nathaniel asks.

Refuse what?

Mom's chest heaves, pressing against my frame. "Then we're both already dead."

We're moving again. *Whine. Snap.* It's warmer. We must be inside, the door closed. Mom shifts. Floorboards groan as she shuffles forward.

It's dark. So dark.

Fizz. A match strikes. *Hiss.* An orange glow washes the ceiling. I only see Mom.

"Father, who is this?" Makai, has to be. He sounds younger, but it's him.

"Ask *her*," Nathaniel harrumphs, as pleasant as ever. "Claims to be running from Tiernan. As far as I'm concerned, you can tell my younger son until he returns what he stole, I'll have nothing to do with him." Having met him, seen the sadness in his eyes, I recognize the wrench in Nathaniel's voice as grief, not hatred. Despite Tiernan's actions, Nathaniel loved his younger son.

"I'm not sure what you're referring to." Mom adjusts me in her arms. "But I promise you I've had no part in his crimes."

"Please forgive my father." Makai sounds closer now. "He is not used to hosting guests."

An inward smile spreads across my middle. I wish I could see my uncle's face. Would I be able to discern his admiration for Mom even then?

"Yes, well." The defense in her tone relaxes. "I understand your hesitation. Tiernan is not the most trustworthy person in the Second." Her voice hitches at that. Is the admission painful? "What reason would you have to believe me?"

"May I see?"

I'm shifting, turning. Makai's face fills my vision. He's younger. No specks of gray streak his hair, and the lines on his face are not so pronounced.

"The child is my brother's. Isn't she?"

"Y-yes." A crack in Mom's voice. "He mentioned this place once. I have no one. I wasn't sure where else to go."

"You cannot stay here," Nathaniel calls from a distant corner of the room. "There's a nice cave deeper into the island. Perhaps you and the child can make a home there."

"Father!" Makai scolds, whipping his head in Nathaniel's direction.

The loudness startles me, sends me wailing again.

Mom coos. Moisture crests her eyelashes. "Please," she whispers. "If Tiernan finds us, I'm afraid he will kill my daughter. And my father . . . I'm not sure we're safe around him either."

"Why?" I could kiss Makai for his kindness. Every single compassionate word trumps ten of Nathaniel's insolent ones.

I quiet.

"He's very old-fashioned," she explains, further hushing her tone. "My indiscretions would be an embarrassment to him. Aside from that, he has released the Void. There's no telling what he'll do."

"Your father is Jasyn Crowe." It's not a question. Makai strokes my forehead, but his eyes remain fastened on Mom.

Mom nods. "My father has never harmed me, but I cannot risk it. I cannot stay there."

"Who helped you escape?"

Huff. "I was raised in the castle. I know my way around."

She was only sixteen. It must've been difficult for her to prove her independence, her credibility, to these two men when she was just a kid herself. I have to give her credit. Even under Nathaniel's skepticism and Makai's kind but unsure questioning, she's holding her own.

"Why come to us? What can we do?"

It's getting hot in here. I wiggle and stretch, trying to loose myself from this constricting mummy wrap. Ah, my arms are free. That's better.

"You're a Guardian, are you not? Is protecting people not your job? I've heard there's a rebel hideout. Someplace inconspicuous. Can you take us there?"

A toddler's cry pierces their whispers.

"I'll get him." Nathaniel tromps past.

My tummy rumbles. I cry again, and Mom resumes her sway. But I won't relent. Must I be so theatrical about it?

"Does she have to be so loud?" Nathaniel half shouts when he returns. Is Joshua on his hip? I can't see past my squinched eyelids.

"She's a baby," Mom counters, still rocking from side to side. "Babies cry. There, there, brave girl."

The teenager part of my brain managing to comprehend things laughs at her nickname for me. She's always called me this. Always thought I was more than I am. Maybe I'm finally starting to live up to the endearment. I'm trying to, anyway.

"It's all right. Shhh," she tries.

Waaahhhh! I guess my pipes developed at an early age. Quite the solo number I'm performing.

"Well hi there, what's your name?" She's not talking to me.

"Jos-wuh," a tiny voice replies.

Be still, my philharmonic heart.

"Do you want to see the baby girl, Joshua?" Mom asks sweetly.

"Uh-huh."

She moves and sits.

I can hardly see or hear through the screams and tears. Would I shut up already? I want to see him too.

Soft skin touches my hand. My pulse slows, and I grow quiet. I turn my head. Three-year-old Joshua stares back at me, his eyes almost green in the firelight's glow, his little-boy hair two shades lighter, all curls. But it's him. He smiles.

"Bee-bee," Joshua announces, as if he's discovered something everyone else has failed to realize.

"Eliyana," Mom says.

"El," Joshua repeats, his *l* sounding more like a *w*, his brows scrunched and serious. "Kwhy?" He cocks his head.

Cry?

"Mmm-hmm." A smile lilts through her voice.

I blink more wetness away. Sniffle.

Joshua pats my hand. "No kwhy, bee-bee El." Then he closes his eyes, leans in, and presses his pudgy pink lips to my right cheek.

A surge of warmth spreads through my skin, tingling, burning. A sensation I've felt only one other time in my life . . . a few moments ago . . . when twenty-one-year-old Joshua kissed me, not for the first time. For the second.

A Tinker Bell giggle escapes my chest, and I wrap my tiny hand around his finger.

Mom gasps.

I don't take my eyes off Joshua. How can I? Even as a baby, it's impossible not to adore him.

"What?" Protective-older-brother worry rushes Makai's breathy question. "What is it? Did he hurt her? He's still learning how to be soft."

"No." Panic coats the word. She adjusts me once again, and light floods my eyes. Squint. "Look."

I grasp Joshua's finger tighter, afraid he'll disappear if I let go.

Nathaniel shoves Makai aside. The old man dons a set of spectacles, gazes along the bridge of his nose. "Now look what you've done." His weathered face is drawn. "This is exactly why I didn't want you here."

"The boy. He's the Verity's new vessel, isn't he?"

"Yes," Nathaniel snaps. "The king and queen died after his birth. And now, because of you, we have a new set of problems. This boy is destined to become king and imprison the Void. Any idea what his connection with the girl will mean?"

Mom's lip quivers, her strong front wavering.

"Here is what we are going to do." My grandfather begins to

pace. "You will stay here. We will prepare the girl, just as I am doing with Joshua. She will be raised to know who she is and what she must do. Her Mirror abilities will strengthen her. We must . . ."

Their voices deaden then, detach as baby me falls asleep, ending the memory. I drift through darkness, through blue and red and green spots dancing over my eyelids. I don't hear Mom's argument, her decision to hide me rather than remain. I don't see them quarrel over what's best for me or for Joshua.

Because the choice is finally mine.

And Jasyn is going down.

THIRTY-SEVEN

our stories end

"Eliyana?"

Lips at my temple.

"El, are you okay?"

Fingers in my hair.

"Say something so I know you're all right."

A hand squeezing mine.

Blink, blink, blink. "How long was I out?"

"Out?" Joshua asks. "You've just been standing here staring at me." He laughs, my favorite sound. "I must be a good kisser. I think I sent you into shock." He brings my knuckles to his lips, kisses them. Then—

Joshua is yanked from—flees?—my embrace, stealing my heart as he goes.

Arms around my middle drag me in the other direction.

The throne room vanishes.

The globe lights. The elegant décor. The dais. Everything is gone. Disappeared. Or so Jasyn would have us believe.

The arena swapped for the throne room is a mix between a modern-day stadium and a Roman coliseum. Stone bleachers scale the oval structure at every angle, creeping out of view beneath high arcs stretching to a starry sky. Every seat is full. The faces blur—a glitch in the façade?

The crowd roars. Angry? Excited? I can't tell.

My captor shoves me to the ground. My gown rips at the knee, and gravel digs into my skin. I hiss through my teeth.

"Don't touch her!"

I crane my neck. A daunting female Soulless with coffee-colored waves to her hips and high cheekbones restrains Joshua a few feet back.

Lark.

Joshua jerks and tugs. Pointless.

Boom, boom, boom. Drums beat an ominous march.

An iron gate twenty yards to my left shudders, sinks into the ground like a carnivorous jaw welcoming dinner. The reverberation travels across the sandy floor. Loosening pebbles. Thrumming into the soles of my ballet flats. Pulsating to my skull.

Jasyn struts into view once the iron teeth disappear, grinning and waving to the crowd. He's dressed in gladiator garb, only adding to the setting he's created. "What do you think?" he asks as he approaches, his voice amplified as if traveling through a megaphone. "Is it not glorious?" He raises his arms and does a 360, basking.

The drumming ceases. The crowd falls silent.

Jasyn tips his chin and Lark releases Joshua.

He's by my side in an instant. "Are you hurt?"

I chomp back the pain emanating from my throbbing wrists. "No," I lie.

He kisses the top of my head and springs to his feet. "Why the theatrics, Crowe?" He shouts above the din, his rigid form bent forward in tackle-ready fashion. "You know your time is up." His voice carries the slightest quaver. Hopefully my grandfather doesn't notice.

"Oh really?" Jasyn lifts his palms. "What are you waiting for then? Everyone is present. Make. Your. Move." With a clap on Joshua's shoulder, Jasyn announces, "Good people of the Second,

I reveal to you your long-awaited king, son to the late Aidan and Ember, the vessel of the Verity himself—Joshua David!"

I hear the unified gasp of every person in the stadium, the beat preluding a Shakespearian death scene.

Jasyn steps to the guard behind me, unsheathes a sword. *Shink.*

This is a game to him. A cruel, twisted game. And it will never end. It will never stop. Not unless Joshua does what he has to do.

Clatter. Jasyn tosses the sword before Joshua's feet, strides ten paces, and pivots.

Joshua glances at the sword only briefly before returning his gaze to my grandfather.

The drums roll again, low and light. Snow drifts toward us, melts in the sand.

"Go ahead." Jasyn almost yawns the words. "Fulfill your destiny and finish me, or inform the people why you cannot. But please, do not waste my time."

Arrogant weasel.

Joshua's arms shake at his sides.

"Very well," Jasyn says. "I suppose I must do everything myself." His gaze flits to me, left eye twitching. "This is the reason your precious vessel refuses to wield his sword." He points a finger. "Bring me the Shield." His arm sweeps in the gate's direction.

Haman emerges, dragging Ky.

His slacks gather dirt with every inch, his boots scraping earth. Chains bind his wrists, coiled so unforgivingly his hands have begun to turn blue.

I link my finger and thumb around one wrist, twisting. Suddenly I realize the throbbing isn't solely due to my fall. My wrists hurt because Ky's do.

Haman stops when he reaches me and chucks him to the ground.

One, two, three shards of my heart land on the broken boy beside me. "Ky," I whisper.

He turns his head away.

Why did they do this to him? Is Jasyn's goal to break me?

Joshua clutches his chest.

I attempt to mute my emotions. Joshua's an Ever. An Ever who loves me. I've no idea if what we shared was a Kiss of Infinity, but it doesn't matter. Because I have the power to break his heart. And Ky? My life is his. I need to restrain myself. My heart is a time bomb, and I control the counter. *Tick-tock, tick-tock.*

"Leave Kyaphus alone." Joshua's resounding timbre ricochets throughout the stadium, unwavering. "He has no part in this."

"You have no idea." Jasyn toes the sand. Chuckles. "Let us play a little game. Every minute you hesitate will be another life I claim for the Void. Shall we begin with Kyaphus?"

"No," I cry. I place my body in front of his. "You'll have to go through me first."

Sweat glistens at Joshua's temple. His ears are bright red.

Jasyn wags two fingers at Lark, who brandishes another murk-filled syringe.

My pulse zooms up my neck, fires to my ears. When my soul was linked to the Verity, the Void couldn't touch Ky. Will it have the same effect now that I'm eighteen? I can only hope since my birthmark remained, somehow the protection on my soul is intact as well. The protection on *Ky's* soul.

Lark approaches and shoves me aside. I kick her shin and pull her hair. Sing, *"Stop. Don't."* But she ignores me. Why—?

There. Inside her left ear. Some sort of plug. She can't hear me. My song is useless.

Lark injects the syringe into Ky's neck without batting an eye. His face contorts. He hisses in pain.

The arena spins. I bite my lip to keep from screaming. Taste salt and rust. When I gain focus again, I watch as the Void is unable to consume Ky just as it had been before.

Relief cools the volcano bubbling in my core. Thank the Verity.

"How very interesting," Jasyn muses as if making a scientific discovery. Except he can't fool me. His casual humming and hawing lets on he expected this to happen. That he's only messing with Ky to torture me, which in turn torments Joshua.

Enough.

Gathering all my strength, I push off the ground, stagger forward, placing myself between my grandfather and his current victim. Time to find out if I have what it takes. Inhale. Exhale. Vision clearing. I turn my focus on Joshua. He wears a drawn expression, mouth turned down in silent anguish. I close my eyes and force myself to sing the lyrics I've spent the past week pairing with my own personal melody. The lyrics meant to persuade him to do what he must.

> *"Every choice you made for me,*
> *The love I always failed to see,*
> *You gave it all to see me free,*
> *Let me give it all for you."*

"El." Joshua shakes his head. Touches his lips. "Wait."

It's working.

> *"Every time you held on tight,*
> *Never let me leave your sight,*
> *Did what you thought was right,*
> *Let me do what's right for you."*

He covers his ears. "El, stop. I'm not ready. I need another minute."

I inhale, ready to begin a new verse. We don't have another minute.

Fingers snap.

I double over. I've experienced Haman's Calling firsthand

before, but this is different. Less, somehow. My insides twist. I cry out. But at the same time, I feel the Shield in me fighting back, building a wall against the Shield in Haman. Healing. Mending. Restoring.

Joshua whirls, fingers clawing his breaking heart.

Ky opens his mouth but doesn't make a sound, his obvious pain finally confirming what I've suspected since our kiss.

He kissed me back. We *shared* a Kiss of Infinity. Our link is complete.

I pick up the sword.

Heavier than it looks. I struggle to wield it.

Joshua's by my side, his pain subsiding as mine does. Hand over mine, he says, "Stop."

I thrust the hilt into his palm. "Then end this. Now."

The determination behind his eyes gives me a semblance of hope. Did my song work? Have I convinced him? The sword arcs, circling his head as his face contorts.

This is it. He's—*no.*

Thud. Haman collapses to his knees, his face a petrified state of shock. The blade has passed through the soft space between his chest and throat. No blood. No scream. Another *thud.* He's on his side.

Gone.

The crowd roars.

Joshua plants his feet in a wide stance. "No more, Crowe."

If the death of his right-hand man shakes Jasyn, he doesn't show it. "I knew when it came right down to it, you could not imprison the Void inside your beloved."

Joshua doesn't respond.

"Say it," Jasyn says. "Say you surrender."

"I will not." The words are ground out through clenched teeth.

Jasyn withdraws the sword impaling Haman. Blood gushes and pools. "Have it your way. The next victim, please." Jasyn waves an arm and a brawny Soulless with tattooed arms and a dark goatee emerges from the space beyond the gate, drags a new captive forward. I don't recognize the Soulless, but I do know the girl he's dragging.

Ebony.

"How many of your people—your *father's* people—will you allow to become Soulless before you either end me or surrender?" Jasyn's eyes are wild. Crazed.

Ebony is tossed to the ground, perfect nails digging into the sand. Shiny hair falling into her eyes. She hangs her head. I barely hear the words she speaks. "You promised me. You said if I served you, the Void would never touch me."

"Yes, well." Jasyn's gaze darkens. "I lied." He nods at Lark, who withdraws another full syringe.

Despite the bad blood, literally, between Ebony and me, I don't want to watch her become Soulless. No one deserves that.

I will not let any of our stories end on Jasyn's terms.

I forget the perfectly chosen lyrics from before. Attempt a desperate plea instead. *"Your mother,"* I sing to Joshua. *"She died giving you life. A life meant to follow in your father's footsteps."* My voice is hoarse. Dry. Cracking. *"Please."* The word is off-key. *"Let me go so others might live."*

He pauses. His gaze flits. And then, what I feared wouldn't come but am terrified to see . . .

Joshua nods.

"I'd rather die," Ebony begs. "I'd rather die than lose my soul to the Void."

"As you wish." Jasyn leers at Ebony. He stands beside her, points the sword at her heart. Lark backs away. "Choose," Jasyn belts. "Surrender or allow this girl to die because of your cowardice."

I look between Joshua and Jasyn. Jasyn and Joshua.

The Verity's vessel creeps forward.

Jasyn laughs. Raises the sword higher.

But neither Jasyn nor Joshua is fast enough. As if sliding into home plate, chained wrists and all, Ky forces Ebony aside with his shoulder and places himself directly beneath Jasyn's sword.

A cry of agony. From me. From Ky.

I watch his blood spill, spill, spill onto the ground as Jasyn withdraws the sword from his middle.

"No!" My throat strangles the word. Too little too late.

Several things happen at once.

I'm beside Ky, on my knees, dirt and blood everywhere, mixing and staining and smelling so vile I want to puke.

Ebony scrambles away, clawing at the sand, stumbling toward the gate.

I can't see Joshua, but I hear him. He cries out. Because he knows what Ky's death will bring.

My heart wrenching, I emit an ugly sob.

And then . . .

Ky dies.

THIRTY-EIGHT

Rewritten

N ow the real storm begins.

Time lags. Each heartbeat a minute apart. I'm screaming but don't hear a sound.

No. My life is supposed to take Ky's place. Yet there he lies. Unbreathing. Unmoving. I pound the sand with my fists. Can I heal him? I've never tested my Physic abilities.

Joshua. Ever blood. I whip my head around, hair slapping my face in drenched columns.

But he's not stirring either. On his back, limbs akimbo, chest still as a stringless guitar.

I bite my lip. Squeeze my eyes. Pull my hair.

What. Is. Happening?

And then I hear it. The heart-wrenching sound of a woman's cry. I'd recognize that voice anywhere.

Mom.

Eyes bigger than bass drums, I search the crowd. I'm standing, running. Where, where, where—?

I trip over something, hands breaking my fall. But the impact ushers in no pain. I feel nothing. Twisting, I seek the culprit. A lifeless girl in a cornflower-blue gown lies facedown on the sand. Ankles crossed, arms framing her head like a ballerina.

Here is the reason for Mom's agony. I am gone too.

Jasyn struts around our triangle of death. Kicking Ky. Pressing a heel to Joshua's head. I can't decipher his reaction. His face gives nothing away. Shocked? Terrified? My grandfather pauses at my body. I want to cover myself, protect my vulnerable form. But he doesn't touch me.

He begins speaking but the sound is warbled, as if coming from underwater. Mounting a foot on Ky's thigh, Jasyn raises the bloody blade high in the air. His back is turned toward me.

That's when I see it.

An aurorean swirl corkscrews from Ky's open wound. Floating. Hovering. It's like nothing I've ever witnessed. Transparent but opaque. Blinding but impossible not to look upon. The color-infused light moves, twirling as it glides in ribbons through the air. Stopping directly above my body. Does Jasyn notice? Am I the only one seeing this?

I scan the arena. All eyes remain fixed on the Void's vessel.

When my gaze finds Joshua, a swirl identical to the one that emerged from Ky rises from the Ever's body. It joins the light hovering over me. Intertwines with it. Completes it.

The Verity. Must be. But it came from both boys—men. Ky and Joshua were two halves of one whole. Both were the Verity's vessel.

How is this possible? What does it mean that pieces of the Void and Verity could coexist in one person?

Reaching, I move toward the rainbow. My fingers graze its surface, my skin sparking, glowing, then dimming. Still, I feel nothing. Circling my body, I examine the thing from all sides, unable to deny or explain the way it draws me. Suddenly I have to know what it feels like. Because I crave feeling. A sensation. A breeze. Anything.

I step into it—the light transporting me like a Threshold.

A rush of wind, similar to what I felt when I kissed Ky, expands my lungs. Filling them. Making them whole. An ache punches my chest, so strong and so deep, I can't help but laugh. Because I feel it. Life. Love. Death. Sorrow.

The Verity has merged with my soul.

Ky sacrificed himself for Ebony. He's rewritten the ending. No time to reason or think or calculate why in the Reflections the Verity would choose my heart as its new home. Because now I have to finish this. No backing down. No second-guesses. No hesitation.

I will follow through.

My gaze sweeps between Ky and Joshua. So different. So undeniably irreplaceable. Mom's out there too. Who will become the Void's new prison?

Eyes open and pulse returned to an even cadence, I peel myself off the sand. So strange. I'm conscious the Verity resides within, but the differences are minute, nearly indistinguishable. Clearer vision. Fear less difficult to suppress. Yet I'm still myself, utterly human. This power, this gift, does not belong to me. It exists to contain the Void. Now, so do I.

My grandfather's back remains turned. The audience notices me first. A child pointing. A woman with a hand to her heart. From the corners of my vision I register the stir of Joshua's leg. The rise and fall of Ky's chest. Each of us canceled out the other. My life for Ky's, Joshua's for mine. I still have no idea if I gave him a Kiss of Infinity earlier, but he must've given me one. When I rose, Joshua's Ever blood took over, reviving him too. We need each other, the three of us.

Unstrapping the mirrorglass blade at my ankle, I grip it with certainty. Five feet. Three. When I can smell the arrogant fumes wafting from my grandfather's person, I raise both arms, aiming straight for his heart.

The knife plunges. It passes through flesh. Muscle. My gut churns. Bile rises.

Jasyn's sword falls. He coughs. Staggers. Left. Right. Then sinks to the ground.

I release the hilt. If I don't withdraw the mirrorglass, the wound will be unable to heal.

A circlet of crimson crowns the blade in Jasyn's back. For a fleeting moment, nothing happens. The crowd doesn't react. Joshua and Ky don't get up. My grandfather doesn't move.

And then the strangest thing occurs. Jasyn breathes. Gulp after gulp of air, inhaling, and gasping, and exhaling again, as if this is his first taste of oxygen in decades. He rotates, grabs my wrist, and drags me to the ground beside him, the collision sending pins and needles into my shins and knees. The soles of my feet.

"Thank you," he croaks. His eyes roll back. Head lolls. He lies in a crumpled heap before me. I watch his façade fall away, the handsome, regal exterior he wanted everyone to see. His skin is ash, darkness leaking like ink from his veins, staining his skin. His eyes are white as marble, the lids around them red and swollen and raw. Inch by inch the Void retracts, melting into itself, as if being absorbed by something outside. Then it's nothing at all.

I lift my head, scanning the Soulless scattered throughout those present. A similar phenomenon affects them, the color returning to their skin, the light restored to their eyes. I experience a moment of panic. Because it isn't just the Void within Jasyn I'm containing—it's the darkness as a whole.

My eyes find the sky, soft light consuming the night. The room swirls. The arena. Everything false peels away as the Void finds its new prison. As if awakened from a spell, the crowd applauds, hugging and crying and celebrating the joyous ending they've all been waiting for.

But I ignore them. Just as I alone beheld the Verity's true form in death, I cannot see the Void's raw state in life. Who will it choose? Which of those I love will have to pay the price for Jasyn's demise?

Joshua's at my side, drawing me into his arms, helping me to stand. He kisses my hair and pushes it off my face. I'm alert enough to register he's still himself.

Which means . . .

I trip over my own feet to get to Ky, breathing and alive, but still lying on his back. His hands are pressed to his soaked middle and his eyes stare at the sky. A lazy snow drifts toward us. Sticking in our hair and eyelashes. Melting into our skin.

"I'm sorry," I spit, seethe, sob. My chest . . . so tight. Hard to breathe. I did what I had to do, but now, in the aftermath, I can't help but feel a wave of regret wash over me.

What have I done?

"Don't be." His eyebrows cinch. "Now I know for sure." And then he smiles. It's weak and doesn't meet his eyes, but it's a smile just the same.

Joshua shouts behind me. Then I'm being hauled in another direction.

Guardians surround Ky, hoisting him up, carrying him away. Where are they taking him?

I don't know what comes next. My head grows light. Stomach churns. Stumble, slip, fall. Strong arms scoop beneath my neck and knees, lifting, supporting. I fight the compulsion to pass out, but the urge is far too tempting. The curtain closes. The audience takes its leave.

It is finished.

changed

"E liyana."

Blink. A blurred face above me.

"She's opening her eyes."

Wince. Ow. My head. Who's talking so loudly?

"Get some water."

Whimper. My bones are lead beneath my skin.

"Lift her head."

Cold. Something cold and wet at my lips.

"Not too fast."

Spit. Sputter. Choke.

I roll my head, force myself to arrive at full consciousness. Where am I? A dimly lit room. Heat on my face. Lavender and vanilla. A fire nearby. And . . .

Oh—

"She's awake! Hurry, get Nathaniel!" Mom barks orders like a drill sergeant. Her face slides into focus above me.

"Mom?" I lift my hand to my head. "What happened?"

"You about sent me to my grave is what happened." Her harsh tone makes me smile.

I sit, glance around. Lavish décor. A fire crackling in the hearth. Mom's suite or one identical to it. "What happened? Where's Joshua? And Ky—?"

"No more worrying, or you'll make yourself sick again. My

brave, brave girl." Mom fusses over me, fluffing my pillow, feeling my forehead with the back of her hand. "We've been taking shifts watching you."

"Who?"

"Makai and me mostly." She looks over her shoulder at the door. "Sometimes Robyn or Stormy."

Robyn was here? That means Joshua healed her. I never asked. Warmth spreads across my chest. "What about Joshua?" Why isn't *he* here?

Mom's gaze shifts.

The warmth dissipates. Oh no. "What's wrong?" I sit straighter, my pulse hurtling. "Is he okay? Is Ky?" The Void. What's it done to him? Will he still be himself? I have to help him. I'm the Verity's vessel now.

He needs me.

Mom pats my hand. "Joshua's fine." A close-lipped smile. "Lots to do. The rebels are making their way from the Haven, returning to their former homes throughout the provinces. Ebony's awaiting trial. Guardians have been dispatched to round up threats to the crown such as Isabeau and Gage. My father"—she swallows before continuing—"he's been buried in the cemetery here on the grounds. By the time the knife was removed, he'd already bled too much." The slightest hint of sadness resides in the creases of her eyes. "Joshua's been very busy tending to his duties as the interim king."

"Interim king?"

"Yes. You are the Verity's vessel now, darling. Once you are well . . ." She pauses, as if allowing me to mentally fill in the blank.

My mouth forms an O. "I'm the queen."

"I don't want you to worry about that now," she says. "There is plenty of time before your official coronation in the spring. You must take this season to rest. Joshua has trained for this. He has things under control for now."

"And Ky?"

One, two, three beats. Why won't she meet my eyes?

"Mom?"

"Nathaniel took care of his wounds. He's okay."

I rip the covers off, not caring I'm only wearing underwear and an oversized tunic. "Great. Just tell me where he is." I need to apologize for our argument at the ball. To thank him for his sacrifice. To see if he can possibly forgive me for ending his life. For making him a slave to the Void.

And the Verity. Did he know it was part of his soul? Did Joshua? Did Jasyn? All the unexplained details make sense now. The reason the Void couldn't take over before. Why it stayed secluded to Ky's arm. Even if I hadn't kissed him, the Verity would've shoved the Void away. I touch my right cheek. My mirrormark didn't remain because of Joshua's love. It stayed because of Ky—the Verity's other vessel. His Kiss of Infinity allowed me to go on as a Mirror even after my link to Joshua broke.

I open my mouth to tell Mom, but something holds me back. Until I speak with Ky, this must remain my secret. I've broken his trust once. I won't do it again.

Mom puts a hand on my shoulder, pushing me back in that gentle way of hers. "You can't see him."

"Why not?"

Knock, knock.

I cinch the covers around me, smooth my hair. How long have I been out? I must look like a wreck.

Mom eyes me as if making sure I'm decent before she calls, "Come in."

Nathaniel enters, offers a tight smile, and meanders to my side. "How are you feeling?" He wraps an arm around Mom.

"I feel fine." Irritation bubbles, then pops. "Will everyone please stop tiptoeing around me?"

They exchange a hesitant glance, and then Nathaniel says, "I overheard your conversation. You cannot see Kyaphus. He left as soon as I released him from my care. Said he needed to find his sister."

The blood drains from my face. Of course he would go after Khloe, but why didn't he come to me first? As long as I'm living, he—the Void—answers to me. How can I help him suppress the darkness inside if I don't know where he is? I should've gone with him. I'm still not sure how this whole Verity-Void relationship works, but the only way to find out is to get through it together.

My worried expression must give me away because Mom's eyes fill with compassion. She squeezes my hand.

I swallow the too-big lump lodged in my throat. I hardly know Ky. But somehow he got under my skin, became a constant during a time when I just needed a friend. Someone to listen and care and see. Finally I swallow and ask, "And Joshua? Can I at least see him?"

"Soon." Nathaniel relays the information as if it's common knowledge, as if repeating something he's been told.

I wait for them to say more. A disconcerting silence follows.

"Give us a minute, Nate?"

Nate?

"As you wish." Nathaniel exits the way he came.

Mom perches on the mattress, rests her hands on her barely showing stomach. "I suppose we have a lot to talk about."

I gaze out the window at the other end of the room. A layer of white ices the forest beyond, daylight turning the snowflakes to diamonds. "I know why you did it." I keep my attention on the trees. White. Pure. "I saw your face. You were so scared for me. If I had a child, I would've done the same thing."

"You remember?" She shakes her head. "Of course you do. You're part Scrib, like me."

I nod. "I hear your voice sometimes too. The things you've taught me, all the encouragements and reminders, they've stayed with me. And when I'm alone or frightened or all feels lost, the memories of your words come back to me. Then I don't feel so afraid."

"When the mark appeared"—Mom swallows—"I knew you were like her—Queen Ember. Makai helped us escape, vowed to protect us. I made him swear we'd never tell you who you were. He agreed, sealing the promise with a—"

"Kiss of Accord." I turn my gaze on her.

A sad smile crinkles her eyes. "Yes. And then Joshua showed up the year you turned fifteen. I begged Makai to make him leave, but Joshua insisted he only had your best interests at heart. So he stayed. I can't remember when I stopped being afraid of him—of what his connection to you meant."

I reach over and cover her hand with mine. We sit that way awhile, sharing a comfortable quiet.

Questions raid my thoughts. Why can't Joshua see my mark? What if his soul hadn't been linked to mine? Would we still have met? So much of our relationship feels . . . unnatural. Like a spell. What happens now? Where do we go from here?

I chew the inside of my cheek.

Mom pats my knee and rises. "I'll let you rest."

The moment she's gone I leap from the sheets, cross to the wardrobe in search of clothes. I've been sleeping too long. I glance outside again, at the awaiting day. No more hiding. No more shadows.

Time to face the sun.

The fresh snow is air beneath my boots. The sky is bright blue, a sight I never thought I'd see this side of the Second. I walk the castle grounds alone. Unguarded. Unhindered. Free.

I've always adored the whiteness of winter. How the flakes transform everything they touch, dusting the world in fresh white, somehow managing to silence even the most intrusive noise. When I was younger, I'd stand on our front stoop. Face the sky. Let the frozen flecks melt on my skin. In my imagination, each powdery kiss washed my birthmark as clean as the city around me. Everything used to center on my ugliness, on my desire to be anyone but myself.

Now I'm learning to recognize my own beauty. An idea that's foreign but welcome. If true love begets a change, perhaps that's where I need to begin. How can I fulfill my purpose as a Mirror unless I can first love myself?

I meander toward the edge of the leveled hill, passing Jasyn's rose garden. Will blossoms adorn its thorns come spring? I pause at the waist-high wall, observing the snowcapped trees below. Their needles have turned evergreen, their trunks now a lovely shade of bark. What will the forest be called now? To keep its current name seems unfitting. Forest of Night? More like Forest of White.

I move left and walk through an archway, trudging down the path I'm sure rests somewhere under the snow. Near the hill's bottom, I find an iron bench nestled beneath a tree. I sit, shrugging my shoulders to my ears. Tilting my head back against the trunk and closing my eyes, I breathe in the quiet. I can't control the melody that slips from my lips then. Ember's poem combined with a piece becoming more ingrained in my soul with each inhale. The lyrics release on fogged breaths. After the final note I remove my hands from my peacoat pockets. Rub them together. Blow.

"Allow me?"

My eyes flash open.

Joshua stands a few feet off. I rise from the bench and he meets me, covers my hands in his, exhales a hot breath onto my icy skin. "I thought I'd find you here." A smile tugs at his lips.

I can't hide my mirroring grin. "And why is that?"

"Just a feeling, that's all." He shrugs in that boyish way of his. "The forest is the closest thing the Second's got to Central Park."

I study our hands. My grin falters.

"The song you were singing?" He cocks his head, questioning. "The rose beyond the thorns. Did you write it?"

I tell him about his mother. How she was a Mirror, like me.

He listens, his cheeks lifting.

As I speak of Ember, my thoughts drift. "Joshua. About Ky—"

His lips flatten. "You don't have to worry about him. He's gone to find his sister. He may be the Void's vessel now, but he can't hurt anyone as long as you live. That's all that matters."

But what about *his* hurt? *His* pain? I pull away and an ache deepens inside me, burrowing its way into my gut. "I did that to him. I guess it makes sense he wouldn't say good-bye." He must hate me.

Neither of us addresses the extraordinary elephant in the forest. We both know the truth but somehow can't find the words to ask the question on both our minds. If the Void enters the one closest to its captor, why didn't it take Joshua? Why Ky? I still don't know if I gave Joshua a Kiss of Infinity, though it's clear he gave me one. Questions, questions, questions.

No answers.

Joshua's shoulders bristle beneath his navy-blue coat. "So where do we go from here? You will be crowned queen come spring. Anything you want is yours."

What *do* I want? "I think I'd like to throw a wedding." I try to veer toward a lighter topic. "Mom and Makai deserve a proper ceremony with family and friends after all they've been through."

"A wedding, huh?" He nods, the spark returned to his eyes. "I think that can be arranged." Then he takes my hand. And kneels.

In.

The.

Snow.

How many times have I imagined this moment?

"Eliyana Olivia Ember . . ."

There's always a choice.

Ky?

". . . I've loved you since before I can remember." His lips brush my hand, sending an explosion of goose bumps up my arm.

You can still choose me.

I—

Joshua raises his eyebrows. "Think of what we can do. Together. As king and queen of the Second, we'll bring this Reflection into a new era. El, will you be my bride?" He withdraws something sparkly from his pocket.

My breath ceases. It's my necklace, the one with the treble clef and heart charm. And there, beside the charm, hangs a new addition—a white-gold band studded with diamonds.

"Where did you find it?"

"At the bottom of Lynbrook Province Threshold." He fastens it to my neck with care, leaning in so close his nose grazes my ear as he pulls away.

My heart beats *yes, yes, yes* as I stare at the treasure resting between my coat lapels. But there's another answer too. Softer. Not as distinct. The one belonging to the rose button necklace hidden beneath my clothes. The one I'm not quite ready to let go.

"I don't want an answer now," Joshua says, helping me breathe. His thumb caresses my cheek. "I know it's a lot to consider, especially after all that's happened." He gathers my hands in his. "But El, I would wait a thousand lifetimes for only one with you."

Of course he would. I *know* he would. "Thank you."

Snow falls, dusts our faces. He draws me in and kisses me on the forehead. Light. Tender. "Come on." He intertwines our fingers. "Let's go home."

I nod and we walk up the hill side by side. Our conversation is easy, and for a moment I forget everything we've faced. The past strips away, wiping the slate as clean as the snow covering this beautiful Reflection. This is an ending, but it's a beginning too. For us. For me.

I glance over my shoulder once. Just once. Saying a silent good-bye to the boy who chose me as I chose him. He gave me a chance. I won't let his sacrifice be in vain.

Thank you, Ky.

I face the castle again, my real-life fairy tale. I never thought I'd be the girl someone wanted—the girl *Joshua* wanted.

But even if he didn't, I think I'd be okay. Because my worth isn't defined by others. My mirrormark is invisible to Joshua. The rebels saw me as the girl to lead them to their savior. To Mom I was the sole person she had to protect. And Ky . . . he's saved me time and time again.

So many people willing to risk everything for my sake. I mean something different to each of them. But it doesn't matter. All that matters is what I mean to me.

As Joshua holds open the massive door leading inside the castle, I catch my reflection in the window and my mouth forms an O. My brown-purple hair is pulled off my face, revealing my mirrormark in its entirety—a mirrormark that shouldn't be there according to Ember's theory. Once the Verity took on a new vessel—me—my Mirror Calling should have vanished. I hadn't even thought about it until now. Somehow I don't mind it's still there. It's an odd feeling, seeing the mark I've always loathed as something else altogether. My strength. My song.

But the present mirrormark isn't what startles me most. There's something else, too, unfamiliar and new and maybe even beautiful. In all the times I've looked in the mirror, this image is one I've never seen.

The girl in my reflection is smiling.

CODA

KY

yesterday

This isn't over.

I clutch the envelope, its corners poking through my gloves and into my skin. Packed snow covers the ground, spreading across the ice-encrusted Threshold before me.

Crunch, crunch, crunch.

I heft the pack on my shoulder higher as he approaches.

When he halts at my side, we don't look at each other. I allow him to speak first. He is, after all, the king.

For now.

"It's better this way," Joshua says.

"For her? Or for you?"

He doesn't answer, shifts, passes me something.

"What's this?" I open the weighty leather pouch. A wad of green paper, Third Reflection currency, taunts me. "A bribe? Do you really believe a wad of cash is going to keep me away from her?"

"Not a bribe, no." He turns toward me. "Just something to get you started."

"I've lived in the Third before. I know how to survive." A dark laugh crosses my lips. I avoid eye contact, study the dead landscape.

"You spoke to Ebony about your sister's whereabouts?"

I nod. "Khloe's with Countess Ambrose in the Fourth. I'm headed there as soon as I can reach the Threshold."

"I've already arranged passage. A ship will be waiting."

Silence stretches. "She'll figure it out eventually," I say. "Ember isn't stupid."

"*Eliyana*," he says as if making a point, "is marrying me. You're going to have to accept that. I've been in her life for years. You, on the other hand, only have claim to mere days."

I face him, shoving his payoff into my coat pocket. I leave my fist submerged—otherwise I just might punch him between his royal-blue eyes. "What lie will you feed her? When she asks about me?"

"*If* she asks about you, I'll tell her the truth." His gaze narrows. "You left to find your sister."

So that's how he wants to play this. Fine. "I want to see it before I go."

"I'll show you mine if you show me yours."

Typical. I clench my teeth. Then I shove up my right sleeve, revealing the blackened veins along my arm. Except, unlike before, they're darker. And cold. But also hot. Burning.

I can't decide which pain is worse. The never-subsiding sensation that my arm is being sliced open. Or the emptiness. The constant craving for . . . something.

Once he's had a good look, he clears his throat. Rolls up the sleeve covering *his* right arm. His veins are identical to mine. "Happy now?"

"How long do you think you can hide it?"

He rolls his sleeve back down. "As long as it takes. There isn't room for both of us in her life, Kyaphus."

"It doesn't matter what distance you put between us. She and I are bound, heart and soul. My taking on part of the Void only makes our bond stronger."

"That may be. But the longer you're away, the more she'll

forget. Her connection to you will become nothing more than an annoyance. An old scar she'll ignore given time. And you . . . you will go on without her. If it's any consolation, your feelings for her will keep the Void inside at bay. As long as you love her, the Void will not spread past your arm. Remember that." It's quiet for a beat. Our breaths fog the air. Then he adds, "I would like to know one thing."

I shrug my shoulders to my ears. Shiver.

"Why didn't you tell her? If you're so sure of her feelings for you, why not use the truth to your advantage?"

Because she's not a toy. Because I have no interest in manipulating her for my gain. Before I can decide against it, I shove the envelope into his hand. "Give this to her for me, okay? You owe me that much."

"I owe you nothing." His lips tighten, but he nods. "However, I'll do as you ask. Just don't expect it to change anything."

I shove my free hand into my empty pocket. Then I turn and trudge onto the frozen lake, toward the hole in the middle, the one that will lead me through frigid water to her former Reflection. *My* former Reflection. Chills dig at my spine like daggers, the snow growing deeper the farther I walk.

When I reach the opening, I glance at the shore. David is gone, already having backtracked the foot-printed path toward the castle. Toward *her.*

I clench my teeth, readying for the sudden burst of pain the subzero water will cause. Before taking the leap, I search the sky for her window. I don't care what David says. He may have known her longer, but I know her better. Once I find Khloe, I won't even need to return. Em will seek answers eventually. When she does, I'll be waiting.

Pulling in a long breath, I step off the edge.

It's only a matter of time before she follows.

acknowledgments—a.k.a. cool nerds in my universe

fun fact: I always, without fail, read this section of a book first. Well, now it's my turn (finally) to thank the people who got me here.

YHWH, my King. My Creator. My Abba Father. Thank you for giving me this gift called writing.

Mom, I miss you every day. Thanks for instilling in me a passion for reading and for always urging me to write things down. You inspired Elizabeth. She is you.

Daddy, you never let me settle for less than an A in English. I totally get it now.

Aunt Terri, you are the other version of myself. Thank you for believing in me.

To my sibs: Karine, Tim, and April, thanks for all the awesome, and sometimes crazy, times. I love you, dudes. Seriously.

To my husband Joe: you've always supported me in whatever crazy dream I had. Thank you for being patient until I found a dream that stuck. I love you.

N and M, you are my sunshines. Thank you for understanding when Mommie is on the computer (sometimes longer than I said I would be). I love you both oh so much!

To the rest of my family, the Larsons, Springer cousins, Pop, and Aunt Cook, I love each and every one of you. You have no idea how much your support means to me.

Carolyn, thank you for letting me read the early chapters of this book aloud to you as we drove to Phoenix. I love you.

Christen and Neysa (a.k.a. WriteNight Girls), I didn't really get serious about this story until you two showed up. I love you awesome nerds.

ACFW, you paved the yellow brick road to my very own Oz. Now every time I attend the annual conference I think, "There's no place like home."

Thanks to Tina Russo Radcliffe for telling me "story begins when change happens." And to Christina Rich for explaining what weasel words are.

Nancy Kimball (a.k.a. Obi-Wan), you're more than a mentor, you're a sister and friend. Thanks for taking a chance on this "inkling in training."

Deirdre Lockhart (a.k.a. Editor the First), thank you for helping shape this story (and this author).

Janalyn, your friendship means the world. You inspire me each day just by being you.

To my agent, Jim Hart, thanks for taking a chance on me. I owe you more than I can say.

Becky Dean, you may not have worked on this story with me in its early stages, but your help since we joined forces warrants a huge "Thanks!"

To my publishing family at Thomas Nelson/HarperCollins, thank you for whatever you saw in me. This is me sending a huge hug to each and every one of you! Becky Monds, thank you for encouraging me, brainstorming with me, and helping me fill in all the holes. Jodi Hughes, you inspire me to try to live up to all the epicness of OUAT. Daisy Hutton, Becky Philpott, and Kristen Golden, thank you all for everything you have done for me. I can't wait to get to know you all better. Amanda Bostic, you were the first to welcome me once I received my contract. Thank you for that and all you do behind the scenes. Samantha Buck, your ideas make marketing fun. I can't wait to see what you cook up next! Julee Schwarzburg, thank you for your amazing attention to detail and for asking all the right questions. Paul Fisher, thanks for your enthusiasm and super exciting ideas! Kristen Vasgaard, I cried when I saw the cover design. It's perfect and fairy tale–ish and so very me. Matt Covington, thank you for bringing the Second Reflection to life with your awesome map. I also want to thank Katie Bond who is no longer with the team. I will be forever grateful for the time I got to spend with you.

To my personal cheerleaders: Ingrid, Cassia, Zara, Kelly P., Janelle, Brooke, Ann, Nick, Denise, and the many others who have cheered me on via social media. I can't thank you enough for your encouragement and support.

Mandi, Abby, and Hope, thank you for the sunshine you bring to all my cloudy days.

To my beta readers, Gabrial, Laura, and Karine, your feedback and all-out fangirling have encouraged me to the moon.

Thanks to my FB buds, Flic and Anson, who helped when I was stuck. And to Mitz, thanks for those NYC descriptions you wrote. Also to Steve (a.k.a. the Lawn Gnome): Thanks for answering my NYC questions in the final stages of revisions.

To my BookTube friends: Thank *you*, (insert your name here). There are quite literally enough of you to fill a separate section of acknowledgments. You know who you are. *waves*

Trina Ruck, thank you for your enthusiasm for this project. Your creativity inspires me.

To my Street Team/Early Reviewers: ABasketCaseyReads, April Sarah, Bekah AwesomeBookNut, Between Chapters, books & tea & all things me, Bre Faucheux, Coffee&Chapters, Danni Darling, gingerreadslainey, Hope Ortego, ISmellBooks, thejordanjournals,

Kayla Rayne, KalesKorner, The Little Librarian, Meagan Precourt, and taylortalksbooks, saidthestory . . . Thank you all for your willingness to read my book baby and tell the world what you think . . . whatever that may be.

Thanks to Jade @bedtimebkworm for telling me about the Combine feature in Word.

Emilie Hendryx (a.k.a. E.A. Creative Photography), thank you for the lovely headshots!

To my author friends, thank you for letting me pester you, among other things: Krista McGee, Lorie Langdon, Mary Weber, Kristy Cambron, Sarah E. Morin, Diana Sharples, Elizabeth VanTassel, Shannon Dittemore, Melissa Landers, Nadine Brandes, Katherine Reay, Elissa Sussman, Patricia Beal, Emileigh Latham, Rachelle Rea, Laura McNeill, Sara Crawford, Morgan Feldman, Bre Faucheux, and *all* the other authors I'm failing to mention.

To Rachel Hauck and Susie May at My Book Therapy, thanks for giving me that extra confidence and help to pitch this story at ACFW.

To you, dear reader: Thank you for giving El's story a chance. Whoever you are, you're beautiful (or handsome!). Inside and out.

And finally I have to mention the King of my heart again. He is, after all, the Beginning and the End. You are my happily ever after, my one true pairing. And like Prince Charming, I know you will always find me.

discussion questions

SPOILER ALERT! Do not read these questions until you have finished the book!

1. Eliyana faces the loss of her mother in the opening chapters. How does her grief affect her decisions and actions in the beginning? Have you experienced a loss similar to El's? How did your grief affect your decisions and actions during that time?

2. Eliyana and Ky both have less-than-perfect physical appearances—El with her birthmark and Ky with his acne. How do they deal with what others think of them? Do you notice a contrast in how El behaves in regard to her appearance versus how Ky behaves in regard to his? Who is more insecure? Why do you think so? Is there any insecurity in your life that has shaped your behavior and attitude toward yourself and others?

3. Throughout the story we see how the Callings relate directly to the different strengths of each character. What Calling do you think the Verity would choose for you? Why?

4. Elizabeth felt that keeping the truth from El was the best way to protect her. Do you agree with her decision? If it

were your child, what would you have done differently?
Why?

5. Joshua struggles with choosing between his duty to the
Second Reflection and his love for El. What would you
do if you were in his situation? Do you think it is right
to sacrifice the well-being of many to save one? Was it
right for him to take the burden upon himself, or should
he have given El the choice to share in his burden? Give
reasons to support your answer.

6. Ky says, "... *appearances can deceive. A jagged surface
doesn't always allude to what truly lies beneath.*" In a culture
of Photoshopping and filtering, we often portray a
rose-colored version of ourselves. Do you consider this
behavior deceitful? Should we be more honest on social
media? Why or why not?

7. Ky and Joshua share the burden of the Void in the end.
According to the story, the Void enters *"the one the vessel
cares for more than any other."* It's clear El's heart is divided
in the end, but what about the guys? Who do you feel
cares more for Eliyana and why?

8. In the final chapter, El thinks, "... *my worth isn't defined
by others.*" If this is true, what or who *does* define our
worth? Do you gauge your worth by what others think
or say about you? Discuss El's inner journey. Her physical
appearance hasn't changed, but how has she transformed?

9. Does the opening poem (*"Once upon a time is ne'er what
it seems ..."*) hold any truth? Oftentimes we romanticize
what love should look like. We think of fairy tales and
Prince or Princess Charming and create expectations that
can be impossible to meet. Is love an action or a feeling?
What does it mean to "fall" in love? What does "true" love
look like to you? Can you share an example?

10. El hasn't known Ky very long. We discover *"a Kiss of*

Infinity isn't something you decide to bestow. It comes from the deepest part of your soul. Stems from desires and emotions you may not even be aware you possess." Why do you think El was able to give Ky a Kiss of Infinity? What does this say about her as a person? What do you predict will come of El and Ky's relationship in the next book? What about El and Joshua?

11. Ky sacrifices himself in the final showdown with Crowe. Do you think Ky knew he carried a piece of the Verity? Why or why not? He not only saved El from taking on the Void, but he also saved Ebony, a traitor. What does this say about him? After all that transpired in the story, are you Team Joshua or Team Ky? Give reasons to support your answer.

12. Ebony sought revenge on El because of their father Tiernan. Do you think Ebony's actions were justified? Should she be punished for her behavior or should she be pardoned? Give reasons to support your answer.

To learn more about
sara Ella and her
upcoming books, check out:

Website: saraella.com
Facebook: writinghistruth
Twitter: @SaraEllaWrites
Instagram: saraellawrites
YouTube: Sara Ella

about the author

Once upon a time, Sara Ella dreamed she would marry a prince and live in a castle, and she did work for Disney! Now she spends her days throwing living room dance parties for her two princesses and conquering realms of her own imaginings. She believes "Happily Ever After Is Never Far Away."

～∞～

Visit Sara online at saraella.com
Facebook: writinghistruth
Twitter: @SaraEllaWrites
Instagram: saraellawrites
YouTube: Sara Ella